Critical acclaim for Edward Wright

The Silver Face

'A very superior whodunit, rich in period detail . . . and aching with the kind of nostalgia produced by that unique movie fusion of trash and true feeling. Wright makes skilful use of old Hollywood scandals in his plot . . . The research is thorough and well digested. But the book's real triumph is one of sensibility . . . Deeply satisfying stuff: exciting, intelligent and tender where it most matters' *Literary Review*

'An entertaining novel set in 1940s Hollywood . . . Wright vividly creates the atmosphere of decadence and superficial glamour of the period' *Sunday Telegraph*

'This haunting novel . . . *The Silver Face* confirms Wright's reputation as a significant talent' *Sunday Times*

'Former big-city newspaper editor Wright's stellar second John Ray Horn novel (after 2003's *Clea's Moon*, which won the CWA's Debut Dagger Award) legitimately merits comparison to the work of James Ellroy . . . Wright does a superb job of integrating a fair-play whodunit plot into a hard-boiled setting rife with personal and official corruption . . . Wright's narrative gifts mark the arrival of a significant new noir voice who hopefully has many more Horn stories in him'
Publishers Weekly (starred review)

Clea's Moon

Edward Wright grew up in Arkansas and has degrees from Vanderbilt University and Northwestern University. His major career has been journalism, and he has worked as an editor at the *Chicago Tribune* and *Los Angeles Times*. His first novel, *Clea's Moon*, won the CWA Debut Dagger for Fiction. He and his wife, Cathy, live in the Los Angeles area.

THE SILVER FACE

Edward Wright

ORION

An Orion paperback

First published in Great Britain in 2004
by Orion
This paperback edition published in 2005
by Orion Books Ltd,
Orion House, 5 Upper St Martin's Lane
London, WC2H 9EA

1 3 5 7 9 10 8 6 4 2

A CIP catalogue record for this book is available
from the British Library.

ISBN 0 75286 451 3

Typeset at The Spartan Press Ltd,
Lymington, Hants

Printed and bound in Great Britain by
Clays Ltd, St Ives plc

www.orionbooks.co.uk

This book is for Jean

My thanks to my wife, Cathy, who is my first line of defense, and my long-term gratitude to Rayburn and Margaret Moore for helping me value the written word. I'm fortunate to have Jane Wood and Sara O'Keeffe as my editors and Jane Conway-Gordon as my agent. And for friendship, support, and help in navigating the rocks and shoals of publishing, I'm grateful to Kate Kennedy, Morrie and Alicia Ruvinsky, Ron and Merle Mardigian, Denise Hamilton, Ed Kaufman, Cara Black, Adrian Muller and, especially, Sheldon McArthur.

Chapter One

The slow rain washed down the windshield, smearing the streetlights and neon signs across the glass, softening the world's edges, melting the features of the people on the sidewalk.

'I can't see good,' Mad Crow grunted. 'Run the wipers.'

'Better not,' Horn replied. 'Right now, we're just another car sitting here. If I start the engine, we'll get attention.'

Mad Crow cursed under his breath, leaned forward in the passenger seat and wiped the inside of the windshield with his hand, then rolled down his window a few inches, letting in a rush of cool air. Outside, the nighttime street surged with cars and people. A block away, one of the movie palaces had finished showing a film, and the crowd began to move past Horn's inconspicuous black Ford, some of them headed for their cars at nearby lots, some ready for a meal at the cafeteria a couple of blocks away, others looking for one of the several bars in this stretch of downtown Los Angeles.

Those in the crowd, young and old, looked well-off and animated, not beaten-down and anxious, as they had only a few years earlier. Many of the men, hats pulled low against the drizzle, wore sharp-looking suits. The younger, gum-chewing girls huddled under their dates' umbrellas and swung their purses like metronomes. *Well, the war's been over for a while*, Horn thought. *People are making money again, having a good time. Funny it didn't work out that way for me.*

Several of the women dabbed at their eyes with handkerchiefs even as they walked and talked. 'What's wrong with them?' the Indian asked.

'That's a Joan Crawford playing up the street there,' Horn replied.

'Oh.' This was their second night here, waiting for a glimpse of a man whose name they didn't even know, and they had exhausted most of their attempts at conversation.

Horn adjusted his rear-view mirror for a look at the young woman in the back seat. 'Nothing else occur to you, Cassie?'

'Huh-uh.' Cassie Montag, her expression uninterested, was working at the braids that held her dark hair. As he watched, she freed one of them, brushed it out, and began teasing at the other with her fingers. Even in the dim light inside the car, Horn could make out the faded rainbow of bruises that marked the left side of her lip and lower jaw.

'You sure he said he likes to drop in at the Green Light Tavern?' Horn asked her. 'You know, there's a Red Lantern Grill just a couple of blocks from here.'

'He said Green Light,' she replied. Mad Crow swivelled around heavily, thick shoulders bunched under his jacket, and studied his niece. She had some of his looks, the dark eyes and the cheekbones. But the rest of her was a mixture of Indian and white, and Mad Crow had once told Horn it was the white part of her that worried him.

'You're just going to have to braid your hair again before you show up for work Monday,' he told her.

'I don't care,' she told him, eyes focused on nothing in particular. She wore a western shirt and a fringed skirt, and Horn could just make out, in reverse, the lettering embroidered on her shirt pocket: Mad Crow Casino. 'I just don't want to look like a goddam squaw all the time.'

Mad Crow's jaw tightened, and he seemed about to speak. But Horn reached over and touched him lightly on the arm. 'Over there,' he said, quickly cranking down the driver's-side window.

They both stared at the bar they'd been watching for two nights. A man who appeared to be in his thirties approached the entrance, loosening the belt of his trenchcoat. 'Looks like him,' Mad Crow said. 'Right, Cassie?'

She took a look. 'That's him,' she said, adding a muttered obscenity.

The man's dark, slicked-back hair shone under the lights. 'If he doesn't introduce himself properly tonight,' Mad Crow said, 'I just might call him Vitalis.'

'Uh, he's got friends,' Horn said. The man had just been joined by a woman of indeterminate age and another man, this one stocky and wearing a slouch cap. The trio went inside.

'You recognize the other one?' Mad Crow asked Cassie without turning around.

'He looks like a guy who was with him that night,' she replied tonelessly.

'So there was somebody with him? Would've been nice if you'd mentioned that.'

Horn could feel the tension building in the car, and he wanted all this to be over. 'Sure you want to do this here?' he asked Mad Crow. 'We can wait, follow him to his hotel, wherever it is, talk to him with nobody around. When a man opens his door in his underwear, you got him at a disadvantage.'

'If he opens the door,' the Indian said.

'I can always get them to open the door,' Horn said. 'That's what I do for you, remember?'

The Indian thought for a moment, his thick hands resting on the dashboard, the big turquoise ring and hammered silver bracelet shining dully in the softened neon light as if they were part of Montezuma's treasure.

'Hell with it,' he said finally. 'I'm tired of waiting. Let's get it done. They've had time to order their drinks and settle in, so let's go join the party. Come on, Cassie.' He rolled heavily out of the car and wrapped his raincoat lightly around his thick chest and torso. The rain had slackened to a light, uncertain drizzle. With his ponytail, his most distinctive feature, tucked under his fedora, he was just a big, copper-skinned man standing on the street.

Horn unfolded his lanky frame and got out. Cassie reluctantly joined them, and they crossed the street. The round green symbol of the tavern flashed slowly off and on, and the name

3

of the place was reflected waveringly upside down in the puddles.

Inside, they stood for a moment in the doorway, getting used to the low light. The tavern was busy, not quite full, with the warm, steamy feel of a place where people have come in from the rain. Somewhere a jukebox played a Dinah Shore tune that had been popular at the end of the war. They saw their man sitting with his male friend one table away from the bar next to the wall. At first there was no sign of the woman, but they spotted her coming out of a back room, adjusting her coat and dress.

Horn thought quickly. 'We should try to separate her,' he said to Mad Crow. 'Okay?'

'Yeah,' the Indian muttered. 'Cassie, we don't want her getting in the way,' he said forcefully. 'Do something, all right?'

His niece hesitated long enough to show her lack of enthusiasm for the whole endeavor. But she approached the woman and spoke quietly to her, motioning toward Horn and Mad Crow. After a few seconds, Cassie and the woman took seats at a nearby table and waited. The two men, who were being served drinks by a waitress, apparently had not noticed.

'We weren't counting on him having company,' Horn said. 'You be careful.'

'You just watch my royal behind,' Mad Crow replied. The sharp planes of his face broke into a wide grin as he crossed the room. Horn had seen the grin before. So had other men. It did not portend a good time.

'You mind?' Mad Crow said to the two strangers as he plucked a wooden chair from the next-door table and sat it down loudly next to the dark-haired man, ignoring his look of mild astonishment. Moving swiftly, Horn found a chair two tables away and set it down to Mad Crow's right, next to the stocky companion in the cap.

Horn brushed the raindrops off his shoulder, slapped his hat lightly against his knee, and unbuttoned his jacket, trying to put a relaxed smile on his face. The stocky man on his right had not moved. His square, outthrust chin had gone a few hours too long

4

between shaves. A toothpick rested on his lower lip, and his gaze went slowly back and forth between Horn and Mad Crow. Horn knew this second man was his responsibility, but he had been careful to position his chair far enough away from the table to allow him to watch everyone else as well.

'Can I help you folks?' The cocktail waitress had shown up. Her expression looked strained, and she seemed to sense that something was going on.

'We're going to think about it, honey,' Mad Crow said to her. When she had left, he turned to Vitalis. 'You know who I am?'

'I think so.' The man wore a well-fitting double-breasted tweed, snug at the waist. His eyes were sleepy and unconcerned.

'You played poker at my place,' Mad Crow said. 'Won a few hands, ordered some drinks, left some nice tips. My guess is you had a good time.'

'That a question?' The man seemed to be enjoying the conversation.

'Sure, let's call it a question.'

'I suppose I had a good time,' Vitalis said, studying his cuffs as he fussed with them until an inch or so showed below his coat sleeve. 'I've been to bigger places, better run. Your bar service is a little slow. But I got no real complaints.'

'That's good,' Mad Crow said, leaning forward slightly. 'I got one, though. One of my waitresses says you roughed her up.'

A look of lazy comprehension passed over Vitalis' face. He looked over his shoulder, searching the room until he spotted Cassie and the other woman, who were now working on drinks. They were sitting too far away to overhear, and they appeared to be talking quietly, eyeing the men occasionally.

'That wouldn't be her, would it?' he asked.

'Says you invited her out in the parking lot, offered her money to go out with you,' Mad Crow went on. 'She turned you down. You grabbed her arm. She tried to get away. You slugged her.'

'That's a lie.' Vitalis didn't move as he spoke, but Toothpick shifted in his chair, hands lightly gripping the arms, and now Horn gave him all his attention. In the background, Dinah Shore

5

had given way to the velvety baritone of Perry Como singing 'Temptation.'

'Which part was a lie?'

'The parking lot was her idea. Meeting me later was her idea. The money—'

'Now you're the liar.' Mad Crow had stopped smiling, and Horn could feel something bad coming, like a train on a downhill grade with a belly full of fiery coal and no engineer at the controls. The unease built in him, the familiar knot in the stomach at the prospect of violence. He glanced at Vitalis. *Why isn't he worried?* he wondered. *He must be counting on his friend. Toothpick. He's the ace in the hole.*

'Here's why I'm here,' Mad Crow went on. 'You bruised her face and chipped a tooth when you hit her. She'll need to get the tooth fixed, and then there's the question of her general discomfort. Way I see it, you owe her an even hundred. You hand it over, we leave you to your drinks and your female companionship. We'll even forget about the apology.'

The other man laughed out loud, and his sleepy eyes came alive. *He's enjoying this*, Horn thought. *Not a good sign*. He tensed himself, waiting for whatever came.

Vitalis reached in his left front trouser pocket and pulled out a wad of bills secured by a money clip. He peeled off a ten and laid it carefully on the table in front of Mad Crow.

'Here's a Hamilton,' he said. 'I think this is the going rate for a halfbreed with a broken tooth.'

Mad Crow leaned forward as if to speak, but instead he reached down and grasped a front and rear leg of the man's chair in each hand, then stood erect, bringing the chair up with him in a surge of arm and leg muscles. Vitalis came up with the chair, then was dumped sideways in a heap on the floor. He scrambled to his knees in a crouch as his right hand shot under his jacket. But in the next instant Mad Crow had swung the chair high, one-handed now, and brought it down in a fearful arc, slamming it into the man's ribs with a sound that everyone in the bar could hear.

Vitalis emitted a cry of pain, then lay there on his side,

wheezing, slowly drawing his legs up, making himself as small as possible in case another blow should follow.

As the chair had struck, Horn saw Toothpick tense, his hands gripping the chair arms tightly, about to commit himself. Horn quickly leaned toward him, speaking in a low but urgent voice. 'Careful,' he said. 'It's all over. It's done. Not your fight anyway. Be sensible, now, all right? Let's leave it right here. We'll be gone real soon, and you can take care of your friend. Nobody else needs to get hurt.'

The man on the floor wheezed again. Everyone in the bar seemed to be holding their breath. Toothpick sat rigidly, unmoving except for his eyes, which were all over the place. *He's figuring the odds*, Horn thought.

'Look,' he told Toothpick, 'I'm just getting comfortable here. If you get up, I've got to get up too. And where do we go from there?'

A few more seconds passed, and then the man, with a lazy roll of his tongue, transferred the toothpick from one corner of his mouth to the other. He relaxed his grip on the chair and sat back. Horn exhaled loudly. Glancing at the bar, he saw the bartender moving toward what Horn guessed was the telephone. 'It's all right,' he called out, making a palms-out gesture. After a moment, the bartender stopped.

Mad Crow reached under the fallen man's midsection, fumbled around for a while, and came up with a switchblade knife, which he pocketed. Then he pried the money out of his victim's clenched fist. When he had it, he looked around the room, re-applied the grin to his face, and said loudly, 'Show's over, folks.'

Sitting down, he removed the money clip and began counting. 'Hey, buddy,' he said to Horn, 'I think this is what they call a Michigan bankroll. Big bills on the outside, mostly singles on the inside. But—' He was snapping the corners of the bills between thumb and forefinger, like an experienced money man. 'But looks like he can cover the tab, and maybe even have enough left over for the train fare back to, uh . . .' He nudged the prone man with the toe of his shoe. 'Where you from, partner?'

7

'Cleveland,' the man croaked.

'How about that? Home of the Indians.' Mad Crow seemed immensely pleased with himself. 'You're headed there tomorrow, aren't you?'

'Right.' The word was muffled.

Horn took the rest of the folded money and passed it to the man on his right. 'Do me a favor,' he said. 'Would you mind helping your friend out the door?'

Toothpick, whose expression had never changed, coaxed the other man to his feet, and they slowly made their way out onto the street.

'Damn, that worked out, didn't it?' Flushed with success, Mad Crow pocketed the hundred. He got up and headed toward the door, stopping for Cassie on the way. Before accompanying him, she spoke a few final words to the other woman, who smiled at her.

Horn started to follow, but his gaze swept over the woman at the other table, then settled on her. The two men had ignored her as they left, and she sat with her drink, head down, as if unaffected by what had happened.

'You two go ahead,' he called out. 'I'll be just a minute.'

As the bar chatter started up again, Horn walked over to get a better look at the woman. From what he could see, she was not young. She wore a serviceable wool coat with a worn fur collar and a felt hat with a floppy brim that partially hid her features, and she sat with both hands cradling her highball, as if it might skitter away from her.

'Those guys friends of yours?' he asked her.

She shook her head. 'Never saw either one of them before tonight,' she said. 'But they seemed nice enough, and they had money to spend. And if a gentleman wants to buy a lady a drink—' She waved one hand gracefully in the air, an almost theatrical gesture. 'The lady doesn't ask to see his pedigree.' Her voice was a soft alto, slightly amused. It hinted at breeding, and it didn't go with her almost threadbare appearance.

'Well, I'm sorry for all the ruckus,' he said. 'Can I buy you another one of those before I go?'

8

'You don't remember me, do you, John Ray?'

'What?'

She looked up at him, and he studied her. There was something about her features, but they wouldn't coalesce into a name or even a memory.

'I can see you don't,' she went on, her words carefully spoken but slightly slurred. She took a big swallow of her drink, and Horn could see that it was already mostly gone. He guessed that it was not her first of the evening. 'You probably don't remember rescuing me from that stampede – all the yelling and shooting, and horses running around. I know it was only a movie, but I wasn't used to horses, and I suppose I was afraid. And you saved me from them, just like it said in the script.'

He lowered himself into the seat opposite her as she went on. 'I had a funny thought right after Joseph hit the man with the chair. I remembered another scene – it was in a bank or a lawyer's office, something like that – when someone hit you with a chair, and it broke into a hundred pieces.' She took a deep breath, as if the memory required too much effort. 'But that was one of those trick chairs, wasn't it? Just a movie trick. I'll bet you've forgotten that too.'

What the hell? He found himself staring at her. A memory was taking shape. Not yet a name, but a memory . . .

She polished off the drink with one long swig and put the glass down heavily. 'Something bad happened to you,' she said thickly. 'I saw it in the paper a long time ago. Something bad. Well, something happened to me too.'

'What happened to you?' As his mind worked to retrieve the memory, a face swam into view, a beautiful face, and the name was somewhere behind it, coming to the surface.

But the memory didn't match the face across the table, and something in his own expression – disappointment, or maybe even pity – gave him away.

'None of your business.' She looked at him fiercely. 'Stop staring at me. I'm sorry I said anything. No, you can't buy me another drink. Why don't you just get out of here?'

Mumbling a goodbye that sounded like an apology, he

left the bar. Across the street, he leaned in the window of the car.

'Where's your Caddy?' he asked.

'A block away,' Mad Crow said. 'It's a lot more comfortable than this heap of yours, so let's go pick it up. Time to celebrate. We're off to the drive-in for a burger and a malt.' Cassie sat in the back, looking idly out the window.

'You two better go ahead,' Horn told him. 'I'm sticking around for a while.'

'What are you talking about? If you want a drink, I know a dozen bars better than—'

'Listen, that woman in there. She knows both of us.'

'What?'

'I know. It sounds crazy, but she worked on one of our pictures. Just one, and it was years ago. She mentioned a stampede . . . Wait a minute.'

He snapped his fingers. 'It's Rose. I'll be damned. Rose Galen.'

'You're out of your mind, John Ray.'

'It's her. I'm going back to talk to her. You go on.' He sprinted across the street, entered the bar, and looked around.

She was gone.

Chapter Two

As Horn approached, the bartender gave him a look. 'Let me guess,' the man said. 'You've come back to buy a round for the house. On account of you and your friend's jackass behavior.' He had a military-style crewcut and wore a crisp white shirt and bow tie, and one rolled-up sleeve revealed a Devil Dogs tattoo on his left forearm.

'I'm afraid I can't afford that,' Horn said, putting on what he hoped was an ingratiating grin. 'But I'm obliged to you for letting things wind down the way they did, without calling in outside help.'

The man shrugged. 'I don't usually need outside help.'

'I can believe that,' Horn said. He slid two singles anchored by a silver dollar across the bar. 'This is for your trouble. And because I need to ask you about the lady who came in with those two men.'

'What about her?'

'Do you know her?'

'Maybe.' The bartender seemed suddenly wary. He hadn't touched the money. 'What's it about?'

'She said she knew me, and I didn't remember her at first. Now I do, and I just want to talk to her.'

'She didn't sound to me like she wanted to talk to you,' the bartender said. 'Told you to get lost, the way I remember it.' The man leaned back on the counter behind him, arms folded. Horn had a sudden thought: *he's trying to protect her*.

'Look,' he said. 'I remember her name is Rose. I knew her years ago. It's kind of embarrassing, you know? Not to recognize her at first. She was a little mad at me, but I promise you I just want to talk to her, ask her what she's been up to all these years.'

It sounded feeble, but the bartender seemed to relax. Finally he said, 'Most people around here call her Rosie.'

'Does she come here a lot?'

'I guess, yeah. I give her credit sometimes, make sure she isn't bothered.'

'Do you know any other places she likes to go?'

'Not really.'

'Any idea where she lives?'

'Somewhere up on Bunker Hill, in one of the rooming houses.' The bartender picked up the bills and the big coin and looked at Horn closely. 'Do I know you from somewhere?'

Over the man's shoulder, near the big mirror behind the bar, Horn could see a handful of framed and autographed celebrity photos, the kind often found in bars and eateries around LA. One of them was a character actor who had a name less familiar than his face. Another photo was of Johnny Mack Brown, complete with Stetson and horse.

If you like the westerns, you just might know me, Horn thought. *My rowdy friend too.* But aloud he said simply, 'I doubt it.'

The man shrugged and went over to take an order from the waitress. Then he stopped and came back, as if remembering something.

'I hope I don't find out you bothered her,' he said.

'I won't bother her,' Horn assured him. 'I don't want to rile the US Marines.' He pointed to the tattoo. 'Pacific?'

'Yeah, a few of those islands,' the bartender said. 'You in too?'

'Army,' Horn said. 'Italy.' He started to add something, but he felt the old wave of shame wash over him, shame that had kept him from talking to anyone about his time in the war. The bartender turned away again, and Horn left.

He rounded a corner and cut over to Hill Street, where he turned north. It was almost eleven, and there was less foot traffic along this street than on Broadway, and almost no neon. The rain was little more than mist now, but his raincoat did little to keep out the January night air. He took fast strides, and it wasn't long before he spotted her up ahead.

She walked a little unsteadily on her high heels, head down, her posture suggesting that she was hugging herself to stay warm. Up ahead to the left was Angels Flight, the short and steep cable railway that carried people up to Bunker Hill. When she reached it, she stopped at the big stone arch that framed the fare booth. That was where he caught up with her as she fumbled in her change purse.

He glanced at the fare sign above. 'Two, please,' he said to the woman behind the glass as he stepped forward, placing a dime on the worn counter.

Rose Galen looked up questioningly, hand still in her purse, then recognized him. Her expression hardened.

'Mind if I ride with you?' he asked her.

'It's a free country.'

'Good.' They passed inside to join the half-dozen passengers waiting for the next car, then stood there awkwardly.

'*Smoke on the Mountain,*' he said after a moment.

'What?'

'That was the name. More than ten years ago, and it was only my second movie, which means you were only my second leading lady. I'm sorry I didn't remember you, Rose. It was just—'

'Just that I've changed so much,' she said, looking him in the eye defiantly. 'How do they say it? The years haven't been kind to her. Isn't that right?'

As he tried to frame an answer, one of the two orange and black cable cars arrived, slowly descending to the pad. They stepped aboard with the others and sat across from each other, the wooden floor sharply tilted but the seats angled so that each passenger sat level. After a few moments the car lurched mildly and began its slow climb.

Horn looked around. In contrast to the crowds on Broadway, the people on the car seemed to belong to another LA, one that was older, more tired, and less prosperous. He took in the scuffed shoes and worn clothes. One man, unshaven, held a paper bag in which the top of a newly purchased bottle of liquor was just visible.

'You know what they call these two cable cars?' Rose Galen asked him abruptly. Across the narrow aisle, he could smell the liquor on her breath.

'Ah, no.'

'You must not get up the hill much.'

'It's been a while,' he said. 'I don't have much reason to go up there.'

'Not many do,' she said. 'Just those of us who live there. They call the cars Sinai and Olivet. They're named after mountains in the Bible.' As before, she spoke with the careful enunciation of those who know that heavy drinking can make them stumble over words. 'We're riding on Sinai. When they built this thing a long time ago, Bunker Hill was where the rich folks lived in the big houses, and riding the cable car up there must have seemed like a trip to heaven.' She laughed harshly as her right hand twisted and released the fabric of her skirt, over and over. 'It's not that kind of a place any more.'

In the unforgiving overhead lights, he got his first good look at her. Time had not been kind to her, it was true, and no one would call her beautiful today. Those years showed in the lines around her eyes and mouth and the twin furrows between her brows. Her hair, once a rich brown, was now half gray and spilled carelessly out from under her hat. And although his emerging memory of her included a sense of serenity, what he saw now was tight-wound tension, characterized by the repetitive, unconscious motion of her right hand half buried in her skirt.

But as he looked, he began to discern the Rose he remembered, the woman he'd known in that brief time before she disappeared. Even though some drinkers get bloated, she appeared to be still trim within those baggy clothes. And although her hair was no longer dark, a lock of it hung over one eye in a way that seemed familiar to him. The full lower lip remained, as did the direct, brown-eyed gaze. Best of all, he had seen those eyes flash at him with anger tonight, telling him life had not dulled all her responses.

14

The humming cable car and its tired passengers faded, and for a few seconds he saw a young woman in a loud western shirt, a kerchief knotted around her neck, sitting astride a skittish mount. Like a camera, his memory moved in for a close-up as she worked the reins, grinning broadly and making a joke about her own horsemanship. He heard himself laugh along with her. Then the scene shifted to a quieter place, and the memory took on a different emotion, one summoned up from a deeper level, a feeling he hadn't touched in a long time. In his mind, he reached out for her . . .

An old woman in the car was seized with a coughing fit, dragging Horn back to the present. He realized Rose was looking at him warily, almost suspiciously, and he felt as if he had been caught in something shameful.

He had questions for her. But he didn't know if he could get past the barrier of booze. Horn liked to drink and had been known to overindulge when the occasion demanded, but he hated habitual drunks, those who let alcohol take them over. He suspected the feeling originated with his father's sermons against the evils of drinking. Horn had spent much of his adult life fleeing the memory of the Reverend John Jacob Horn, but the old man had a way of surprising him even today, of infiltrating his thinking, of ambushing him with his convictions, his absolute certitude on questions of good and evil. Horn knew, of course, that there was no such thing as absolute good or evil but only those slippery regions in between. Except in that sleepless time before dawn, when he sometimes lay awake, heard the faint thunder of his father's voice, and wondered . . .

'We're here,' Rose said as the car gently stopped at the top of the incline. They stepped off with the others, and a moment later he stood with her, looking around at Bunker Hill.

The years had not been kind to the hill either. Early in the century, the city's merchant princes had built their grand homes up here, tall Victorians and Italianates and Gothic revival showcases with turrets and gables and balustrades and ornate detail hand-carved into the wood. Three and sometimes four stories they stood, with servants' quarters in the upper levels. Proudly their owners looked down on the raw young city from high on their hill, and they sent their servants down by cable car to do business and buy goods and then return by the route of the angels. It must have been a good life, Horn reflected.

But it lasted less than half a century. By the end of the war, the merchant princes and their descendants had fled the heart of the city, and their homes had begun to decay. Looking around, Horn could see that the once-dense blocks were now pocked with vacant lots here and there. The homes that remained had been converted into rooming houses, shabby and in need of paint. In place of a single wealthy family, most of them now housed a whole collection of the down and out.

The rain had stopped. They stood on a street lit only by street-lamps. The tall houses loomed up on either side, with dim lights visible behind windowshades.

'Not exactly heaven, is it?' Rose said. Something caught in her throat, and she coughed repeatedly.

Horn turned and looked behind them, where the downtown lay ablaze, the lights of its streets and buildings reflected from a layer of angry, gray, low-lying clouds. 'It's not heaven down below either, Rose,' he said. 'I live there, and I should know.'

She gestured down the street to the right, and they began walking. 'So you're a philosopher now,' she said almost play-fully. 'When I met you, you were pretending to be a cowboy. And I was impersonating an actress. We made an odd pair, didn't we?'

'You were good,' he said forcefully. 'Don't shortchange your-self. I learned a few things from you. I couldn't understand what you were doing in that no-count little B-movie. You were better than any actress I ever worked with, before or since.'

'Well, golly,' she said in exaggerated modesty. 'Listen to you. I'm all—'

'I never found out what became of you,' he said suddenly. 'You just disappeared at the end of shooting. Why did—'

'We have arrived,' she said, gesturing grandly. The old house had little of its grandeur left. It still bore all its architectural flourishes, but it seemed to have settled onto its foundation like an elderly woman who can no longer hold herself erect. The hand-painted sign over the porch read: *Rook House. Week or Month*.

'This is where I leave you,' she said. 'Time for some beauty rest.'

'What happened, Rose?'

'All you and I have are a few memories, and I don't enjoy most of my memories,' she said, patting him tentatively on the arm. 'Goodbye, John Ray.'

As usual, the birdcalls woke him just after first light. Walking into the curtained-off alcove that functioned as a kitchen, he found he was out of both bread and eggs. Even though he was already hungry, he took the time to make a batch of drop biscuits, then fried up some bacon to go with a couple of them. There was just enough buttermilk left from the biscuits for him to enjoy with his breakfast. He ate out on his front porch, listening to the morning sounds of the canyon. Each day, he found, went a little better if he could start and finish it by spending some time on his porch.

It wasn't much of a porch, or much of a house either. The place was just a cabin, made of wood and stone, originally intended to house the caretaker of the old Aguilar estate. It sat a hundred feet above the road that marked the floor of Culebra Canyon, and beside the cabin a gravel road wound up a steep, wooded hillside to the estate itself, up on the ridge that formed the western rim of the canyon.

The buildings on the ridge had burned down long ago, and the estate was now a blackened ruin. But its current owner, while deciding what to do with the property, allowed Horn to live in the cabin rent-free in exchange for caretaker duties.

Today those duties focused on a crumbling wall, just off the road, that marked the lower edge of the property. After breakfast, Horn turned on the hose by the cabin and ran some water in a wheelbarrow, then mixed in some cement with a shovel. Wheeling the mixture down the slope, he went to work on the rock-and-cement wall. Wherever he found a loose stone, he

17

pried it out with a crowbar, troweled some cement into the cavity, then re-seated the rock. Periodically he freshened the cement mixture from a jug of water he kept nearby.

The day was perfect, one of those crisp, sunny, blustery winter days that periodically visited there. Horn wore a light cotton jacket. When his work placed him in a sunny patch, he quickly warmed, but as soon as he moved into the shade, it turned chilly. From the wall, he could glimpse stretches of the asphalt road below, but there was no traffic on it, nor was there usually, since the cutoff to the Aguilar estate was the last side road before the canyon dead-ended. Horn's nearest neighbor was a half-mile away.

Los Angeles, his home off and on for more than a decade, had not always been good to him. But along with its many unkindnesses, it offered a geography of a thousand choices. Last night he had seen Rose's world, a place where worn-out people lived too close together. Horn had made his own choice. He lived almost as far away from civilization as one could get and still say he lived in the LA area. He liked it that way. After a few hours, he took a break for a sandwich and a bottle of beer, then went back to it. The sun was high now, so he left his jacket on the porch.

As he labored, every now and then he glanced up the hill where the narrow road disappeared into the trees. His work sometimes took him up to the site of the old estate, for weeding and general maintenance around the scorched remnants of the manor house and outbuildings. Once he had enjoyed walking up the road, or climbing the trail that led up there, to sit among the ruins and reflect on the kind of wealth that could build such a place, and what had become of it.

But no longer. Not since that night he had spent there, waiting for men to come and kill him and a young girl named Clea. The waiting was followed by terror, gunshots and sudden death in the dark. And now that he knew three bodies lay buried up there, somewhere among the oak and eucalyptus that ranged along the ridgeline, he could never think about the old estate in quite the same way.

18

So, as he pried another cantaloupe-sized rock out of the wall, he thought instead about Rose Galen and the shock of seeing her again. About the years that had accumulated on her face like a road map of worry. About the eyes that could still bore in on him. But his thoughts soon turned to older memories. Of *Smoke on the Mountain,* and the actress who showed up on the set one day, who stuck out her hand and said, 'I'm Rose. Never done a western, but I'm willing to learn. If you'll bear with me, maybe we can make this fun.'

He hadn't seen the irony at first. He was Medallion Pictures' newest cowboy actor, in his second starring role, and pretty full of himself. It took a while for him to realize that Rose was not only a few years older than he but also much more experienced at acting. He never found out whether her experience originated in movies or the theater, only that he was learning to rely on it. The truth was, he was not a very good actor. He was stiff and clumsy and often unable to commit the simplest dialogue to memory. His value to Medallion, such as it was, lay in his looks and his ability on horseback.

Time and again, Rose would step in whenever he stumbled and quietly offer the advice he needed. 'Remember, the camera's not there,' she whispered once. 'Look at me and Joseph and the others, and when we're talking, don't look like you're ready to say your line. Act like you're absolutely fascinated by what we have to say. Especially me,' she laughed. 'You could listen to me go on all day.'

Another time, after he blew a line over and over, she asked the director for a break, took him aside, grinned, and said, 'It's a stupid line, so don't worry about the exact words. Here's what's important: the man's a crooked lawyer, the contract is phony, and people are being cheated. Here's what else is important: you're the only one who cares about this. Now go give him hell.'

He surprised himself by doing just that. The director wasn't happy with the improvised dialogue, but it worked.

Beyond her abilities, though, he knew she was troubled. Even while doing her usual good work, there might be liquor on her breath. When the crew was setting up for a new shot, she would sometimes walk away and sit under a tree, and he knew not to interrupt her. In the midst of being helpful to him, she seemed to need help herself, and he didn't know how to offer it.

After several more hours of work, Horn reached the south end of the wall and re-cemented the last loose rock. Then he rolled the wheelbarrow up to the cabin, where he used the shovel to scrape out the remnants of cement from the wheelbarrow, then hosed down everything. Most of the canyon was in shadow now, the late afternoon sun painting a bright stripe of brown and green across the top of the far canyon wall. He was mounting the uneven stone steps of the cabin, beginning to think about supper, when he heard the phone ring inside.

'I couldn't remember if you had paid your phone bill lately,' Mad Crow said. 'Glad to hear you're still hooked up with the outside world.'

'Whenever you pay me on time, my bills get paid,' Horn said. It was an old joke.

'So was that really Rose, or just the bad lighting in there? How did it go?'

'Not very well. Maybe I'll tell you about it sometime.'

'You could make it now.'

'I don't know, Indian . . .'

'Look, I had my heart set on a hamburger last night, and you ducked out on me. Now I've got the grill fired up, and the meat laid out, and you're going to help me eat these little critters. So climb in that beat-up thing you call a car and come on over here, all right?'

Chapter Three

The coals in the fifty-gallon drum had died down to hot ash. The burgers had been consumed, along with the beans and the ears of corn. The two sat in large, rough-hewn chairs out on the uneven lawn in front of Mad Crow's ranch house, each man with a bottle of Pabst Blue Ribbon nestled comfortably in his crotch.

'Want to do a collection?' the Indian asked. 'Guy out in Westwood. A professor at UCLA, for God's sake. He teaches math, and he's supposed to have come up with this system to beat the table at poker. Only thing is, he keeps losing.'

'Guess he still needs to work out a few bugs,' Horn said.

'That's right. Meantime, he's into me for more than three hundred. I know he's good for it, but here's the thing: the other day his wife calls and begs me to stop him playing. Says she's afraid he's going to go off the deep end one of these days. I told her I can't bar him from my place as long as he respects the rules. But I got to thinking that maybe I shouldn't carry him any more, 'cause that just encourages him. So why don't you go collect what he owes? For the usual percentage.'

'Sure,' Horn said. 'I'll get the address when we go inside.'

'Got it right here.' Mad Crow leaned over to hand him a slip of paper. 'Try not to embarrass him in front of his wife.'

'Don't worry. You know, you wouldn't have any of these problems if you'd just—'

'Just run the casino, and forget about shylocking? I know. Maybe I like it. Maybe I'd rather be the banker to some of these dopes instead of sending them out on the street for their money, where they pay twenty percent and get their fingers broken when they can't come up with it.'

21

'Maybe you like the extra income.'

'That too.' Mad Crow pulled at his beer and grinned over at Horn. 'But if I didn't have the occasional bad loan that needs collecting, what would you do for a career, my out-of-work cowboy buddy?'

When Horn didn't answer, Mad Crow cleared his throat. The knotted ropes beneath his seat cushion groaned as he shifted his bulk. 'That was some asshole of an idiot talking just now,' he said after a moment. 'Had no business saying that. I think I'll kick that dumb ass out of this yard so's we can get back to our beer drinking.'

'You go right ahead,' Horn said. 'Give him a kick for me too.'

Off in the stable, one of Mad Crow's horses whinnied in an excess of equine emotion. It was now fully dark, the only illumination coming from the dim glow of the coals and the light behind them on the front porch of the house.

Mad Crow cleared his throat again, a sign Horn had learned to read as unease or embarrassment. 'I get a little worked up on the subject of earning a living,' the Indian said. 'Don't pay me no nevermind, all right? Only thing is, I'm the first one in my family to have anything like this.' In the near-dark, Horn saw him sweep an arm around to indicate the whole of his ranch. 'I'm not saying my relatives are all poor and miserable. Hell, my oldest brother lives by himself out on the reservation, doesn't have a pot to piss in, but hunts and fishes and lives his own kind of life. I guess I'd call him happy.

'But I'm the one that came to the big city. And after a while, some of them followed me here.'

Horn had heard the story before, but he didn't mind. 'And now they work for you,' he prompted.

'That's right. Now I got seven cousins and nephews – and a niece – on my payroll. And they're doing pretty good. I got a right to be proud of myself.'

'So be proud.'

'You know what he called me?'

'Who?'

'My brother.' Mad Crow got up and went to the ice bucket,

22

where he fished out two more beers. He opened them and handed one to Horn, who waited to hear the rest.

'Last time I visited, a bunch of us were in town, eating and drinking. My brother called me a civilized Indian. He said it like it was something I should be ashamed of. I almost uncorked one on him, but my sister was there – Cassie's mama – and I didn't do anything. Maybe I should've.'

'No, maybe you shouldn't have.' Mad Crow seemed to be getting morose, and Horn wanted to change the subject. He heard another whinny from the stable, followed by the sound of a heavy body against boards. 'You've got an unhappy horse in there,' he said. 'Is he lonesome?'

'I suppose,' Mad Crow said. 'He's a mustang I bought at auction couple of weeks ago. Got him cheap, and I thought I'd make him into a saddle horse, but it was probably a mistake. He's mean and bad-tempered. The hands are afraid of him. He broke Paco's thumb.'

'That never stopped you before,' Horn said. 'I never saw a horse you couldn't—'

'Why don't you do it for me?'

'Me? Why would I want to—'

'Twenty bucks in it for you.'

'I'm too old to get stomped by some horse. And besides, you're a lot better at that than I am.'

'Flattering me won't work. Tell you what, I'll flip you for it.' He pulled a coin out of his pocket. 'You call it.'

'I'm not calling anything. It's too dark to see, anyway. Handle the horse yourself, and leave me out of it.'

'In the old days I would've, but I'm getting tired,' Mad Crow said with a sigh. 'This thing with Cassie. What with her and the business, I got no time to spend on some ornery stallion. Maybe I'll just sell him.'

'Suit yourself. How's she doing?'

'Cassie? Oh, just great. She hates the job I gave her, the clothes she has to wear at work. Says it doesn't make sense to have her hair in braids like an Indian girl while she wears cowboy boots and a fancy skirt and a Stetson.'

23

'Well, it doesn't,' Horn said. 'You got to admit that.'

'It's just business,' Mad Crow said defensively. 'The customers like it. But you can't talk to her. I only took her in, gave her a job and a place to stay, because her mother's my favorite sister. I thought Cassie wanted to work, earn some money, maybe go to college – she'd be the first girl in our family to do that, and she's smart enough. But she spends all of her time carousing – the booze and the boys. She's wilder'n any of her brothers. Reminds me a little bit of the way I used to behave back when I was a young buck, before I became a pillar of the business community.'

'So she takes after you. Aren't you flattered?'

'God help me. And you haven't heard all of it: that guy we messed with at the bar last night? Turns out he wasn't exactly lying about the way it happened with her. I had a talk with one of my dealers today. He said it looked to him like she invited that guy out to the parking lot.'

'Oh, Jesus.'

'I know. If it happened that way, then maybe the rest happened like he said. Maybe she suggested they get together later. Maybe the money wasn't even his idea . . .' Mad Crow's voice trailed off, as if he lacked the heart to go on.

'I'm sorry, Indian.'

'And it's not like she's some kid I can send home to her mama if she doesn't behave herself,' Mad Crow said. 'She's pretty much grown – turns twenty-one in a few months.'

'Is she around tonight?'

'Hell, no. She's never around. Borrows a car almost every night, heads out to have a good time someplace. Tonight she's got the Caddy.' He snorted. 'Must want to impress somebody.' Mad Crow cursed almost inaudibly. 'Let's talk about something else,' he said. 'Tell me about Rose.'

Horn recounted the events of the previous night, ending with the farewell on the steps of the rooming house. 'Doesn't make a good story, does it?'

'No,' Mad Crow said. 'When you get to like somebody and then lose track of them, you hope they go on to a happy ending

24

somewhere, like the kind our movies used to have. Hers doesn't sound like that.'

'I guess not.'

'You know why I liked her? Because she had class, but she acted like plain folks. Because the movie business is full of people in love with themselves, and she wasn't like that. She was better at what she did than most people we worked with, but she wasn't all puffed up with herself. I saw her working on you, giving you tips. Let me tell you something: it helped.'

'I was pretty bad, wasn't I?'

'You were pretty bad. But you got better, and she was the reason. You had some good years out there on horseback, with your faithful Indian trailing along . . .'

'Until it all went bad. You saying I owe it all to her?'

'Well, I'd say at least part of it.'

'Did you have a little bit of a crush on her, Indian?'

'You bet.' In the dark, Horn couldn't see the grin, but he could sense it. 'Didn't you?'

Before he could answer, they heard the faint ring of the telephone from the house, and Mad Crow heaved himself up to answer it. A few minutes later he returned. 'Damn.'

'What's the matter?'

'That was Rusty, over at the Dust Bowl. Cassie's there, and she's making some kind of trouble. I'm going to have to go get her.' Horn heard the jingle of car keys. 'I'll take the truck.'

'I'll drive you over,' Horn said, getting up.

'I think you've done me enough favors in the last day or so.'

'Bullshit,' Horn said. 'Let's go.'

The Dust Bowl, a honky tonk popular with farm and ranch workers, was a few miles from Mad Crow's spread in the northern San Fernando Valley. The place stood on a county road surrounded by flat, open land, bean fields and lemon groves. They could see the winking neon sign long before they reached it.

'Shouldn't have told her about this place,' Mad Crow muttered as Horn pulled off the road and into the Dust Bowl's

25

half-full parking lot. They spotted Rusty Baird, the owner, coming out to meet them.

Baird nodded to both men before speaking to Mad Crow. 'It's okay, Joseph,' he said. 'I guess it's over. She's gone.'

'Any damages?' the Indian asked.

'A light fixture and a few broken beer bottles,' Baird said. 'She got a little wild with a pool cue. You don't owe me anything. I'm just glad it—'

'You let girls shoot pool in this establishment of yours?'

'Well, not usually,' Baird said a little defensively. 'But it's hard to say no when she's got her mind set on doing something. You know that.'

Horn pointed over to where the Cadillac convertible sat in the lot. 'How did she leave?' he asked Baird.

'She went off with a couple of guys she was shooting a game with. Don't know where to.'

'Describe them for me.' Mad Crow's voice was flat.

'Mexican boys,' Baird said. 'They were in a truck, headed north.'

In seconds, they were on the road. Horn had the accelerator near the floor, and the big Mercury engine – installed by the head mechanic of the Medallion Pictures motor pool to create a stunt car with a high-performance heart inside a drab exterior – pushed the Ford up to seventy. The road was narrow and straight and illuminated only by the car's headlights.

Barely two minutes later they saw the truck. It had stopped on the right shoulder, and Horn cut his lights and slowed, finally halting about twenty yards short. They got out quietly and advanced. The truck, with weathered slats rimming the bed, was used for hauling produce. It sat with its engine off but headlights on.

As they drew up to the rear, they heard a retching noise. Off in the ditch that bordered a walnut grove, a young man knelt, heaving. He seemed oblivious to all but his own distress.

'Never mind him,' Mad Crow whispered. 'You hear that?' It was music, coming from the truck's radio. Peering around, they could see Cassie and the other young man dancing in the bright headlights, like a couple of ballroom dancers on a spotlighted stage.

'What do you think?' Mad Crow asked.

'I think we do this quick and easy, no trouble,' Horn said. 'Listen, we know the key's in the ignition, right? So here's what we do . . .'

They split up, Mad Crow to the right. Horn quietly got behind the wheel of the truck. Up ahead, Cassie, in a brightly colored dress, clung to her partner, who wore boots and dungarees and a faded shirt. The song was Al Dexter's raucous 'Pistol Packin' Mama' but they were attempting a clumsy and drunken waltz. Every now and then she threw her head back in a mock swoon. The man gripped her tightly, his right hand cupped around her rear.

Mad Crow moved into the light and grabbed her by the arm, wrenching Cassie away from her partner and dragging her back along the side of the truck. She screamed in rage, and the Mexican stumbled, caught himself, and then muttered something as he prepared to go for the intruder. Just then Horn fired up the truck's engine, jammed it into gear, and tromped on the accelerator. The man jumped aside with a startled yell, then started after the truck. But it was out on the road now, lurching along, and Horn soon left him far behind. He drove for about a half-mile, then stopped and got out, leaving the key in the ignition. After a minute, the Ford pulled up, Mad Crow behind the wheel and Cassie, grim-faced, sitting up front. Horn squeezed in beside her, and they turned around and drove back. When they passed the two young men trudging along, one of them still holding his stomach, Mad Crow stopped and leaned out the window.

'Your truck's up the road,' he said. 'Shouldn't drink if you can't hold your beer. And by the way, if you see this young lady again, you stay away from her.' Then he drove on.

They rode in silence all the way back to the Dust Bowl. But as Mad Crow pulled up next to the Cadillac and he and his niece got out, she exploded at him.

'You make me sick!' she shrieked at him, the neon light

27

painting eerie colors on the Caddy's white finish and garish pinto hide upholstery. 'I hate working for you. And I hate you.'

'You're a cartoon Indian,' he yelled back at her. 'You're right out of the funny papers. You've got no pride. Wonder why people look down on us, laugh at us? Just look at yourself.'

'Oh, I'm supposed to be like *you*?' Her sarcasm was venomous. 'Dress like some kind of wild west show? Pretend I'm still acting in cheap movies? I don't know if you've looked at any of them lately, but all you ever did was tag along after *him*.' She indicated Horn. 'I suppose you're proud of that.'

'I did my work,' he said grimly. 'And I built a life out here. And when your mother asked me to take you in . . .'

'I don't want your charity,' she yelled. 'If this is what it's like to be Indian, I'll just be white, thank you very—'

He hit her before she could finish, slapping her face with his big open hand, and the sound was sharp and loud in the parking lot, even over the music coming from inside.

Cassie gasped and sucked in air, and in the next moment dissolved in breathless sobs. Horn helped her into the Caddy's passenger seat, and moments later Mad Crow, his face set in stone, drove off.

Horn got in the Ford and began driving home, crossing the Valley southbound until he struck the pass over the Santa Monica Mountains, which led him to the ocean. He turned up the coast until he came to the road that cut inland and wound several miles up Culebra Canyon to his place. It was a long drive, and he could find no listenable music on the radio, so he focused on his thoughts.

He felt sorry for Cassie, sorry she had no clear idea of the world where she belonged. Everybody had problems, but most people knew who they were from the day they were born. They either accepted who they were or ran from it, but at least they knew it, and drew in the knowledge with their mother's milk. Cassie didn't even know that much.

Mad Crow might be thinking of kicking her out, Horn speculated, and Cassie wasn't likely to want to go back to that little

South Dakota town, back to the dirt roads and the shabby homes and the junked cars, now that she had had a taste of LA. He tried to imagine her adrift in this sprawling city, with its bright sun and dark shadows, its noisy streets and its quiet open spaces. Its temptations and contradictions. The thought made him uneasy. Cassie was wily and tough, but she was no match for this place.

And suddenly he thought of Rose Galen. Another lost soul. Once, he recalled, he had been the lost one and she had been his guide. Mad Crow was right: whatever success he had attained was partly her doing.

But during the shooting of *Smoke on the Mountain*, he was still aware of how inadequate he must seem to the others around him – Rose, Mad Crow, and the technicians on the film crew, who had seen cowboy actors come and go over the years. At times the director, a decent but harried man, looked ready to trade in Horn for the first ranch hand with a clean shirt and a good profile who rode up and volunteered.

Rose's work ended on the next to last day of shooting. When they wrapped that day, she caught up with him. 'Feel like going for a ride?' she asked. They mounted their horses, and he led the way across the Medallion Ranch, over a low range of hills and into an adjoining valley where no film crews were working. Rose had made off with some extra ham sandwiches and two bottles of soda pop from the lunch wagon. Horn unsaddled the horses to let them graze and spread his bedroll on the grass. They sat there, ate and talked.

'You don't think much of yourself, do you?' she said.

'No,' he said around a mouthful of sandwich, shaking his head emphatically.

'Well, why are you doing this?'

'I'm not sure,' he said wonderingly. 'I just fell into it. A year ago I was pumping gas and wiping windshields out in Santa Monica, and on weekends I looked after horses on a ranch out in Chatsworth. One day I was giving a riding lesson to this guy. Turned out he was some kind of producer. He asked me if I wanted to pick up some extra money doing bit parts in westerns.

I said sure. Six months later the same guy asked me if I wanted to star in—'

She laughed delightedly. ' "Do you want to be a movie star?" That's the question we all want to be asked, isn't it?'

'I guess. Did they say that to you too?'

'Something like that.' The smile left her face, and she seemed far away. 'A long time ago.'

'But I'm no good, Rose. I know that now. I'm tired of embarrassing everybody.'

'Listen to me.' She sat forward on the bedroll and fixed him with her gaze. 'You're right, you're not a very good actor. Not yet. Maybe you'll never be a great actor. But you've got something, John Ray. Something the camera likes. I can see it, even if you don't. All you need to do is identify it and use it.'

'I appreciate all your help. But—'

'I won't be able to help you after today. But you won't need me any more. All you need is the self-confidence to stand up in front of the camera, say your lines, and know that there's something in you that comes across, something the audience likes. You don't have to be glib, like some of these guys. You don't have to be good with the girls, or good with a guitar, God help us. All you have to do is be honest.'

He gave her a crooked grin. The sun was down, and the valley floor had gone from bronze to pink to gray. The grass had lost whatever warmth it had absorbed from the sun. 'You're really something,' he said. 'Have you got a guy?'

'No, and I don't particularly want one. But—' She looked up at the darkening sky. 'Can you see the stars out here?'

'A million or so. You're out in the country now.'

'That's nice. Well, I was about to say I'd like to sleep here under the stars with you tonight, if you don't mind.'

Her words stunned him, but not for long. He hobbled the horses, cleared a spot on the ground, and spread her bedroll next to his. They made love, hungrily and hurriedly, even before the stars came out. Then they lay side by side.

'Thank you for that,' he said.

'Thank *you*.'

'Don't worry. It'll go slower next time. And better.'

They were silent for a while, listening to the crickets and the night birds and the occasional sounds of the horses shifting their weight in the grass nearby. Then she said, 'I'm jealous of you, John Ray.'

'Why's that?'

'Because you've got it all ahead of you. You have an appetite for life, and when the choices come your way, I think you'll choose the right things.'

He laughed softly. 'Listen to you, the experienced old lady. You sound like you've really been around. What about the choices you get to make?'

'I think I made mine very early,' she said, her words so faint he had to strain to hear. 'And the ones I have left are mostly unimportant ones.'

'You're not making any sense.'

'Look,' she said, pointing. 'Here they come.' He looked, and there was a faint spray of stars all over the inverted bowl of the sky. They seemed to brighten as he watched.

'What's the worst thing anyone can do?' she asked, and her voice had such a dreamlike quality she might have been addressing the question to the sky, or to herself.

'Well,' he said, 'my daddy is a preacher. He would probably say the worst thing you can do, after denying God, is to take a life.'

'Isn't that funny?' she said, turning toward him. 'Your daddy must be a very smart man. I'd say the same thing. Taking a life.'

'Rose, what—'

'*Shhh.*' She put a finger on his lips and rolled closer to him, her other hand suddenly busy. 'We have some unfinished business.'

In the midst of what followed, he found the presence of mind to reflect, for just a second: *She was right. It is better the second time. Much better*.

He awoke groggily a few hours later. It was still dark. She had saddled her horse and was kneeling by him. 'Don't get up,' she said quietly. 'I have to leave. You sleep for a while.' She touched his cheek and was gone.

For more than ten years.

Chapter Four

Horn slept late, then drove down the canyon road to a diner on Pacific Coast Highway, where he sat at the counter and ate ham and eggs. The door of the diner was open, and he could smell the ocean and hear the cars on the highway and, beyond the road, the sound of the surf.

Back at his place, he started on a long-planned job, clearing weeds along the road that led up to the estate. Later, he thought, he might head over to Westwood and make the collection for the Indian. He worked for two hours, stooped over as he stuffed weeds into a big canvas bag he dragged up the road behind him. By eleven, he had made his way almost up to the grounds of the estate. Tired and sweaty, he ran a hot bath in the battered, claw-footed tub that took up most of his small bathroom and soaked for a while, then made a salami sandwich, opened an RC, and sat on the porch to eat.

As he sat there, the thought of visiting the professor with the foolproof poker system began to seem less important. Instead, he went inside, looked up a number, and dialed it.

'Hello, Dex. It's John Ray Horn.'

'John Ray. How you been?'

'Not bad. I didn't know if you had the same number, or if I'd find you at home today. Haven't they put you out to pasture yet?'

Dexter Diggs laughed. 'To stud, you mean? That'd be the life. Hell, I can't afford to retire. No, they've decided they're going to kill me instead, with all the aggravation. I finished shooting one on Friday. Evelyn's going to have me underfoot for a couple of weeks, then I start shooting another one, something about stolen atomic secrets.'

'Sounds pretty exciting.'

There was no response. After an awkward silence, the other man said, 'I got nothing for you, John Ray.'

'What do you mean?'

'Work. Aren't you calling about—'

'I don't need a job, Dex. And if I did, I'd know better than to try to come back to Medallion anyway.'

'All right, then.' Diggs sounded relieved. 'You know, the last time you came around, that day we were shooting out at the ranch, Junior almost had a heart attack when he saw you. Started yelling about calling the police, getting you thrown off the property. And you almost cost me my job just for talking to you.'

'I know, Dex. Sorry – except about the heart attack. Listen, here's why I called: you remember Rose Galen?'

A silence, and Horn could almost hear him reaching back a decade for the memory. Then: 'Sure. *Smoke on the Mountain*, right?'

'That's it. I want to ask you about her. Who hired her, where she came from, what happened to her later.'

'Well, I hired her. I mean, I recommended her for the movie.'

'How come?'

'I knew her. I'd worked with her before.'

'What happened to her? After we finished?'

'I don't know,' Diggs said. 'I lost track of her. One thing I know: she never worked in the business after that. Have you heard anything?'

'I've seen her, Dex. Just the other night. It was in a bar downtown, and she was . . . well, she was not in good shape.'

'Damn.' The word came out quietly. 'I'm sorry to hear that.'

'I'm just trying to find out what happened. You said you worked with her before. When was that, and where?'

Diggs took his time answering. Finally he chuckled and said, 'You were a nice guy, John Ray, and we turned out some good shoot-em-ups together. But I sometimes forget how little you knew about things. Remember that time we were driving down Hollywood Boulevard and I pointed out John Barrymore coming out of Musso and Frank? And you said, "Who's John Barrymore?" '

'All right, Dex. I know who he is now.'

'But you didn't then. See, even though you were an actor—'

'I know a few people who'd argue with you about that.'

'Maybe so. At least the studio called you one. You worked in Hollywood, but you were pretty ignorant about what went on in this town before you showed up. Let me ask you this: when you met Rose, that day she walked onto the set, you knew nothing about her?'

'No,' Horn said with irritation. 'What the hell are you getting at?'

'I'm going to answer your question,' Diggs said with some satisfaction. 'But in my own way.'

'Come on, Dex . . .'

'No, I'm going to give you the long answer, not the short one. You'll have to come over here for it. How's Saturday night, about seven? It's Evelyn's bridge night, but we'll see what's in the fridge.' Diggs paused. 'You going to talk to her again?'

'I don't know. But I think I'm going to try.'

'Say hello for me. And tell her I'd like to see her sometime.'

It was close to one o'clock when Horn parked the Ford across the street from Rose Galen's rooming house and got out. On his side of the street stood more rooming houses interrupted by a junk-strewn vacant lot, like a gap in a row of old and yellowing teeth. Through the gap he could look out beyond the east rim of the hill and across much of downtown, where the last of the morning haze was burning off. The pointed-top City Hall dominated the skyline, an ersatz Babylonian transplant looming over this newest and most American of cities.

Below sleepy Bunker Hill the noise of traffic hummed away, and the smell of exhaust worked its way up the steep streets. Downtown was dirty, he knew, and the smoke from cars was foul, but he didn't always mind. Years earlier, when he had come here as a refugee from the hill country of the South, Los Angeles had taken him in with no questions. He had embraced the raw young city, with its fast pace and bustling streets, and even today the lung-biting smell of cars on the road both repelled and excited him.

He went up the worn steps of Rose's rooming house to the spacious front porch. A woman, not Rose, sat on the porch swing. Inside, he found the manager's office, a converted room with a Dutch door, top half open. The manager was short, round, and balding.

'Rose Galen?'

'Third floor, south front,' the man said, barely glancing at Horn.

The stairs squeaked, and the air in the stairway was close and still, bearing the smell of years of boiled cabbage and beans and other dishes he'd rather not know about. On the third floor, he knocked at her door but got no answer.

Retracing his steps, he stood on the porch, considering asking the manager if he knew her whereabouts.

'Who you looking for?' It was the woman on the swing. He walked over. She was tiny, birdlike, swaddled in a heavy coat buttoned up to her neck. Her feet stopped well short of the planking, and she gently rocked the swing back and forth on its two heavy, rusting chains. She could have been anywhere between fifty and seventy.

'Rose Galen,' he said. 'Do you know her?'

'Rosie? Sure. She lives right over me.' Her voice was tiny as she was, and animated. He had a quick image of a small animal in one of the cartoons shown before a movie. A mouse, a rabbit. 'Who are you?'

'I'm an old friend. Do you know where she is?'

'Yeah.' The little woman smiled open-mouthed, as if enjoying a secret joke. She had not visited a dentist lately. 'You sure you're not a bill collector?'

'No,' he said. At least not today.

'What's your name?'

'John Ray Horn.'

'I usually roll my own,' he said. 'You probably—'

'I don't mind,' she said, patting the seat of the swing next to her. 'My late husband, Earl, used to do that, all through hard times, until the war came along and we could get regular work. I got used to smoking handmades.'

He sat next to her and dug into his shirt pocket for a pack of papers and his pouch of Bull Durham. He laid a paper into the hollow formed by the thumb and forefinger of his left hand, delicately shaped it into a trough, carefully sprinkled the tobacco into the trough, and smoothed it with his index finger. He closed the pouch by yanking the string with his teeth and pocketed it. Then, with two quick motions, he licked the edge of the paper and rolled the bundle into a tight little cigarette, which he offered her.

'You do that real nice,' she said, leaning over to accept a light. 'Just like Earl did.' She sucked the smoke in greedily, then coughed lightly. 'Going to kill me, if a dozen other things don't first.'

'About Rose?'

She eyed him appraisingly. 'Well, if you were a good friend, you'd know where she was, 'cause she goes there most every day.'

'We go way back,' he said. 'It's just that I haven't seen her for a long time.'

'You the guy who walked her over here the other night?'

'Uh, that's right. How do you know about that?'

'Not much happens around here I don't know about. I've lived here longer than anybody, even the manager. During the war, I was the one made sure everybody kept their blackout curtains closed.'

'That's a big job,' he said. He waited.

She took another drag, burning up half of what remained. 'Anybody who can roll a good smoke can't be all bad,' she said finally. 'Besides, I could see right away you're not the gray man. You don't look anything like him.'

'Who's the gray man?'

'Just somebody we've noticed hanging around. She's down at the Anchor. You know where that is?'

'On Main Street?'

She nodded. 'She goes there to help out with the noon meal.'

'Thanks, Madge.'

He drove over to First Street and down the steep hill to the fortress-like newspaper building that housed the *Times* and the *Mirror*, then passed City Hall, towering smooth and white, on his left. After turning onto Main, he parked and began walking south.

Just a block to the west ran Spring Street, the financial center, where deals were cut involving water and power and land, where banks hoarded money and insurance companies calculated odds.

Main Street was different. If Spring wore a public face, Main was the street of more private pursuits. For as long as Horn could remember, Main had been the haunt of men and women out of luck and out of pride. During the war, the street had jumped to a manic rhythm as servicemen thronged to its bars and liquor stores and strip joints and tattoo parlors. Now it was just shabby and sad.

He passed a pawnshop, its barred window display crammed with weapons of more or less lethal character: rifles, nickel-plated pistols, hunting knives, switchblades, leather saps, a set of brass knuckles. Up ahead was the Follies burlesque house, all seats seventy-five cents, the marquee advertising Ruby Renfrew, the Detroit Firecracker. Just beyond the Follies, up ahead on the left, was his destination, the Anchor Mission and Traveler's Rest.

Horn knew the Anchor. When he first arrived in LA at age twenty-two, after two years on the rodeo circuit, hard times had descended on America, those same hard times experienced by Madge and her husband. He had spent several weeks at the mission while looking for his first job. The memories were not pleasant – nights spent on a cot in the big hall, the sour smell of other men as poor and unwashed as he, the minister's long and droning sermons imposed as the price of meals. But all was not bleak there: the food was regular and plentiful, the bed linens were changed once a week, and Horn learned the valuable lesson of always sleeping with his shoes under his pillow.

The big neon sign out front showed an anchor, slightly askew, superimposed over an upright cross. Underneath was a phrase, also outlined in neon: *Ye Who Are Weary, Come and Take Your Rest*. Horn pushed through the big front door and found himself at a reception desk behind which sat a man in shirtsleeves and suspenders. The man, his long face permanently creased into a hound dog's sad-eyed expression, looked up as Horn came in, then looked again, paying special attention to his clothes. 'You hungry, friend?' he asked.

Horn had intended to ask for Rose, but he changed his mind. 'Yeah, I'm hungry,' he said. 'Can I get something to eat?'

The man tore a ticket off a roll and handed it to him. It said *Admit One*. 'This is good for lunch,' he said. 'If you want dinner, you got to be here for the sermon at six. You need a place to sleep?'

'Not tonight,' Horn said and, following the wave of the man's hand, headed down a long corridor lit by a single feeble bulb. Through the door at the end he could hear many voices and the clink of cutlery. He paused there to take off his tie and put it in his pocket, almost smiling at his sudden and unusual desire to appear down and out. Usually, he reflected, people took one look at his pre-war, out-of-fashion suit and his scuffed, government-issue shoes and assumed a look of mild disdain.

The room was as he remembered it, big and noisy, full of people putting away food. At the far end stood a cafeteria line where a half-dozen of the staff stood ladling out big portions to the men and women who shuffled along with their trays. He scanned the food servers, trying to find Rose, then looked around the room once, then again, before returning to the serving line. It was there he finally spotted her.

She wore an apron over a plain, short-sleeved dress and she was hatless, her hair pinned back from her face. As she served up mashed potatoes and gravy onto the passing trays, she smiled, laughed, and joked with those in the line, her face free of make-up and shiny in the steam from the table. She was almost a different woman from the sad character he had seen two nights ago.

He stood there, debating whether to pick up a tray and take his place in line, when he heard a voice at his side.

'So, what's the deal?'

Horn turned to find a man facing him. He was a shade under medium height, spare and muscular, with a nose just slightly off center, and he wore a work shirt and khakis. He stood balanced on the balls of his feet, full of nervous energy that might need to be worked off at any moment.

'Beg your pardon?'

'I noticed you standing here. You got a ticket, but you're not in any hurry to eat, and you don't look like you're particularly hard up. So what do you need?'

Horn didn't like the man's manner. 'I thought everybody was welcome here,' he said. 'You know, to take their rest, like the sign says.'

'Well, I'm the pastor here, name's Quinn, and I'm also the doorman and the bouncer, and if I decide you're not a hard-luck case, ticket or no ticket, you don't get to eat.' He folded his arms.

Horn decided to try the conciliatory approach. 'Sorry to make trouble,' he said with a grin. 'I don't really need a meal, but I came looking for Rose Galen.'

'Don't know her.'

'Look, I'm an old friend,' Horn said. 'That's her over there, in the serving line. I just want to—'

'Nobody bothers people here,' the pastor said. 'You need to leave.'

'Wait a minute—'

'Out.' Quinn was three inches shorter than Horn, but his jaw jutted upward as he stepped into Horn's face. 'Or I call some friends over.'

'Easy.' Horn held up his hands. 'I'm leaving. But you really need to go back and brush up on one or two of your Beatitudes.'

Quinn looked at him curiously as he left.

40

Outside, he crossed the street and took up station in front of a liquor store, where he rolled a smoke and waited. Thirty minutes later, Rose came out just as a shiny maroon Lincoln Continental sedan, driven by a woman, pulled up in front of the mission. Rose waved. The woman got out and, taking long-legged strides, joined her on the sidewalk. They seemed glad to see each other and talked animatedly. Then the woman opened the trunk, and they began pulling out armloads of clothing, some of it still on hangers, and taking it inside. Soon the sad-faced man from the desk came out to help, extracting more clothes from the back seat. When they were finished, he huddled with the other woman over some paperwork on the hood of the car.

Afraid that Rose might leave with her friend, Horn quickly crossed the street, careful to dodge a passing trolley that clanged and sparked as it went by. He stepped up behind Rose and tapped her lightly on the shoulder.

'Remember me?' he asked. 'The guy with the bad memory?'

'*Oh.*' She backed away from him, panic washing over her face for an instant. Then she recognized him.

'I'm sorry, Rose,' he said. 'I didn't mean to—'

'Hey!' He turned to find the other woman standing inches away. 'Who the hell are you?'

'Uh . . .'

'Is he bothering you?' she asked Rose.

'It's all right,' Rose told her. 'I know him.' Her face was pale but composed.

'Yeah?' The woman had turned to face Horn again. 'How well?' She was tall, with a mass of auburn hair barely covered by a beret perched precariously on one side. She wore a tweed suit, man's style but woman-tailored, and appeared well put together underneath it. Horn guessed her age at somewhere around Rose's, but she was doing a much better job of holding back the years. For an instant, he had the feeling he had seen her before.

'It's all right, really,' Rose said. 'We're old friends. He won't do me any harm, so you can call off your dogs.'

The redhead gave Horn a last once-over. 'I don't think I like his looks,' she said, but this time she spoke with a lighter touch.

'Too bad,' he said. 'I like yours.'

'Lot of good it'll do you,' the woman said. Then, ignoring him, she gave Rose a quick hug. 'Got to go, hon. Much shopping to do. Say hi to Saint Emory for me.' Seconds later she gunned her engine and was gone.

'Who the hell was that?' he asked Rose.

'What are you doing here, John Ray?' she demanded. 'Emory mentioned there was a man looking for me in there. Was it you?'

'Yes, it was. And if Emory is the pastor, I thought he behaved in a very un-Christian way.'

'He was just trying to protect me.'

'From what?'

'Oh . . .' She looked uncomfortable, as if she'd said too much. 'He's protective of everyone who comes to the Anchor. He says some people are poor through no fault of their own, and we can't give them much, but we can allow them their privacy. He doesn't want people coming in and gawking at them. Or at those who try to help them.' Then, as if remembering to be angry, her voice took on an edge. 'How did you find me?'

'Your friend Madge,' he said. 'I rolled her a cigarette and made a friend for life.'

'Madge.' She shook her head. 'She's a dear, but she loves to gab.'

'So who's your redheaded friend in the shiny car?'

'Oh, that's Doll. You didn't recognize her?'

'I'm not sure. Why?'

'I just wondered.' A chilly breeze swept across the sidewalk where they stood. She took a near-shapeless wool cap out of her pocket and put it on, then wrapped her coat more tightly around her. 'I really should go.'

He took a step toward her. 'Rose, I came looking for you today, and I'm not leaving until you talk to me.' When she didn't reply, he pressed on. 'Have you had lunch?'

She laughed. 'Of course. Stewed chicken, mashed potatoes and gravy. One of the best meals I'll get this week.'

'Well, your friend Emory wouldn't let me have any, so I'm still hungry. Will you sit with me for a while?'

Doubt crossed her face, then resignation. Finally she sighed. 'All right, I know a place. Do you like Chinese food?'

Chapter Five

They walked back down Main to First and turned right. After a few blocks they entered a doorway under a sign that read *Far East Cafe. Chop Suey.* The inside was high-ceilinged and dimly lit, and dark wood partitions divided the space into many curtained-off alcoves. The Chinese hostess greeted Rose with affection and showed them to a booth. Soon they had a steaming pot of tea, and Horn ordered wonton soup.

'This neighborhood is mostly Japanese,' Rose told him, 'but the owner here told me once that Japanese like Chinese food, which explains this place. A little farther down the street is a Buddhist temple. Early in the war I was walking by, and I saw hundreds of Japanese waiting outside the temple with suitcases. Before long, trucks began pulling up and taking them away.'

'I remember,' he said. 'It seemed right then, didn't it?'

'Not to me.' She took off her cap and shook out her graying hair. It was cut shorter than the style of the day, but he decided that it looked good on her.

'This is quite a spot,' she said, indicating the restaurant. 'They say politicians from City Hall come in here and make deals behind their private little curtains. And since police head-quarters is not far from here, you see a lot of . . .' She stopped, noticing his expression. 'You don't like the police, do you?'

'I don't like the police.'

His soup arrived, and he started on it, surreptitiously studying her as he ate. Strangely, although the worry lines still played around the edges of her eyes, the lack of make-up only en-hanced her strong features. Her movements showed no sign of the other night's nervousness. He found himself comparing her face to that of the haggard-looking creature in the bar. *Sober and in the light of day, she's still a good-looking woman*, he decided.

'You're staring at me,' she said.

'Sorry.'

'I know what you're thinking. Which is the real Rose, the one you see today or the drunk?'

'Well, which one?'

'Both.' She held her cup in both hands, blew off some of the steam, and took a sip. Her fingernails were clean but not very well tended. 'Both. Today I served food to a lot of people who are worse off than I am. Tonight, if I feel like it, I'll go back down to Broadway and . . .'

'I don't get it.'

'You don't have to get it.'

'Do you need money?' As soon as he asked the question, he realized how pointless it sounded.

She laughed. 'Well, doesn't everybody? But are you offering me a loan? No offense, John Ray, but look at yourself. You're not much better off than I am.'

His expression reflected his frustration. 'At least tell me where you've been and what's been happening to you,' he said.

She reached over to refill both cups, moving slowly, as if she was using the time to marshal her thoughts. 'You're being polite,' she said. 'You want to know how I wound up the way I did.'

'Maybe I do.'

'Maybe you're prying.'

'I know. That's what I'm doing. But I have an excuse. I like you, and I want to know about you.'

She rolled her eyes, looking almost playful for the first time. 'It's boring.'

'Bore me.'

'Well, here goes. I grew up in Kansas and came out here a *long* time ago – even before you lived here – to work in the movies. I was lucky and got a few parts. Later, when things didn't go so well, I decided to move back home to Wichita and live with my folks for a while. I didn't fit in there, so I moved to New York. I worked at different things—'

'What kind of things?'

'I sold gloves in a department store. I was a waitress for a while.' He saw that she was looking him in the eye now, daring him to say something. 'I worked in an escort service, dating men who could afford to pay for an evening's company.'

He didn't meet the challenge. 'All right,' he said. 'What then?'

'I moved back to LA to give the movies one more try. I should have known there weren't many jobs available for a has-been actress who drank too much. That's when I met you. *Smoke on the Mountain* was my last film. You probably didn't know your co-star was at the very end of her not-so-glorious career.'

'No, I didn't,' he said. 'What happened then?'

'Not much. My parents died, and although they didn't leave me much, it was just enough to keep me at Rook House and allow me to eat out every now and then, and buy an occasional bottle to take back to my room. Although, as you saw the other night, it's always better if a kind gentleman comes along and offers to—'

'All right, Rose.'

She reached across the table and touched his arm briefly. 'Enough of that. Let's change the subject. If you can eat and talk at the same time, I want you to tell me about yourself, everything you've done since we worked together. First of all . . . well, that night I saw you, I knew something bad had happened to you, but I was drinking, and I couldn't quite remember what it was. Now I know: you were in prison.'

'That's right.'

'Do you want to tell me what happened?'

'I don't mind.' He finished the last of his soup. 'I'll back up a little first. After that picture we were on together, I worked steady and did all right. In 1940, I was Medallion Pictures' top cowboy, and if you looked at all the studios I ranked pretty high, right after Gene and Roy and a few others. When the war came along I was drafted, and when it was over I went back to work. One day . . . Do you remember Bernie Rome Junior?'

'Mr Rome's son? Vaguely,' she said. 'I think he was off at college, but I saw him once when he visited the set.'

'Uh-huh. Well, by the end of the war, his daddy was starting to train him to take over Medallion, even though the only thing that seemed to interest Junior was polo and spending Daddy's money. One day, Junior brought some East Coast gal out to the lot, someone he was trying to impress. He had some of the boys saddle up my horse, Raincloud, so he could jump a few fences for her. Raincloud broke a leg against the fence and had to be put down.'

'Oh, no,' Rose said. 'I remember your beautiful horse. I never heard about it. I'm so sorry.'

'I took it out on Junior. They called it felony assault. He got a busted jaw, and I got two years.' He pushed the empty bowl away from him. The waiter silently parted the curtain and laid the bill on the table, then departed as silently.

'That's terrible,' she said.

'I don't talk about it very often, but you're a good listener. Now it's your turn again. The other night, you said something bad had happened to you too. What was it?'

'Oh, I was just feeling full of self-pity,' she said, making a face. 'I do that when I drink. But don't stop now. Are you married?'

He pulled out his makings and questioned her with a look. When she said, 'No, thanks,' he began rolling a smoke. 'I got married about a year after I knew you,' he said. 'It didn't last. She divorced me while I was in prison.'

'I'm sorry to hear that,' she said. 'Any children?'

'She had a daughter when I married her. Name's Clea, and she's seventeen. I see her every now and then. Her mother too.'

'That's good,' Rose said. 'So now we're up to the present. Are you still in the business?'

'No,' he said, and it came out a growl. 'Mr Rome saw to that. He made sure no studio would hire me. For anything. I'm working for Joseph. You saw him the other night—'

'I liked him. How is he?'

'He liked you too. He's doing all right. Or would be, except for this niece of his who's staying with him and working in his

47

business. She grew up in a little town just outside the Lakota reservation, and now that she's living here in LA, she's gone kind of wild.'

'Is she the one who came into the Green Light with the two of you the other night, the one with the bruises?'

'That's her. It was your friend who gave her the bruises. That's the reason we were there.'

'He wasn't my friend, just an acquaintance. If he hit her, I'm sorry I spent any time with him. But the girl and I had a nice talk.' She smiled. 'I liked her.'

'I'm afraid she's trouble, Rose. Drinks too much, gets in fights, runs around with the wrong guys. Joseph feels responsible for her.' Horn shook his head. 'Being a father doesn't come naturally to him. She even seems to enjoy getting on his nerves. Every time she goes over the edge, he gets a little crazy and goes right over the edge himself.'

'Poor Joseph. Poor girl, too. I know what it's like to be young and pretty and on the loose in LA.' Rose shook her head. 'What's her name?'

'Cassie. Cassie Montag.'

'That doesn't sound like an Indian name.'

'Not all Indian names do. But Cassie happens to be half white.'

'I know what this town can do to people, especially young girls,' she said wryly. 'Maybe I should have a talk with her.'

'Thanks, anyway, Rose.' He looked uncomfortable.

She inclined her head slightly, regarding him. 'What's the matter? Oh, I get it.' Her expression hardened. 'I'm such a mess, I'm not entitled to give advice to anyone, is that it? Well, that's not very kind of you, John Ray. Or very fair.'

When he said nothing, she sat back in her chair, eyes still boring in. After a while, her face softened, and she smiled. 'It *was* nice to see the two of you together, just like the old days. Of course, Joseph didn't recognize the old dame across the room either. Looked right past me, just like you did the first time.'

'Well, I guess we can be proud of the Indian,' Horn said. 'He's made something of himself. Runs a card parlor out in an unincorporated part of the county, and I help out. It's called the Mad Crow Casino.'

'Sounds pretty grand.'

'It's not really. Just some poker tables and a roulette wheel and a few other things. But Joseph likes running a business, along with all the attention that goes with it.'

She seemed to be studying the tea in her cup, suddenly quiet. 'I know,' he said. 'You're wondering how it feels for Sierra Lane, the big cowboy hero, to be working for the Indian who used to follow him around in all those movies. But you're too polite to ask. Well, I don't exactly feel wonderful about it. But it's a job, and Joseph's a friend, and I'm glad to have it.'

'Sorry,' she said. 'You're right, I was wondering, and it's none of my business.' She got up suddenly. 'Thank you for the tea. You don't need to walk me back. Goodbye, John Ray.'

Quickly laying some money on the table, Horn followed her out. The sidewalk was busy with people, most of them orientals, heading for nearby shops and grocery stores and outdoor food stalls.

'Wait.' He caught up with her and took her sleeve. As they stopped, Horn was bumped from behind by a baby carriage propelled by a young Japanese woman. The baby boy leaned out, arms waving, and Rose reached down and allowed him to curl his tiny hand around her index finger. She smiled at the baby as the mother steered around them.

'Dammit, Rose.' She looked up at him, her face impassive, as he searched for something to say. 'Do you have a telephone?'

'A pay phone,' she replied. 'In the hall, under the stairs.'

Fumbling in his pocket, he came up with the meal ticket from the mission, then the stub of a pencil. He handed them to her, and she wrote down the number as he went on talking.

'Joseph and I were together last night, and he said I owed you for some of the good things that happened to me in the movies.'

'Well, that was nice of him,' she said.

'He was right,' Horn said. 'I never got a chance to thank you for it. Look . . .' He plowed ahead, knowing he sounded foolish but not caring if he did. 'Something went wrong for you, and you don't want to talk about it. Well, I've got secrets too.' He took a deep breath. 'In the war, I folded up. I've never told anybody. I spent months in a hospital while they tried to figure out what was wrong. They finally called it battle fatigue and discharged me. Everybody thought I came home some kind of hero, like Sierra Lane would have done. But I want you to know the truth. So, whatever secrets you have . . .'

'Did you kill anyone in the war?' she asked, her gaze elsewhere.

'Yes.'

'Was it self-defense?'

'I guess you could call it that,' he said. 'We always called it that. Look, Rose . . . Whatever you tell me about yourself, chances are I've done something worse.'

They stood there for a moment amid the noise and stream of pedestrians, the smell of cooked food and fresh produce drifting out of open doors.

She looked up at him and shook her head slightly, as if silently willing him to know that there were things he could never understand.

'Have you?' she asked. Then she turned and left him there on the sidewalk.

He drove back to his cabin. For a couple of hours he weeded some more along the driveway, this time making it all the way up to the burned-out estate. Once there, where the ground evened out, he used a scythe to cut them down, swinging the blade in broad, easy strokes, hearing the satisfying *snick*, seeing the weeds topple and lie down in bunches, like soldiers mowed down by machine-gun fire as they marched across a field in precise formation. He had last performed this chore just a few weeks ago. But the owner, a real estate speculator, liked to show prospective buyers around on short notice and had instructed Horn to keep the grounds from becoming overgrown.

In the early evening, he grilled a pork steak for his supper. Then he took a quick bath and changed into clean clothes.

When collecting, he always tried to dress well – suit, tie, hat, and fresh shirt.

The drive into Westwood took about half an hour. The neighborhood was a prosperous little enclave around the University of California campus. He found the professor's address on a quiet side street of small but well-tended homes. The house was vaguely Spanish in design, a popular look ever since the 1920s.

A youngish, pleasant-faced woman in an apron opened the door and, after some hesitation, called her husband. Henry Otis was younger than Horn had expected, somewhere in his mid-thirties and almost boyish-looking, clean-shaven and wearing wire-rimmed spectacles. Otis showed Horn into a kind of study and closed the door.

'You're from Joseph Mad Crow?' the man asked.

'That's right. I need to collect what you owe.'

'Well, I'd have preferred a phone call first,' Otis said. 'We're just about to have dinner.'

'I apologize,' Horn said. 'If I can just collect the amount, I'll be gone and won't bother you any more.'

'Coming into a man's house, in front of his wife,' the man said resentfully. 'Did your employer think I wasn't going to pay him? Is this the way you always work?'

'I do whatever I need to do,' Horn told him, trying to keep his tone friendly. 'As for your wife, I didn't tell her anything. And no, Mad Crow didn't think you'd try to welsh. He just doesn't want you to take on more debt than you can handle. He wants you to keep coming to the casino, but he's not going to extend you any more credit.'

'Well . . .' Otis sat at his desk, moved some papers around a little longer than necessary, then wrote out a check and handed it to Horn. 'Is that the amount?'

'That's it.' Horn folded the check and stuck it in his shirt pocket. 'Thank you, professor.'

'You don't have to call me that,' Otis said. 'I'm just an instructor.'

Horn looked around the room and noted that it was decorated in a western motif, with a painting of a roundup on one wall, a

51

set of polished longhorns over the desk, and a handsome, tooled-leather saddle on a stand in a corner.

'Do you ride?' he asked.

'I do,' the man said, still a little stiff but no longer quite so angry. 'There's a group of us who teach at UCLA. We like to rent horses and take them up into the hills. We call ourselves the Riders of the Purple Sage – you know, after the Zane Grey book. It's our little—' He stopped, staring at Horn. 'Good Lord,' he said. 'I know you. You made those movies with Mad Crow. You're Sierra Lane.'

'John Ray Horn, actually.'

'You look different now,' the man said, looking Horn up and down. 'Sometimes, for fun, we take our wives and girlfriends to that theater on Hollywood Boulevard that shows westerns—'

'The Hitching Post,' Horn said.

'That's right. We're usually the oldest people in the theater. We carry on just like the kids. I guess it's our way of getting away from the academic life, which can be pretty stuffy. Some of us have our favorite cowboys. One friend of mine, in the biology department, decided that Johnny Mack Brown is the best. Another likes the Durango Kid. I seem to recall you got somebody's vote too.'

They stood at the front door. Inside, Horn could hear Otis' wife finishing up in the kitchen, and he thought he could smell grilled fish.

'I'll go now,' he said.

'So, this job of yours,' Otis said, looking beyond him, out into the street. 'Do you ever have to get tough? That's the way I think of people who collect gambling money. Tough guys. I mean, suppose I'd told you to get out of my house? What would you have done? Hit me? Broken one of my fingers? Maybe threatened my wife?'

'Come on,' Horn said.

'Oh, hell,' Otis said. 'Why should I lie to you? I was the one who said Sierra Lane was the best of them all. You see, even though it was just the movies and acting and all that, still I thought you were pretty damned heroic. And I came back from the war thinking that heroes were very hard to find. But still worth looking for . . . And here you are, walking into my house to collect a gambling debt. Isn't that funny?' Otis smiled a little sadly, his eyes cold behind the glasses, and Horn knew what was coming. He was halfway down the sidewalk when he heard the man's parting words.

'I wonder if you're ashamed of yourself.'

Chapter Six

Horn was in a sour mood by the time he got home. In the small, curtained-off kitchen, he reached into the cupboard for his bottle of Evan Williams and poured a generous serving into a large glass. He sat on the front porch staring into the dark that was the canyon, listening to the small night sounds, waiting for Henry Otis' bespectacled face to take shape out there in the void. When it did, it wore a familiar expression, one Horn had come to dread: disappointed expectations, thinly veiled contempt. Sipping at his drink, he softly cursed all those who expected things of him, especially those who walked out of cowboy movies confusing the real person with the screen image.

Otis' face dissolved into Rose Galen's, and to his surprise he almost cursed her too. Even Rose, with all her problems, had shown a trace of pity when she regarded him and what he'd become. *She's got no room to pity me*, he thought.

But his other memories of her soon crowded out the anger, and he remembered his talk with Dexter Diggs. Her old director wanted to see her again, and he had forgotten to mention it to her.

Picking up the receiver of the telephone by his sofa bed, he fished out the meal ticket and dialed her number. After several rings, a man answered, and Horn asked for Rose.

'If she's here, I'll tell her you called,' the man said. Horn thought he recognized the manager's voice.

'Can't you take a look?'

'She's two floors up,' the man said impatiently. 'We don't like to tie up the phone.'

Horn grudgingly left his number and hung up. His watch told

him that it was after ten, and he wondered if Rose had gone down the hill to the bars on Broadway. But a few minutes later he heard her voice.

'Hello, there,' she said. He could tell she was drunk.

'How are you doing, Rose?'

'I'm doing . . . I'm just *mar*velous.' She drew the words out slowly, languorously, as if examining each one before letting go of it. 'I've been sitting with a friend, and we're having a wonderful time.' She giggled. 'Wish you could be here. Except you have a way of interrupting a girl when she's drinking.'

'I hope it's not that character we saw you with the other night.'

'And what if it is?' She tried a teasing tone, but it lay heavy.

'I mean it, Rose. He's a dangerous man—'

'Oh, I know all about him. Don't be such a *policeman*,' she said. 'If you must know, he's not the one. No, this is a new friend, a very nice new friend.' She sounded pleased with herself, as if she knew something he didn't. 'You'd have no objection.'

He felt a wave of anger toward her, for being a lush, for not being the Rose he wanted to remember. But he tried to suppress it. 'Listen,' he said. 'You can get back to him. I just wanted to ask if I can see you tomorrow and if I can bring someone along. Do you remember Dexter Diggs?'

She repeated the name, giving it three distinct syllables.

'You remember Dex. He directed us together. And he worked with you a long time ago.'

'Oh,' she said faintly. 'Dex.'

'I'll see if he can come over tomorrow night, all right?'

'No.'

'What's the matter?'

'I don't want him to see me.' It was almost a whisper.

'Dammit, Rose, I've seen you.'

'I didn't want you to. Now that you have, I can't do anything about it. But I don't have to see Dex. And I won't. Now you'll have to excuse me, while I . . . disappear.'

'What does that mean?'

'Nothing,' she said almost playfully. 'It's just a line from a song. You're way too serious sometimes, you know that?'

He made a sound of frustration, trying to think of another approach. Almost in desperation, he said, 'You know, I remember you.'

All he could hear on the line were the faint sounds of the rooming house. It was almost as if she were holding her breath. 'Remember what?' she said finally.

'How important you were to me.' He began speaking quickly, to overpower her denials. 'I remember two things. The way you turned this dumb-ass country boy into something resembling an actor and gave him a chance at a career.' She made a dismissive sound, but he went on. 'And I remember that night I saw you for the last time. With everything that's gone wrong in my life, I'd just about forgotten that night. But not any more. I'm not Sierra Lane, and I can't rescue anybody. I'm just a guy who never got a chance to say thank you. For all of it.'

Another long pause, and then she spoke. 'Well, if you'd like to come calling tomorrow night, come right ahead. No Dex. Just you.'

'Fine.'

'I remember you too,' she said in a small voice, and hung up.

He spent the next morning doing chores around the property. As he took a break for a midday meal, Harry Flye, the owner, drove up in his big Chrysler with a couple who had come to look at the Aguilar estate. Unlocking the gate, Flye steered the car up the rutted driveway past the caretaker's cabin and on up the hill. Although Horn stood there regarding them, Flye didn't acknowledge him. The two men had a scratchy relationship based strictly on mutual need. Flye, an inveterate penny-pincher, needed an employee who would work hard for no wages, and he knew that Horn was grateful to have a place where he could live rent-free.

Too bad I'm not wearing my hat, Horn thought. *I could take it off and hold it in both hands, ducking my head just a little to show him respect.*

card parlor to deliver the money he had collected from Henry Otis and to get his cut. The place sat on what before the war had been a rural road, its only neighbor a gas station a hundred yards away. Now, with Los Angeles filling in around its edges and pushing outward into farmland, the road had grown busier, with a cafe and a roadhouse and a scattering of little homes nearby.

The casino itself, which the Indian had built while he was still on the payroll at Medallion Pictures, resembled an oversize barn. It was painted white, with a red roof, a few small windows, and a flickering neon sign over the door that read *Mad Crow Casino*. The inside was mostly one big, high-ceilinged room, with offices for Mad Crow and his secretary upstairs and storage rooms in the back. When Horn entered, the place was quiet, not due to open for a couple of hours. The Indian was at the bar, conducting a liquor inventory with a couple of his employees.

'How you doing?' he muttered distractedly to Horn. The bar glittered with bottles lined up neatly in twin ranks. The place smelled of ammonia as one of his workers wiped down the glass shelves and the mirrored wall behind them. His mind clearly elsewhere, Mad Crow took the check, extracted a small roll of bills from his pocket, and peeled off an amount for Horn.

'Lula!' he bellowed for his secretary. 'I need those invoices!' He looked around. 'Where the hell is she?'

'You're busy,' Horn said. 'I'll just—'

'No, uh . . .' Mad Crow's eyes focused on Horn. 'Oh, shit. Stick around. Got my mind on other things, that's all.' He leaned back against the bar and exhaled heavily. 'It's Cassie.'

Horn made a face. 'What is it this time?'

'She took off from work last night without telling me. I wasn't paying attention. One of the boys told me she got a call from somebody and up and left.'

'Steal your Caddy again?'

'No. I've been letting her use the Chevy. But I think she lifted one of the bottles from the bar.' He looked disgusted. 'Now she's stealing from me. And she probably ran off to be with that Mexican boy.'

'You don't know where she went.'

'I know she came home late last night, drunk on my liquor, and slept till noon. And I don't know if she's going to bother to show up for work tonight.'

'What are you going to do?'

'I'm going to quit playing wet nurse, that's what.' He slammed the edge of the bar with the heels of both hands, as if to make the thought go away, and focused on Horn again. 'So now that you're flush, you going out to spend some of it?'

'Guess I am,' Horn said. 'Going to see Rose tonight.'

Mad Crow brightened visibly. 'Well, that's real nice. You say hi for me.' His expression shifted as a thought struck him. 'Maybe you can ask her if she, uh, needs a job,' he said slowly.

'You thinking of firing Cassie? Don't you think Rose is a little old to wait on tables here? And she's . . .' The rest remained unspoken: *And she's a drunk.*

'I guess she is. But if she needs work, I could ask around, maybe help her find something, you know? See if she's interested.'

Horn's watch showed a few minutes after seven when he parked near Rook House. It had rained in the late afternoon, a winter shower too brief to cleanse the air or the streets. The old rooming house stood huddled in the cold, the dampness only adding to its bedraggled look, the way a dog seems to lose some of its pride when wet. A faint smell of engine oil rose off the newly slick street.

He had a plan. He was going to take Rose out for a good dinner. He would buy her a few drinks if necessary, and then make her tell him what he wanted to know. It would not be easy, but he would not stop pushing until he knew what had happened to her, what had made her give up.

He would have found it hard to explain why he was there. The drive for self-knowledge did not come naturally to him. But two years in prison and the collapse of his career and his marriage had forced him into a grudging examination of what had gone wrong, and Horn now knew that he carried within him great flaws – anger, suspicion, resentment – that had laid him low and could destroy him if he allowed them to take over again.

He had fallen. So had Rose. And her fall had been much more profound and hopeless. Seeing her and what she had become made him uncomfortably aware of the parallels in his own life. It was like seeing his own distorted image in a funhouse mirror and being unable to look away.

It wasn't exactly charity that brought him back to Rook House. If he could lift her up just a little, maybe he could do the same for himself.

He went inside and climbed the two flights of uneven stairs to her room, then knocked and waited. No answer. He knocked again, louder. 'Rose, it's John Ray.' He retraced his steps down to the first floor, where he knocked on the manager's door. Again, no answer.

Undecided, he stood there for a moment. Then he began to recall something from his talk with Madge, the little woman on the porch swing, the day before. What was it she had said? *She lives right over me.*

Up on the second floor, he knocked on the door of the south front room. After a few seconds, Madge opened it. She wore a thin, limp robe, one hand holding it tightly closed around her neck. Standing, she looked even smaller.

'Evening, Madge,' he said. 'Remember me?'

She looked him over quickly, her eyes moving over his clothing and features with tiny, abrupt motions. 'Sure I do,' she said, with a trace of irritation. 'On the porch yesterday.' She waited.

'Well, I found Rose, and I want to thank you for the directions,' he went on. 'I just can't seem to find her tonight. She knew I was coming . . .' He paused, recalling that Rose had been clearly drunk when they spoke; she might have simply forgotten. 'But I got no answer at her door. Or the manager's either. Any idea where she might be?'

Madge stood there a moment, appraising him. 'She usually goes out at night,' she said.

'I don't think she would have gone out tonight. She was expecting me.'

'Well . . .' She seemed about to close the door.

'Can you help me?'

'Oh, shoot. I don't know what I can do.' But she went for her slippers and, cinching the sash of her robe about her waist, led him up the stairs. 'She naps sometimes,' Madge explained on the way. 'Air raid siren wouldn't wake her. Maybe you knocked, but you're too polite. I know how to rouse her.' Reaching Rose's door, she made a tight little fist and banged loudly on the door several times. 'Rosie! You got a visitor!' She banged again, then stopped. 'You hear that?'

'What?'

'That music.'

From inside the room, Horn could hear a faint melody. 'Radio's on,' he said. 'Maybe she was—'

He stopped when he saw Madge's face. She looked suddenly pale and fearful. 'I been hearing music all day long,' she said. 'All last night too. Didn't know where it was coming from. Wait a minute.' She bit her lip. 'We give each other keys,' she said. 'Just in case, you know? One time I got chest pains, and she . . . Anyway, I'll go get it.'

She scurried down the stairs. As he waited, Horn idly tried the knob, and the door opened. The sound of the radio came up. It was Tex Beneke's band doing 'Give Me Five Minutes More,' and the lightweight tune seemed oddly buoyant and out of place in this tired building.

He wasn't sure how he knew there was death in the room. Maybe it was the radio playing all night and day, with no one to turn it off. Maybe it was the faint ammoniac smell that struck him suddenly, making him think at first of someone wiping down Mad Crow's bar. But this was earthier and more sour, a smell that took him back to a young German soldier sitting under a tree somewhere in southern Italy. He was dead only minutes, a neat American-made bullet hole in his throat, and his winter-issue wool trousers were sodden down to his knees. *Happens a lot when they die*, Horn's sergeant said, hustling his men along.

As the door swung fully open, he saw her on the bed. He had encountered death many times, both in the war and later, but this was different. He had never seen anyone dead by strangulation, never seen that particular violence done to a person.

Rose seemed to be resting after great exertion, her arms and legs still frozen in the effort of trying to escape the thing around her throat. As he drew nearer, he saw that it was a thin pull-cord of the sort used for curtains. It was tied once around her neck, buried until nearly invisible in the discolored skin, and the remaining cord was looped around some of the upright posts of the bed's headboard, with the trailing end lying on the floor. She was fully dressed except for her shoes, which lay by the bed.

He looked once at her face, swollen and nearly purple, and then did not look at it again.

He heard quick footsteps, then a hiss of breath from behind him. He swung on Madge as she entered the room, moved to block her view, took her by the shoulders more roughly than he intended. 'Don't look at her,' he said sharply.

Madge swallowed audibly. 'Is Rosie dead?' the small voice asked.

'That's right. She's dead. Someone . . . It wasn't an accident. There's nothing we can do for her. Listen . . .' He bent close to her. 'You're going to need to call the police. Go down to the phone and do that, will you? And Madge—' He tilted her chin up until she looked directly at him. 'Don't tell them I was here. Can you remember that? I wasn't here.'

'You weren't here,' she almost whispered, and then left.

He closed the door and looked urgently around the room. The radio made it hard for him to think clearly, so he turned the volume down. If the police found him here, they would see him as a perfect suspect, a felon, a man of violence. He might even go back to prison; things sometimes worked that way.

But he was reluctant to leave the room where she lay. Without quite knowing why, he wanted to take a mental photograph of the place. She had lived here. She had once been important to him. It was no more complicated than that.

He began to look around. The cord, he soon found, had been yanked from one of the tattered curtains that framed the two windows. Whoever killed Rose had cleverly arranged the rope so that when he pulled on it, her head and neck were forced up against the headboard until they could go no farther. He kept pulling, and she died.

The place was a single furnished room, the bath apparently down the hall. The bed took up a third of the room. In one corner was a crude sink and counter top with a coffee pot and hot plate. Over the sink, behind a flimsy curtain, were shelves of glasses, dishes, and canned goods. By the window was a small kitchen table with two chairs, where Rose may have taken her meals. On the table were an almost empty bottle of Scotch and two glasses with small amounts of liquor. Had Rose's killer had a drink with her first?

Rose's purse lay against the baseboard, as if discarded hastily. It was empty. He found no money, no documents, cards or other papers – only an old wartime sugar ration stamp that had been wedged in a seam.

There was something wrong with the room. No pictures, no mementos, nothing to suggest a life, a history, friends, family. He looked quickly through the dresser drawers and found nothing but clothes. Then, digging deeper in the top drawer, he brought out a hard object that had been wrapped in a wool muffler. It was a small, framed photo of a young woman. The picture was oval-shaped and expertly hand-tinted, the way photographers had once added color to a black and white portrait before color film became readily available.

The young woman was not Rose. She had dark hair in spit curls that had long since gone out of fashion. She wore a blouse with a Peter Pan collar, and she was lovely.

Horn turned over the frame and saw on the back a faded sticker bearing the name of a photo studio in Oklahoma City. He slipped the frame in his jacket pocket and looked quickly around the room once more. Then he crossed to the bed, bent over and, averting his eyes once again from Rose's face, touched her leg lightly. Her nylons were wrinkled from her struggling, and along a seam he saw the remains of an old split and the shiny spot where she had repaired it with clear fingernail polish.

He knew that when someone died, you were supposed to say words. But he could think of none. He patted the leg once again, then left.

As he descended to the first floor, he heard Madge talking to the police on the phone under the stairs. Her voice quavered, but she spoke slowly and distinctly. *She's handling this all right,* he thought. He went out the door without looking back.

Horn sat in his darkened car for a long time. He saw the police arrive, followed by a black coroner's wagon. He watched them trundle Rose's body out under a sheet, and noted lights going on in some of the windows as detectives moved around the building talking to residents.

Finally, the old building was dark and quiet again, and still Horn sat there, unwilling to leave. He tried to roll a smoke but found himself unable to control the paper and tobacco. He felt a rage building in him. But it had no focus, and instead of strengthening him to lash out at something, it left him feeling breathless and weak.

He became aware of a repetitive, high-pitched sound. Over on the front porch of Rook House sat a small figure, swathed in a heavy coat, rocking in the swing, the rusty chain making a plaintive squeak in the night.

Chapter Seven

It was after midnight when he started the engine and pulled away from Rook House. But sleep seemed impossible, so he drove aimlessly through the city. Broadway with its towering movie marquees now dark, MacArthur Park and its palm-ringed lake full of secrets, the giant Ambassador Hotel, the whimsical Brown Derby restaurant. Then back north, and up to the hills and shabby houses of Chavez Ravine, where he parked above the lights of downtown and listened to the whispers and giggles of couples in cars parked nearby.

After a couple of hours he found himself at an all-night diner in the warehouse district not far from Alameda and the railroad tracks. He went in for a cup of coffee and a couple of doughnuts. He watched the night people come and go – a cabby on a break, a tired hooker wrapped in a pathetic feather boa, an unshaven guy with an army knapsack who looked as if he had just rolled out of a boxcar. All of them perched wearily on stools at the counter for a while and then moved on.

Her face materialized before him among the cracks on the linoleum countertop, the earliest one first: *I'm Rose. Never done a western, but I'm willing to learn* . . . Then, years later: *You don't remember me, do you, John Ray?* For the moment, the picture of her face in death was put away in one of the drawers of his mind. But those drawers, he knew, never stayed closed.

Wanting to stay in motion, he drove south through down-town to Central Avenue, the dark-skinned thoroughfare that never closed, the place of lights and jazz and food and drink. He found a 'blind pig', an unlicensed, after-hours bar, where he stood at a counter made of three wooden packing crates laid end to end and ordered a bourbon. Horn's was one of the few white faces in the bar, and the bartender looked at him hard, smelling cop, but then took in the weary look, unpressed suit, and prison-made belt buckle, and poured the drink.

Waste, Horn thought, taking his first swig. It was all waste. A decent woman dead. A foolish woman, true, one who had been broken by life and chosen to hide behind the bottle. Foolish enough to live in a mean and dangerous neighborhood, to invite men to her room. But a decent woman nonetheless. Horn wondered if he would ever know who had killed her and for what trivial reason.

The bartender, who resembled Jersey Joe Walcott with the addition of a belly and a perpetual scowl, moved around sluggishly, refilling glasses. At a table in one corner of the room sat several men with instrument cases, apparently musicians who had finished their gig at one of Central Avenue's many jazz clubs. One of them blew idly into a tenor saxophone, and Horn recognized a few bars of 'Lili Marlene' – an odd choice for this place, but no one seemed to mind.

As he stood there, Horn went over the mental snapshot of Rose's room again. His eyes focused on the bartender's hands, and something in the fuzzy mental image of the room stood out, so suddenly and unexpectedly that he put down his drink, quickly laid a half-dollar on the bar, and left.

He arrived at Mad Crow's ranch house not long after first light. The sun would be up soon, but house and trees were still gray and indistinct in the early light. When he got out of the car, his breath showed lightly on the air, and his shoes made tracks in the dew-wet grass.

He knew the layout of the house and carefully counted the windows in the rear until he found the one he wanted. He tapped a few times on the glass with his fingernail. He waited, and the curtain parted and Cassie lifted the window a few inches. She squinted at him in the pale light.

'I need to talk to you, Cassie,' he said in a low voice. 'I don't want to wake anyone else. You can either come out or let me in the front door. But be quiet.'

65

A question crossed her face and she started to ask it, but she changed her mind and lowered the window. A minute later she opened the front door and let him in.

The living room was big and high-ceilinged and finished in rough-cut wood. Years earlier, Mad Crow had gotten to know William S. Hart and had liked the rugged western look of the retired actor's hilltop home out in Newhall. This room was full of Indian rugs, mounted buffalo horns, antique weapons, paintings with Indian motifs, and one-sheet posters from some of the films he and Horn had made.

They sat across a table in big leather chairs. Cassie was barefoot, wearing rolled-up dungarees and an oversize plaid shirt. The bruise had mostly faded from her jaw. She had once again worked the braids out of her shoulder-length hair. Even free of make-up and with the sleep still clouding her slightly sullen face, she was striking.

'Sorry if I woke you up,' he began, keeping his voice low. 'I just need to find out where you were night before last.'

She yawned exaggeratedly. 'Is it any of your business?'

'Yes,' he said.

'I don't think so.' She looked around the room, feigning boredom. 'You doing some kind of errand for my uncle? If that's it, he can ask me himself.'

'You don't like him very much, do you?'

'He called my father white trash,' she said, her face now hard in the half-light of the unlit room. 'I know, because my mother told me. I've seen the way he looks at my father. He looks at me the same way.'

'I bet you're wrong about that,' Horn said carefully. 'Joseph doesn't judge people.'

She laughed. 'He judges white people,' she said. 'You think he likes you?'

'I know he does.'

'Maybe it's just because you're such a good errand boy.'

He decided to let the insult pass. 'Things aren't as simple as you think. I'm sure your father—'

'And if you're going to stand up for him, don't bother,' she said heatedly. 'He *is* trash. Why do you suppose I left?'

'You tell me.'

'Because I was tired of watching him get drunk and hit my mother. Even worse, I was tired of hearing her make excuses for him. Not long ago he hit her again, and I stuck him with a kitchen knife. I swore if he did it again, I'd cut his throat. Next thing I knew, she had packed me off to this place.'

He sighed. He had come here with a clear intent, only to find her leading him down this side road. 'All right. I'm sorry it's like that. But I need to talk to you about something else.'

'I know. Where I was night before last. Maybe I'm not in the mood to talk.'

He studied her, trying to equate this angry young woman with the shy youngster he had once met on a visit to Mad Crow's home ground in South Dakota. He had sensed that her mixed blood assigned her a questionable status in the extended family. But he had warmed to her right away, and soon was able to coax her into showing him some of her favorite places. They spent hours together roaming the fields and fishing the streams.

'I can't quite figure out why you don't like me very much,' he said.

She shrugged. 'You're just a white guy, like all the others. You used to boss my uncle around—'

'I never did that.'

'Well, look at these.' She indicated two posters bracketing one of the windows. 'You're the big hero, and he's the loyal Indian somewhere in the background.'

'It was a job, Cassie. For both of us. It was also the Depression, and we were glad to have the work.'

'And now you're hard up,' she went on as if she hadn't heard him, 'so you come around looking for a handout.'

'I work for Joseph, just like you do.'

'Maybe not for long.' Her mouth twisted into a grin.

'What do you mean?'

'He wants me out of his house. And he said if I feel like quitting my job, that's all right with him too.'

67

'Well,' Horn said, 'none of this would have happened if you'd stayed out of trouble.'

'Go to hell, Mr Horn. You want to know something?' The anger tightened her voice. 'I'm ready to be on my own. I don't need his handouts. He's just been waiting for the little halfbreed girl to fall down, embarrass herself, embarrass her family.'

'Are you going home?'

She didn't answer.

'Are you really going to take a knife to your father?'

'Won't know about that until it happens.' She sank back in her chair and mumbled the words, sounding irritated and resentful.

'All right, listen to me.' He sat up in the big chair, leaning forward. 'If you won't talk to me about the other night, let me tell you a story, and maybe you'll want to join in. I met up with an old friend, a woman named Rose. You sat with her for a while that night at the Green Light Tavern, and I got together with her a couple of days later. We had a long talk, and I told her about you, about how you've been having trouble. She knew a lot about trouble, and also about helping people, and she offered to talk to you. I didn't ask her; in fact, I didn't particularly want her to. But she offered.

'As I said, she had problems of her own, and I had no idea if she'd follow through or not. But then Joseph told me you took off work and lifted a bottle from the bar. I was at Rose's place later, and I noticed she and someone else had been drinking from a bottle. There was one little thing I didn't remember until after I'd left. Funny how you can almost miss something that's right under your nose. The bottle hadn't been bought at a store. It had a bar spout stuck in the top. Now that doesn't mean a lot, I suppose. But I know that if a bartender wanted to give away some of his stock, he'd never hand out a bottle with a spout still in it. He'd pull the spout and cap the bottle first.' He paused. 'Any of this make sense to you?'

Cassie slowly twisted a lock of hair around one of her fingers. 'Well, suppose I was there,' she said finally. 'She called me at the casino. Invited me over. We had a few drinks.'

'What did you talk about?'

'Nothing much. Things I should watch out for. All the terrible things that are waiting for a little girl out there in the big city.' She laughed. 'She sounded like my mother.'

'Did she give you any good advice?'

She shrugged. 'Who knows? I guess she tried.'

A door opened, and Mad Crow's aunt came out in her night-dress. Her broad, sharp-planed face regarded them impassively.

'Good morning, Nee Nee,' Horn said quietly.

'Make some coffee?' the old woman asked.

'Don't go to any trouble.'

'Make some coffee.' She headed for the kitchen.

He felt immensely tired. It was time to get to the point. 'What time did you leave Rose's place?'

'I don't know,' she said, looking bored again. 'Sometime after midnight. She got sleepy, and I said good night.'

'Did you lock the door?'

Her eyes narrowed. She seemed to understand that his ques-tions were not idle ones. 'No,' she said. 'I couldn't. What's this about?'

You're stalling, Horn, he said to himself angrily. *Spit it out*. 'Sometime that night, someone came into Rose's room and killed her.'

Her jaw went slack. 'What?'

'Killed her. Strangled her with a piece of rope. I found her last night.'

'No.' Without taking her eyes off him, she slowly brought her knees up and hugged them, as if suddenly cold. 'Who?'

'I don't know. In that neighborhood, it could have been anyone. Her purse had been emptied. Did you see anyone there? Did anyone see you?'

Her face still vacant, she shook her head. 'No. I mean, I don't remember. There were a few people around. I suppose someone could have seen me.'

'Cassie, if the police get your name, they'll be coming around asking questions. So I have to ask you first: do you know anything about what happened there?'

69

'Why don't you say what you mean?' she said slowly, her eyes fixed on the tabletop. 'You want to know if I killed her.'

'All right. Did you kill her?'

'No.' The word came out gutturally.

They sat there in silence for a minute or two, listening to the stirring sounds in the back of the house. Nee Nee came out of the kitchen with two cups of black coffee, which she put on the table between them, then left without a word.

Cassie spoke in a voice too low for him to hear.

'What?'

'She was a nice woman. She didn't deserve that.'

'I know.'

A door opened, and heavy footsteps came down the hall, followed by the sight of Mad Crow in a garishly patterned robe and slippers. 'What the hell?' he muttered as he spotted them. 'Thought I heard talking.' He came over and sank into one of the chairs, raised his eyebrows at Horn. 'Let me guess. You're sitting here in my living room because you want my permission to court my niece. If so, you're a stupider cowboy than I thought.' He noticed the coffee. 'Think I could get a cup of that?' His eyes darted between the two of them, and he caught the tension. 'All right, what's going on?'

Horn took a long breath and began talking. He told everything. As he spoke, Mad Crow's face went from shock to anger to something more guarded.

'Sonofabitch,' the Indian muttered when Horn had finished. 'Poor Rose.' All three sat motionless, the windows now bright around them. Horn was about to speak when he saw that Mad Crow was regarding his niece through narrowed eyes. There was suspicion in the look.

Cassie saw it too.

'You sure you want to throw her out?'

The two men sat at Mad Crow's kitchen table while Nee Nee fixed them breakfast. Cassie had gone to her room. When the food arrived, Mad Crow splashed liberal amounts of hot sauce on the scrambled eggs, then studied his plate as if deciding what to do with the food. Finally he shoved a forkful in his mouth. 'I don't think you want to get involved in this,' he said around the eggs.

Horn started to say something, then looked questioningly toward the aunt.

'She's all right,' Mad Crow said.

'Okay. Just thinking out loud. Cassie was in a place where a murder happened. Maybe somebody saw her, maybe not. If the cops ever put her on their list, you know it won't make any difference to them whether she did anything or not. I'm not particularly happy about the treatment I got from the police, but at least I'm white. An Indian—'

'I know.' Mad Crow reached over to refill Horn's coffee cup. 'But she's on her own now. She hates my guts, and she's told me too many lies. My sister's just gonna have to understand. Cassie's a big girl, and I'm through looking out for her, covering up for her. If she needs some help finding another place to stay, even getting another job, she can ask me, and I'll try to help. That's all.' Mad Crow's wide mouth was set in a hard line. The rest of his eggs sat untouched. 'Something else you want to say?'

'Just this. If you ever hear that Cassie's headed back home, you need to call your sister right away.'

'Why's that?'

'You may not know everything about why Cassie's here. She went after her father with a knife.'

'What?'

'Said he'd been hitting her mother.'

'Why, that . . .' Mad Crow let his fork drop to the table, and Horn saw the old look steal into his eyes, the same look the Indian had shown that night in the Green Light Tavern. Only this time there was no grin.

'All right,' Mad Crow said quietly. 'That's between me and him. Some day it's going to happen.'

'Do you mind if I talk to her again?'

'What about?'

'Just things.'

71

'Be my guest.' He looked sideways at Horn. 'You, uh . . . You think she did it?'

'Did what?'

'You know.'

'Hell, no, I don't think so. And you better not either.'

Chapter Eight

The police came that night. He had tried to get some work done around the place but, exhausted, he finally turned in before sunset, while the rim of the far side of the canyon was still painted orange by the lowering sun. He slept soundly until something awakened him around nine. He lay on his couch under a sheet and blanket, listening, then saw a bright light rake through the trees outside the front windows. A second later it was gone. Then it returned, this time illuminating his front porch.

He got up and dressed quickly. Stepping out the front door, he saw a large, dark-colored sedan parked just beyond the locked gate. It had twin searchlights, and both were busily playing around the cabin and property.

He walked down to the gate. Two men stood on both sides of the car, leaning casually against the doors, operating the light handles with small, expert wrist motions.

'You Mr Horn?' asked the man standing on the passenger side.

'That's right. You want something?'

'Yes, indeed.' The man flipped his suit lapel to one side, and the shield pinned underneath it shone dully in the reflected light. 'My name's Coby, and this is Stiles. We're with the police, and we'd like you to unlock the gate so's we can come on up and have a talk with you.'

'Happy to.' He pulled the key from his pocket, freed the big lock, and swung the gate open. Stiles got in and, tires crunching on the gravel, drove the sedan twenty yards up the estate road and then turned off and parked in front of the cabin. Horn and the man's partner followed on foot.

'You're way the hell out in the middle of nowhere, aren't you?' Coby asked as the three mounted the steps to the porch.

'I suppose,' Horn said. 'I work here, looking after the property.'

'What property?' Coby was heavy-set and slow-moving, with a soft face and an amiable grin fixed onto it. He leaned against one of the front posts, hands in his pockets. Stiles, who was younger and apparently the junior partner, sat on the top step, playing with the crease in his fedora.

'Up on the hill,' Horn said. 'It's the old Aguilar estate.'

'Never heard of it.'

'Well, unless you used to go to the movies a lot twenty years ago, you wouldn't have,' Horn said. 'Place was built by Ricardo Aguilar. He was big in the silents.'

'I think I've heard of him,' Stiles said. 'Didn't he play Ben-Hur?'

'That was Ramon Novarro,' Horn said. 'But Aguilar was the same kind of actor. Big movies like that.' *If you like, I could give you the tour*, Horn thought. *If we had the time and a few shovels, maybe I could even show you where a few bodies are buried.*

'You know a lot about the movies?' Stiles asked from where he was seated, and Horn thought he detected a small secret joke in the question.

'Sure he does,' Coby said before Horn could answer. ' 'Cause he used to be *in* the movies.' He turned to Horn. 'Didn't you?'

'That's right,' Horn said.

'Cowboy movies,' Coby went on. 'You used to saddle up and ride after the bad guys, get into shootouts, all that stuff.'

'I guess so.'

'I never heard of you before today,' the detective said. He pulled out a book of matches, extracted one, and began scouring the inside of one ear. His face took on a reflective look. 'But I dug out your record, and there were some newspaper clippings in there. I guess you were hot stuff. Me, I always liked Gene Autry.'

'You like the singing cowboys,' Horn said. 'The ones with the guitars.'

making fun of him. 'Just Gene. Anyway, a few years ago, you
got put away for something. That right?'

'You saw the record.'

'Nearly beat a man to death, what I heard.'

'It wasn't as bad as that.'

'Did two years for it. Must've been pretty bad.'

'Whatever you say.'

Having apparently quelled the itching in his ear, Coby flipped
the match over the porch railing. 'Anyway, brings us to the
reason we're here. Woman got killed downtown the other night.
A barfly named—' He pulled a small notebook out of an inside
coat pocket, turned a few pages until he found what he wanted.
'Named Rose Galen. She lived in one of those old places up on
Bunker Hill. That neighborhood's crawling with winos and
derelicts, all kinds of people like that, you know? It's about one
step up from skid row. They fight over cigarettes, over bottles of
booze, and every now and then, one of them winds up murdered. Looks like she was one of those.'

'So why are you talking to me?'

'Well, interesting thing,' Coby said, warming to the subject.
'Couple of people saw you with this gal in the last few days. One
was a bartender down on Broadway who spotted you at the
same table with her and some other characters. There was a
scuffle, and everybody left. He said he wasn't sure who anybody
was, but then you came back for a minute and he got a good
look. Said he finally placed your face after you left. You know,
from the movies.'

'You said a couple of people,' Horn said.

'Did I say a couple? I don't remember. Anyway, this is the part
where I quit talking and you start.'

He had to be careful about what he said. He couldn't lie about
knowing Rose. If he denied being at her place, they might force
Madge to contradict him. Someone could also place him at the
Anchor Mission when she was there. All he had was the truth,
and it offered dismal protection.

'Let me say something first,' Horn began. 'Since I got out, I've been doing my job and trying to stay out of trouble. I work at the Mad Crow Casino—'

'I know,' Coby said. 'I hear Mickey Cohen's got a piece of that place.'

'That's the owner's business, not mine. Thing I'm trying to say is, since Cold Creek I've had a clean record. I don't go around killing people.'

'Fine,' Coby said. He and Stiles waited.

'I ran into Rose at that tavern. There was a little trouble, but the bartender can probably tell you it was between two other men. Rose was an old friend, and I caught up with her later and walked her home. Two days later, I looked her up at the Anchor Mission, where she sometimes volunteered. We walked over to Little Tokyo for some lunch. That night – the night she was killed – I called her, and she said I could come by the following night. When I showed up, her door was unlocked. I found her dead.'

'You found her?' Coby asked quietly.

'That's right. There was another old gal there, friend of Rose. She went off to call the police—'

'We talked to her. Funny she didn't say anything about you being there.'

Horn laughed. 'Well, I'm not surprised. She looked like she was in shock. I don't know how she even found her way to the phone. Anyway, I thought I'd better just leave – you know, with my record and all. I guess that was a mistake, but I'm not used to walking up on dead bodies, and I wasn't thinking very well.'

'I hear you were in the war,' Coby said casually. 'You must have seen a few bodies over there.'

'Sure,' Horn said. 'But not like this.'

'Uh-huh.' The detective flipped through the notebook pages again. 'You know any of her friends?'

'Not really. Just that woman. Madge, she said her name was. And the pastor over at the mission.'

'Emory Quinn,' Coby said after a glance at his notebook. 'We talked to him. You want to tell me where you were two nights ago?'

Horn told Coby about his visit with Henry Otis over by UCLA

in the early evening. The detective wrote down the address in his notebook. 'After that,' Horn said, 'I came home and stayed here.'

'And no one saw you here.'

'Nope. I live alone.'

Coby wrote that down too.

'One of the roomers said they saw a stranger going up the stairs in the building the night Rose Galen was killed. A young woman, dark hair. Ring any bells?'

'No. Sorry.'

'Okay. Anything else you want to tell us?'

'If I made a problem by not sticking around last night, I'm sorry.'

'Sure.' Coby stood there studying him, that half-smile still stuck on his face.

'I'd sure like to know if you're arresting me,' Horn said. 'If so, I'll finish getting dressed. If not, I guess I'll get back to bed.'

Coby laughed, made a meaty fist, and brushed Horn's shoulder with it good-naturedly. 'Might be fun to arrest you. That's one of those things I always wanted to do – take a movie actor downtown. Friend of mine, he's in Vice. Got his picture in the paper the night he nailed Robert Mitchum for smoking a little weed. Never let me forget it. I always told him I'd get my own movie actor someday. Maybe it's going to be you, huh? Now, Stiles here—' He indicated his partner with a nod of his head. 'Thing he likes to do most is beat up Mexicans. That, and pumping his girlfriend.'

'All right, Luther,' Stiles said, sounding bored.

'Me, though, I just want to collar a movie star. Since I can't get Robert Mitchum, I'd settle for a washed-up cowboy actor. No offense, of course.'

'I'd be a disappointment,' Horn said. 'You wouldn't see a single photographer turn up.'

Coby looked around at the shabby cabin. 'Maybe so. Anyway, I don't have enough on you. Hell, maybe you're clean. But just for fun, let's say you killed this Galen woman. I'll get what I need, and I'll be back. I'll be the sheriff, and you'll be the horse thief who gets to ride out to the hanging tree, just like in those old movies of yours.'

As if catching an unspoken signal from his partner, Stiles rose to his feet. Coby stepped closer to Horn, looked him up and down.

'Something tells me you were a better actor than they gave you credit for,' he said. 'Let's talk again sometime, all right?'

A wind off the ocean found its way up the canyon during the night, and Horn awoke to a chilly mist blanketing the trees. He drove down to the coast highway and had breakfast at the diner where the canyon road met the Pacific. Later, he worked around the property for a few hours, trying not to think about Rose. Then, as lunchtime approached and he began cleaning up, he felt his spirits lifting. It was Saturday, and he was going to see Clea.

Forty-five minutes later, he drove up to an imposing white house in the Hancock Park neighborhood, and she ran out the front door, skirt flying over her long legs and saddle shoes, and reached through the window and hugged him before he even had a chance to get out.

'Damn, it's good to see you, little girl,' he said.

'You're not supposed to call me that any more,' she said in mock anger. 'I'm a *senior*.'

'Oops. Pardon me.'

He studied the seventeen-year-old. He had not known exactly what to expect, for it had been only a few months ago . . . He thought back to that night on the scorched grounds among the ruins of the Aguilar estate, when Iris' new husband had died violently, when Horn and Clea had come close to death, and when Clea herself had been forced to kill in order to save both of them. No one could come away unmarked from such a night, and he had feared for her. But here she was, looking guilelessly happy and full of energy.

Iris came out to join them. 'Hello, John Ray.' She wore a stylishly long camel's-hair coat, her hair done in a new kind of wave. She had the same strong, attractive features, but she seemed to look older. Horn wondered how much Clea had told her about that night. But Iris had been through enough, and he had decided never to ask.

'Iris.' He leaned out to kiss her cheek. 'Where do you girls want to eat?'

'Dolores's!' Clea shouted before Iris could speak.

'I guess it's Dolores's,' Iris said. 'Would you like to take the Packard?' she asked diplomatically, glancing at Horn's cramped and dirt-streaked old Ford. 'We'd have more room.'

'Sure.' They switched cars, with Clea in the back, and he drove them to the drive-in on Wilshire, about fifteen minutes away. A car hop came out to take their orders, and Clea self-importantly specified crisp French fries and extra malt in her chocolate malt.

They tore into the food, and he was happy just to listen to the talk of school, boys, Frank Sinatra, clothes, boys, dances, and . . . oh yes, boys. While he and Iris had been married, Clea was his stepdaughter. When he went to prison and Iris divorced him, then remarried, he had no reason to expect that he would ever see mother or daughter again. Now her third husband was dead, leaving behind secrets that Horn prayed his widow would never unearth. Iris and Clea were once again a part of his life. And Horn, a man not especially skilled at forming attachments, found himself immensely grateful.

'And you,' he said to Iris around a bite of his hamburger. 'How are you doing?'

'All right, I suppose,' she answered with a small smile. 'I miss Paul, of course.'

She's entitled to her memories, he told himself. *And so is her daughter. Let it rest.* 'You need to move on,' he said to her, aware of how feeble his advice must sound.

'I know,' she said. 'I'm trying.' In the back seat, Clea seemed oblivious to their conversation. As she ate, she hummed along to a tune from a nearby car radio.

'Don't misunderstand. I'm not seeing anyone,' Iris said with a half-hearted laugh. 'I've sworn off men forever. But I've been thinking of going through the house, clearing out some of Paul's things. Do you think that's wrong?'

'Of course not.'

'Paul had some nice clothes. I think he would have wanted them put to good use.'

'You'll think of something.'

'How about you?' she asked. 'Would you have any—'

'No,' he said, more forcefully than he intended. He had an image of Rose's tall, redheaded friend delivering clothing to the mission. 'But I might be able to help you find a good place for them.'

'I'd appreciate that.' She leaned back in her seat, looking as relaxed as she was capable of looking. 'This is fun,' she said. 'I'm glad we came here.'

'Can I get another malt?' Clea called out from the back seat.

As they ate, rain began to spot the windshield, and the car hops ferrying trays to and from the cars looked increasingly bedraggled. By the time he dropped off Iris and Clea and headed home, it was raining steadily, with the radio warning of a Pacific storm about to move ashore.

Once home, he built a fire in the small stone fireplace and listened to the rain and wind outside. He poured a small glass of Evan Williams and settled on the couch with a copy of Zane Grey's *Fighting Caravans*. He didn't realize he had dozed off until the phone rang.

'John Ray? It's Dex.'

'Dex?' He sat up quickly, knocking the book to the floor. 'What time is it?'

'A little after seven. You forgot, didn't you? My feelings are hurt.'

His mind struggled to recall. Dex was going to tell him about Rose. And now there was no need. 'Oh, no.'

'It's not that bad. They say at your age, it's normal to forget little things, like going to visit a friend. Now when you get to *my* age, you'll find it's going to be a lot—'

'Listen to me. She's dead.'

'Who?'

'Rose.' He let out a deep breath and sank back onto the couch. 'Rose is dead. Somebody killed her.'

There was a long silence on the other end. Outside, the wind was still troubling the trees, and every now and then he heard something skitter across the roof of the cabin.

'Sorry,' Horn said. 'I should have called you. But I've been trying not to think about Rose or anybody connected with her.'

'Who did it?' Diggs asked quietly.

'They don't know. Police were here, muscling me a little to see if I had anything to do with it. But they seem to think it was just somebody in the neighborhood, one of the drunks or junkies that hang out around her building. They called her a barfly, Dex. It made me mad to hear it, but I couldn't help thinking: maybe that's what she was. Rose was a nice lady, but she was a drunk too, and people who live the way she did sometimes wind up—'

Diggs interrupted him. 'John Ray, I know we're friends, but I wish to hell you'd just shut up.'

'What's the matter?'

'That's what I want to know. All this talk about her—'

'It's true, Dex.'

'I don't care.' He stopped, and Horn could almost hear him thinking hard. 'Can you still come over tonight?'

'What? We've got a storm out there, or haven't you noticed?'

'I promised to tell you what I know about Rose. And from those noises you've been making, that she deserved what she got—'

'I never said that, Dex.'

'You need an education in Rose Galen, even more than you did before. And I guess I'm in the best position to give it to you, and there's no better time than tonight. If you'll come over here now, I'll throw in a free dinner.'

When Horn didn't speak, he pressed on. 'Like I said, it's important. To me, and to you too.'

Horn sighed. 'Directors. You sound like Cecil B. De Mille with his megaphone, ordering the peasants around. All right, Dex. I'm on my way.'

Chapter Nine

Dexter Diggs' house stood on an unremarkable street in the Valley a few blocks north of Ventura Boulevard. Before going in, Horn sat in the car for a few minutes, the rain drumming on the roof like Gene Krupa gone berserk. The last time he had visited here, he was married, with a wife and daughter, making good money working at a job he enjoyed. He had never been in a war, never fired a shot in anger, never seen the inside of a prison. Much had happened since then, but the little house stood just as before, half obscured by ivy and bougainvillea, like a picture postcard in the back of a forgotten drawer.

Diggs answered his knock. 'Hi, there,' he said. 'Plenty wet, huh? Well, we're going back out in it. But first, come in here with me for a minute.' He was stocky and square-featured, a little below medium height. Although close to sixty, he was tanned and strong-looking. The only detail that seemed out of place was a natty, almost delicate moustache. Over the course of a long career, Horn knew, Diggs had been an all-purpose director, as much at home doing drawing-room comedies as outdoor sagas. In his glory days, he had lived much more grandly. But those days were behind him, and he was now settled in at the B-movie factory known as Medallion Pictures.

Diggs opened an interior door leading to the garage, stepped inside and flicked on the light. Walking around the front of his Plymouth, he stood for a moment in front of a large set of shelves that held dozens of film canisters, looking for something. Spotting the one he wanted, he lifted it off the shelf. 'Open the garage door for me, will you?' he asked Horn. Moments later, they were in his car, backing out of the driveway.

houses,' Diggs said as he steered the car down the street, wipers going furiously. 'Mine's in my garage.'

'I know,' Horn said, remembering. 'You showed me a few there. Mostly, I remember a lot of beer drinking. And Evelyn's popcorn.'

'I never showed you any of the old ones,' Diggs said. 'When I started out, back before sound, the life expectancy for a lot of studios was a few months. Every time one of those fly-by-night companies would go belly-up, I'd try to salvage some of my work before I went out the door. When sound came in, everybody said silent film was dead, and a lot of the studios melted down their old inventory for the silver content. Meanwhile, I'd built up a pretty good collection. Be worth a little money some day.'

'What are you going to show me?'

'You'll see.'

'Why not show me at home?'

'You'll see that too.' Although Rose's death had darkened his demeanor, Diggs was enjoying being mysterious.

'So where are we going?'

'Just a few blocks. To the studio.'

'Medallion? They won't let me in, Dex.'

'We'll see.' They drove in silence for a few minutes. Then Diggs turned in at the main gate of Medallion Pictures and drove up to the guard shack. 'Looks like Al's on tonight,' he said to Horn, cranking down his window. 'I thought he would be. Remember him?'

The guard, a stocky, florid-faced man in a tight-fitting rain slicker, leaned over the car. 'Evening, Mr Diggs.'

'Evening, Al. I've got a little work to do.'

The guard looked past him to his passenger. 'Hello there, John Ray,' he said hesitantly. Then, turning to the driver: 'I'm sorry. He . . . uh, he can't go in. You know that.'

'We won't be long.'

'I can't let him in. You know what would happen.'

'You're absolutely right. If you see him, you can't let him in.'

Diggs' tone was friendly. 'But if you never saw him, then you haven't done anything wrong. Now, if I were to try to bring my friend here onto the lot, I'd probably hide him in the trunk. And if anybody asked me later on, I'd say there was no way anyone could have seen him.'

The guard pondered this, obviously reluctant. 'I don't know.'

Diggs had one more card to play. 'Al, I hope your wife and kids had a good time on the set a few months ago. *City in Danger*, wasn't it? The bank robbery scene?'

The guard nodded. After hesitating a few more seconds, he went over and threw up the gate. 'Don't work too late,' he said.

The lot was mostly dark, and pools of rainwater glistened on the asphalt between the structures. Diggs passed the main administration building and the commissary and guided the Plymouth between two rows of giant sound stages.

It had been about three years since Horn had been here, but the memories went back at least a dozen. Over on the right was Sound Stage Number Three, where he had walked into his first speaking part. The movie was something called *Arizona Gun Law*, and it had taken them less than two weeks to shoot. Horn had only a few lines, and he still remembered them: *I ain't looking for trouble, Marshal*, and *We'll never catch him, boys. He's got too much of a head start*.

Up ahead was Sound Stage Number One, where they had shot the interiors for *Smoke on the Mountain*, and where he had first met Rose. Number One was also where he and Mad Crow had worked together for the first time, in a movie called *Vengeance Trail*. Their first scene was a fight in a saloon. Over-eager, the Indian dislocated a shoulder during a fall, and Horn feared they would lose a day's shooting. But Mad Crow wedged his forearm high up between two stair railings, put his weight on it, and popped the shoulder back in place. Then, his face impassive but shiny with sweat, he turned to Horn and said, 'I love this business.' Horn knew they were going to get along.

'Looks the same to me,' Horn said to Diggs, indicating the row of dark and bulky buildings.

'It is, pretty much,' the director said. 'At least on the surface.

This place still cranks out an average of a picture a week. But not as many of those cheap westerns you and I used to make. We're doing more crime movies now, the kind I call "wet streets", because we go for the nighttime look. Everything's supposed to be dark and mysterious. I don't know . . . The war did something to us. It's gotten harder to tell the good guys, John Ray. Even in the movies.'

Diggs pulled up in front of a long, one-story building. 'And then there's this television thing,' he said as he set the brake. 'All they show now is junk. But it's going to get better, and it's not good for our business. I wonder if any of us will have jobs a year from now.'

Horn could think of nothing to say. It was hard for him to feel any sympathy for an industry that had turned its back on him.

Diggs unlocked a door and led Horn down a corridor past several screening rooms until they came to the last in the row. He produced another key and unlocked the door, and they went in.

The room was medium-sized and austere, with a large screen, concrete floor, exposed pipes and ducts across the ceiling and, on a series of four elevated platforms, a few rows of bolted-together folding wooden chairs of the sort found in some classrooms.

They shook the water off their hats and coats and laid them down. Carrying the film canister, Diggs climbed up to the tiny projection booth and busied himself inside. 'This is the only old-fashioned projector I know of that's still plugged in and running,' he said, raising his voice as he worked. 'That's why we had to come down here. This antique was used for silent films. It runs at sixteen frames per second, too slow for today's film. If we threaded a silent onto a regular projector, it would make everybody jump around like puppets.'

'What's this one doing here?'

'The old man, Mr Rome, he keeps it for sentimental reasons. Word is, he's still got a crush on Mary Pickford and likes to sequester himself down here every now and then with his brandy flask and run her old movies.' Diggs went on, 'I told you I worked for half the studios in this town, even some of the biggies. I'd still be at MGM or Fox or one of those if I hadn't started hitting the bottle. Only got myself to blame for that. I directed Gloria Swanson at Paramount – twice.' He stuck his head out of the booth. 'You know who she is, don't you?'

'I know who Swanson is, Dex.'

'Never sure about you,' Diggs said, getting back to work. 'This was before sound, when you had to do everything visually, with light and shadow and gestures and faces. Anyway, I know a few things about stars. They're not like you and me, John Ray—'

'You don't think I was a movie star? I'm going to feel bad, Dex.'

'You know what I mean. The real stars have got something extra. Maybe it gets turned on only when they step in front of a camera, but it doesn't matter. They've got it. I'm going to show you somebody who's got it.'

Horn heard the whine of the projector. 'Hit the light, will you?' Diggs asked, coming out. They took seats together as the blank leader ran through the projector, throwing a bright white square up onto the screen.

'In the late twenties I worked for a studio named Pinnacle. The place was run badly and lasted only a few years. But while I was there, we did one called *Hawk of Tramonti*. This is the last reel.'

An image sprang up on the screen. It was the great hall of a castle, with tapestried walls and towering stone columns. At the far end, a small figure stood on a balcony beyond an arched portal that framed distant, snow-streaked mountains. In the foreground, a richly robed man, back to the camera, began walking toward the balcony.

'The duke,' Diggs said. 'The actor who played him was a bit of a ham. I had to warn him about overacting all the time. But he was fun to have around. After wrapping each day, he and I hit a few bars, as I recall.'

The small figure turned as the camera cut in to a medium shot, and Horn recognized a much younger Rose Galen.

'She was about twenty,' Diggs said. 'She plays Lucia, the duke's daughter. This was her first big part. We weren't sure if she was up to it, until . . . Well, you'll see. Sorry we've got no music, but this isn't Grauman's Chinese.'

A title card flashed on the screen, and Horn began to follow the story when Diggs interrupted. 'Bunch of illiterates wrote this stuff,' he said disgustedly. 'I can tell it better. This is, oh, fifteenth-century Italy, if I remember. Her old man's a tyrant, and the people hate him. She falls in love with the leader of the revolutionaries, a dashing young fellow called the Hawk, spends some time with him and his merry men in the mountains. Daddy captures her boyfriend, threatens to execute him unless she renounces both him and his cause and agrees to marry this pansy who has his own little principality next door.'

'Let me guess,' Horn said. 'She saves the Hawk, and they ride off together.'

'Not exactly,' Diggs said. 'It's coming up. Just watch.'

Down below in the courtyard, men with crossbows were taking aim at the young revolutionary, who stood proudly against a wall, his eyes on the figure on the balcony. Then, as drums rolled – silently, of course – the camera began cutting between Lucia, her lover, and the drums, each shot of Rose moving in closer until her face filled the screen. Horn saw a range of emotions pass over her features – first shock at her father's words, then horror at the moment of execution, then a steely determination as she turned to face her father.

Horn sat quietly, his eyes fixed on her. The rest of the film unfolded quickly. That night, Lucia crept into her father's bedroom with a dagger, intending to murder him as he slept. In the candlelight, her face once again reflected a series of changes. First it showed her hatred for him. But as her glance swept past a bedside portrait of her dead mother, her expression softened into a trace of the love she still held for him. Finally, she placed the portrait on the pillow beside his head, and her expression took on a look of peace. In the final scenes of the movie, she mounted her horse and, as the sun rose and a hawk circled above her, she rode into the mountains to join the revolution against her father.

When it was over, Diggs went up to shut off the projector and begin rewinding the reel. Then he took his seat again. 'We liked to lay it on pretty thick back then, huh?' His tone was self-effacing, but Horn could hear the pride underneath.

Horn turned to him. 'Good Lord, Dex,' he said. 'I've never seen anything like that.'

Diggs looked grimly satisfied. 'When I promised you an education, I wanted you to see how wonderful she had been at that time in her life. That's the way I remember her. You should too, my friend, no matter how she ended up.'

Horn nodded, still searching for words. 'She was really something.'

'I know. One in a million. Her face, the way she moved. And did you notice how natural she was? Most silent actors came out of the theater, where they exaggerated everything for those in the back rows. Somehow, Rose understood that the camera was different, it could handle subtlety.'

'You weren't so bad yourself.'

'Hmm?'

'That footage. It's pretty good stuff, Dex.'

'Oh, yeah.' Diggs allowed himself a smile of self-approval. 'It *was* good, wasn't it? These days, when I'm shoveling 'em out every few weeks, I forget what it was like to be absolutely passionate about making movies – working with the actors, setting up the camera, getting the look just right. I was a man in love, John Ray. In love with the idea of putting beautiful pictures on a long strip of celluloid. It'll never be that way again—'

'Maybe it could be.'

'Nope. Not for me, and certainly not for Rose. But damn, we did some good work together, didn't we?'

He heard the film finish rewinding. 'Come on,' he said, getting up. 'Let me get this baby back in the can, then there's that little matter of dinner.'

They sat at Diggs' kitchen table eating roast beef sandwiches and sliced pickles and drinking beer. Horn had finished telling the other man what he knew about Rose's death. They sat in silence for a while, then Diggs began speaking in a reflective tone.

'She called herself Rosemary Gale back then,' he said between bites. 'It was just a name the studio gave her, because they thought her real name didn't have enough pizzazz.' He seemed to be studying his sandwich. 'You know, back when the three of us worked on that horse opera,' he said, 'you probably thought I was busy with camera setups all the time, but I saw the looks you two shot each other. Anything going on there?'

'I guess there was,' Horn said. 'But it was over real fast, and she was gone.'

'The lady had a habit of disappearing, didn't she?'

'When I had lunch with her, she told me she left the business the first time around because things didn't work out. What did she mean?'

'I have no idea. I mean . . . granted, Pinnacle sank out of sight not long after we made *Hawk of Tramonti*, so she would have been out of work. But she was an amazing talent, John Ray, right at the beginning of what could have been a spectacular career. You saw how beautiful she was. I'm not exaggerating when I say she was the best natural actress I ever worked with, and one of the best I ever saw anywhere. Better than Swanson, better than Dietrich, and – hell, I know this is heresy – almost as good as Garbo. All she needed was the right roles and a little time to prove herself.'

'But none of that happened,' Horn said. 'What brought her down so far?'

'Maybe it was nothing more than the bottle, John Ray. It's done in a lot of people. I can tell you about that.'

'I'd be surprised—'

'You shouldn't be,' Diggs said forcefully. 'When I first worked with her, young as she was, she already had a problem.'

'Booze?'

'That, and other things. This was Prohibition, you know? It seemed like everything we liked was illegal, and we were all a little wild. I think Hollywood was one of the craziest places on earth. Everyone drank, everyone played around with dope. If you showed up at a party, people would hand you things – drinks, reefers, it didn't matter. Things were so out of control, I remember somebody dying at one of those parties.' He shook his head. 'Rose was . . . well, she was part of all that. We ran into each other at some of the same places, and I always left before she did. When we were making that movie you just saw, she would amaze me. She'd be up half the night dancing, then show up early the next morning, face the camera, turn on some kind of interior light, and . . .' He shrugged. 'As I said, she had something.'

'That doesn't sound like the Rose I knew,' Horn said. 'The wild part.'

Diggs shrugged. 'People change.' He opened the fridge. 'You want another beer?'

Horn didn't reply, his thoughts off somewhere. Diggs put the bottle in front of him.

'How did she look?' Diggs asked.

The sight of Rose's face in death rose up again, dark and awful. But Horn knew that was not what his friend had meant.

'Worn down,' he said. 'But there was still something there.'

'I wish I'd been able to see her,' Diggs said.

'Like I said . . .'

'I know. Stubborn woman. It was her damn vanity, I imagine. She didn't want me to see what she looked like. I wouldn't have minded.' Horn was surprised at the man's vehemence. 'And for her to die like that, at the hands of some piece of vermin who wanted whatever money she had in her purse,' Diggs went on. 'She deserved better.'

'You're not the first person to say that,' Horn replied. 'I wonder if it's all as simple as we think. Her death, I mean.'

'Why wouldn't it be?'

'I'm not sure. I just remember small things. For one, Madge – her friend at the rooming house – mentioned a man, someone Rose knew about. She called him the gray man, and it sounded as if he had been hanging around the place for some reason.'

'Well . . .'

'And Rose may have been afraid of something.'

Diggs waited, head cocked to one side.

'I found her at the Anchor Mission down on skid row,' Horn said. 'When I asked the guy in charge where she was, he lied, said he didn't know her. Later, she told me he was just trying to protect her privacy.'

'Maybe that's all it was,' Diggs said.

'Maybe. But I'd already told him I knew she was there, so why lie? A bartender on Broadway behaved the same way, as if he was watching over her. And when I crossed the street outside the mission to see her, she panicked for just a second, as if she thought someone was after her.'

'That's a rough part of town, John Ray.'

'I know. Maybe I'm wrong. Then, later on, just before we said goodbye, she hinted that . . . I can't even remember her words, but the gist of it was that she might have done something terrible, something she was ashamed of.'

'No offense, but maybe she had a lot to be ashamed of,' Diggs said, shaking his head. 'It's a sad story, and a lot of the murders in this town never get solved. Tell you what—' He lifted his beer bottle. 'Let's drink a toast to her and remember her the way she would want us to.'

Horn didn't move. 'Not long ago, I told myself I was going to find out why she wound up in that fleabag of a rooming house,' he said. 'I thought I owed her something, and that maybe if I found out what had gone wrong with her, I could help.'

'Well, it's too late, John Ray. Even with good intentions, you don't always get to do what you—'

'It's not too late to find out who killed her.'

'Now wait,' Diggs said. 'That's for the police. Don't you think you've had enough dealings with them? If you get in their way, they'll come down on you.'

'They've already written her off,' Horn said. 'You can hear it in their voices when they talk about her. She was a nobody, and she was killed by a nobody. They don't care. I do.'

'All right, you care,' Diggs said with resignation. His face was lined under the strong kitchen light, and Horn was struck by how old and tired he looked. 'And what happens if you find the one who did it?'

'Then we'll see.'

Chapter Ten

The few tables in the cafe were taken, so they sat side by side at the counter. Madge ordered a bowl of chili, the lunch special, and Horn had a grilled sausage sandwich.

'Rosie liked the grilled cheese here,' Madge said. 'She'd order it almost every time we . . .' She stopped, unwilling to take the memory any farther.

The cafe was two blocks south of Rook House, and the customers seemed representative of the neighborhood. Most were shabbily dressed, although some still wore signs of gentility – a worn-down fur stole, perhaps, or an old pair of shoes that had been expensive when new. All were older, except for a young deliveryman in an Air Corps surplus bomber jacket whose truck was parked at the curb.

'See him?' Madge said, indicating a thin, white-haired man at the end of the counter. 'They say he's the last one here on the hill who still owns his house.' The man wore a dark suit and tie, and he held his coffee spoon delicately. 'He used to be rich as Croesus, but he was wiped out in the crash. His wife died, and his kids scattered. Now he keeps taking in roomers, to buy groceries and pay taxes. He's down to almost nothing, and his place is full of strangers, but he still has his house.'

'Can I ask you about Rose?' When he had met her at the rooming house, she had seemed to be still stricken by her friend's murder. He didn't want to make her unhappier, but he felt he had little choice.

'I don't mind,' she said. 'Maybe I'll feel better, talking about her. I like to talk anyway. I was going to call you sometime.' She crumbled some of the plump, round crackers into her chili and shook some hot sauce over all of it.

'Why's that?'

' 'Cause I knew she liked you. She told me so, after that time you went down to the mission to find her.'

'I'm glad to hear that,' he said. 'But how could you call me?'

'I had your number. Remember that time you called Rosie? The manager scribbled it on the wall, along with your name.'

The news troubled him. It sounded like one more thing the police might use against him if they discovered it.

Seeing the expression on his face, she patted his arm. 'Don't worry. I scratched it off soon as I noticed it.'

'Then how—'

'I memorized it. PRospect 3391. Right?'

'You've got quite a memory, Madge.'

'I know,' she said, her mouth full of chili. 'All my life, I've been able to remember almost anything I set my mind to, especially words or numbers. When me and Earl were on our way out here about fifteen years ago, we'd stop by the roadside and camp with other people. Everybody was hard up for entertainment. Some folks would play guitar or mouth harp and sing. Me, I'd do memory tricks. You got a dollar bill on you? If you'll read the serial number off of it, I'll say it right back to you.'

'I believe you,' he said.

'And if there's anything I don't want to remember, I just forget it.' She chuckled. 'I guess that leaves room for the things that take up space in my head.'

'About Rose,' he prompted her. 'Did she ever have arguments with anyone? You know anybody who didn't like her?'

'Everybody liked Rosie,' she said in a tone that did not invite disagreement.

'What about this gray man you mentioned? Who is he?' He motioned to the counterman to freshen his coffee and bring Madge another grape soda.

'Just somebody I see around every now and then. Eugene, the manager, seems to know him, but he won't tell me anything about him. Once I saw him talking to Rose, out on the sidewalk, and later I asked her about him, being my usual nosy self.'

'What did she say?'

'Nothing. She just looked . . . very far away, almost like she didn't even hear me.'

'Did she seem afraid of him? When they were talking?'

Madge paused. 'I don't know,' she said. 'Agitated. A little nervous, maybe.'

'How did he get that name?'

'I gave him that,' she said, looking amused. 'Not 'cause he wore gray. He wore dark colors, mostly. But his complexion looked almost gray. You know, unhealthy. He looked like an old guy who didn't get out much.'

'If you see him around again, would you let me know? It's important.'

She nodded, busy again with her chili.

'What about her friends? I understand she'd sometimes run into people—'

'Down on Broadway? I wouldn't know about that. I don't like to go in bars. Rose and me would share a bottle in her room sometimes. Maybe I like to snoop, but what she did on Broadway was her business.'

'Anybody ever visit her?'

'Just me. Sometimes Doll.'

'Tall redhead? Drives a big Lincoln?'

'That's right. You know her?'

'Kind of. I bumped into her down at the mission. She thought I was giving Rose a hard time, and she almost chewed my head off. Who is she?'

'Rosie said if I went to the movies more, I'd know her. I don't go much, though.' Madge went on, 'Earl and me, we got out of the habit during hard times. Seemed like all the movies back then were about rich folks wearing evening gowns and sitting on white upholstery. Some people liked that, 'cause it helped 'em forget their troubles. But it just reminded us how bad off we were.'

'What about Doll?'

'Well,' Madge said between sips of grape soda, 'she'd come by every few weeks. Sometimes she'd leave a bundle of old clothes for Rosie, but Rosie'd usually just take 'em down to the mission. Once, though, I saw a hat I liked, and Rosie gave it to me. It's velvet, with a beautiful feather. I've still got it, but I don't get many chances to wear it.'

'Maybe you will. Any other friends you can think of?'

'She talks – talked – about this guy Emory something or other. He's down at the mission. I know she liked him. With him, I think it was even more than that.'

'How so?'

'She said he was sweet on her,' Madge said with the confidential air of a gossip. 'But she knew he was too young for her, and he had problems of his own, and they'd be awful for each other. So she told him they should just stay friends.'

One of his problems is his manners, Horn thought. He called for the check and paid up. 'I'll walk you back,' he said to Madge.

The day was cool and crisp, and the sun bounced blindingly off the puddles that stood in the street. The old houses, and the stores scattered among them, looked cleaner but no less time-worn after the night's rain.

'Why all the questions?' Madge asked as they walked.

'Oh . . . I was talking with a friend last night, someone who knew Rose. And I felt bad just talking about her. And suddenly I knew that there was only one thing that would make me feel better – finding out who killed her. Does that sound crazy?'

'No,' she said. 'I hope you find out. If you do, you going to tell the police?' He was silent, and she glanced sideways at him as she tried to match his long strides. 'Have you ever been in trouble yourself?'

'Yes. How did you know?'

'Didn't take much. The way you acted that time in her room, I could tell you didn't want coppers around you. Earl was like that, since the cops never treated us fair either. With you, it's just something you give off. Like the way you can tell a dog who's been beaten . . .' She stopped. 'I guess that's not a very nice thing to say, is it?'

He laughed. 'That bad, huh?'

'Didn't mean any offense. But you're going to have to be careful, aren't you?'

'You're the second person to tell me that. Don't worry.'

They had reached the steps of the rooming house, and she paused. 'I think there's something else.'

'Tell me.'

'A few weeks ago,' she said, 'Rosie asked me to do her a favor. Said she had to meet somebody at the Biltmore, and she wanted me to come along – not to be with her, but just to watch, in case.'

'In case what?'

'She didn't say. But I could tell she was a little worried and would feel better knowing she had a friend somewhere around her. So we got all dressed up, me in my special velvet hat. I'd never even been in the Biltmore, and she said she hadn't been there in years. She was supposed to meet this person in the lounge, and I went in first, so nobody would see us together. The man at the door was wearing a tux, and he looked at me kind of funny, like he knew I didn't belong, but I put on my best face and told myself, *I'm as good as anybody here.* And next thing I knew, a girl showed me to a table, and I ordered a drink. Everything's really overpriced there, I can—'

'I know,' he said. 'So what happened?'

'Well, after a while Rosie came in and spoke to the man at the door, and he took her across the room himself, over to a table where a man was already sitting.'

'Do you know who he was?'

'Let me just tell it. He bought her a drink, and they talked for about half an hour, very serious, heads bent over close to each other. Then she got up and left. After a minute, the man waved his arm to a man who was sitting not far away, and that guy came over and sat where Rosie had been. They talked for a few minutes and then left together.'

'Can you describe them?'

'Sure I can, even though I'm better with numbers,' she said proudly. 'See, I made an effort to remember them. First man was thin and not very tall, with kind of a long face, maybe in his late fifties, hair mostly turning gray and combed back. He was well dressed, and he had a pearl stickpin in his tie. Even though I wasn't close, I could see the light shining on it no matter which way he sat.'

'Good. And the other man?'

'Heavier, not as well dressed. He wasn't much taller than the other one, but he looked a little bit like the strong man in the carnival, the way his clothes fit him too tight. Not fat, but—'

'Beefy?'

'That's right. Beefy.'

'Good, Madge. Thanks. That's—'

'Don't you want to know who the other man was?'

He gaped at her. 'You know his name?'

'Uh-huh.' She grinned broadly, showing her darkened and irregular teeth. 'It was just a fluke, how I found out. Nothing happened for a week or so after that night. Then I was visiting with Rose one day, and she went down the hall to use the facilities, and, uh . . .' A look of embarrassment quickly crossed her face. 'I was just looking around, you know? Not much, just a little. I guess I was curious, like people say I always am. She has this bedside table, and in the top drawer was a page torn out of the *Evening Herald*. Part of a page, really. And there he was.'

Horn waited. He knew there was no hurrying her.

'It was a story about this doctor who was on trial for hiring somebody to kill his wife. He'd just been found not guilty, and there was a picture of him and his lawyer outside the court-house. The lawyer was the man Rosie saw at the Biltmore.'

She paused for effect. 'His name was Jay Lombard. The story said he defends all kinds of people, including gangsters, and usually gets them off.'

Jay Lombard. Horn thought he might have heard the name before. 'Did you mention anything to Rose?'

She shook her head. 'I didn't want her to know I knew his name,' she said. 'If she had wanted me to know, she would have told me. I thought it would be smart just to keep quiet.'

'Thank you, Madge.' He took her hand awkwardly. 'You've been a big help.'

'I'm glad,' she said cheerfully. 'Now I think I'll head down the hill to the market. Saw some pretty good-looking pork chops there the other day, and I want to see what they have today. I usually can't afford pork chops, but . . .' She stopped, looking at him expectantly.

Horn understood. 'Madge, I'd be real pleased if you'd allow me to treat you to a couple of pork chops,' he said, pulling out his wallet. 'And maybe something on the side?' He handed her a couple of singles.

'Well, if you insist.' She put the money in her purse. 'Do you think this man could have killed Rosie?'

'I don't know,' he said. 'Right now I think anybody could have killed her.' He felt a stirring of the old unfocused rage. 'I want you to be careful. Don't walk around after dark, don't let strangers into your room. You hear me?'

He could feel the tight-wound tension in his voice, along with the sound of hopelessness. He knew his words were addressed to Rose, who could no longer hear them.

Horn half sat, half leaned on a liquor crate in the stock room behind Mad Crow's bar. Cassie had taken the only comfortable seat, a bottom-sprung easy chair the casino staff used when on their breaks. Since Mad Crow didn't want music in the club – 'Distracts the good people from the business at hand,' he would say – the only noises coming through from the main room were the low murmur of voices, the faint click of chips, and the occasional sound of the croupier calling the spin of the wheel.

Cassie wore her work outfit of fringed skirt with boots, silk blouse, and cowboy hat pushed back on her head. She had the resentful expression she usually adopted when Horn or her uncle was around, and Horn once again marveled at how she could look so sour and so attractive at the same time. *Maybe there's something fascinating,* he thought, *about a girl capable of dancing close with a man she likes and sticking a knife in a man she doesn't.*

'I've only got a few minutes,' she said. She pulled heavily on an Old Gold and tapped it nervously in one of the casino's glass ashtrays balanced uneasily on the arm of the chair.

'Have you found a place to stay?' he asked her.

'No, but I will.'

'What about a job?'

She shrugged. 'I'm looking around. Anything where I won't have to dress like Dale Evans. And my uncle's got a couple of ideas too.'

'You need any money?'

She looked momentarily surprised at the question. 'Not right now,' she said. 'I've saved part of my salary, whatever I wasn't spending on booze and wild times.'

He ignored the sarcasm, and refrained from pointing out that she was still a few months shy of legal drinking age. 'Just asking. Reason is, Joseph is an old friend, and even though you two aren't on speaking terms right now, I know he's concerned about you. So . . . I am too. And you need every friend you can get.'

'I've got friends,' she said.

'Sure you have. I've seen some of them. The guy you followed out to the parking lot, for one. That's a real friendly wallop he gave you. And the two boys out at the Dust Bowl. I've got a good idea of the kind of friendship they wanted from you. Cassie . . .' He searched for the words to reach her. 'You go looking for a certain kind of man, that's what you'll find. But not all of them are like that.' He stopped and laughed suddenly. 'If I'm not careful, I'm going to start preaching. Like my father.'

'Hmm?' Her thoughts seemed elsewhere.

'He's the Reverend John Jacob Horn. He never had any doubt about anything – about who he was, about sin and damnation, faith and salvation. He used to beat me and my little brother whenever we didn't measure up to his idea of goodness. He's the reason I left home a long time ago.'

Cassie nodded and looked thoughtful. He wondered if she was thinking of her own father, and he wondered how many fathers in this world showed a face of violence to their children.

'Actually . . .' she began.

'What?'

'Actually, you sounded a little like Rose.'

'Really?' He wondered if she could see how much that pleased him. 'I'd like to hear more about what she told you the night you went over to see her.'

'It really started earlier, in the bar,' she said. 'We didn't get a chance to talk much there, but she asked me what happened to my face, and when I told her, she got this angry look. Then, when I went to see her, she said I should be careful here in big, bad LA. But I never got the feeling that she was preaching, just that she cared about what happened to me.' She took a drag on her cigarette, stuck out her lower lip, and exhaled a stream of smoke that climbed lazily toward the ceiling. The expression on her face softened.

'We must've made a picture, her in her worn-out clothes and me with bruises on my face. There we were, sitting around a table getting quietly drunk on Uncle Joseph's Scotch. And her talking like we were old friends and what happened to me was important to her.'

'Maybe it was.'

'She said whatever I've been getting into, she'd already done it, or worse. Told me she'd done some wild things herself, and it was too late to go back and change any of it. I asked her for details, but she just shook her head. She said it wasn't too late for me. That she could tell I was smart – not many people say that – and I could do almost anything I want to.'

'I believe that too, Cassie. So does your uncle. If Rose were alive today, she'd be a real friend, the kind you'd want to keep.'

She inclined her head slightly, as if seeing him from a different perspective. 'She said some nice things about you. Are you the reason she called me?'

'Uh-huh. Joseph too. She liked both of us.'

'Was she your girlfriend once?'

'Once, a long time ago.'

'You think they'll find out who killed her?'

'I don't know,' he said, the disgust audible in his voice. 'I've talked to the police. They don't look very hard for people who kill women like Rose.'

Cassie considered his answer. She knocked another Old Gold out of the pack but held it without reaching for a light. 'Are you going to look for him yourself?'

'Why would I do that?'

'I've heard a few things,' she said quietly. She gestured over her shoulder toward a dark corner of the room. 'There's an old tarp on the floor behind some boxes. Good place to relax when you're on your break. I was lying down there the other day, and I heard my uncle and another man come in. They sat for a while, talking. The other one sounded like my cousin Billy. You know him; he handles security and tends bar sometimes.'

'Billy Looks Ahead. I know him.'

'I didn't get all of it, but it was about some men who came after you one night, and Billy and my uncle went to help, and when it was all over, people were dead.'

'I'm not sure you heard it right, Cassie.'

'I heard that part just fine. Is that how you got hurt?'

She was looking at the place on his neck where the tip of the wound showed above the collar, like a writhing white worm. It looked even worse below the collar, he knew, and the memory swept over him again – the jagged glass twisting its way through flesh and muscle and nerve, the screaming pain . . . He fought the urge to raise his hand and rub the place. Instead, he sat there silently, staring stubbornly at her.

The door opened, and one of the other waitresses looked in. 'You about ready, Cassie?' she asked. 'I'm dying for a break.'

'I'll be right there.'

'I dropped off three orders for table twelve at the bar,' the waitress said. 'Be a sweetie and deliver them, will you?'

'One more minute.'

The door closed, and Cassie turned to him. 'Who did the killing that night?' she demanded. 'Was it you? My uncle? Billy? Or all three of you?'

'This is not something you need to know, Cassie. Nobody's going to talk to you about it.'

'All right.' She placed her hands squarely on the wide arms of the chair. The position made her look immovable. 'I want to help you find him.'

'That's crazy, Cassie.'

'No, it's not. I can help.'

'If you're about to tell me you're doing it for Rose, she'd tell you to take care of yourself.' He thought for a moment. 'You blame yourself, don't you?'

She shook her head, but after a few seconds her defiant expression melted into something that resembled hurt. 'She said she was tired and wanted to lie down,' Cassie said almost inaudibly, her gaze fixed somewhere on the floor between them. 'I said good night and turned out the light. I tried to lock the door. I did try.' She looked at him as if seeking proof that he believed her. 'But it was one of those old locks. You can't lock it without the key. So I just . . . closed it . . .'

'It's not your fault,' he said forcefully.

'Maybe not,' she said. 'But I've made up my mind.' She glared at him. 'I'll keep your secret. And I'll show you I'm good for something.'

Shaking his head, he left her there. As he entered the main room, he looked around for Mad Crow. It was well into the evening, and the casino was full of the subdued noise made by people keyed up to win or lose money on the turn of a card or the spin of a wheel. Card players sat around poker tables covered in dark green baize. Some of the men wore suits, but most were in sportcoats or shirtsleeves. The women were similarly dressed, some elegantly in cocktail dresses, others in slacks and blouses.

The walls and beamed ceiling were of varnished pine. High up, the bright ceiling lights were lightly fogged over by a haze of cigarette and cigar smoke. The interior smelled of tobacco smoke, alcohol, perfume, and nervous energy.

He spotted Mad Crow's bulk and distinctive ponytail across the room. The Indian was standing at one of the poker tables, laughing loudly. The man at the table who had apparently told the joke looked familiar, a second-banana comic actor that Horn thought he might have seen in one of the Hope and Crosby

103

movies. He caught Mad Crow's eye, and they met in the center of the big room.

'Man named Jay Lombard,' Horn said. 'You know anything about him?'

Mad Crow took his time answering. 'Sure. Why?'

'I hear Rose knew him.'

Mad Crow looked around, then pointed with his chin. 'Upstairs, okay?'

They mounted the stairs to Mad Crow's small, pine-paneled office, which looked through a large window down onto the casino floor. Horn sat in a straight-backed chair, and the Indian perched precariously on the edge of the desk.

'How would Rose know somebody like that?' Mad Crow asked.

'Don't know.' Horn related Madge's story, then asked, 'So what do you know about him?'

'He's a shyster lawyer who's very good at what he does, which is mostly defending trash. He's also an investor who puts a lot of money around, here and there, some of it in real estate. He likes to bet, too. He's partial to the horses and the fights, but I hear he'll bet on almost anything. They say he once bet a fifty on which raindrop would make it to the bottom of the window pane first. He'll give you odds on whether the next woman through the door is going to be a blonde or a brunette, on how long it'll take for your cigar ash to break off, that sort of thing.' Although he was only imparting information, Mad Crow's voice conveyed something else, something darker. Horn decided to wait for the rest of it.

'I get the picture.'

'He owns an interest in a few downtown buildings. He also owns some fighters, a piece or a whole, and a couple of thoroughbreds.'

'Sounds like you two sometimes hang out in the same general neck of the woods.'

Mad Crow shrugged. 'Not really. He's never been in here. He'd consider this place a two-bit operation. If he wanted to bet on cards, he'd head for one of those clubs where everybody wears tuxes and they have to know your name before they let you in.'

'Is he at all dangerous?'

'Dangerous how?'

'Could he kill somebody?'

'Rose, you mean.' Mad Crow's brow furrowed. 'You're wondering if he's anything like my esteemed silent partner, who goes around waving his cute little nickel-plated popgun in people's faces.' The Indian didn't bother to hide his distaste for Mickey Cohen, and Horn knew better than to follow this line of conversation. Mad Crow had resisted giving the Mick a piece of the casino until he had no more options. Their partnership was built purely on mutual convenience, not affection.

'I'd say no,' Mad Crow went on. 'Lawyers aren't dangerous, unless you're on the wrong side of the courtroom from them.'

He stared at the floor. 'Still . . .' His meaty fingers drummed loudly on the scarred edges of the desk, which sometimes doubled as a bottle opener.

'What are you thinking?'

'Oh, just things. Like a long time before he got his law degree, there are stories that he ran booze down from Canada back in the twenties, during Prohibition. I never met a former bootlegger who wasn't a genuine tough guy.' He looked out the window, as if studying the activity down on the floor. 'One other thing.'

'What's that?'

'I tangled with him once. Or with a friend of his.'

'Uh-huh?'

'It was a long time ago, before the war. I was pulling down my regular paycheck at Medallion, wearing my eagle feather, blowing smoke signals and using words of one syllable. You remember.'

'Sure.'

'But I was starting to put aside money for this business, borrowing whatever I could. Lombard was one of the people I went to. He turned me down, so I moved on. But I found it harder to get in to see people, and I started hearing that Lombard was using whatever influence he had to close doors on me. I asked around, and I learned he owned a small piece of the Rex, the old gambling ship that used to be anchored off Santa Monica. He didn't want the competition from me.'

'A business decision.'

'Right. I ran into him at some watering hole out on Wilshire – this was back when I still had a serious night life, as I believe you also did. I had a few drinks. And I made the mistake of calling him out. Guess I forgot about this hunk of granite he travels around with, Willie something or other. Strongest son of a bitch I've ever met,' he said soberly. 'He got a hammerlock on me. I grabbed hold of a bottle, and I recall hitting him about the head and ears and anything else I could find, and he didn't seem to feel any of it. I think he would have broken my neck if Lombard hadn't called him off. And only because there was a crowd. Anyway, I hear those two still travel together, sort of a Mutt and Jeff act.' His lips formed a thin smile. 'So does this answer your question?'

'I suppose. I'd just like to know why Rose was spending time with him.'

'Maybe she decided she needed a lawyer.'

'Maybe. But why pick him?' Horn got up and headed for the door. On his way out, he turned and said, 'Cassie wants to help find out who killed Rose.'

'God help us,' Mad Crow muttered.

Chapter Eleven

When Horn was a young man, thumbing his way around the West during the Depression, working any job he could get and occasionally riding the rodeo circuit, he had become familiar with the places where the down and out gathered. Every big city had a skid row, each with its different character, its different meanness.

The one time when they all seemed alike was early morning. Gray light, stained sidewalks, shuttered stores, a kind of worn-out quiet. Few cars or people, and the people looked either furtive or exhausted, some huddled or crouched in doorways or stretched out on the sidewalks, others standing and staring at nothing, still clutching last night's blankets.

It was a little after eight when Horn parked in front of the Anchor and got out of his car. Across the street, atop the marquee of the Follies, was a blown-up photo of Ruby Renfrew. Retouched in unlifelike colors that made her hair jet black, her skin almost orange and her lips, pasties, and G-string a blazing red, she gazed with an incongruously wholesome smile over toward the mission and those sprawled on the sidewalk in front of it.

At the desk inside, he asked for the pastor and was directed down the same long corridor, which he followed past the dining room to the chapel. That room, windowless but skylighted, was somewhat smaller than the dining room. It held several rows of folding chairs and, at the far end, a platform with a lectern and an upright piano. A large wooden cross looked down on everything. The only person in the room was an elderly man wielding a mop down the center aisle. The odor of Lysol did battle with the leftover effluvium of last night's congregation.

Behind the piano was an unmarked door, which stood slightly open. He knocked and called out, getting no answer. But he could hear sounds, so he opened the door and stepped inside.

It was a small office, furnished only with a scarred desk and a couple of straight chairs and a handmade bookcase holding an assortment of books and magazines. In the far wall was another door, this one also open, and it was from this doorway the sounds came – abrupt thuds, irregularly spaced, accompanied by explosive breathing. Horn knew the sounds. He called out again, and they stopped. A moment later, Emory Quinn came out. He wore a sweat-soaked gray jersey and nondescript pants. His face was flushed and his hair shone with sweat.

'I know you,' he panted, wiping his face with a towel that hung around his neck. 'You're the guy who didn't need to eat.'

'John Ray Horn. I wouldn't expect to find a gym in a place like this.'

'Just a big closet,' Quinn said. 'Where we keep the hymn books and other stuff. But there's room for a heavy bag.'

'Sounds like you were punishing the hell out of it.'

'We're pretty evenly matched,' Quinn said. 'Sometimes I beat the bag, and sometimes the bag beats me.'

'There was a Boston Quinn I saw fight at the Olympic about fifteen years ago. Middleweight. He lost a decision to a colored boy named Jace or something—'

'Everett Jacey,' Quinn said. 'Best fighter I ever went up against. Couple of years later, he got in some kind of a brawl outside a club down in Watts. One of the other men had a gun, Everett didn't.'

'Too bad,' Horn said. 'Anyway, I thought it was close that night at the Olympic. Could've gone either way.'

'Nice of you to say so,' Quinn said. 'That was my last pro fight. I knew it was time, I'd gone as far as I could.' He draped the towel back around his neck and sat behind the desk. When he turned his head, Horn could see that his left ear was slightly enlarged and misshapen, the mark of too many right hooks.

'I was a good counterpuncher, but one of the newspaper guys

said there was something missing. The thing that makes you
want to . . .' He stopped.

'The killer instinct?'

'Something like that.' Quinn shrugged. 'Maybe the guy was
right.' He motioned Horn to the chair across the desk.

'What brought you here from there?' Horn asked, taking a
seat and laying his hat on the desk. He wasn't particularly
interested in Quinn's history, but he wanted to get him started
talking.

'The Lord,' Quinn said simply. 'He decided I'd spent enough
time sinning – drinking, whoring, profaning his name, trying to
hurt other men with my fists for my own personal gain. When I
began losing fights, I started drinking for real. One night I left a
bar and wandered down this very street. I heard singing here,
and I came right in. Do you know what happened?'

'I have an idea.'

'You're a doubter; I can tell. I heard a sermon about com-
mitting your life to God, about being a fighter for Jesus. It was
aimed right at me. I volunteered to help out here at the mission.
Before I knew it, the old pastor who'd been here for years died,
and the church asked me to take over his work.'

'Do you have any training?'

'You mean did I go to Bible school? No, this place is run by the
Light of the Trinity Church. We believe that if the Holy Spirit is
in you, it's worth more than a truckload of degrees.'

Quinn nodded his head as he spoke, as if in agreement with
his own words, his mouth set in a thin, curved half-smile. Horn
thought he knew the man now. Not the individual, but the type.
The reformed sinner. Burning with the fire of renewal, secure in
the knowledge of his own salvation, impatient that others
couldn't see the same truth.

Quinn looked quizzically at Horn. 'You mentioned the Beatitudes the other day. Are you a man of religion?'

'No. I just grew up in the house of a man like that.'

'Then you should be a believer, not a doubter.'

How would you know? Horn shifted uncomfortably in his chair.
'I didn't come here to talk about me,' he said. 'I was a friend of

Rose. I was looking for her that day you saw me. I under-stand you were trying to protect her when you sent me away, and I don't want to bring you any trouble now. I just want to talk.'

'Rose is dead,' Quinn said in a flat voice.

'I know.'

'So why do we need to talk?'

'You may not need to. But I'm trying to find out about everyone who knew her, who liked her and disliked her. I don't think the police are going to try very hard to find out who killed her.'

'So you've elected yourself?'

'Something like that.'

'You got qualifications?'

'No.' *No more than you*. 'Just curiosity.'

Quinn reached into a drawer and pulled out a pack of Lucky Strikes. 'One of my last vices,' he said almost apologetically. 'Satan can be strong, and I'm no saint.' He held out the pack and Horn took one. Quinn struck a kitchen match on his thumbnail and lit both cigarettes, then pushed a chipped glass ashtray toward the center of the desk.

'The way people are talking,' Quinn said, 'it was probably some drifter, the kind of lowlife who hangs around Bunker Hill looking for easy scores. He found her door open, came in to rob her, she fought back, he killed her. Something like that. He could've caught the next freight out of here.'

Horn studied Quinn carefully. It was impossible to know if he believed the theory he'd just sketched out. 'Could've happened that way,' Horn said. 'Me, I just want to know for sure. How about you?'

Quinn had gotten his breath back and sat quietly, tapping one foot on the floor under the desk, reminding Horn of the nervous energy he had given off that time they had first met.

Finally Quinn spoke. 'She talked about you once,' he said.

Horn waited.

'She said she had known you a long time ago, and she happened to see you at a bar on Broadway. She said she was

110

annoyed when you asked her too many questions. But I could tell she liked you.'

'I liked her too. And those questions – I finally got to ask some of them the day I came here looking for her. But I have a lot more, and that's why I'm here now. So let me ask you again: do you want to know who killed her?'

'Yes,' Quinn said quietly.

'Then tell me what you know about her. Especially if you know of anyone who had anything against her.'

'That's hard to say,' Quinn said cautiously. 'Rose told me about some of the people she knew, but I'm sure she kept a lot private. And I didn't ask. That's the thing about this place. People come here for some kind of help – a meal, a clean place to sleep, the word of God. I owe it to them to help them out without asking a lot of questions.'

'But she wasn't looking for a place to sleep,' Horn prompted him.

'That's right. A few times a week, she helped us serve the noon meal.'

'Why?'

There was pity in Quinn's expression. 'Is it hard for you to understand that some people want to help others?'

'Depends on the person,' Horn said curtly, unwilling to let Quinn lead him back into the topic of religion. 'Do you know anything about this woman she called Doll?'

'She started coming around a month or two ago. I know she and Rose were good friends. I spoke to her a couple of times to thank her for donating clothing and other things to the mission. She's been generous, and she's never asked us for anything in return.'

'What's her last name?'

'I never asked.' Quinn looked embarrassed. 'We don't always keep the most complete records around here. We only ask if someone's heart is in the right place. Rose said her friend was generous and could afford to help us out, and that was good enough for me.'

'Back to Rose,' Horn said. 'Did she tell you anything about her life?'

'Yes, but only what she thought I needed to know. She said she'd acted in the movies a long time ago but that her life had taken a wrong turn and she'd thrown away her success. She said she was a drunk, and it was too late to do anything about that or anything else. I think she came to the Anchor in order to try to make amends in some small way for her sins.'

'Did she call them sins?'

'That's my word, I suppose. Rose wasn't particularly religious, but I didn't let that get in the way of our friendship any more than her drinking did.'

'What kind of friendship was it?'

Quinn glanced at his watch. 'I'm going to have to start getting our people ready for the noon meal,' he said. 'Rose isn't here to help out any more, and we're stretched very thin.'

'What kind of friendship?' Horn repeated.

'Some things should be private,' Quinn said. 'Especially if they don't have anything to do with what you're trying to find out.'

'I'm sorry if I raised the wrong subject,' Horn said. 'She told you her life took a bad turn. I got the same impression from talking to her, but she wouldn't tell me any more. I'm thinking, though, that if I were Rose, you might be the one person I'd talk to. Who better than a minister? If she did, maybe you should talk about it now. She's dead; you can't hurt her by telling. And it just might have something to do with her death.'

He waited. Quinn said nothing, just sat with his foot tapping faintly under the desk. A single drop of sweat worked its way out from under his hairline at the temple and poised itself for the journey down his cheek.

'I think she'd forgive me,' he said.

Horn nodded.

'She killed someone.'

'What?'

'Years ago.'

'Who? How did it happen?'

Quinn shook his head. 'She didn't say. It came out one day

when we were in the chapel, just the two of us. It was almost like a confession, except our church doesn't have that kind of thing. But I could tell it made her feel better. She said she had never told anyone until then.'

'When was this?'

'A few weeks ago. She asked me what she should do about it. I said I couldn't give her advice on that, but she shouldn't have to carry the burden all alone. She started talking, almost to herself, saying maybe she should just tell about it, once and for all. Let it out. I thought she might be talking about going to the police and confessing, although she didn't exactly say that. But as soon as she said it, it was like a weight being lifted off her. I could tell that she had made a big decision and was going to do something about it.'

'Telling somebody about it.'

'I think so.'

Suddenly, Rose hiring a lawyer makes sense, he thought. 'Did she say anything else about the killing? Anything at all?'

'She said more, but I didn't exactly understand it. Something about how it happened in the least likely place, surrounded by people and noise and celebration, a place where you'd never expect to find death. And how, in that instant, she lost everything.'

'That's it? That's all she said?'

'Yes.' Quinn got up from behind his desk. 'I have to get back to work. Would you like to stay for the meal?'

'No, thanks, I'm meeting a friend. Do you know where Rose is buried?'

'She's going to be buried by the county,' Quinn said harshly. 'As soon as they finish the autopsy – maybe as early as today. There are no relatives. We had a memorial service for her yesterday, but this mission is poor, and we can't afford to bury her privately. Not that it matters, really. Heaven is what's important, not what happens to our body after we leave it.'

Horn considered asking Quinn if he believed that anyone who committed murder could end up in heaven. Instead, he said, 'Have you ever heard of a man named Jay Lombard?'

'Sure. Why?'

'I hear he goes to the fights a lot.'

'I used to see him around when I was fighting. We never met, but I knew about him.'

'What did you hear?'

'I try not to judge people any more.'

'Come on, Quinn. I'm not just making conversation. This is about Rose.'

Quinn glared at him. If Horn had seen that look across the ring, he would have thought twice about going up against this man.

'All right,' Quinn said. 'He's a lawyer who likes to hang around the fights. It's kind of a rich man's hobby for him. But he doesn't love it, the way real fight people do; he just dabbles. To me, he was the kind of person who spends a lot of money to get inside a sport and then ruins it from the inside. I heard he sometimes tried to fix bouts. Lombard used to own a light-weight, a man I knew. He tried to move him up too fast. In my friend's last fight, he was so overmatched, the other man knocked him out for two hours. He was never the same after that. Sometimes, I see him on the streets around here, just wandering . . .' He stopped.

'Do you still go to the fights?'

'Every now and then,' Quinn said. 'Maybe that's another of my weaknesses. Understand, I don't miss being in the ring; that life's behind me. And I don't wager. But I can still appreciate a display of courage in the midst of struggle. After all, we were put on this earth to struggle, weren't we?'

way. He was to meet Diggs for lunch at a Mexican place in the bustling arcade known as the Grand Central Market. As he passed the market, he caught a rush of pungent smells from the food stalls inside, a mixture of fresh vegetables, spices, grilled fish, and raw meat, some of it leaning toward exotic fare such as pig's feet and sheep's heads. He slowed, ready to turn into a parking lot. But just then he spotted Diggs, waving to him from the sidewalk. Diggs sprinted over and got in.

'Look, Dex, I turned down a banquet at the Anchor mission to have lunch with you. Aren't we going to eat?'

'I found out something. Necessitates a little trip.'

'Yeah, well, I'm hungry.'

'Here. Got us a couple of these.' Diggs opened a paper bag and passed Horn a bulging taco wrapped in a soft tortilla. 'I had them put extra hot sauce on yours. I imagined an old southern boy would like it that way. There are napkins in the bag in case you make a mess. You know the way to Glendale?'

'What?'

'You know, where Mildred Pierce made all those pies.'

'I know where Glendale is. Are you being mysterious again?'

'Maybe. All will be revealed at our destination. Just drive, and enjoy the taco.'

They ate on the way, and Diggs fiddled with the radio, eventually finding a station he liked. He turned up the volume a notch, and the strains of 'Sleepy Time Gal' filled the car.

'Harry James,' Diggs said. 'Hell of a trumpet player. But I always thought Betty Grable could have done better.'

'You and half of America,' Horn said.

Horn began telling him about his talk with Quinn. 'He's like a lot of reformed drunks,' he said. 'With religion added on top of it, which makes him even more—'

'Insufferable?'

'No. Just real intense, you know? He talks a lot about how much Jesus has done for him, but you get the feeling that underneath he still doesn't like himself very much.'

'What did he say about Rose?'

Horn described some of their conversation. But he stopped

117

short of relating Rose's admission of murder. Something told him Diggs wasn't ready to hear it yet.

'He told me she's going to be buried in some potter's field, wherever the county—'

'That's not exactly true,' Diggs interrupted. 'Stay on this street for about a mile. You know where Forest Lawn is?'

'I've been to a couple of funerals there.'

'That's where we're going.'

Twenty minutes later, Horn pulled in at the ornate iron gate, beyond which they could see the green expanse of the cemetery. After Diggs got out briefly and inquired at the gatehouse, Horn followed one of the winding drives up into the hills. Soon they came to a hillside dotted with markers lying flush with the ground.

'They don't allow tombstones here,' Diggs said. 'Guess they're afraid the place will look too much like a cemetery.' He spotted something. 'Over there.'

Horn stopped the Ford behind a car that looked familiar. A man sat behind the wheel. Horn and Diggs walked over the grass about thirty yards to a freshly filled grave being fussed over by a groundskeeper. A woman stood nearby, watching the man work. She was tall and wore a stylish black dress and a large hat under which most of her red hair had been gathered. She turned her head briefly as they approached, then went back to watching. Horn recognized her.

'I didn't know she'd be here,' Diggs said in a low voice. 'But I shouldn't be surprised. Yesterday I called the coroner's office in the Hall of Justice. I wanted to see what arrangements had been made for Rose. They told me that since no one had claimed the body, she would be buried in the public cemetery. This morning I called to get particulars, and they told me the body had been transferred to Forest Lawn for burial today.'

'Why the change?'

'She offered to pay for the burial,' Diggs said, indicating the woman.

'I saw her at the mission, talking to Rose. Who is she?'

'You really should get out to the movies more, John Ray. And

I don't mean the ones with all the horses. That's Dolores Winter. Doll to her friends. I've never met her, but I know her work.'

The woman approached the groundskeeper, spoke to him briefly, and pressed something into his hand. Then she walked over to the two men and stood waiting, her sunglasses hiding any hint of expression.

'Miss Winter, I hope we're not disturbing you,' Diggs said with a touch of courtliness in his voice, and Horn was reminded of the man's skill at working with actresses.

'I was just saying goodbye to my old friend,' the woman said casually, her voice a pleasant alto. 'I'm finished.'

'I'm Dexter Diggs,' he said to her. 'I suppose we've never formally met. I admired what you did in *Tropic Wind*.'

'Thank you.' Although her eyes were hidden, Horn noted that the rest of her features were strong and well sculpted. 'I know you worked with Rose. And didn't you do one of the Bette Davis things at Warners?' she asked Diggs. 'The one where she has amnesia?'

'Guilty.'

'I liked the way you didn't let her get away with much. Jack Warner should have used you more.'

'There's a good reason why he didn't,' Diggs said wryly. 'But I won't bore you.'

'Rose said you were the best director she ever had.' She paused. 'That's not all she told me.'

'Well, it was a long time ago.' Diggs looked slightly uncomfortable.

'She could have used a friend from a long time ago,' Dolores Winter said deliberately.

When Diggs didn't respond, she turned to Horn. 'What are you doing here?'

'This is John Ray Horn,' Diggs said. 'Another friend of Rose.'

'From a long time ago,' she said, and the sarcasm lay just under the words.

'This is a nice thing you did for her,' Horn said.

She took off the dark glasses and looked Horn up and down, as if measuring him. She wore high heels, and her eyes – pale hazel, he noted – were almost on a level with his. But there was no friendliness in them.

'She mentioned you too,' Dolores Winter said. 'Reading between the lines, sounds to me like you had a roll in the hay with her once. Then you showed up, making a nuisance out of yourself when she didn't want to talk to you. And not long after that, someone came into her room and killed her.'

'You've got the wrong idea,' he said.

She stepped closer. 'If I find out you had anything to do with it, I won't wait for the police. I'll make sure somebody takes care of you.'

They watched as Dolores Winter strode up the gentle grassy slope to the road and, without looking back, got in the front passenger seat of the Lincoln. The driver pulled away.

Horn whistled softly between his teeth. 'Remind me never to make an enemy of that particular redhead.'

'Too late. I'd heard she was a tough one. On the way back, I'll tell you a few tales about her.'

'Sure,' Horn said, looking toward the mound of earth. 'But first I want to spend some time with Rose.'

Horn dug two quarters out of his pocket and dropped them in the near-shapeless upturned hat that lay on the concrete. Beside the hat a man of about thirty sat crosslegged, wearing an old suit, a khaki shirt and no tie. Sightless eyes crisscrossed with old shrapnel scars looked up vaguely at passers-by. Propped against his knees was a roughly lettered sign on cardboard: *War Vet. 5th Army, Italy.*

As they walked on, Diggs turned to him. 'Wasn't that where you fought?'

'Hmm?'

'Italy.'

'Oh. That's right.'

'You're the only one I knew who didn't come back from the war with a bunch of stories.'

'Well, I'm not much of a storyteller.' *But since you're interested, how's this? Two-fisted cowboy goes to war, finds out all his heroics were just play-acting. The real Sierra Lane comes back with a different kind of war wound – a missing spine. Almost sounds like a movie, doesn't it? I could play myself.*

'Why don't we sit over here?' Horn indicated a vacant bench. Around them, Pershing Square was an oasis of grass and concrete, banana trees and bird of paradise flowers, in the middle of downtown LA. They had stopped there on impulse, a few blocks from Grand Central Market and Diggs' car, in order to sit and talk for a while. The winter sun glared off the windows of the tall buildings around them and brightened the ornate brick facade of the Biltmore Hotel across the plaza. Office workers strolled around and bums lolled on the grass, unshaven faces turned to the sky.

'My uneducated theory is, they never quite knew what to do with Doll Winter,' Diggs said, continuing part of their earlier conversation in the car. 'She's spent most of her career at Magnum Arts and done pretty well in supporting parts – you know, the wisecracking best friend, the gun moll, that kind of thing. But most people thought she was too tall and too unconventional to be a leading lady. She sometimes did her own make-up, which offended a few people who thought that movie stars should just sit back and be pampered. And there was a little talk, here and there, that she liked girls as much as she liked boys.'

'Oh?'

'It was probably bullshit. Maybe she's not all delicate and fluttery like Luise Rainer. Who cares? But in this town, that kind of talk isn't good for anybody's career. So she never got a chance to show what she could do. Until *Tropic Wind* came along. Did you see it?'

Horn shook his head.

'It's based on a novel about a madam at this bordello in Honolulu just before the war. The studio took a gamble on her, and she was perfect for it. Big, brassy, a little beaten down by life, but unstoppable. She was directed by J. J. Drummond, who gets good work out of women. Of course, they had to tone down a lot of the racier stuff. In the movie, she's a "hostess", for God's

121

sake, and her girls are "escorts". But the spirit of it comes through. Trouble is, she's too old for most of the best parts, and now, once again, they don't know what to do with her. That's Hollywood. I would've liked working with her about ten years ago. We could have made beautiful music.'

'She's something to look at,' Horn said. 'Too bad she hates my guts.'

'I'm sure she'll change her mind when she finds out how lovable you can be,' Diggs said. 'But don't make any plans in her direction. That man in the car with her was her husband. Wait a minute.' He snapped his fingers. 'Now I remember. He's her ex-husband, several years younger than she is. Used to be a big-shot screenwriter over at MagArts, but he lost his job. She took him back in, and they live together in one of those peculiar Hollywood relationships that no one has thought up a name for yet.'

'Well, she must be a generous soul,' Horn said. 'When she's not snarling at people.'

Diggs excused himself, walked over to a vendor's cart and returned with a bag of hot peanuts. They began cracking the shells.

'Besides talking to Quinn,' Diggs said, 'have you found out anything else about Rose?'

'A little.' Horn told him Madge's story about Jay Lombard. 'They met right over there,' Horn said, gesturing toward the Biltmore. 'Mad Crow knows a few things about this guy, and I don't like any of what I hear. I want to know more about Mr Lombard.'

'Be careful, John Ray. He sounds like trouble.'

'I will.'

'You're acting a little like one of those private detectives in the movies. And you're not exactly . . .' Diggs trailed off uneasily.

'I know. An ex-con should watch where he sticks his nose. Don't worry. This really isn't all that different from what I do already – looking for Joseph's deadbeats. I've gotten pretty good at that.'

'Well, for what it's worth, I hope you find the son of a bitch who did it,' Diggs said, working to extract a recalcitrant peanut with his thumbnail. But just remember, in the movies, those private dicks get beat up a lot.'

Seeking to change the subject, Horn reached into the inside pocket of his sport jacket and pulled out the photo of the young woman he'd found in Rose's room, which he had carefully removed from its frame. He briefly told Diggs about it as he showed it to him.

'Very pretty,' Diggs said. 'I'd guess this was made about twenty years ago, judging by the hairstyle. But who knows what it means? She could be a long-lost relative, or someone Rose went to school with.'

'I know. But it's an unanswered question, so . . .' Horn flipped a shelled nut in the direction of one of the square's many pigeons. The bird hopped over and, in quick, jerky motions, made a snack of it.

'Something I didn't tell you about my talk with Quinn,' Horn said. 'I didn't know whether you needed to hear it or not.'

'Well?'

'He said Rose told him she killed someone.'

Diggs swiveled around on the bench and gave him his full attention. 'Killed someone?'

'She wouldn't give him any details. An accident, maybe, but it sounded worse than that. When she told him about the place where it happened, her description made it sound almost like some kind of celebration. Maybe a party. Remember when we talked at your place? You told me about the parties you and Rose went to, how wild they were, and you said someone died.'

Diggs nodded slowly.

'What do you know about that?'

'John Ray, it was a long time ago. I just remember hearing about some woman who died of . . . who knows what? She could have been drinking too much or getting too high on this or that. People talked about it for a day or so, and then life went right on, just as crazy as before. It took the Depression to sober us up—'

'Dex, this is important. Can you try to find out who she was,

123

and how it happened? There may be no connection with Rose, but I need to know.'

'All right, my friend.' Diggs got up heavily. 'I'll ask around. But I hope it's nothing. There's been enough sadness around here lately.' He gave a tired wave. 'I think I'll walk back to my car.'

As Horn drove home, he twisted the dial on his radio but could not find a clear music station. He found himself listening to the distinctive whine of Louella Parsons as she gossiped about the famous, about their marriages and divorces and fracas with their studios. She seemed to take special delight in their misfortune.

Today, though, it was mostly good news. Horn caught the end of a comment about Rita Hayworth and Prince Somebody-or-Other, then a breathless rumor: are Joe Louis and Lena Horne about to take a trip to the altar? Finally, Louella reminded her listeners that after two years on Broadway, it was still hard to get tickets to *Annie Get Your Gun*. Horn was puzzled by this news. He had heard Ethel Merman singing on the radio once, found her voice even more grating than Louella Parsons', and quickly changed the station.

Nearing the end of the canyon and approaching the turnoff that led up to the cabin, he saw a bright splash of color in the trees just off the road. It was a Yellow Cab, one of the big De Sotos, and it sat just outside the locked gate. As he drew nearer, he could see the outline of the driver but no passenger.

Horn halted on the canyon road and honked his horn once. 'You looking for an address?' he yelled. The driver got out and walked down the gravel road toward him. Horn looked once, then again in surprise. It was Cassie.

She wore the cabby's uniform of slacks and a company jacket over a white shirt and one of those clip-on plastic bow ties. Her dark hair was gathered under a hard-billed cap. It was an outfit that some women would avoid at the risk of looking mannish or just foolish. But Cassie, he decided, handled it well. She stopped by his door.

'What is this?' he demanded.

'My new job,' she said. 'I started driving this morning. What do you think?'

'I think it's crazy,' he said. 'But do you care what I think?'

'Not really.' She seemed uncomfortable, as if she had been sent to deliver an unpleasant message and wanted to hurry through it.

'You don't just walk into a taxi company and ask them to give you one of their cabs,' he said. 'How—'

'My uncle,' she said. 'One of the Yellow Cab managers likes to play poker.'

'Don't tell me. He owes Joseph money. Or a favor. Or something.'

'Or something.'

'Your uncle's still looking after you, isn't he?'

Her mouth tightened. 'He would probably say so, but then he expects me to be grateful and do things his way. He has two ways of getting what he wants – doing you favors or muscling it out of you.'

'When has he muscled you?'

'You saw him hit me.'

'Cassie, I know he's sorry about that. He's not a violent man.'

'Tell that to his horses.'

'What are you talking about?'

'I heard some of his ranch hands talking about how he's going to break that mustang, the one he bought. On the reservation, I've seen horses handled by men who shouldn't ever be allowed near them, and I've seen horses with blood on them . . .'

Her words trailed off, and Horn remembered something about the little girl he'd met on his visit with Mad Crow years earlier. She loved horses, especially young ones. Once, pledging him to silence, she snuck him onto a neighbor's ranch, where they stealthily approached a corral fence so Cassie could feed chunks of carrot to her best friend, a chestnut filly. She'd given it a name, even though it wasn't hers.

'Cassie, that's just crazy,' he said. 'Your uncle is wonderful with horses.' She seemed not to have heard him and looked as if she was about to leave, so he changed the subject.

'You think you can find your way around this town in that cab? I've lived here for years, and I still get lost.'

'I've got a big map,' she said. 'And an Indian's natural sense of direction.'

'That's a joke,' he said. 'Joseph gets lost as much as I do.'

'Well, if that ever happens, I'll just turn to the fare and say, "I'm having a little trouble finding it. Do you know the best way to get to this place?"'

'And if he doesn't?'

'I pull over, kick him out, and go looking for another fare.'

Horn shook his head. 'It's dangerous out there, Cassie. For anybody driving a cab.'

She parted her jacket, and he saw the hilt of a sheathed hunting knife at her belt. 'I've got this,' she said, without apparent concern. 'I don't expect any trouble.'

He was beginning to feel like her uncle, angered by her risk-taking but powerless to do anything about it. 'I guess you don't want my advice,' he said. 'So why did you look me up?'

'I just wanted to see where you live,' she said. 'And . . .'

'And what?'

'The other night at the casino, you acted a little worried about me finding a job and a place to stay. I just wanted to tell you I'm all right, so stop worrying.'

'In other words, leave you alone,' he said, trying not to sound like a sarcastic parent. Her reasons for looking him up struck him as feeble. He didn't flatter himself that she enjoyed his company. He wondered idly if she had come in order to find out if he'd uncovered anything about Rose. But she'd asked him nothing about that. Maybe, he thought, this is her way of staying in touch with her uncle.

'I know where you're living these days,' he said. 'You think that's smart?'

'I think Rose would have liked the idea,' Cassie said defiantly. 'I'm getting along with everybody there. Even the manager. He told me he saw Buffalo Bill's Wild West Show in Chicago when he was a little boy, and ever since then he's had a thing for Indian girls in braids and buckskin.'

Horn was not amused. 'I'm glad all this strikes you as funny,' he said. 'Just understand that there's nothing you can do about Rose's death. If she were here, she'd be telling you the same thing.'

'Maybe. But if I ask a few questions, what harm does that do?' For the first time, she allowed herself to grin, but the expression bore a touch of wildness. Then it went away, and she looked around, seeming bored. 'Like I said, I needed work and a place to stay. Now I'm fixed up.'

He didn't want her to leave yet. 'So if I ever need a cab, I'll call you, okay?'

'You won't need a cab.'

'But if I do.'

She pulled a Yellow Cab card from her pocket. 'My hack number's written on the back.'

He sighed. 'You want to come in for a minute?'

'No thanks,' she said, heading back to the big De Soto. 'Gotta go earn some money.'

Chapter Thirteen

The Italian kid from Philly caught the Mexican with a stinging left hook, sending the sweat flying off his face and almost dislodging his mouthpiece. The Mexican kid was a local favorite, and the crowd's displeasure echoed off the walls like the bellow of a single animal.

Horn sat with Emory Quinn about twenty rows from ringside. It was Thursday night, fight night at the Olympic Auditorium, Eighteenth and Grand, and all around them the huge hall pulsed with noise and energy. Fight fans, gamblers, hangers-on, the occasional celebrity, all gabbed and smoked and jostled and yelled at the spectacle of two men pounding each other with padded fists. Near ringside were the French cuffs and the gold watches, the easy-money boys and their women, even a movie star face here and there. The men wore flashy suits, and the women were in night-out regalia. Farther back, where Horn and Quinn sat, both sexes were more casually dressed but no less enthusiastic. About two-thirds of the 15,000 seats were occupied. The air was spiked with the mingled scents of aftershave, perfume, sweat, and mustard, all of it overlaid with the smell of cigarette and cigar smoke, which swam lazily in a dense cloud around the lights above the ring, barely stirred by the ceiling fans.

The Mexican landed a quick combination, and the crowd loved it. In the early rounds, Quinn had kept up a steady stream of muttering, mostly to himself. Now his inhibitions were gone. 'That's right, stick him!' he yelled. 'You're waiting too long! Whenever he drops the right, use the left!' He bobbed and weaved slightly in his seat, his fists clenched.

Horn had focused on the fight for the first few rounds, but now he grew restless. Although he had seen many bouts at the Olympic – sometimes with Mad Crow or other friends, sometimes with Iris – tonight he wasn't here for the boxing. He started to nudge Quinn, but the other man was totally engrossed in the action, so he decided to wait.

Two more rounds, and it was over: decision to the hometown boy, a decision loudly endorsed by the crowd. Many began to surge up the aisles toward the rest rooms and hot dog stands, some of them unlimbering silvery flasks from inside jacket pockets.

The main attraction on the night's card, a heavyweight bout, was thirty minutes away. Now was a good time, Horn decided. 'I don't suppose you've seen him,' he said.

Quinn's face shone with sweat and excitement, and it took him a moment to comprehend. 'Sorry,' he said. 'It's just that . . .'

'I know,' Horn said. 'Pretty exciting, huh?'

'Once you've been down there, under the lights, there's nothing quite like it. Raul could have fought better tonight. He knows the moves, but he hasn't been training hard lately. He's got too many people around him telling him how wonderful he is.' Quinn shook his head. 'Anyway . . .' He looked around. 'No, I haven't seen him. But if he's here tonight, he'll be close to ringside, and it'll be easier to spot him now that people are out of their seats.'

'Good.' They both stood up, looking casually around the vast interior.

'You think ancient Rome was anything like this?' Horn asked.

Quinn understood the question. 'I'm sure it was worse then,' he said. 'But they thought they were civilized too, just like we do. Man is an animal with a spiritual side, but still an animal, and boxing appeals to that side of him. I was in another fighter's corner years ago, and I saw something I'll never forget. My man was on the ropes, the other man pounding him. Down there at ringside was a beautiful woman, all dressed up. A cut had opened up over my man's eye, and the blood flew. A drop of it landed on this woman's glove. I just happened to see it. Her expression when she raised the glove close to her face . . . She looked horrified and fascinated all at once. For just a second, she looked as if she wanted to taste it – I think she would have done it if she hadn't been surrounded by thousands of people. Does that make sense?'

'I think so,' Horn said. But he was only half listening, because he had noticed something. 'I hear Lombard hangs out with a big man, kind of a bodyguard.'

'That's right. At least he used to.'

'See that man over there?' Horn pointed to the other side of the ring, where a block-like figure was slowly moving down the aisle. The man was not above average height, but even from that distance, his solidity was apparent. His head appeared too large for his frame. As they watched, he settled himself into the third row, next to a smaller, gray-haired man.

Quinn stood on tiptoe for a second, studying the big man's companion, then turned to Horn. 'Lombard,' he said.

'All right,' Horn said. 'Let's do it the way we said.'

They made their way down the aisle and around the ring. The two men they sought were sitting in the third row. The gray-haired man was talking with a woman who sat beside him.

Horn held back as Quinn went over and introduced himself. Horn saw the gray-haired man put out his hand without standing. He appeared polite but reserved. Quinn was friendly and animated, trying his best to keep the conversation going. After a while, he turned and motioned Horn over.

'My friend, John Ray Horn,' he said. 'This is Jay Lombard.' Horn put out his hand, reaching past the big man on the aisle, and they shook. Lombard was thin and spare, with a full head of gray-white hair, and his movements were quick and precise. His face was long and somewhat sad, and his eyes were alert and penetrating.

'Glad to meet you. Ever see this guy fight?' Horn asked, indicating Quinn.

'Boston? Saw him a lot. Good footwork, I remember. I liked his style. He went up against one of my boys a few times. I think

130

I came out on the short end.' He gestured toward his companions, the woman first. 'This is Eden Lamont,' he said, 'and Willie Apples.'

As they shook hands, Horn tried to study the big man without seeming obvious. Willie Apples was about five-ten and well over two hundred, but none of it looked soft. He wore an ill-fitting double-breasted dark gray suit with a tie that looked like an afterthought. His neck bulged away from his collar, and his oversize head, topped by a GI haircut, was not quite symmetrical, as if his birth had been an especially violent occurrence. His features, although coarse, were not unpleasant. His brow was creased, suggesting perpetual worry.

'Willie wrestled for a while,' Lombard said. 'He had some good matches. One time he took on the Swedish Angel right here in this place. But we decided his talents lay in other directions.'

Willie Apples nodded in agreement. 'I was too small to rassle,' he said good-naturedly. 'But nobody ever said I wasn't strong.' He turned his attention to the crowd around them.

Eden Lamont, Horn noted, was quite possibly the best-looking woman at the Olympic that night. She wore a tricky burgundy gown that left one shoulder bare except for the fox fur stole draped negligently around her, its color dyed an almost exact match to her abundant dark brown hair. The fox, its glassy eyes vacant, nipped its own tail in an endless chase around her neck.

She looked at Horn closely. 'Are you an actor?' she asked.

'I used to be, ma'am.'

'But you're not any more?'

'I thought I recognized you,' Lombard interrupted. 'You did some westerns. You were away for a while, weren't you?'

He's being diplomatic. 'That's right.'

'Up north,' Lombard went on. 'It's coming back to me now. You and I just might have some friends in common.'

'Could be.'

'Eden's in the movies too,' he said. 'Have you seen the new Danny Kaye?'

'I don't go to many musicals.'

'This is actually more of a comedy than a musical, and you'll see her in it. She's one of the Goldwyn Girls. The most beautiful one, I might add.'

'Stop it, Jay,' she said in a voice that added, *But not right away.*

'I can't argue with that,' Horn said.

The crowd was returning, and once again the noise level rose.

'I don't suppose you all would be interested in going out for a drink afterward,' Horn said casually to Lombard.

'Why not?' the other man answered. 'We could talk boxing and movies and the vagaries of the criminal justice system. And you and I could see how many people we both know. In fact, let's get out of here right now.'

'What about the next bout?'

'I know how that one turns out,' Lombard said with a straight face, waiting for the response.

'Really?'

'No, I'm joking. But I've got a good idea. Anyway, Raul was the one I came to see tonight. He won, I have money coming to me, and I'm feeling generous. What do you say?' His voice was a pleasant baritone, one that would have gone over well in the courtroom, and every now and then his lugubrious features dissolved in a broad smile. Horn decided that Jay Lombard could be likable.

'If you don't mind, I'll stay for the heavyweights,' Quinn broke in. He and Horn had decided that if Horn was able to attach himself to Lombard, Quinn would find an excuse for not coming along.

'Too bad,' Lombard said. 'Mr Horn, would you like to ride along with us?'

'That's kind of you.' He handed Quinn the keys to the Ford. 'Why don't you take my car?' he said to him. 'Just leave it parked in front of the Anchor with the keys stuffed down between the cushions.'

Outside, they walked a short distance to Lombard's car, which was parked on the street. A young boy, wearing an army surplus jacket several sizes too large for him, leaned against it.

'Anyone bother my car?' Lombard asked him.

'No, sir,' the boy said.

'Thank you, young man. Put this together and go buy yourself some nifty clothes.' He handed him half of a two-dollar bill, and the boy took off running. 'He is now the richest kid on his block,' Lombard said.

Horn wasn't listening. He was looking at the car. It was a Duesenberg Model J, long and low, with a bold, standup grille and twin horns riding below the lights. Even the front bumper looked graceful. It was a rich man's car, and Horn had seen only a couple of them.

'What do you think?' Lombard asked.

'This is a beautiful machine.'

'Well, I like expensive things,' the lawyer said, winking at Eden. 'This one was made in 'twenty-nine. I saw Clark Gable pull up in front of the Trocadero in one of these, and I decided I wanted one too. Shall we go? Willie, kindly take us out to the Strip.'

Half an hour later Lombard was being greeted warmly at the entrance to Ciro's on the Sunset Strip. Smooth dance music drifted out from the main room, along with the heady mixture of perfume and alcohol. The maitre d' looked long and hard at Horn's cotton sport jacket and tieless sport shirt, but Lombard slipped something into the man's pocket, and moments later they were shown to a table not far from the dance floor.

Instead of accompanying them, Willie Apples took up station at the bar, where two men made instant room for him.

'Have you ever been here?' Lombard asked.

'Once or twice,' Horn replied, looking around at the gaudy interior – red ceiling, crystal chandeliers, a giant Venetian gondola decoration dominating one wall. Couples danced as the orchestra played a rumba. The crowd looked elegant, many of the men in black tie, women in evening gowns and long gloves. Iris had enjoyed dressing up and going out, and he had occasionally indulged her. But even in his days as a minor celebrity, he had never felt comfortable in nightclubs. Although role-playing was part of his job, nightclubs seemed to be populated with people who played roles as part of life.

Lombard ordered champagne and began talking about his

background. He had an attorney's courtroom voice, and he told the story with practiced ease. 'I grew up in an Italian neighborhood in Chicago,' he said. 'My family name was Lombardi until I decided that didn't look very good on a business card. Where I grew up, you were either in a gang or you were dead, so I joined a gang. I was this little runt of a character, but I learned early on that if you acted tough, people thought of you that way.' He smiled as he set up his punchline. 'That also works in the practice of law.'

Horn recalled Mad Crow's comment about Lombard as a bootlegger. 'So you're not a violent man.'

'I don't resort to it personally,' Lombard answered carefully. 'Obviously, some of the people I defend are not so cautious. But I saw enough violence in my first sixteen years to last a lifetime—'

'Tell him about your ear,' Eden prompted him.

'This?' Lombard indicated a line of scar tissue, studded with beads of flesh, that ran along the front of his right ear from top to bottom. 'Kid a couple of years older than me found me on the wrong street one day, left me with this. He was too big for me to go after, but I knew another kid who was big enough for the job, so I bribed him with a half-dozen comic books and a couple of packs of cigarettes. He went after the other guy a little too enthusiastically. Cut off his ear lobe, brought it back to me in a matchbox.'

'It must be nice when other people are willing to get their hands dirty for you,' Horn said.

Lombard gave him a sharp glance. 'You could say that. But violence should be a last resort. I always prefer peaceful means. I get paid to flap my lips eloquently and persuade people to see things my way. I've tried it both ways, and believe me, it's much more satisfying to win a victory through reason and rhetoric.' He adjusted the cuff of his shirt enough to allow the cufflink to show. It was a sizable pearl, first cousin to the one pinned to his tie, the one Madge had mentioned. A neatly folded silk handkerchief in his breast pocket was of the same pearl gray, only slightly lighter than the hue of his well-cut wool suit.

Horn put an appreciative smile on his face as he glanced at Eden. 'How did you two meet?'

'I was visiting the studio,' Lombard said. 'Her boss, Mr Goldwyn, was having a little union trouble and asked my advice. He invited me back to the sound stage to watch them shoot a scene.'

'It was *The Secret Life of Walter Mitty*,' Eden said. 'The scene in the department store where Danny Kaye's surrounded by girls who are modeling corsets, and he's all flustered—'

'Danny Kaye. A waste of pretty girls, if you ask me,' Lombard broke in.

'Don't be unkind, Jay,' she said. 'Anyway, I was one of the girls.'

'Must have been a half-dozen of them, standing around in their undies,' Lombard went on, 'and she was the only one I noticed. Couldn't take my eyes off her. I know I'm no Tyrone Power, all right? Mr Goldwyn said he doubted she'd be interested in me. I bet him fifty dollars I'd have dinner with her that very evening. He lost.'

'And just what's so fascinating about him?' Horn asked her.

Eden hesitated, thinking, as she extracted a cigarette from a shiny case and Lombard lit it for her. 'I'm tired of pretty boys,' she said, exhaling a stream of smoke across the table. 'The studio is always trying to fix me up with some contract player with perfect teeth and hair. I like Jay because he's smart and successful, and because he has more self-confidence than any man I've ever met.'

Lombard seemed quietly satisfied with her answer. The orchestra moved into 'Embraceable You'. The waiter brought a second iced bottle of champagne, and Lombard deposited something in the man's pocket as he left.

'So how long were you up there?' he asked Horn. 'Cold Creek, wasn't it?'

'Two years.'

'That seems a little stiff for a first offense. I might have been able to cut a deal for you.'

'Maybe,' Horn said. 'But I had a studio chief testifying against me while his son sat there with bandages on his face. Nobody offered me a deal.'

'Did you make out all right?'

'I suppose. Every now and then, somebody would get the urge to pick a fight with an ex-movie actor, and I'd have to roll around in the dirt with him.'

'At least you've got a sense of humor about it,' Lombard said. 'I've known a few men who came out of the pen with serious problems. You might know some of them yourself. Did you ever—'

'Eden's probably bored by all this,' Horn cut in.

'Didn't mean to embarrass you,' Lombard said smoothly. 'Let's change the subject. I believe I know an old friend of yours from the movies. The Indian.'

'Joseph Mad Crow. We made a lot of them together. I work for him now.'

'Is that right? Doing what?'

'Collecting debts.'

Lombard tilted his head slightly, as if seeing Horn with fresh eyes. 'Interesting job. But nothing like what you used to do.'

Horn shrugged. 'Joseph tells me you tried to keep him from getting his hands on money to start his casino.'

Lombard laughed. 'Not really. I simply wouldn't lend him any myself. If his feelings were hurt, I'm sorry. I hope his operation is doing well.'

Be careful, Horn told himself. He couldn't afford to alienate the man before he got around to asking him about Rose.

'How many movies did you make?' Eden asked him.

'I lost count,' Horn laughed. 'But you could've made ten of mine for the cost of one of Mr Goldwyn's. You haven't heard of any of them. They had titles like *Bloody Trail* and *Wyoming Thunder*, and each one took about two weeks to shoot.'

'You must have spent a lot of time on horseback,' she said. 'I love horses.'

'I had a fine horse,' Horn said. 'I still miss him.'

'Eden's going to be a leading lady some day,' Lombard said. 'She already has the name. All she needs now is the right break.'

'My real name is Peggy Jean Turner,' she said to Horn. 'I didn't think it sounded dramatic enough.'

He tried to imagine her as Peggy Jean Turner and failed. 'I'm sure your new name will look good in lights,' he said.

'I'm keeping an eye on her career,' Lombard said. 'You have any advice for her?'

'I'll give you the best advice anybody ever gave me,' Horn said. 'Remember your lines, don't bump into the furniture, and never think you're better than the people behind the camera.'

Eden looked at him so searchingly that he was suddenly uneasy, so he tried to make a joke. 'Too bad I never took that advice,' he said. 'I always thought I was hot stuff.' He suddenly saw an opening. 'The person who told me that,' he said, tracing the rim of the champagne glass with his finger, 'I think you knew her. A woman named Rose Galen.'

When Lombard appeared to hesitate, Horn resisted the impulse to raise his eyes and look at the man. He waited.

'No, never heard of her,' Lombard said.

'All that riding and fighting,' Eden said to Horn. 'I imagine you must be pretty tough to do all that.'

'Well, some of the boys I knew were the real thing,' Horn said. 'Ken Maynard was a champion rodeo rider before he became a movie cowboy. And Johnny Mack Brown was an All-American at Alabama before he came out here. But most of us were just people doing a job. When it got really hard, they called in the stunt men. In the fight scenes, we mostly faked it – you know, pretending to throw a punch. If the camera angle is right, you can miss the other guy's chin by six inches and it'll still look realistic.'

'So you're not a tough guy,' Lombard said with an exaggerated smile, and Horn couldn't tell if there was anything behind the remark.

'Not me.'

The Duesenberg headed east back toward downtown, drawing occasional stares from other drivers. Horn sat in front next to Willie Apples, talking over his shoulder with the two in the back seat. He paid little attention to the conversation. All he could think about was that he was running out of time to get anything useful out of Jay Lombard. He would have preferred a private talk with the man, but he didn't know if he would ever get a better chance – or, in fact, if he would ever see him again.

'Willie, would you swing up by Chavez Ravine?' Lombard said to his driver. 'Eden likes to see the lights from up there.'

Willie Apples guided the big car carefully up a barely paved road that led past old houses that seemed to sag in the moonlight. There were no streetlights up here. The night air was clear, and the lights of downtown glowed like costume jewelry strewn in a shallow bowl. Horn wondered if Rose had ever come up here and seen the same lights, and what they might have said to her.

Then they descended, finally reaching a bleak stretch of rail yards, where their driver turned south. Horn decided it was time to try again.

'We started to talk about people we both know,' he said to Lombard. 'You sure you've never heard of Rose Galen?'

'I'm sure.' Horn heard an edge of impatience in the voice.

'Maybe you've forgotten her, or maybe you knew her by another name,' Horn said. 'But a friend of mine said she saw the two of you in the lounge at the Biltmore not too long ago, sitting and talking. It occurred to me that she might have needed a good lawyer, one who knew the angles.'

He glanced sideways at Willie Apples, but the other man appeared to be interested only in his driving. Horn felt as if he had opened a door and stepped into a dark room. His words could be taking him into a dangerous place, but he was no longer trying to be smart, calculating the odds. He was running out of time, and this time he had to push as far as he could.

'I'm afraid your friend's wrong,' Lombard said.

'Maybe I can help you remember,' Horn said. 'She had a career in the movies for a while, but she wasn't very successful. Last few years, she lived in one of the rooming houses up on Bunker Hill. She kept a newspaper clipping about you in her room. And—' He turned around to face the man in the back seat. 'And a few days ago somebody killed her.'

In the shifting lights from passing cars, it was impossible to read Lombard's expression. He said nothing.

'I've seen a few people die,' Horn said, trying to keep the tension out of his voice. 'Maybe you have too. I've noticed that when someone dies violently, it's almost always without dignity. For some reason, that bothers me. Whoever killed Rose didn't leave her any dignity.'

Lombard leaned forward deliberately, tapped Willie Apples on the shoulder, and spoke quickly into his ear. Then he sat back.

'Mr Horn, I don't think this was a coincidence, our meeting tonight,' he said quietly.

Their driver slowed the car and turned left out of the traffic and onto a darker and narrower street.

'No coincidence,' Horn admitted. 'Not to say I haven't enjoyed the champagne and the conversation, along with the chance to meet Eden. But I need to find out—'

'I'm forced to be rude to you,' Lombard cut in. 'I have to say I'm not interested in your story about some woman. Quite simply, you've made a mistake, and I'm afraid your ride is over. Please get out.'

Willie Apples stopped the car, and Horn looked around. They were on a street of warehouses and loading docks, dark except for a few streetlights.

'This is not very hospitable,' Horn said. He opened the door and got out. It would be a long walk to his car.

Just then, Willie Apples cut the engine, got out from behind the wheel, stripped off his suit jacket, and laid it carefully on the seat, then stood looking at Horn over the roof of the Duesenberg, his brow furrowed as usual. Horn knew something was wrong. 'What's going on?' he asked Lombard through the window.

'I tried to be friendly toward you, but you insisted on crowding me about this Rosemary—' Lombard caught himself. 'This Rose person. I told you I didn't know her, and you implied I was lying. If I felt particularly unkind, I'd point out that you are a broken-down actor and an ex-con, a man not to be taken seriously. Willie here, who has a different attitude about violence than I do, is going to leave you with a souvenir. Nothing

139

permanent, just enough to make you remember that I'm not someone who responds well to disrespect.'

Horn took off his fedora and let it drop to the pavement. He caught a glimpse of Eden Lamont's face in the back seat. Her eyes were wide with fear and something else. He thought fleetingly of the woman with the spot of blood on her glove.

Willie Apples came around the car, arms wide, flexing his big fingers, moving in an exaggerated crouch like an ape Horn had once seen in a zoo. 'Come here,' the man said.

Horn's stomach knotted. He could try running, but they had a car, and eventually it would come down to him and Willie Apples out here on the street. He might as well save his wind. His right hand started for the pocket of his sport jacket, but he stopped it. No sense in giving anything away too soon. He backed off some more, looking over his shoulder. He was a few feet from a darkened loading dock. He might be able to use the darkness, but he could also get trapped up there on the platform. Better to stay on street level.

As Willie approached, Horn angled to the right until he and the other man were in the full glare of the car's lights, like players onstage in a violent drama. Bile churned up into his throat. It was the familiar taste of fear, the fear that had paralyzed and unmanned him during the war. All he could do was try to forget the source of the fear – the man who wanted to hurt him – and focus on the reason he was here.

Rose. He allowed her face to drift upward from the secret place where he kept it. In death, it was ugly and terrible. But it might be enough.

Moving lightly for such a big man, Willie rushed him. Horn threw a solid right at him, but it glanced harmlessly off his shoulder, and in the next instant Horn felt himself enclosed in the other man's arms. Willie lifted him off his feet and lumbered toward a tin-sided warehouse wall a few yards away. With a bang, he slammed Horn against the wall and pinned him there.

'Jay said to break something,' he said in a conversational tone. His knuckles ground into Horn's spine, sending jolts up and down his back. 'You get to pick.'

Horn struggled with all his strength. Sliding slowly down the wall, he felt his feet touch the ground. He raised one foot and brought it down hard on the other man's instep. Willie groaned and loosened his grip a bit.

'How about a couple of ribs?' he asked. When Horn didn't answer, he dropped his arms, stepped back, doubled up a giant fist, and aimed a right hook at Horn's ribcage. Horn saw it coming and barely had time to twist to the right. Instead of the ribs, the big man's fist slammed into the muscles to the left of his spine, sending a shock down to his knees. *If he lands a solid one, I'm finished*, Horn thought desperately.

Before Horn could recover from the blow, the other man stepped in close to fashion a quick wrestler's hold, slipping his right arm up under Horn's left as he grabbed a handful of hair with the other hand. Horn knew what was coming, but he couldn't stop it. An instant later, he flew through the air, landing heavily and painfully on his right shoulder. As he rolled onto his stomach, his opponent dropped on him from behind, aiming a heavy knee at the base of his spine with all his weight behind it. Horn's breath was driven out of him.

Next the weight shifted up to Horn's shoulders, pinning him to the pavement. He felt Willie grab his hair with both hands and rake his face across the concrete in a quick scrubbing motion. The pain was ferocious.

Willie lifted him by his collar to his feet and spun him around. His face on fire, Horn fought to give himself a few seconds' time. He jammed a thumb toward the man's left eye, but Willie merely squeezed his eyes tightly shut and shook his head. 'You fight dirty,' he said. 'I don't mind.'

I learned in the joint, Horn answered the man silently. *Nobody fights clean there.*

Another giant fist, a left this time, and Horn could not avoid it. The blow caught him dead center in the chest, bouncing him loudly off the tin wall and back out onto the pavement.

Willie stood about six feet away, grinning slightly.

Fighting for breath from the blow to his chest and unable to see well out of his right eye, Horn dug into the pocket of his jacket, but he found only a large rip in the pocket seam. The object he sought had dropped down into the lining. Frantically he dug farther until he found it, then tried to drag it out, but the heavy object snagged on the torn pocket.

'What you got there?' Willie asked without much concern. 'Can't be a piece. An ex-con'd be crazy to—'

Horn jerked his hand free, wrapped his fingers around the grip of the brass knuckles and, in a single motion, stepped forward and drove his fist into Willie's stomach, just grazing the lowest rib. The other man grunted loudly, bent over, and clutched his midsection. Without pausing, Horn brought the knuckles around in a right hook that exploded on the man's left temple. Willie went down on one knee. Another blow, this one cracking on the crown of the head, and the big man went down all the way, curled up, one cheek resting on the asphalt. The trickle of blood from his temple looked black in the light from the faraway street lamp.

But Willie wasn't finished. Slowly, noises coming from his throat, he pushed up from the pavement, then rose to his knees. There he stayed, swaying slightly, as if wondering what he should do next.

Horn had forgotten everything except his rage. It was like the moment after the needless death of his horse when he went after Bernie Rome Junior. He stepped forward, ready to follow up, to use the brass knuckles decisively, to break a bone in the man who had threatened to break one of his. But a wave of pain and dizziness swept over him. He reached out for support, found none. The next thing he knew, he was sitting down about ten feet from Willie, watching the car's headlights rotate crazily in giant circles.

'I think I'd call that a draw.' It was Lombard's voice. The lawyer walked over and stood over him. 'Even better than Raul's bout. And this time I had a ringside seat.'

He turned to his employee, who was rising painfully to his feet. 'Not bad, Willie, although I was a little disappointed in the outcome. Let's go.' They walked toward the car.

Horn got up too, found his hat, and followed them. As he

walked, everything hurt. Expressionlessly, Lombard sat in the back seat and watched him approach. 'You want another round?' he asked.

Horn leaned in the window closest to Eden and spoke past her. 'No,' he said, his voice a shaky whisper. 'I just wanted to say this isn't over. Whoever killed Rose Galen probably thought everyone had forgotten her. But she had friends. We're going to get her dignity back for her.'

His own language sounded alien to him, like a speech from the hero of a bad movie, but he couldn't stop. 'You still have something to tell me. If she was a friend or a client of yours, you should want to help. But if you're the one who killed her, I'm going to find out.'

He turned to Eden, who was staring at the fresh wound on his cheek, her eyes still wide and face pale except for the dark slash of lipstick. 'Before it's too late, you may want to ask yourself if you belong with him,' he said. 'And by the way, I like your real name better.'

Chapter Fourteen

'He called her Rosemary.'

Horn and Mad Crow sat at the weathered bar of the Dust Bowl amid the comforting fragrance of spilled beer and cigarette smoke and the familiar talk of the regular patrons. Sometimes it seemed that everyone in LA came from somewhere else, and many of those in the Dust Bowl spoke in the distinctive twang of Oklahoma, Arkansas, and East Texas.

It was early afternoon, and the customers were low-key and few in number. The place was one-story, ramshackle and finished in whitewashed clapboard.

'He called her Rosemary,' Mad Crow responded, not comprehending. 'That's not her name.'

'It used to be. Dex told me that. Back when she was in the silents, that's the name she used. But only then. When Lombard called her that, he stumbled and then caught himself and called her Rose. But I heard him.'

'So . . .'

'So he didn't just know her. He knew her a good twenty years ago. Back around the time when she left the business without telling anybody why. Something happened to her back then, and I'll bet you Lombard knows what it was.'

'Maybe it wasn't something that happened to *her*,' Mad Crow suggested. 'Maybe she really did—'

'Kill somebody.' Horn absent-mindedly scraped at the label of his Blue Ribbon with his thumbnail. A large, rectangular bandage was taped to the right side of his face, covering it from temple to jaw. 'Maybe.' He drained the bottle and waggled it in the air. 'Hey, Rusty. A couple more?'

Rusty Baird, who was tending bar, came over and uncapped two bottles and set them in place. 'How's Cassie?' he asked.

'Who knows?' Mad Crow responded. 'At least she's on her own now. Instead of tearing up saloons, she's got herself a job driving a cab, terrorizing innocent pedestrains.'

'You got yourself quite a niece there,' the bartender said with a grin. Rusty Baird had come out to California with his family during the Depression. He started as a fruit picker but, after discovering Marx and Steinbeck in the public library, found his calling as a labor organizer. When a blow from a strikebreaker's club left him deaf in one ear and near-blind in one eye, he bought a big fruit stand, put a roof on it, turned it into a honky tonk, and named it the Dust Bowl. It now drew an eclectic mix of ranchers, cowboys – both real and Hollywood – and Mexican farm workers.

Baird moved down the bar to wait on someone else, and Mad Crow looked at his watch. 'Guess I should head out pretty soon. The boys'll be opening up, and the customers like to see me standing around looking colorful.' But he didn't move. 'Do you think I was too rough on her?'

'No. You did what you thought was best. She's got problems with you, but she's going to have to work them out herself. Why don't you invite her out for a meal this weekend?'

'I'll see. I'm gonna be busy. Since you turned lily-livered on me and wouldn't help with the mustang, looks like tomorrow's the day I'll have to go out to the corral and get myself all dirty.'

'Can I come watch? Maybe bring a friend?'

'Hell, I don't care. Come around noon. Bring a brass band.'

When Baird returned, he and Mad Crow began discussing the virtues of beer in the new aluminum cans, and Horn's mind wandered. He lifted his eyes to his own reflection in the mirror behind the bar, lazily scanned some of the familiar black-and-white pictures obscuring part of the glass. There was Gene Autry holding a guitar, Roy Rogers resplendent in a fringed shirt, and others: Charles Starrett as the masked Durango Kid, Al 'Lash' La Rue wielding a wicked-looking bullwhip, silver-haired William Boyd as Hopalong Cassidy. And the sidekicks: George 'Gabby'

Hayes, Smiley Burnette, Andy Devine and, in a prominent spot, Joseph Mad Crow. Horn's eyes stopped on a newly framed photo. 'What the hell is that, Rusty?'

Baird had an almost boyish, freckled, open face, a look that had fooled many a drunk into thinking he was a pushover. He looked slightly guilty and shifted his eyes to Mad Crow, saying nothing.

'Did you give him that?' Horn asked Mad Crow.

'Hell, yes, I did,' Mad Crow responded belligerently. 'You belong up there as much as him. Or him. Or him.'

'Take it down, Rusty,' Horn said. 'I mean it.'

'All right,' Baird said, removing the offending photo and putting it beneath the bar.

'I don't know about you, partner,' Mad Crow said, shaking his head. 'You got no reason to be embarrassed—'

'Don't worry about me, Indian,' Horn said, eyes straight ahead. 'Just don't go around doing things behind my back, all right?'

'At your service. Put your six-gun away, and let's get back to Lombard. You want to tell me where you managed to get your hands on a pair of brass knuckles? Far as I know, you don't keep those down there with the nickels and dimes and all the lint in your pocket.'

'I'd seen them in the window of a pawnshop by the Anchor,' Horn said. 'You'd already told me about this Willie Apples. When I went over to pick up Emory Quinn to go out to the Olympic, something told me I might need a little equalizer. As it turned out, things just barely got equalized.' He paused, think-ing. 'You know, Quinn said something to me about not having the killer instinct when he was in the ring. I think that about myself sometimes. I don't like to fight. But out on that street, all I could think about was how that big son of a bitch might have been the one who went into Rose's room, put that rope around her neck . . .'

'I know,' Mad Crow said quietly. 'Damn, I wish I'd been there last night to see it.'

Rusty Baird stepped away from the jukebox, and a voice filled

146

the bar, backed by steel guitar and little else. The voice sang about the time when you're so lonesome you could cry, and it carried a whole world of knowledge and pain.

'Who's that?' Horn asked.

'Fellow named Hank Williams,' Baird replied. 'Alabama boy. He's on the radio sometimes, the 'Louisiana Hayride'. Good, ain't he?'

'Sounds like he's been there and back.'

'Well, he's just a kid. In his twenties, I hear.'

'Somewhere inside,' Horn said, 'he's old.'

Back at the cabin he found a handwritten note in his mailbox that said simply *Drainage*. It needed no translation. Harry Flye, his landlord, had amassed a fortune speculating in real estate without ever acquiring manners or much of a vocabulary. He and Horn had spoken of the need to clear the estate's old drainage canal of weeds and brush. The note said it was time to begin.

Carrying a shovel and dragging a moldy, discolored tarpaulin, he climbed the road up to the ruins of the estate on the plateau. At the edge of the property, he found the spot where the concrete-lined drainage canal began its course down the hill, paralleling the road. Over the years, the concrete had been breached by roots and tough weeds and choked by debris. He began digging with the shovel, flinging the contents onto the spread-out tarp. After digging out the caked mud and brush until the concrete was exposed, he began pulling weeds.

Even in the cool air, he quickly worked up a sweat. After almost two hours, he had barely covered twenty yards. But it was a start. He dragged the tarpaulin and its contents down the road. The mud looked like rich soil. He could spread it over the grounds around the cabin where, years earlier, someone had planted an array of flowering shrubs. The rest he would burn.

Inside, he drew a hot bath, poured a glass of Evan Williams and soaked away some of the soreness. Tired as he was, he let his guard down, and for an instant Rose's face in death emerged, like a too-quick image in a badly edited film. An involuntary noise came from his throat, and the image dissolved. To keep it from returning, he decided to deliberately go back over the events of the last few days.

He had learned some things.

Rose had killed someone. Or so she had said. An accident, or murder. Given what he knew about her, he could barely make room in his mind for the idea, but he allowed it there anyway. If it was true, it was no great stretch from there to the notion that Rose herself might have been murdered in retribution.

Jay Lombard. He had known Rose years ago and met her quietly not long before her death. Horn had no idea yet of the shape of his relationship with her. But he knew Lombard and his thug-companion were men of violence. Were they capable of murder?

Whether or not she was a killer, the Rose he had known had touched people, left them changed in some way by her friendship and decency. Horn himself was one of those. Dexter Diggs and Emory Quinn were others. Dolores Winter might be another, he thought, and could possibly be a helpful ally. If only she didn't dislike him so much.

The phone interrupted his thoughts. It was Dex.

'I've found out something,' he said. 'Someone died, remember? At a party? I've got the name.'

'Good for you, Dex. Who was it?'

'A girl named Tess Shockley.' Diggs spelled the name. 'She was eighteen. She—'

'How did you find out?'

'Luck, partly. An old friend of mine is now in the advertising department at the *Examiner*. He put me in touch with one of their police reporters, who agreed to dig some clippings out of their morgue. I now owe him a bottle of his favorite sour mash. By great good fortune, this character has been working there since the Woodrow Wilson administration and, once he pulled the clips, realized he'd been one of the reporters who worked on the story. He began to recall it and was able to embroider some of the details that didn't make it into the paper. Anyway—' He paused to catch his breath.

'Tess Shockley. She came here fresh out of high school to make it in the movies. Sound familiar? She was only here for a year before she died, and she never did make it, although she did land some bit parts. Being pretty, she got invited to a lot of parties, including some where the Hollywood people would show up. There was some talk of her dating for money, but that was probably just yellow journalism talking, people looking for another Black Dahlia. Indications are she was just another one of these nice, star-struck kids.

'One night she turned up on the doorstep of the emergency room at Cedars of Lebanon, bleeding uncontrollably. They took her in, but they couldn't stop the bleeding. She died a few hours later.'

'Where did she—'

'Wait. Let me finish reading from these notes. At first they thought it was a botched abortion, but she was too well dressed, as if she'd been to a party. Emergency room doctor found alcohol and cocaine in her system. He also concluded – and this wasn't in the paper – that she'd been penetrated by a hard object with enough force to rupture the wall of the uterus.'

'She wasn't pregnant?'

'No. She was a very unlucky young lady who went to the wrong party. Someone got her high and raped her, most likely using something. And killed her.'

'Maybe she got *herself* high, Dex.'

'You mean maybe it was just one of those jolly, madcap parties full of coke and copulation? All right, maybe she got herself high. But she didn't do the rest of it to herself, my friend. She had some bruises on her arms, suggesting a struggle. The coroner called it homicide, and it wound up just another unsolved killing. A little juicier than most, but no Black Dahlia. After a while, people forgot.'

'Do they know where she'd been?'

'The party, you mean? No. She was dumped at the hospital, like a bag of dirty laundry. The police talked to her landlady and any friends they could locate, trying to find where she had gone that night. Nothing. She died in the early hours of New Year's Day, so I'm sure she had plenty of parties to choose from the night before.'

'How about relatives?'

'A day later, another story mentioned that her parents showed up to claim the body. But they had asked the police to keep their names out of the paper, and it was done.'

'Well, this is all interesting stuff,' Horn said. 'But we don't know yet if this Shockley girl—'

'Is connected with Rose? Let me finish,' Diggs said urgently. 'Although the paper didn't name the parents, it didn't have to. It mentioned where they came from, which was enough.'

Horn waited, but Diggs said nothing. He filled in the silence himself. 'Oklahoma City?'

'That's right. And the first day's story ran a picture of Tess Shockley. It's her, John Ray.'

'Same picture Rose had?'

'Exact same. Tess probably had it in her apartment, and some reporter swiped it for the paper. Common practice among the gentlemen of the press, my friend tells me.'

'So this is who Rose meant when she said—'

'We don't know that for sure. But it's a natural assumption to make, isn't it?'

Neither man spoke for a moment. 'I don't like where this is going,' Diggs said finally.

'Me neither. But we can't stop now. I'm going to see if I can track down her folks, if they're still alive.'

'Rose couldn't kill anyone.'

'I want to believe that. Thanks, Dex. I'll be in touch.'

He was up early the next morning, thinking about things he needed to do. He started some coffee and fried a couple of eggs. Adding a few slices of white bread and a splash of hot sauce on the eggs, he carried the breakfast outside, eating and gazing through the dense growth of trees to the far rim of the canyon. Sitting quietly for a while in the mornings helped him prepare for a day that might include confrontations in the service of the Mad Crow Casino. Evenings, it helped him journey back to a peaceful place inside his head.

On this day, it seemed most important to try to locate relatives or friends of Tess Shockley. He had to know why Rose had kept her photo all those years. Would a murderer keep a photo of her victim?

Two decades had passed. He hadn't the name of a single friend of the dead girl. He hadn't even the full names or address of her parents, assuming either was still alive. But he knew they were from Oklahoma City.

And he had the name of the photo studio that had once taken her picture.

He went inside, retrieved the photo from his jacket pocket, and studied the back of it. *Beasley Studio, Oklahoma City*, it said. He picked up the phone, got the long-distance operator, and asked for Oklahoma City information. The Beasley Studio, it seemed, was still there, and a minute later the operator was ringing the number.

'Beasley's,' said a male voice in a familiar accent.

'Good morning,' he said. 'My name is Horn, and I've got kind of a funny request.' The sounds of Oklahoma and Arkansas speech have a lot in common. Almost unconsciously, like an actor learning a part, Horn found himself lapsing into an exaggerated version of the accent of his early years.

'I've got an old picture of a cousin of mine, taken at your studio maybe twenty years ago. Her name is Tess Shockley. She's deceased, I'm afraid. I'm looking into my family tree and trying to get addresses on everybody who's still alive. I believe her folks may still live in Oklahoma City, and I'm wondering if you'd mind seeing if you have an address for them.'

'Well, I don't know,' the man said slowly. 'Twenty years ago, you said?'

'That's right,' Horn said, laughing as if in embarrassment. 'I know it's asking a lot . . .'

'You see, Mr Beasley, he cleaned out a bunch of the records and moved them upstairs not long before he died.'

'Uh-huh,' Horn said. 'Prob'ly a big job to go through 'em. Listen . . . what did you say your name was?'

'Ernest.'

'Ernest, I'm calling long-distance from Los Angeles, California.'

'Is that right?'

'Yes, sir. I wouldn't be calling if this wasn't real important. I have to be honest with you. This isn't for me, it's for my wife. She's been ailing lately, and she wants to get in touch with all the family before she . . . well, you know.'

'I see.' Ernest sounded vaguely sympathetic.

'All I can do is hope you understand how important this is for our family. If you'd be willing to take a little extra time and go through those records, my wife and I would be really grateful to you.'

'Well, I suppose I could take a few minutes during my lunch.'

'You're very kind to do this. May I call you back later?'

He hung up. Another concern, he reflected, was money. He wondered briefly if he needed to take on a quick job for the Indian, either a collection or something else. Horn pulled out his wallet. He had enough cash, he estimated, to last several days if he was frugal. There was no need to go to work just yet.

He went back outside to plan his day, but the rocking chair had barely reached its usual tempo when the phone rang again.

'This is Dolores Winter.' He thought he would have recognized her voice anyway – direct, low, almost husky. A voice that sounded like cigarette smoke. 'I had some bad words for you the other day.'

'I remember.'

'Well, I don't like to apologize. It spoils my image as a tough broad, one I've spent years building up. But after I ran into Dexter Diggs, I started thinking about old times. I called him just now, to say thanks for coming out to Rose's grave. He told me a few things about you. One was that you thought a lot of her. Another was that generally you're an all-right guy, even if your reputation is shot to hell these days.'

'Thanks for putting it so delicately.'

'So, as long as we don't call it an apology, what say we start over?'

'Fine with me.'

'I'd like to buy you lunch. At my place, next Thursday. Dexter and his wife will be there. I hope a weekday's all right with you. I'm not working right now. You want to come over?' She gave him the address, and he wrote it down. 'We can talk about Rose, if you want to. Dexter said you'd like to know who killed her. So would I. If there's anything I can do—'

'I'm grateful for lunch,' he said. 'That's a start.'

Chapter Fifteen

'What do you want?' Cassie leaned out the window of the cab, a cigarette hanging lazily off her lower lip.

'I want a cab. Just like I told the dispatcher.' Horn had to raise his voice to be heard over the buzz of activity in front of Union Station. The big white stucco building loomed behind him like a modern-day Spanish mission. It was late morning, the Super Chief had just pulled in, and travelers, many toting luggage, jostled each other on the concrete expanse in front of the terminal.

'You asked for me.'

'That's right. Any crime in that?'

'What's wrong with your car?'

He walked over and leaned both hands on the roof, looking down at her. 'I came down here to see someone off for San Francisco. Now my car won't start. Battery, I think. I'll take care of it later, but I need to go someplace now.' It was the first of many lies he planned to tell her.

She exhaled, squinting through the cigarette smoke, one elbow resting on the open window. Her cap rode at a jaunty angle. *She's got the cabby look down real good,* he thought admiringly.

'Where do you need to go?'

'Out to Joseph's place.'

She removed the drawn-down stub from her mouth and flipped it away. 'Get somebody else.'

'Come on, Cassie, give me a ride. It's a long way out there. You'll get a two-way fare. All I ask is that you take me off the meter while we're there. You can have some lunch while I take care of my business.'

She looked doubtful. 'Are you going to see my uncle?'

'Maybe,' he said, trying to sound as casual as possible. 'If he's there. But he's not the reason I'm going. You know Two-Step, his mare? She's for sale, and a friend of mine who's looking for a horse for his wife asked me to check her out. I'm going to throw a saddle on her and take her for a ride.' He indicated the change of clothes he carried in a large paper bag. 'Then I'm going to see if Nee Nee will make me a sandwich, and then I'll come back.' He paused. 'It's good money.'

'All right,' she said, still sounding dubious. 'Get in.'

The drive over the Santa Monica Mountains and across the San Fernando Valley took almost an hour, even with Cassie's aggressive driving. Horn tried to talk to her, but several abrupt lane changes and hair's-breadth escapes at intersections made it hard for him to concentrate on conversation.

When she pulled into the drive of Mad Crow's place, she stopped short of the house. 'I'll wait here,' she said.

'Hey,' he said. 'Didn't you leave some riding stuff in the stable? Pants and boots and that kind of thing?'

'I suppose.'

'Well, come on. Ride with me.'

'I'm working.'

'Who cares? Let's saddle up and go for a ride up into the foothills. We'll be back in less than an hour, get some lunch, and you can take me back.'

When she hesitated, he said, 'One of the hands told me you get along well with Doodle Bug. I bet she'd enjoy getting out.'

Fifteen minutes later, they led their freshly saddled horses out of the stable, mounted up, and guided them out to the road that led behind Mad Crow's place and northward up into the foot-hills. They proceeded until the road gave out, then began climbing steadily up a dirt path, rutted by recent rains and dotted with occasional piles of horse dung. When they reached a kind of plateau, they stopped to rest their horses, turned and looked back.

The light breeze was warmed by a bright midday sun that burned down through a high scattering of streaked clouds.

Below them and off into the distance sprawled the ranches, farms, and orchards that for recent generations had defined the San Fernando Valley. Farther off was the newer face of the Valley, the denser collections of houses and businesses butting up against the Santa Monica range. Beyond that line of mountains lay the great, raw, sprawling city itself.

Horn had lived and worked and ridden all over this end of the Valley. Ten years ago, it had seemed almost like wilderness to him, well hidden from the distant noise of Los Angeles. But not any more. Looking south, he could see that LA had spilled over those hills and was fast coming this way.

Horn's mount shifted its weight restlessly and swatted at something with its tail.

'How's she doing?' Cassie asked. She wore dungarees, boots, and a plaid shirt. Her hair was in a loose ponytail under a wide-brimmed straw hat.

'Little Two-Step? Just fine,' Horn said. 'Nice and gentle. Good saddle horse.'

'I think Doodle Bug missed me,' Cassie said, leaning forward to tousle the mare's forelock and rub the spot between her huge eyes.

'Bet she did. You should come out and ride her more often.'

'Sure,' she said sarcastically. 'Me and my uncle, we could go riding together.'

'You used to love horses. Remember the filly back home? The one you introduced me to?'

'One of her owners spooked her, and she ran off and got tangled in some barbed wire,' Cassie said evenly. 'By the time they found her, she'd lost so much blood they had to put her down.'

'I'm sorry.'

'People don't treat horses like they should.'

'And I suppose that includes your uncle.'

Cassie began to answer, but a loud splashing announced that her horse was taking a leak. During the long time it lasted, she stood up in the stirrups to relieve the pressure on the mare's kidneys.

Horn began rolling a smoke, but Cassie offered him one of her Old Golds. They shared a light.

'What happened to your face?' she asked.

'Just an accident. Have you learned anything about Rose?'

'A few things,' she said. Seeing the look on his face, she added: 'I know you think I'm sneaking around the place like some kind of cab-driving Nancy Drew. I'm not, really. I'm getting to know some of the people, asking a few questions about Rose, that's all. Maybe I'll learn something important, maybe not. But the place is affordable, and I like living in her room.'

'In a room where somebody died?'

She shrugged. 'That doesn't bother me. I remember her alive, not dead.'

He thought about that. 'Well, I guess she'd probably like having you there too.'

'There's a woman who lives in the building, named Madge—'

'I know her,' Horn said. 'She was a good friend of Rose. Did you tell her you know me?'

'No reason to. She's a strange old gal, gabs a lot. I like her, though. She mentioned some odd character who used to hang around the rooming house, who never talked to anybody except Rose.'

'The gray man?'

'That's right. Funny name. Anyway, I think I may have seen him the other night. He was standing on the sidewalk across the street, just looking up at my window. When I went outside, he was gone.'

Horn had a quick, troubling image of Willie Apples. 'Was he big? I mean really big?'

'No. I don't think so. Tall, but thin.'

'If you see him, call me,' Horn said. 'That's what I told Madge. You don't know what he's up to, and there's no need for you to approach him by yourself.'

'You keep thinking I'm helpless,' Cassie laughed. 'And if this person killed Rose, why would he keep coming back to her building?'

'I just want you to let me know,' he said, trying to sound stern but knowing that sternness was largely wasted on Cassie.

'Well, if it's that important to you, maybe I will.' He could hear the joshing in her voice. But then she turned serious. 'The people who live there are already forgetting about it, even the ones who liked her,' she said. 'I don't think anybody really cares who killed Rose.'

'We do.' They sat in silence for a while, horses and riders relaxed. 'So . . . when you were little, did you want to be Nancy Drew?'

She laughed, so suddenly that Doodle Bug's ears pricked up lightly at the sound. 'Sure I did. Every red-blooded American girl did, even the ones who grew up around the reservation. Who did you want to be?'

'William S. Hart.'

'Who's that?'

'Cowboy actor, back in the silent days. He had traveled the West as a boy and actually knew real cowboys and Indians. I was seven or eight first time I saw one of his movies, and I remember how solid and serious he seemed, how believable, even to a little kid like me. I also think he reminded me of my father – very stern, very sure of the difference between right and wrong. That was back when I worshiped my father—'

'Before you learned to hate him?'

'That's right.' He was growing uncomfortable with the subject. 'We better start back,' he said. 'Hungry?'

Mad Crow, they learned, had lunched and was busy in the stable. His aunt, happy to see Cassie, sat them down in the kitchen and built them fat sandwiches of sliced beef with tomatoes, onions and mayonnaise. 'She puts mayonnaise on everything,' Mad Crow told him once. 'Even for breakfast.'

The old woman spoke little English, and Mad Crow's Lakota vocabulary had shrunk over the years, but she seemed to fit comfortably in this world far from the reservation where she had spent most of her life. She claimed to have been born the year of the battle that was fought by the Little Bighorn, the river known to her people as the Greasy Grass. As a girl, she said, she had heard the great Sitting Bull himself tell of how he had dreamed of a great victory against the Bluecoats and how the Sioux and Cheyenne, swarming like bees from a hive, had descended on the white soldiers and fulfilled his vision.

'I don't know,' Mad Crow once said to Horn. 'Sitting Bull was killed about four years after the battle, so I'm not sure she would remember him. But if you think I'm going to contradict her on that, you're crazy.'

When they had finished eating, Nee Nee hugged Cassie and solemnly shook Horn's hand. Outside, he spotted Mad Crow and a couple of his ranch hands with a horse in the corral abutting the stable. 'I do believe he's going to work on the mustang,' he said to Cassie. 'I think I'll watch this for a few minutes. Then we can leave.'

'I don't want to see it,' she responded. 'I'll wait over there.' She indicated one of the lawn chairs nearby, under a sprawling oak.

Horn leaned against the top rail of the corral fence. The other hands had closed the gate and stood outside the corral, leaving Mad Crow alone with the mustang. Mad Crow noticed Horn and nodded silently, then returned his attention to the job at hand.

The stallion was a brown two-year-old with black mane and tail and a silver dollar-sized star between the eyes. Its coat was matted with straw and dirt. It paced nervously at the far end of the corral, always aware of Mad Crow, who stood relaxed in the center with the coils of a lariat looped in his left hand. Slowly he began stalking the horse, and the stud responded by running in quick bursts until stopped by the fence, then wheeling around and starting off in another direction. But the corral was too small to afford it much freedom, and Mad Crow remained in motion, adjusting his angles so as to head off the stallion whenever it decided to go right or left. After ten minutes of this, the horse stood still, breathing heavily, eyes on Mad Crow.

Horn felt pressure on the top rail and turned to find Cassie standing beside him, her face grim. 'Watch this,' he said to her in a low voice. 'It might surprise you. But don't talk loud.'

'I'm watching,' she said, sounding bored.

'He's quarter horse stock, bred on the open range, never handled by anybody,' Horn said.

'He looks afraid,' she said, almost in a whisper.

'He is, because horses have it in them to be afraid. Out there, especially when they're young, they're chased by cougars and wolves. They don't prey on anything; other animals prey on them. This guy's instinct is to turn away and run from the man with the lariat. But Joseph needs to get him to the point where he's tired of turning away, where he'll face the man and concentrate on him. That's where he is now.'

As they watched, Mad Crow stood about fifteen feet from the stallion. The horse, which had been shifting its hind quarters right and left, now stood squarely facing its adversary, head bobbing nervously. Mad Crow took a step forward, then waited. The head bobbed again. Each time the horse's attention seemed to stray, Mad Crow took another step. The horse snorted, bobbed its head again, then eyeballed the man.

'He's puzzled,' Horn said quietly. 'But he's curious, too.'

Easing the loop free of the lariat's coils, Mad Crow made a few easy moves with it, to no response. Then, from a distance of about ten feet and with delicate motion, he flicked the loop over the stallion's head. The horse took off, running and bucking around the corral. Mad Crow kept a strain on the lariat. Each time the horse tried to head away, Mad Crow tightened his grip. The stallion, clearly troubled by the feel of the loop on its neck, shook its head as it ran. Little by little, the radius between man and horse tightened. Finally, winded, the horse stood as before, facing the man, breathing heavily.

'Horse just learned something,' Horn said. 'It's more comfortable to stand close to the guy with the rope.'

Mad Crow gathered in a big length of lariat, shortening the distance to about five feet, then slowly extended his hand. The stallion bobbed its head one more time, testing the air. Mad Crow took a half-step closer, hand still extended. Then, as Cassie audibly drew in her breath, the horse leaned out and sniffed the hand.

'First time he's been touched by a human,' Horn said.

The wrinkled muzzle lingered over Mad Crow's hand. 'Watch the ears,' Horn said to her. 'This is the dangerous part. If the ears flatten, he's going for Joseph, and he could hurt him. If not . . .'

But the ears stayed erect, and the horse delicately lifted its lip as it sniffed.

'Joseph talks about this,' Horn said. 'He says there's a place where the horse just . . . *lets go*. Where he decides to trust you. His head drops, and you can see things in the eyes and the face. The horse has just learned that it can trust a human and not get hurt. You know your uncle's not a particularly emotional man, but when he talks about this . . . Well, you should hear him.'

'He never told me about that,' Cassie said.

'Maybe you never gave him a chance.'

Moving slowly, Mad Crow knelt, gently lifted the horse's left foreleg, and began to stroke it. He repeated the gesture with the right leg. The horse continued to bob its head, wondering about all this strange behavior, but accepting it.

For a long time, Mad Crow remained on the ground, stroking the leg. Then he slowly straightened, shrugged his left shoulder, and caught a bridle as it slid down his arm. With no sudden motions, he slid the bridle up over the long, bony head and secured it.

'Bitless bridle,' Horn said. 'It won't bother him much.'

Leaving the stallion for a moment to get used to the feel of the bridle, Mad Crow fetched a blanket and saddle from the top rail of the fence. Returning, he laid the blanket over the horse's back, then stood for a moment, waiting. Nothing happened. Stooping, he picked up the saddle and effortlessly swung it up and onto the blanket, keeping a grip on the saddle horn and cantle. The horse made a nervous whuffling sound and stepped away, and Mad Crow let it go. After a few seconds, he followed, raising the saddle into place again. Once again, the stud moved away.

A third time, Mad Crow followed with the saddle, laying it onto the horse's back with what looked like a feather touch. This time, the mustang stood still, head bobbing slightly, body shuddering with the new sensation.

Horn had witnessed this several times but never failed to appreciate what it meant. 'This is an animal who's afraid of predators,' he said almost wonderingly, 'and he's just agreed to take a strange weight on his back. It's really something, isn't it?'

'Yes, it is.'

As gently as possible, Mad Crow went through the motions of securing the saddle in place and stepped back. Then, as if to prove Horn wrong, the stud bucked a couple of times, turned to look at the saddle, then bucked some more. But after pacing a little, the horse finally stood still.

Taking a last look over his shoulder at the stallion, Mad Crow came to join them. 'Hi, Cassie,' he said casually. Then, to both of them: 'I'll leave the saddle on him a while, let him get used to it. Tomorrow, I'll bring in some other horses for company, put the saddle on him, and see if he'll let me ride.'

'I got a nickel says he throws you,' Horn said.

'Wouldn't be the first time in my illustrious career. If so, I'll keep trying until he lets me. It'll take a while, but he's going to be one great horse. I can tell.'

He noticed the expression on Cassie's face. 'What's wrong?'

'Nothing,' Horn said with a grin. 'Just that she thought she knew all about breaking wild horses. She thought it always left them bloody and sweaty and . . . well, *broken*.'

'We've all known some idiots who work that way,' Mad Crow said, then turned to her. 'I never used a whip or a spur on any animal,' he said quietly.

'I'm glad to hear that.'

'Something else,' Mad Crow said, looking ill at ease. 'I don't know if there's any good time or good way to say this, but . . . I'm sorry I hit you.'

Cassie nodded, swallowing hard. 'Sorry for the things I said.'

On the way back, Cassie invited Horn to sit up front. Half turning to him as she changed lanes suddenly, almost dusting the fender of the Buick Roadmaster behind them, she said, 'There's nothing wrong with your car.'

'You're pretty smart,' he said. 'For a cabby.'

'It's my Indian half.'

Horn got home mid-afternoon. While he was debating tackling one of several chores around the place, the phone rang. It was Luther Coby, the police detective.

'How are you doing, Mr Horn?' There was a slight wheeze in his voice, the sound of an overweight man who smoked too much.

'I'm just fine.'

'I mentioned we'd be talking again. You mind if we get together for a little while tomorrow?'

'I suppose not. You have some more questions for me?' Horn was on his guard. He felt he had told Coby enough already.

'A few, I guess, and I may even have some news for you. I don't particularly relish the idea of driving out to the sticks where you live. You plan on being downtown any time tomorrow?' The suggestion was plain.

'Well . . . I plan on being halfway there around midday, and I guess I could come the rest of the way in the afternoon.'

'That's obliging of you. You know the Hall of Justice? I'll meet you out front on the sidewalk. How's three o'clock?'

Horn hung up. Even though he knew he was innocent of Rose's murder, he felt the ex-convict's sense of shame whenever confronted by a badge. The police had the power to keep their own secrets while uncovering those of others. And who does not have secrets?

Realizing it was getting late in Oklahoma City, he went to the telephone and asked the long-distance operator to place the call. Before long, he heard Ernest's familiar twang.

'Hello, my name is Horn. I spoke to you yesterday, remember? About the Shockley family?'

'Yes, sir. You're the gentleman out in Los Angeles. Well, I looked around upstairs, where Mr Beasley moved everything. It's a mess up there, I tell you—'

'I'm sorry I had to put you out like that.'

'No, I don't mind. Happy to do what I can to help your wife

locate her relatives. Well, sir, I finally turned up our file on that family. You got a pencil?'

'I sure do.'

'All right, then. It's Willis and Edith Shockley.' He gave Horn the address and phone number. 'That's out by McKinley Park, if you know the city.'

'Since this is old information, I guess there's a chance they don't live there any more.'

'Well, sir, I can tell you they do.' Ernest sounded proud of himself. 'I called the number, just to make sure. Spoke to Mr Shockley himself. He's a high school principal, and it turns out we've done some of the class photos for his school.'

'Ernest, that was very kind of you.'

'Least I can do. You know, for your wife and all.'

A minute later, with the help of the operator, Horn heard the phone ring in the Shockley residence, and a man answered.

'Mr Shockley, my name is John Ray Horn, and I'm calling from Los Angeles.'

'Yes?' The man drew out the single syllable in a flat tone, and Horn thought he could already hear a barrier being thrown up. *If it's Los Angeles calling, he may have an idea what this is about.*

'I apologize for disturbing you. I'm hoping I might speak to you about your daughter, Tess.'

'Are you the man who's looking for a relative? Someone from Beasley's called.'

'Well, I mentioned something about that. But it wasn't exactly true. I thought it was the simplest way I could—'

'So you lied to him.'

'I made up a story so he would give me your phone number. I'm sorry that was necessary.'

'Are you with the police?'

'No.'

'One of those newspapermen?'

'No.'

'Then who are you?'

'I'm just . . . just a man. Someone who heard about your

164

daughter's death and thinks it might be connected with the death of another person.'

'Did you know my daughter?'

'No, sir.'

'Why should I talk to you?'

It was the question Horn had anticipated and feared. He had only one answer that might work.

'Mr Shockley, would you like to know who killed Tess?'

For what seemed like minutes, Horn heard only the other man's breathing. It sounded tired and ragged, an old man's breathing. Then he heard what sounded like the scrape of chair legs and a weight settling in.

'How can you ask me that?'

'I'm sorry. This must be hard on you, I'm sure, but—'

'Of course I want to know.' He exhaled into the phone. A long breath, as if pent up for years. 'Both of us did. Almost until the day my wife died, the thing she wanted most was just to know what happened to Tess. And why.'

'I didn't know she had died. I'm sorry.'

'Five months ago.' A pause. 'Do you have children, Mr Horn?'

'Yes. A daughter.' It was only a small lie.

'Can you imagine losing her?'

In a way, you could say I have. But not like this. 'No, I can't.'

'Of course not. But then it happens, and . . . and you get an idea of hell. Only God knows why Tess had to die, and He hasn't chosen to let me know. I'm just glad I had my faith to keep me going. I wish I could say the same about my wife, but Edith lost her faith in everything the day we heard about Tessie.'

He paused to take a breath. Horn was somewhat surprised to hear the man confiding in him, but then he thought: *Why not me? Sometimes it's easier to talk to a stranger.*

Shockley spoke again. 'You said something about another person dying.'

'Yes, sir. A woman named Rose Galen—'

'Oh, God.' Horn heard the chair squeak violently, as if the man had been seized by some force. 'Rose is dead?'

'You knew her?'

165

'Dear God. What happened to her?'

'I'm afraid someone killed her, in the room where she was living. How did you know her?'

'Edith called her our angel, because she was so kind to us after Tess's death,' Shockley said, his voice thickened by emotion. 'Rose got in touch with us, told us she and Tess had been friends, and offered her sympathy. At first she wrote, and then she called a few times. We stayed in touch with her over the years, off and on. Then, finally . . .' He stopped and cleared his throat.

Horn waited, but nothing happened. 'Mr Shockley?' he prompted.

'I'm sorry. This is not easy. About six months ago, a new letter arrived, and Rose said something strange. She asked us how we would feel if she were to tell us that she had some responsibility for Tess's death. That was how she put it. Indirectly, as if she were asking our permission to tell us something terrible. We couldn't face it. We couldn't bear hearing that, if it was true. Edith and I talked about it, and she said hearing that kind of thing from Rose would be like reopening an old wound. I wrote back to Rose and said we no longer wanted to hear from her. We wished her well, but we didn't want to know anything further. It was too painful.'

'I understand,' Horn said.

'Edith died soon after that. For a while, I wondered if Rose's letter might have contributed to her death. Then I told myself to stop wondering. It did no good. Rose wrote one more time. I never opened the letter.'

'Did you go to the police? About Rose, I mean.'

'No.' He seemed surprised at the question. 'I never considered it.'

'I'm sorry for all of this. I'll try not to keep you much longer. Mr Shockley, did Rose tell you anything about Tess's friends, the kind of life she lived?'

'Oh, yes. She talked about the two of them double-dating college boys, going bowling, going to the drive-in. Rose, you know, was an established actress, and she was trying to help Tess with her own career. So far, Tess had gotten only small parts, but the studio was encouraging. She was getting invited to parties and things. Once, Rose told us, Tess went to the premiere of a new movie as the guest of Cecil B. De Mille and his wife. We thought that was nice, because Mr De Mille has done some wonderful movies based on the Bible. We wondered why Tess never told us about that . . .'

'Maybe she didn't want you to think she was bragging,' Horn said.

'Wouldn't surprise me,' Shockley said. 'We raised her to be modest.'

'Did Tess mention Rose?'

'Yes, but only in passing. In fact, it was something of a surprise when we found out later that they had been so close. In her letters, Tess mostly talked about how hard it was getting started out there. But she always told us she was enjoying herself and for us not to worry.'

'Do you still have the letters from Rose?'

'Yes. Somewhere.'

'Do you think I might see them?'

'I don't know . . .'

'I would greatly appreciate it. Mr Shockley, I realize you've got no reason to trust me. I'm just a voice on the phone. But I swear to you I want to find out who killed Rose. And despite what you've told me, I believe you still want to know what happened to your daughter. Maybe Rose was responsible, but maybe it was more complicated than that. And if, along the way, I turn up anything about Tess's killer – and if you decide you want to know – I'll share it with you.'

'Why do you think there's any connection—'

'Between the two deaths? I'm not sure. It's kind of an instinct, you might say. Sir, if you think of anything else that might help me, would you call me, collect?' Horn gave him his phone number, then added his mailing address.

'I have a feeling you're not telling me everything,' Shockley said. 'But I'm not sure I care. I only want to find some way to put all this to rest.'

'I know.'

After the other man hung up, Horn sat on his couch holding the receiver for a few moments until the dial tone interrupted his thoughts.

Whatever your daughter was doing, he said silently to Willis Shockley, *I don't think it involved going bowling with college boys.*

Chapter Sixteen

He found Dolores Winter's address on a quiet, narrow street in the Hollywood Hills. Those who inhabited the highest reaches of the Hollywood firmament tended to live in Beverly Hills, a place of emerald-green lawns and busy yard men and shiny Packards and Cadillacs and more exotic conveyances parked in the driveways. Dolores Winter's hillside home was not nearly that grand, but it was elegant and expensive-looking by his standards.

Just off the street, he found the number set in Spanish tile on a high, peach-colored stucco wall interrupted by a heavy wooden door. He knocked and, when no one answered, opened it. Inside was a small, lush garden with a fountain rimmed by the same green and yellow tile. To the right, the garden sloped up through a series of narrow terraces topped by a large eucalyptus tree that threw its shadow over the entire front of the house. On one of the terraces a man was working. He was large, pale-haired and thick-chested, wearing only a pair of shorts and sandals, and he was intent on setting what looked like fifty-pound stones in between the jade plants and flowering bushes that ranged along each of the terraces.

'Excuse me,' Horn called up to the man. 'I'm looking for Miss Winter.'

The man straightened up, turned, and slowly picked his way down the terraces to the garden floor. Wiping his hand on his shorts, he extended it as he wiped the sweat from his face with the other. 'Lewis De Loach,' he said. 'Doll's inside with the others. Knock loud and they'll hear you.'

The hand was calloused and hard. De Loach's face could have been called boyish were it not for the strong jawline. His pale

169

complexion had been left slightly pink by the feeble winter sun. 'You used to work at Medallion, didn't you?' he asked.

'Uh-huh,' Horn said. 'Now I do other things. How about you?'

'Screenwriter. These days, I like to tell people I'm taking stock of my career. That's a way of saying I'm between jobs.'

'Happens a lot in this town,' Horn said.

'I knew a couple of the writers at your studio,' the man said. 'No offense, but it all sounded very formulaic to me, the things they did.'

'That's Medallion, all right,' Horn said with a grin. 'If it works, stick with it.'

De Loach gave a wave and climbed back up to his rocks. Horn approached the front door. The house, done in the popular Spanish style, echoed the peach of the outer wall, reminding him of a candy he had enjoyed as a child, and how its artificial color would stain his fingers. He knocked hard on the wooden door and heard a voice call out from inside. A moment later, Dolores Winter opened the door.

'The cowboy,' she said with a grin, tossing her hair out of her face. She wore a sailor's striped boat-neck pullover with canvas deck shoes and a pair of trim, well-cut white slacks. Her hair was loose. 'Come on in. Dexter and Evelyn are here.'

She took him through a tiled entryway that led directly back to a patio, where a table was set up amid ficus trees and more flowering plants. He shook hands with Dexter Diggs and went over to give a hug to Evelyn, whom he'd not seen since before his time in prison.

Evelyn, who had possessed what her husband called a motherly look ever since her thirties, took his face in her hands, gently avoiding the bandaged area, and looked at him for a long moment. 'Are you all right?' she asked.

'Hell, Evelyn, I'm fine,' he said, a little too brusquely. 'Had a little accident working around the house. But it does me good to see you.'

'You look skinny,' she said. 'Come over for dinner some-time.'

'Yes, ma'am,' he said dutifully as he took a seat.

Dolores Winter was watching the exchange with an unreadable expression. 'Didn't know this character had so many friends,' she said. 'First time I met him, I didn't like his looks. I was ready to take a swing at him just on general principles.'

'Might have done him some good,' Diggs said.

'If you'll remember, Miss Winter,' Horn said, 'I liked your looks right from the beginning.'

'If you don't start calling me Doll,' she said menacingly, 'things are going to get nasty around here. Now, who's hungry?'

A Mexican maid in a brightly colored peasant dress brought out cold drinks followed by shrimp cocktails on ice. The three guests had mixed drinks while their hostess had iced tea.

'Love to join you, but no booze for me for a while,' Doll said. 'I've got a movie coming up. We go into pre-production in a few days, and I want to make sure I can get into the outfits.'

'What is it?'

'*Yukon Queen*. From a Jack London story. I'm a dance hall hostess. With a tragic past and a heart of gold.' She made a face.

'You don't want to do it,' Diggs said.

'Well, it's got a nice budget, and we're borrowing Bob Taylor from MGM to be my leading man. And ain't *he* something? But . . . I don't want to do madams and hostesses and bar girls and hookers all my life. And did I mention big sisters and wisecracking shopgirls?'

'It's your own fault,' Diggs said, 'for being so good in *Tropic Wind*. What do you want to do?'

'I don't know,' she said. 'But every time I see a really good part going to Davis or Crawford over at Warners, something with red meat in it, I think: *I* could have done that. Even Missy Stanwyck – did you see *Sorry, Wrong Number*? God, I'd like to have gotten my teeth into that one. I wouldn't have played her spineless and whimpering all the way through. I know she's an invalid, but she should be a stronger personality at the beginning, loving and capable, and then slowly come apart until, at the end, she's this screaming mess.'

'Interesting,' Diggs said. 'I'd like to have seen your version.'

171

'Me too.' Doll adopted a wicked grin. 'So, I march into Ben Greene's office and tell him exactly what kind of part I want. And the old weasel takes my hand in his paws, gazes into my eyes, and tells me how much he loves my talent. But it's a *unique* talent, he says, one that those schmucks Louis B. Mayer and Jack Warner could never appreciate. Then he tells me how his writers are working overtime to provide the perfect vehicle for my oh-so-unique talent. And meanwhile, he says, while we're waiting for that vehicle to pull up at the curb, he'd like me to do just one more gum-chewing girl reporter, business tycoon's mistress, or whore with a heart of . . . you know.'

She stopped, aware that everyone was staring at her. The maid appeared with steaming bowls of chowder. 'Hell with it,' Doll said. 'Down the hatch.' She lifted her iced tea. 'Let's have a good time, and stop talking about how poor little girls get trampled by the studio system. What am I complaining about? I'm doing leading roles now, and I've got it better than most gals. Let's talk about the rest of you.'

The conversation meandered for a while. When Doll tried to steer things around to Horn, he politely deflected her. He didn't want to get into his illustrious acting career, his failed marriage, or his unemployability. So she turned to her other guests, who were happy to talk about their children and grandchildren.

They heard the front door open, and De Loach looked out into the patio. His legs and chest were caked in sweat and dirt. 'Pardon my filth, everybody,' he said to the group. Then, to Doll: 'I'm going to the hardware store for a few things. You need anything on the way?'

'Pick up some fresh oranges and lemons, sweetie,' she said to him. 'And bring me a part. A good one this time. Something about a beautiful woman with a brain tumor who . . . Wait a minute. Bette Davis has done that one. Never mind; just oranges and lemons.'

Doll turned to them when he had gone. 'Poor Lewis, he's trying to stop drinking – he doesn't mind my talking about it; he'll tell you himself. And the only way he can take his mind off it is to stay busy, run errands, or go out in the garden and move boulders. That, or drive over to Muscle Beach and lift lovely young things over his head.'

'Really?' Evelyn asked.

'You've never seen them? There's this bunch of muscle boys, they have their own spot out on Santa Monica Beach. They lift barbells and do handstands and generally show off. Lewis isn't as serious as some of them, but now that he's not drinking, he's decided that his body is his temple and he wants to keep the temple all spruced up.' She laughed. 'I say good for him. At least he's not gambling or snorting God knows what up his nose, like some screenwriters I could name.'

'He told me he's between jobs,' Horn said.

'That's a creative way of putting it. I think it's best we don't talk about that, good people.' Doll watched as the maid cleared the table and freshened the drinks. 'How about some more gossip?' She told an affectionate story about her last leading man, lingering on a detailed physical description of his most notorious attribute. When the laughter had died down, Diggs and his wife got up to say their goodbyes.

'You're sweet people,' Doll said to them at the door. 'I'm sorry it took such a sad event to bring us together. Let's see each other again.'

When they had left, Horn began to phrase his own good-bye, but she tapped him lightly on the chest. 'Don't go yet,' she said. She led him back to the patio. 'I'm curious about you. Dexter told me just enough to make me want to know more.'

'He told you we worked together?'

She nodded. 'You did westerns. I'm sorry I never saw any of them.'

'You didn't miss much.'

'He said you were good.'

'Well, he's very kind, old Dex.'

'He said you went to prison for assault.' Her eyes lingered on his bandage. 'Don't worry, I'm not going to ask you if you're still up to your old tricks. But since then, Dexter said, you've had trouble finding work.'

173

'That's not quite true. I'm not welcome at any of the studios. But I have a job.'

She stared at him with a half-smile, as if she knew about his job and was too polite to pursue the subject. Then she said, 'According to Dexter, you're someone who's good to have for a friend. He said back when you were in the movies, your studio had somebody lined up to play your Indian sidekick, but you wanted a real Indian, not some imitation, and you made a lot of noise until they hired . . . What was his name?'

'Joseph Mad Crow.'

'Uh-huh. And he said you and Joseph are still friends.'

'We trade favors back and forth. He's done a lot for me.'

'You don't like to talk about yourself, do you?'

'No.'

'Well, I find that pretty damn refreshing. Most of the men I know won't shut up about themselves.' They heard the front gate open and close. 'That's Lewis,' she said. 'I suppose we've been putting this off, but we were going to talk about Rose.'

'That's right. Before we do, can I ask you something?'

'Sure, as long as it's personal.'

'I had a visit from the police not long after Rose was killed. According to them, a couple of people told them they should take a hard look at me. One was a bartender. The other they wouldn't name. It could have been this old gal who lived in Rose's rooming house, but if it had been her, I think they would have just gone ahead and said so.'

'Uh-huh.' She drew small, wet designs on the top of the patio table with her iced tea glass. Up close, he decided she was gorgeous – not a perfect look, like George Hurrell's airbrushed photos of Norma Shearer or Jean Harlow, but a more flawed and down-to-earth beauty. Nothing about her was delicate. She was, he reflected, a little too tall, a little too broad in the shoulder and hip. When taken separately, certain details, such as mouth and nose and eyebrows, were a little too abundant. But in some kind of physical alchemy, he decided, the parts added up to a package that worked. He was attracted to her in a way that almost startled him. It had nothing to do with her smart conversation

174

or wicked sense of humor. Doll Winter simply exuded sexuality like a faint perfume. He wondered if she could see the effect she had on him.

'I can think of one other person,' he said, 'who saw us together not long before Rose was killed.'

'You mean me, don't you?'

'If you tell me it wasn't you, I'll believe you.'

'And if I tell you it *was* me?'

'I'll believe you, but I won't be happy about it.'

'All right, here it is,' she said. 'They got in touch with me because they knew Rose and I were friends. They asked me for ideas about anyone who might have wanted to . . . you know. All I knew about you was that I'd seen you talking to her on the street, and you were pushing yourself on her. I described you. They seemed to know who I was talking about. That's all.' She reached for a pack of cigarettes on the table. He didn't offer a light. 'Sorry if it made problems for you, but—'

'I thought you never apologized.'

She lit up, inhaled greedily, and exhaled audibly. 'That was a slip. It won't happen again.'

'You said we could talk about Rose. Do you mind if I ask you some things?'

'Ask away.'

'When did you meet her?'

'I don't remember the exact year, but it was a long time ago. She was only a year or two older than I was, and she was already working in Hollywood. She called herself Rosemary Gale back then, and she was everything I wanted to be. I was this pathetic little thing, nineteen or so – well, not so little, actually, since I was already pretty grown-up looking. But there I was, fresh out of Long Beach, all star-struck and desperate to become an actress. I don't know if you remember what it was like back then—'

'No,' he said. 'I didn't move here until later.'

'I can't tell you how glamorous Hollywood was. It was near the end of the silents, although we didn't realize it at the time. I'm talking about Valentino and Garbo and Swanson and John

Gilbert and Theda Bara. They had amazing faces. To the rest of us, they were almost like gods. For a while, I worked in wardrobe at Magnum Arts. The job was terrible, but I didn't care. I could see the gods and goddesses strolling around the back lot, and I was in heaven.'

'About Rose,' he prompted her. 'How did you meet her?'

'It must have been at a party, since she never worked at MagArts.'

'Dex tells me the parties were wild.'

'They were.' She seemed lost in thought for a moment. 'Drinking and doping and people pairing off in the bedrooms – men, women, any combination you could think of. Now that I'm a lady of a certain age, with a house and a mortgage and an ex-husband, I look back at little Dolores Winter from Long Beach, the outrageous things she did, and I don't recognize her.'

'What about Rose? According to Dex, she could be—'

'She was,' Doll said emphatically. 'Once I got to know her, I thought she was a wonderful girl. I loved her like a sister. But I won't lie to you: Rose was a hellion. She was the one who got me into the best parties – or worst, depending on your point of view. She got me dates too. She fixed me up with Howard Hughes once, back when he was young and rich and horny and just beginning to understand how much fun he could have in this town. And little Dolores must have been ripe for corruption, because she went along with all of it.'

'Dex said there was one party where somebody died. A young girl.'

'Really? That sounds vaguely familiar. I may have heard about it.'

'Her name was Tess Shockley.'

'Sorry, I don't remember. It was a long time ago.'

'What happened to Rose? Her career, I mean.'

'I wish I knew. Dexter asked me the same question. One day she was just . . . *gone*. Dropped out of sight. I lost track of her for the longest time, right up until a few months ago, when she sent me a note through the studio publicity department. She said she'd seen one of my movies, complimented me. I looked her up. I was horrified to see where she was living, but she didn't seem to be particularly ashamed. Anyway, we picked up again just like old friends.'

'You've been helping out at the mission.'

She waved that away. 'I was glad to,' she said. 'I've been lucky. Why not spread some of it around?'

'Do you have any idea who might have killed her?'

She shook her head. 'No. Or why. Unless it was just one of those random things. The place she lived . . .'

'I don't think it was random,' he said. 'I think it was revenge.'

She narrowed her eyes. 'What do you mean?'

'I don't know if I can explain all of it,' he said. 'It's too complicated. But you know Emory Quinn at the mission, don't you?'

'Sure. A little strange, like a lot of fanatics, but I like him.' Noting Horn's expression, she went on. 'Most people have their own narcotic; it may be good or bad for them. For Lewis, it's booze. He knew it was going to kill him some day, so he's trying to beat it. For Emory Quinn, it used to be booze, but he's replaced that with Jesus.'

'How about you?'

'Me?' She made an exaggerated gesture, hand to her bosom. '*Fame*, darling. What is it they call her? The bitch goddess. But what were you going to say about Emory?'

'Rose made a kind of confession to him, told him she killed someone a long time ago. I think it was Tess Shockley, the girl who died after one of the parties. The police called it murder, and it was in the papers. I think someone came after Rose because of that.'

'After all these years?'

'Yes.'

'Good Lord. And you're looking for this person?'

He nodded.

'And what will you do—'

'If I find him? I'll be a good citizen and turn him over to the police, that's what I'll do. Maybe even call up that fat detective, our good friend Coby. He's going to be disappointed if it doesn't turn out to be me, though. He's had his heart set on arresting somebody who's been in the movies.'

'Maybe he could try me,' she said, pretending to reflect on it. 'I've never seen the inside of a jail. Think of it: just little Dolores and all those desperate, primitive, unshaven men.' She paused for effect. 'And I'm just talking about the cops.'

Laughing, he got up. 'I should go. Thanks for lunch, and for talking to me.'

There was no sign of Lewis De Loach outside. She walked out to the street with him.

'Have you ever heard of Jay Lombard?'

She hesitated. 'I think so. A lawyer, right? He's been in the paper. Why?'

'Rose knew him. I'm trying to find out their connection.'

'Will you let me know whatever you find out? I'm interested. And will you let me know if I can help?'

'I sure will.'

She looked at the battered old Ford. 'Your trusty steed?'

'Yep.'

'I've always had a thing about cowboys,' she said, leaning against his car. 'Long time ago, I danced with Tom Mix. What a spectacular-looking man. I could feel muscles under his jacket, all along his back.'

'Careful, there, ma'am. Lewis might hear you.'

'Maybe I should explain something,' she said slowly, straightening up and taking a step closer. 'Lewis and I aren't married any more. He's a sweet man, but he's an out-of-work screenwriter and probably always will be. He's been having problems, and I gave him a place to live. That's all.'

'I see. Thanks for clearing that up.'

She studied him. 'I like you,' she said slowly. 'I'm probably not very likable myself, and I don't like many people. You could take this as a warning. Having me like you could be kind of a . . . burden.'

'I guess I can handle it.'

She grinned broadly. 'Hey, maybe you'd like to come by the studio sometime, watch me work.'

'Didn't Mae West say that to somebody?'

'Well, something like that. It was Cary Grant. And he took her up on it.'

'I don't think your studio would let me in the gate.'

'Bullshit. You've got an invitation.' She tapped him lightly on the chest again. It was an affectionate and slightly proprietary gesture, and despite his earlier caution to himself, he decided that he liked it.

'All right.' He turned to go. 'Thanks for having us over.'

'It was fun,' she said, facing him over the car. 'I was a little surprised that Dexter took me up on it, but since we never touched on Rose while he was here, I suppose it was all right.'

'What difference would that make?'

'You don't know?'

He shook his head.

'Well,' she said, looking embarrassed. 'Maybe I should have been more careful. It's just that . . . Back before Rose disappeared, she told me she was having an affair with one of her directors, the one who did the Italian movie—'

'*Hawk of Tramonti*?'

'That's the one. Apparently it was very serious. She said he was even talking about leaving his wife. I assumed Dexter would have told you about that. But now that I think about it, why would he?'

Chapter Seventeen

Horn drove toward downtown. He had to meet Coby, the police detective, and he wanted to make another stop first.

He took Sunset east, keeping the Hollywood Hills to his left. As he approached downtown, he could see clouds and bright haze layered over the City Hall tower, the sun making a futile effort to punch through. The Andrews Sisters were jiving their way through 'Rum and Coca-Cola' on the car radio. Everyone had gotten to know the song's goofy lyrics during the war. The tune seemed curiously old and silly now. It was as if the war, even with its blood and loss and despair, had also been the last manifestation of a kind of innocence that the country had now left behind, along with 'Kilroy Was Here' and Rosie the Riveter and movies about patriotic Americans pulling together for a common cause.

He parked in front of the Follies, across the street from the Anchor mission. The figure of Ruby Renfrew, the Detroit Fire-cracker, loomed overhead. Up close, her red gape of a smile seemed no longer good-natured but depraved. Her eyes stared right down at him. *Do you want to know how all this is going to turn out, cowboy?* they asked him.

Yes, he said silently. *Tell me, Ruby.*

Not 'til the end of the movie, the eyes said. *But if you're looking for a happy ending, you wandered into the wrong theater*. Then she went back to being just a big, garishly painted thing atop a marquee.

Inside the Anchor, he asked for Emory Quinn. The beaten-down man sitting behind the desk, only a few steps removed from the sidewalk himself, told him he hadn't seen the pastor for a while but thought he might be in his office. Horn made the now-familiar journey down the corridor. This time the door to the office at the far end of the chapel was closed. Horn knocked and, when he heard nothing, opened the door.

Quinn lay on the sofa, mouth open and hanging slightly askew. Horn was alarmed at first, but then he saw the empty half-pint bottle lying on the floor and caught the sour smell of alcohol permeating the room. As he stepped closer, he heard soft snoring and saw spit glistening on the man's chin.

'Quinn.' He leaned over and nudged him, but got no response. He tried again, none too gently this time. 'Wake up, Quinn.'

The other man opened his eyes and looked at Horn, but there was no recognition in them. His hands were clasped loosely over his chest, and Horn noted that the knuckles were taped like a fighter's and the tape was stained with patches of dark red.

Horn got up and looked around the room, as if searching for a reason for Quinn's stupor. Noticing a light in the storeroom, he looked in there. A heavy body bag, worn by years of punching, hung suspended from the low ceiling. Its midsection was wrapped in layers of adhesive tape to preserve the life of the bag. On the tape, Horn saw a few smears of blood.

He went back out to the office, pulled a chair over to the sofa, and sat down. Quinn's eyes were now focused on him.

'I came to tell you about what happened with Lombard the other night, but you don't look like you're in shape to hear about it,' Horn said. 'What's wrong with you?'

'Oh . . . just taking a nap.' Quinn's voice was shaky, and his breath was foul. His eyes looked watery.

'I thought you didn't drink.'

Quinn giggled. 'Drink whenever I need to,' he mumbled. 'Don't need to, usually. But drink always . . . always there when I need it. Like a good friend.'

'You're really something,' Horn said in disgust. He noticed that Quinn's folded hands covered what looked like a piece of paper. Reaching over, Horn extracted it and saw that it was a photograph. It had been taken in front of the mission, and it showed Quinn and his volunteer staff of a dozen or so lined up on the sidewalk. Turning it over, Horn saw written in pencil the words *Thanksgiving for the needy, 1947.* Returning to the photo, he studied the faces of the men and women, some of them looking relatively well-fed and prosperous, others looking very much in need themselves. He had a feeling he'd find Rose, and there she was, smiling next to Quinn, wearing the same shapeless wool hat.

He handed the photo back. 'Is this what did it to you?' he asked. 'You miss Rose, and you decide to get soused and go punish the bag, because that's the only way you can handle her being dead? I thought you were tough. You know, she was something special to me too, and you don't see me sliding into the bottle. I think it's time you were straight about what there was between the two of you. Are you afraid? Talk to me, goddammit.'

Quinn's mouth twisted into a knowing, drunken smile. 'Kind of late for talk.'

'It's not too late for you to help me find out who killed her.'

'You had your chance,' Quinn said, squinting at Horn's bandage. 'One round. Overmatched, though.' He nodded his head knowingly. 'Mistake. You missed your target.'

'What target? What the hell are you talking about?'

'The lawyer. The fixer.' A noiseless belch. 'The one who . . .' His eyes lost focus.

'What do you know about him?'

'Leave me alone.' Quinn's jaw hung slack, his tongue barely forming the words. 'You had your chance.'

Horn stood over him, furious. 'Dolores Winter told me you've replaced booze with Jesus,' Horn said. 'She doesn't know you very well, does she?'

'Tired of talking to you,' Quinn said almost inaudibly. 'Don't bother to come around any more. If you do—'

'I know. You'll have me thrown out.'

Outside, Horn sat in his car for a few minutes, wondering why Quinn was suddenly shunning him. And whether the man had some new reason to suspect Lombard. And about the photograph underneath the wounded hands. One evening years earlier, while his father had sat working on a sermon, he began telling John Ray and his little brother about the various roads to sanctity. 'Some so-called Christians,' the Reverend Horn said, 'preach that you can find God by mortifying the flesh. We don't go that far. We believe in self-denial, in avoiding the temptations that we find so abundant on this earth. But wearing the hair shirt, flogging one's own body, dragging a heavy cross to the church on Good Friday – all that is a perversion of the Word. And that has more to do with human guilt than with any desire to sanctify the self.'

Horn thought of Quinn and the stigmata of his bloodied knuckles. Was it simply sorrow over losing Rose, he wondered, that drove the man to punish himself? Or was it rage directed at Lombard, and shame over his own inability to take action? Or was it something else?

He parked the Ford in a lot near the Hall of Justice, then walked over to the massive, thirteen-story Greco-Roman building and waited outside the Broadway entrance. At precisely three o'clock, Luther Coby came out.

Cassie was with him.

She wore a wrinkled dress and scuffed penny loafers without socks. Her face wore its familiar sullen expression, but underneath Horn could discern anger, barely held in check.

'Are you all right?' he asked her. Then, turning to Coby, 'What's she doing here?'

'You know her, don't you?' Coby asked. Without waiting for an answer, he went on. 'Sure you do. She's related to that fellow you work for. And, it turns out, she's the woman who was spotted by one of the neighbors in that rooming house the night Rose Galen was killed. She's been identified. You know what else? She's living in the Galen woman's room.'

'I know all that,' Horn said. 'I'll vouch for her.'

'You?' Coby seemed to find that an irresistible joke. 'I'm not sure that would do her much good, since I've got my own doubts about you. But don't get yourself all upset. I just wanted to ask her a few things. Went over there this morning and invited her to come in for a talk. She didn't like the idea . . . Did you,

183

Girlie?' he asked, turning to her. Although Cassie remained silent, the look she gave him was venomous. 'But she came along. And she explained how she went over there that night just to talk, and how she moved in just because she needed a place to stay.' He seemed vaguely amused at the recitation.

'You didn't arrest her?' Horn asked.

'No, no,' Coby said expansively. 'I don't like to arrest anybody until I've got everything I need. My conviction rate is one of the best in the department, 'cause I'm careful. I've even got a plaque on the wall upstairs. Maybe you'll see it someday. But that doesn't mean I'm not watching,' he went on. 'If somebody looks good to me I stay on their tails, let 'em know I'm there. You'd be amazed how many people get nervous, trip up and do something crazy when they know I've got my eye on them. You ever read *Crime and Punishment*?'

'No,' Horn said.

'You should. This old detective I started out with in the department gave me a copy years ago. Some Russian wrote it. It's really long and it has some big words, but you can skip over the boring places. It teaches you a lot about the way guilty people behave. You can see that some people *want* to confess. I don't suppose that ever happens in any of your movies, does it?'

'No,' Horn said. 'Can she go now?'

'Sure.' Coby turned to her. 'I want to thank you for your cooperation,' he said with some formality.

'Don't mention it,' she said icily.

Horn took her aside. 'Did anybody hurt you?' he asked quietly.

She shook her head. 'They just wanted to scare me,' she said. 'It didn't work.' She looked shaken but in control.

'Fine. Maybe I'd like it better if you were a little scared, as long as it made you careful.'

'I have to go,' she said. 'I should be working.'

'If you'd like to wait, I can drive you.'

'It's not far. I can walk.' She turned and left them, striding purposefully.

'Come on,' Coby said as they watched her walk away. 'I'll buy you a cup of coffee.'

They went north a block, then over to a cafe on Spring Street, where they sat at the counter.

'Where's your partner?' Horn asked.

'Stiles? Doing paperwork. Says he can't wait 'til he's old and fat and got enough seniority to order around his junior partner.' Coby summoned the waitress and ordered a cup of coffee and a cinnamon bun. Horn asked for an orange soda and looked around the place. The cafe's customers were a cross-section of the civic center: lawyers in good suits, court workers, jurors on a break, and off-duty police, both in and out of uniform.

Getting his first good look at the detective in broad daylight, Horn decided the man wasn't fat after all. His waist was thick, and his bullish head and neck made him look heavy, but the extra weight seemed to be solidly distributed. The fingers delicately holding the coffee cup were stubby and strong-looking. He resembled a more compact version of Willie Apples, only marginally better dressed.

'You're on the wrong track with Cassie,' Horn said. 'She's had some problems back where she grew up, and some problems getting used to living here. But—'

'Don't be so sure I'm on the wrong track,' Coby said lightly, blowing into his cup. 'She's a tough little halfbreed, that one. Carries a knife.'

'Sure she does. Driving a cab is dangerous in this town. Everybody knows that. But Rose wasn't killed with a knife. And Cassie had no reason to hurt her anyway. The woman had been good to her.'

'Well, I have to go with what I see,' the detective said, sawing off a sizable wedge of his bun and spearing it with his fork. 'Now if you've got any other information for me . . .'

'What do you mean?'

'You've been looking around,' Coby said, chewing vigorously while he studied the sugary contours of the bun, planning his next assault. 'Stiles and me, we hear things. You've been talking to the guy who runs that mission down on Main. You – or somebody who looks an awful lot like you – were at the fights with him the other night, making nice with Jay Lombard. Late that night, Lombard's right-hand muscle, guy named Willie Apples, showed up at the Good Samaritan emergency room with a bruised rib and a slight head wound. Told the doc he had a little car accident. And . . .' He stared intently at Horn. 'And you show up here today with a bandage big enough for the Bride of Frankenstein.'

'So?'

'So you're sniffing around and butting heads with people, telling 'em you want to find out who killed your friend. You probably don't realize what a big joke this is. Maybe you used to be some kind of movie hero, but now you're just an ex-con, and eventually you'll get the other side of your face pushed in for your trouble.'

'It's my face. What I want to know is how come you're suddenly worried about who killed Rose Galen. First time I saw you, you acted bored by the whole thing. She was just a barfly, you told me. Life is cheap where she lived, you told me, and anybody could have killed her. Today it sounds like you've decided to take this seriously.'

'I don't like to see anybody get killed,' Coby said mildly. 'I get paid to bring in the ones who do it, and I enjoy my work. But I will say that I've changed my mind about Rose Galen. That actress, the great-looking redhead, told me a little about her background, and I dug up some more. Seems that long before her barfly days, she was in the movies, and she was pretty good.'

'Oh, that's right,' Horn said. 'You like it when they're famous. Either the victims or the criminals.'

'Sure.' Coby wiped his mouth. 'Anyway, I'll tell you what I told Cassie Montag: I'm as serious about this one as anything I'm working on right now. And if you've turned up anything I can use, I want it. You give me a good reason, and I'll forget my fascination for this Indian girl and go focus it on somebody else.'

Horn was silent.

'The next time I bring her in,' the detective continued quietly, 'she'll spend the night in our facilities up on the top floor.

186

There's a lot of yelling and screaming in the ladies' block. I don't know how any of 'em manage to get a good night's sleep, what with—'

'All right,' Horn said. 'What do you want to know?'

'Start with Lombard,' Coby said. 'What's that slick son of a bitch got to do with Rose Galen?'

'Sounds like he's not one of your favorite people.'

The detective made a what-the-hell gesture with his fork. 'He'll defend anybody who's got money,' he said. 'There was a trucking company owner who stabbed his wife with a steak knife over dinner; he got him off. I heard he even defended Dolores Winter's husband when the guy got fired by his studio.' He resumed eating.

'How did that turn out?'

'Not so good, I guess,' Coby said, his mouth full. 'He's still out of work, right? I bumped heads with Lombard once when I brought in this fence. I'd caught him with the goods, everything. By the time Lombard got finished, the jury believed the guy just happened to be in a room with all the stuff and that I was an overzealous cop. I suppose he's good at what he does, but him and me, we play on different teams. Now answer my question. What's he got to do with Rose Galen?'

'He knew Rose years ago, but I'm not sure exactly how or where. A few weeks before she was killed, he met her for a drink,' Horn said. 'They talked for a while. I don't know about what. I tried to ask him the other night, after the fights, and that's when he turned his bulldog loose on me.'

'So he's touchy about her,' Coby said reflectively. He pushed his plate away, then waved the waitress over to refill his cup.

'He is.'

'What would you guess they talked about?'

'I'm not sure, but I think she might have wanted him to represent her.'

'Why would she need a lawyer?'

Horn sighed. 'It's a long story.' He began talking. He told Coby about Tess Shockley and her death, about Rose's hints that she had something to do with it. He talked about Tess's grieving parents, about Emory Quinn and his apparent suspicion of Lombard, about Dexter Diggs and the old days before the movies learned to talk. He held back only the suggestion that Rose and Dex had been involved. He wanted to ask his old friend about that first.

'Sounds like I should have another talk with the preacher,' Coby said. 'Nothing I'd like better than to hang this on my little shyster friend. Anything else?'

'Well, there's Dolores Winter,' Horn continued. 'You already know she and Rose were friends.'

'That's right,' the detective said. 'Some kind of woman, huh? Makes me wish I'd seen some of her movies. But she's not one you want to fool with. When I find the guy who did this, I'd better have him locked up before she has a chance to get at him. I wouldn't want her after me.' He looked pointedly at Horn.

'She's not after me any more,' he told Coby. 'We're buddies now.'

'Well, that's just fine. I envy you.' Coby swung heavily off the counter stool and laid six bits on the counter. Then something occurred to him. He pulled a well-chewed pencil out of his shirt pocket and wrote a phone number down on a corner of his paper napkin and slid it over to Horn. 'I'm all out of fancy calling cards,' he said. 'You can usually reach me at this number, or leave a message, if anything occurs to you.'

'You mean if I suddenly get the urge to confess?'

'Something like that.' He looked at Horn for an extra second. 'That cost you a lot, didn't it? Telling me what you know.'

'No offense,' Horn said, getting up. 'I don't like the police. Never had any reason to.'

'Now you're going to tell me you were railroaded.'

'No. I did what they said. I'm just not sure it was worth two years of my time, that's all.'

'You know something? I'm not sure it was either. But you made an enemy of an important man. In this town, that's all it takes.'

The detective's chunky features eased into a grin. 'Not all us cops are bad guys. Some of us are just working stiffs trying to pile up enough years for that pension. You want to see something?' With two stubby fingers, he dipped into a vest pocket and came up with a folded snapshot. Horn took it and unfolded it. It was a photo, in garish colors, of a cottage with a small porch and a vine-colored trellis over half the porch.

'Color didn't turn out good,' he said apologetically. 'I'm having trouble with that film. But this is going to be my retirement place down in Del Mar. Sweet, huh? It's a ten-minute walk from the racetrack and fifteen minutes from the ocean. In a few more years, old Luther Coby will be sitting on that porch, breathing salty air and forgetting all about big, dirty LA.'

'Good for you.'

They walked to the lot where Horn had parked.

'You want to come up?' Coby asked. 'I can show you where Mitchum was a guest of the county for sixty days.'

'No, thanks. I'm familiar with the place.'

'Oh, hell.' Coby slapped his forehead. 'What a memory I've got. Sure you are. You must've spent a night or two up top, then got tried in one of the courtrooms down below. For all I know, you and Mitchum had the same cell. The celebrity cell. He didn't really have a bad time. Just mopped a few floors, that kind of thing. You probably saw that picture in the paper, him and his mop. Did you mop any floors, or did they have you cleaning toilets?'

All of Horn's initial distaste for Coby was returning. Ignoring the question, he said, 'You want to tell me who you think killed Rose?'

Coby's stare was without expression. 'I'm not ready to say yet. But I'll tell you one thing: you're still on the list. The Indian girl too.'

The flag was up on the mailbox that stood on a post just outside his gate. In the box he found a large manila envelope, sent air mail special delivery and containing something thick. The return address bore the name of the Oklahoma City Board of Education, under which someone had written a street address in

189

the same precise hand used to address the envelope. He took it inside and opened it, finding a small bundle of letters tied with a violet ribbon.

'Thank you, Mr Shockley,' he muttered.

He flipped through the envelopes, noting that they were arranged in reverse chronological order of postmarks, with the most recent on top.

He considered fixing a drink or something to eat, but his curiosity was too strong. Settling into the wooden rocker on the porch, he opened the letter with the earliest postmark and began reading.

Dear Mr and Mrs Shockley,
My name is Rose Galen, and I was a friend of your daughter, Tess. I'm writing to say how sorry I am about her death. She was a fine young woman, and she spoke often of you . . .

He read quickly through the rest. Rose expressed her condolences, spoke a little about her friendship with Tess, and promised to write again. The next letter was similar but mentioned a phone conversation she had had with the couple. *You sound like good people,* she said. *You can be justifiably proud of your daughter . . .*

The letters settled into a rhythm then, coming at the rate of about one a year. Rose thanked the Shockleys for sending her a photo of their daughter. She told stories about Tess, always stressing how happy the girl had been and how she seemed just on the brink of some kind of success in Hollywood. But the physical appearance of the letters changed. At first they had been written in a careful, almost elegant hand on good stationery. Later, the postmarks changed from Los Angeles to Wichita and then New York, and the quality of the paper declined. Sometimes the notes were written in pencil on stationery marked with the names of hotels Horn did not recognize. Sometimes the penmanship declined as well, the words carelessly formed.

The last few years' worth of letters again originated in Los Angeles, with the return address at the Bunker Hill room. The next to last letter, dated six months earlier, was the one Horn had been expecting.

Dear Edith and Willis,

Forgive me for what I'm about to say. I've been carrying it around with me for years, and the burden has become too great.

How would you feel – what would you say – if I were to tell you that I was present when Tess was killed? Not killed, I mean, but so horribly injured that she would die because of it. And further, that I was not innocent but had a role in what happened.

This is so hard. You have been dear friends to me, and I fear what you must think of me now. I tell myself I'm no murderer, but I cannot deny what I did. I know that if I had not been there that awful night, she almost certainly would still be alive. So, does this make me a murderer? I dread what you will say.

What I have to tell you is not for a letter. I feel we should talk. If you want, I will call you whenever you like. If you prefer, I will even come to see you. I have one or two friends who would lend me the money for a bus ticket. Once we have talked, whatever you decide to do – even if it involves going to the police – will be, I am sure, the right decision.

God bless you,

Rose

He picked up the last letter. It was postmarked not quite two months ago. The envelope was still sealed.

He wasn't ready. Going inside, he removed the last piece of leftover ham from the icebox, fried it quickly in a skillet, then used the salty and fragrant grease to scramble a couple of eggs. He shook some hot sauce on the eggs, then sat on the sofa, plate balanced on his lap, and ate, chewing slowly.

The winter light was fading outside, and the air became cold, carrying with it a hint of rain. When he finished eating, he closed the door against the weather and carried his plate into the kitchen, where he poured some Evan Williams into a glass and added a splash of water. Still putting off reading the last letter, he picked up the phone and dialed the number for the Anchor mission. The man who answered the phone went to get

Quinn but returned moments later to say the preacher was unavailable.

Quinn was dodging him for some reason. It may have been Horn's insistent questions about Rose, or the newly sensitive subject of Jay Lombard. Or, as Quinn had put it in his alcoholic mumble, maybe he was simply tired of talking to Horn. But Horn still needed to talk to him.

He suddenly thought of another approach. Soon he had Iris on the line and was explaining his idea. They spoke for several minutes until Horn was satisfied.

'Just make sure it's tomorrow,' he told her.

'I will. Thank you for your help.'

'How's Clea?'

'Fine. She's over at a friend's. They're having a record party.'

'Boys too?'

'Of course boys too.'

'How did she get there?'

'One of the boys picked her up.'

'He drives?'

'John Ray.' She sounded impatient. 'They're both seniors. He has his driver's license. Listen to yourself.'

'What's the matter?'

'Just stop worrying about her.' Iris's tone grew warmer. 'She's growing up just fine. Paul would have been proud of her. And you can be too.'

'All right. Just tell her I said hello.'

'I will.'

'And tell her to stay away from boys 'til she's twenty-one.'

'Goodbye, John Ray.'

Back in the front room, he settled back onto the sofa and switched on the table light. The envelope was addressed in pencil in a shaky, barely legible script. The thin paper of the envelope slit easily. Inside he found four sheets of ruled note paper with more pencil writing, and he was puzzled to note that the letter began with the words written in a strong and clear hand.

Dear Edith and Willis (Rose was obviously unaware of Edith Shockley's death),

Thank you for answering. You made it clear in your letter that you choose not to talk to me, and I will honor that wish. But I have to write this letter. There are words I must say, either in writing or aloud. I'm sure I will say them to others at some point, but I must say them to you first. If you return this unopened, I'll understand. (In fact, I think I draw some comfort from that possibility. If I knew for sure you would read this, I'm not sure I could write everything I plan to write.) I only hope you will understand why I need to put this down on paper. As to whether I will have the courage to mail it, I'll know that only when I'm finished.

I killed your daughter. I – and someone else. There. It's said. Whatever else I say to you, nothing else will be as hard. All that remains is to explain how and why, but these are just details next to the awfulness of those four words. I don't intend to implicate anyone else. Each of us must carry our separate guilt. The only reason for this letter is to tell you what I did. As for an explanation, how do you explain the unspeakable? Perhaps God can do that; I can't.

It was New Year's Eve, 1927. As I write this, it seems like a story from a history book or the kind of melodramatic film I once appeared in. But the time I'm describing was real. And exciting. I can't begin to tell you how exciting it was to be a part of that world, to glitter in it, to be regarded as beautiful and talented, an ornament of that dazzling time.

The party was in a home, a rich and grand place. The host was a colorful and somewhat dangerous man. I was his hostess that night, because I loved flirting with danger.

I had known Tess casually – I lied to you when I said we were best friends. I thought that was something you might have wanted to hear. Around the time of the party, we had become, in my mind, enemies, or at least rivals. You see, I had been involved with another man, the director of my last film. I had thought we would eventually be married, but one night he told me that was impossible. He mentioned his wife. I had known about her, of course,

193

but I knew there was more. Tess had had a small role in my latest film, and I had seen the two of them looking at each other, talking quietly. I had seen the look in his eyes when he had first become smitten with me, and it was easy to recognize the same look directed at another woman. In my imagination, he saw me now as wild and promiscuous – an opinion that was not wholly unjustified – and saw her as fresh and unspoiled. The fact that I was a leading actress and she a bit player was even more reason for my pride to feel injured.

Rose's handwriting began to loosen up, as if she were writing faster, more carelessly.

After we rang in the new year, the party changed. The band was still playing in the living room, but the music was slower now. The sounds carried throughout the house. Our host had made sure there was cocaine. (As I write this, I wonder what you are beginning to think of me, of all of us. I suspect the life we lived then was nothing like yours. Can you understand any of it?) Some couples danced, but others went off to find secluded spots in rooms or behind curtained alcoves by the windows on the staircase, where only animals could see. The guests were dressed in every way you could imagine. I wore a short beaded dress in dark blue. Many were in formal dress, some were in costume. One couple wore Roman togas. One attractive woman I knew was dressed like a man; she drew glances from both men and women. Another woman, an actress whose face I recognized but whose name I didn't know, wandered up the stairs carrying a glass of champagne and wearing only high heels and a long strand of pearls.

  All this, the description, is to help you see things as they were. But I realize I have been putting off the hardest part.

The words grew more scrawled, some of them crossed out, and Horn was having trouble reading. This no longer seemed due to haste or nervousness. He now thought the letter was being written by someone who was growing more and more drunk.

As hostess, I had taken a small bedroom for my own. I had a plan. Tess was somewhere in the house, and so was he. I wanted to show him her ~~morecoseumex~~ true nature. I was sure she had been with men, and if he could see how she behaved, she would no longer seem so virginal to him. I would ~~sext~~ make her dirty in front of him.

I found Tess. Wearing my favorite perfume. Gave her a bottle when she admired it. Made me hate her all the more. Said she had never tried cocaine. Good. Cocaine and champagne – powerful effect on her. I got her undressed, and then I went looking for a man to join her. Didn't take long. I did not even know him, but no matter. Just a nameless, red-faced man with a look that said he was ready for anything.

I took him back to the room. Then I planned to get her lover to come and see my little play. But Tess understood. Fear and horror on her face. And understanding. She tried to run out. I caught her, so did the man. We wrestled with her.

Then lights went out. I found out later someone had decided party would go better if house was dark. People lose inhibitions in dark, don't you think? He had found fuse box in the basement . . .

More words were crossed out here, so energetically that the note paper was pierced and smudged. Rose had apparently broken the tip of her pencil.

In the next line, and for the remainder of the letter, the penmanship was a messy scrawl, the letters exaggerated, the words slanting off precariously.

Enough. ENOUGH. Why write more? Why describe more? You know who I am now. Writing this won't bring her back. Read this or burn it. At least words are written now. If you read them, you'll hate me, as you should, but I hate myself enough for all of us.
   Rose

The signature was barely legible. Horn put the letter with the others. He felt exhausted. A picture was taking shape, still blurred like the emerging image in a photographer's darkroom. Against his will, he saw a Rose he didn't know, someone involved in a young woman's rape, driven by pettiness and spite. But key details were missing, most of all the identity of the man she referred to as 'another'. Dexter Diggs was there that night, but he was clearly not the man Rose brought to the room. And how could Dex have been involved in any way in the attack on Tess? The man had been Horn's mentor and friend for years. The thought that he could have played a role in a rape-murder made Horn feel sick.

You won't get anywhere on this now, he told himself, *so don't waste your time*. He undressed quickly, fetched his accustomed blanket from a nearby chair, and settled into the sofa for the night.

He slept fitfully for a few hours. Then he awoke suddenly and lay there, listening. The canyon, which at times seemed almost sleepy during the day, came alive after dark, and he had become used to all the sounds of the night. He strained his ears for the sounds, sorting them out one by one. A soft, low breeze carried ocean smells and ruffled the trees. A lone bird that should have been asleep called out lyrically. Half a mile off, a neighbor's dog barked once. He could imagine other, fainter sounds, of rodents and insects digging in the earth, of coyote and deer stepping delicately through the dew-wet grass. But none of this had disturbed him.

Then he heard it again. A sharp click of rock against rock. Something heavy stepping along the short gravel drive that linked the cabin to the roughly paved road. It could have been an animal, he thought, but animals usually don't broadcast news of their passing. At least not more than once.

He rolled out of bed and quickly pulled on pants, shoes, and undershirt in the dark, then fumbled along the wall by the door until he located the stout, gnarled stick he kept there. Grasping it, he quietly opened the door and stepped out onto the porch.

The cool night air hit him like a tonic. He inhaled deeply, looking around, his eyes already accustomed to the dark. The half-moon was riding high, and he could see reasonably well. Nothing stirred, and the sounds were the ones he already knew.

He stood there for about three minutes, motionless and listening. Then, far back down the canyon road, he heard a car start up, engine rev briefly, and climb through its gears. Someone was leaving.

Someone had been there, possibly getting the lay of the cabin and its surroundings. He suddenly felt very vulnerable. The feeling took him back to the war and made him angry at whoever had inspired the fear and at himself for feeling it.

Taking a flashlight from the kitchen alcove and a shovel from the tool shed outside, he made his way up the slope a couple of dozen yards until he came to three rocks laid in a seemingly haphazard pattern on the ground. There he dug down a foot, finally extracting a bundle wrapped in oilcloth. He carried it into the cabin and unwrapped it on the low table by the sofa.

The light from the table lamp glinted on the handgun. It was a working replica of a .45-caliber single-action Army Colt pistol, 1873 model. It had been the gun worn by Sierra Lane through countless B-westerns, each plot offering little variation from the last. Since Sierra was a man of peace generally opposed to gunplay, the weapon usually rode comfortably in his worn leather holster through several reels. But then, driven to extraordinary measures by his adversaries' evil ways, the cowboy would unholster the gun in the last reel and blaze his way loudly through an entire box of blanks until bodies littered the landscape.

The gun Horn held, turning it slowly in the light, was a copy of a weapon with a proud history. Known as the Peacemaker, it was the handgun most associated with the American West, used by the cavalry in the Indian wars, by prospectors, by lawmen, and by outlaws. Wyatt Earp carried one, as did Bat Masterson and Pat Garrett.

This one, however, was mostly a fraud, designed to simulate gunfire for the movie cameras. Only once had it been loaded with lead and fired in anger. That night up at the old estate, Horn had shot at a human target, feeling the unaccustomed kick of a real bullet, and downed a man with it. But it was not like the movies. None of what he felt that night had resembled heroism.

Ever since then, as an ex-convict, he had considered it too

risky to keep the gun close by. But fear, his familiar enemy from the war, was back. And he needed the old Colt.

Unwrapping the box of cartridges from the oilcloth, he loaded five shells into the cylinder, careful to leave vacant the chamber under the hammer. Then, laying the gun carefully on the floor beside the sofa, he turned out the light.

Chapter Eighteen

His sleep was troubled by hazy, shifting images of people in evening dress, their faces obscured, going in and out of darkened rooms as an unseen band played a frenzied Charleston.

In the morning, he stood in front of the bathroom mirror and picked the bandage off his face. He found a network of freshly scabbed skin stretching from his brow to just above his right jaw, a collection of small, dark islands connected by delicate strands, as if a spider had spun a clumsy web the color of blood. But his cheek no longer throbbed.

He shaved carefully and dressed, and before the sun had topped the far side of the canyon, he was back at work on the drainage ditch. Using a shovel and his bare hands, he dug out more of the mud and debris choking the shallow, concrete-lined canal.

As he worked, he thought of Rose Galen and Dexter Diggs and what he now knew about them. He would have to confront Dex about it, demand answers, and it was not a job he wanted.

Another idea was growing. Rose's last letter said plainly that she was not solely responsible for Tess Shockley's death. *I – and someone else*. Was she simply referring to the stranger she had invited to the bedroom? But Dex clearly had not been truthful with him, and a nagging doubt remained.

And one more notion: if another person shared responsibility, what did this say about Horn's theory that Rose's death had been an act of revenge? He needed to consider another, equally chilling possibility: that Rose had been killed to keep the details of that night secret.

After about twenty yards of progress, he came to a section of the ditch where mud from the last few heavy rains had over-flowed on each side. Thick brush had concealed the spot from the road, so he had not noticed it until now. One more winter storm, it appeared, and the road could be washed out. He quickly saw the problem: during one of the storms, a heavy, fifteen-foot limb had broken off a nearby oak and fallen into the ditch, blocking the passage of water. The limb was now all but buried in dried mud, and debris had backed up for yards behind it.

The shovel was useless, so Horn went to his tool shed for a hand saw and slowly began sawing off smaller branches. He needed to reduce the weight of the limb to the point where he could pry it out of the mud. The work was slow and exhausting. After an hour, he had piled his tarpaulin high with branches, mud, dead leaves, and other debris, but the main body of the limb was still stuck fast. Another storm could come any day, he knew. He needed to have the ditch cleared out soon.

He paused for a sandwich and a bottle of High Life on the porch, then went back to work. After another hour, he dragged the heavy tarp down to the cabin and took a bath. Then he went to the telephone with the scrap of paper napkin. Coby picked up after one ring.

'This is Horn.'

'Well, hello. You decide to take me up on the grand tour?'

'Not today. I just wanted to tell you something. Rose Galen said she wasn't alone when the Shockley girl died. Somebody else was there, and that somebody was responsible too.'

'And just how did you hear that?'

Horn hesitated but could think of no reason to be evasive. 'It's in a letter she wrote to Tess's father.'

Coby was silent for a moment. 'All right, then,' he said. 'But so what?'

'Don't you see? I've had the idea that Rose was killed by somebody who was getting back at her for Tess. But if there was a second killer, and if this person is still alive . . .'

'I get you.' Coby didn't sound particularly interested.

'Then anybody Rose talked to could be in trouble now. Any-body who knew what she knew.'

'The father?'

'Maybe, but I don't think so,' Horn said. 'He never read the letter. He sent it to me unopened.'

'That preacher?'

'Yes. She told him something. Then there's Madge, the woman at Rose's rooming house. She and Rose would drink together, and sometimes people talk when they drink.'

'Anybody else?'

'I don't know.'

'Well . . .' Horn could hear Coby chewing on something, a match or a toothpick. 'Thanks.'

'What are you going to do?'

'What do you think I should do?'

'Well, dammit, at least look in on Madge and Cassie at the rooming house, make sure they're all right, tell them to be careful. Quinn too. Last time I saw him, he was passed out on his sofa, dead drunk, muttering about Jay Lombard. Anybody could have walked in on him.'

'Don't particularly like your tone of voice,' Coby said. 'I appreciate the advice, though.' He hung up.

Horn berated himself for losing his temper. Policemen, he knew, liked to be in control, disliked getting suggestions from civilians unless they were politely phrased. *That respectful attitude of yours needs a little work*, he told himself.

He knew it was time to arrange to see Dexter Diggs, to confront him with some painful questions. He dialed the number. Evelyn answered and told him Dex was scouting locations for his next movie up in the Santa Clarita Valley and would not be back until the following evening. She sounded glad to hear from him. 'When are you coming over to collect that dinner?' she asked him.

'Soon, I hope,' he said. 'I want to spend time with both of you. First, though, I need to talk to Dex about something, and I don't want to bore you with it. I was wondering if I could stop by tomorrow night after dinner and see him for a few minutes.'

'Well . . . he'll be a little tired. But of course you can. Why don't you come by around nine? You know, John Ray, it occurs to me you've never turned down a dinner before. You must not be well.' Underneath the light tone he thought he could discern a note of concern, and he wondered how much she knew.

'Maybe that's it. Anyway . . . thanks, Evelyn.'

It was past three when he got dressed and drove into town, headed for Iris's place. He wanted to time his arrival just right, and he was pleased to see a nondescript Chevy sedan parked in the driveway. And Emory Quinn emerging from the garage with an armload of clothes.

Spotting Horn as he got out of his car, Quinn regarded him with undisguised hostility.

'Funny thing, us running into each other here,' Horn said. 'Since this is not the kind of address where you'd normally find either one of us.'

Leaning into the car, Quinn deposited his load on the back seat, which was already overflowing with suits, shirts, shoes, and other items.

'Nice clothes,' Horn said, peering in. 'Guess the owner won't be needing them any more. And the people at the mission sure will appreciate them, won't they?'

Quinn, still hostile, was clearly puzzled. 'What are you doing here?' he demanded.

'Me and the lady who's being so generous to you, we're old friends,' Horn said. He spotted Iris inside the garage, carrying a cardboard box from inside the house and depositing it on the hood of the Packard. He waved, and she waved back.

'Matter of fact, it was me suggested she donate some of her late husband's things to your mission. She's a nice lady, and she agreed.' Horn took a step toward Quinn, who stood with arms folded, bouncing nervously up and down on the balls of his feet. 'My feelings were hurt yesterday when you said I couldn't visit you any more. I thought I'd catch you someplace off your home ground, see if you felt more friendly.'

'There's nothing you can do about Rose,' Quinn said sullenly. 'And I'm tired of talking about it.' He started for the garage. 'I've got work to do.'

'Talk to me, Quinn,' Horn said. 'Or I'll have a talk with Mrs

Fairbrass, and you can forget about all these nice clothes and how many people they'll keep warm.'

Quinn stopped, and Horn pressed on. 'You're a hypocrite preacher who drinks too much, and you probably weren't much of a fighter, truth be told. But I think you do some good at that place where you work, and I respect that. I also think you haven't told me everything you know. So talk to me, and then I'll help you finish loading your car, and you can go back to the people you're trying to help.'

Quinn blinked and wiped his nose with a reddened knuckle, an old fighter's gesture. His face lost some of its tightness.

'You need to understand,' he said. 'Not talking to you wasn't my idea.'

'Whose, then?'

Quinn leaned back against the fender of his car, head down, as if winded. 'The other day Willie Apples came around. You know, he's not very smart, but he was just delivering a message. Told me Lombard had decided that you were asking too many questions about Rose. He said Lombard didn't have anything to do with her murder, but you were making things awkward for him. Said he was mad at me for bringing you around to the fights, helping you out. That's going to stop, he said. I don't spend any more time with you, or else.'

'You afraid of him? Willie, I mean?'

'I'm not afraid of any man,' Quinn said with so much conviction that Horn believed him. 'But Willie talked about the Anchor and all the people who depend on it. There could be a fire, he said. You never know. Things just happen.' He shrugged. 'I got the message.'

'I think I understand,' Horn said.

'I'm sure I'll have to deal with Lombard at some point,' Quinn said. 'But I'm not ready yet. For now, I just want to protect the mission.'

'You did right,' Horn said. 'And if it turns out he sent Willie after Rose, people will be standing in line to deal with both of them. Come on, let's finish loading up. You've got a delivery to make.'

After Quinn had driven away, Iris invited him in for a cup of coffee. Clea was on her way home from school, she said. Part of him hoped she'd invite him to stay for dinner, but she did not, so he left.

Not ready to go home, he drove down to Wilshire for steak and a baked potato, then headed over to the theater on Fairfax that showed silent movies. The newspaper had told him there was a western double feature, one starring William S. Hart and the other Tom Mix. He got to the theater just as the first show, the Hart film, was starting. It was *Hell's Hinges*, which Horn had seen for the first time as a small boy. Its good-versus-evil story had impressed him strongly, and he was curious now to see how it looked decades later. The Hart character is a bad man, a gunfighter, who nevertheless has a spark of decency that responds to the love of a preacher's daughter. At the end he becomes a kind of avenging angel, wiping out the evil in the town.

As he sat watching the movie unfold, Horn was struck by its sense of certainty. Since the war, something unsettling had crept into certain American films – a darkness, a moral ambiguity, a sense that the average man had little chance against the world. He loved the movies, and this change troubled him. Watching the exaggerated acting of the characters in this old silent western, he knew he was revisiting, if only for a short time, something he had gotten from the movies since childhood – the notion that good will prevail. He felt the power of the Hart character, its almost biblical dimensions, and once again he recalled seeing something of his father there, both the good and the evil. The thought did not bring him comfort, and he considered how long it had been since he had tried to call or write home.

After *Hell's Hinges*, Tom Mix's athletic derring-do seemed trivial by comparison, and Horn left before the second movie was over.

It was not yet ten o'clock. Still restless, he drove over the hill and into the Valley, making his way eventually to the Dust Bowl, its neon-lit exterior glowing like a beacon surrounded by the darkness of open fields. Inside, he went to the bar and had just gotten a Blue Ribbon when someone called to him. It was Mad Crow, who was at a table with Cassie and Rusty Baird. Horn carried his beer over to them.

'Take a seat,' Mad Crow said. 'We're involved in something deep and significant, and we need a fresh opinion.' He belched behind a big fist. 'Also some refills.' He waved to the bartender. 'More tea,' he called out. 'And don't forget the crumpets this time.' A minute later, he and Cassie had fresh beers in front of them, along with a bowl of peanuts salted in the shell.

'What's so deep and significant?' Horn asked.

'Joseph got to talking about how no Indians ever get to play the leads,' Baird said, taking a sip from his cup of black coffee. 'Then he said, hell, sometimes they don't even get to play Indians. I said what about Anthony Quinn? Wasn't he Crazy Horse once?'

'And I pointed out that he's Irish and Mexican,' Mad Crow said with a grin. 'Okay, he looks the part, but it's not the same thing. And Rusty said what about Iron Eyes Cody? He's been in a lot of movies, right? And I had to give him the bad news—'

'Iron Eyes Cody isn't an Indian?' Horn asked.

Mad Crow shook his head. 'Italian, basically. Name used to be DeCorti, and he's from Louisiana. But don't spread it around. He's a nice guy, and I don't want to see him lose any work.'

'We could make a list of the ones who did the worst job of playing an Indian,' Cassie said. She was wearing her cabby's outfit and appeared relaxed, her sense of humor once again in place after her bad experience with the police the day before.

'How about Boris Karloff?' Horn suggested. 'In that Gary Cooper movie, the one with Paulette Goddard.'

'I thought Boris wasn't too bad, really,' Mad Crow said. 'The old chief was supposed to be scary, and so they just went out and hired Frankenstein.'

'Jennifer Jones,' Cassie said. '*Duel in the Sun*. She might have fooled Gregory Peck, but she didn't fool me.'

'I'm going to exempt her,' Mad Crow said expansively.

'Why?' Baird asked.

'Because she was only supposed to be half Indian,' Mad Crow said, glancing quickly at Cassie. 'And, uh . . .'

'You had a crush on her, that's why,' Horn suggested.

'You can't change the rules,' Cassie said.

'Wait a minute.' Mad Crow took a swig of his beer and thought hard for a moment. 'Don Ameche,' he said finally. 'In *Ramona*. They re-released it about a year ago, and Nee Nee made me take her. All through that idiotic movie I kept seeing him in a suit and tie, inventing the telephone.'

'I think you just won,' Horn said. The others nodded in agreement.

A tall, jug-eared young man in a plaid shirt and chinos walked over to the jukebox, popped in a dime and made his selections. Seconds later, Woody Guthrie's version of the haunting 'Will You Miss Me?' began to play. The young man approached the table and asked Cassie to dance. She jumped to her feet.

As Mad Crow watched them walk over to the small dance floor – really just a space with no tables near the bar – Baird leaned over and said quietly, 'He's all right. I know him and his daddy. They work a few acres of hazelnuts over in Canoga Park.'

'Sure,' Mad Crow said. 'I'm not worried.'

Baird excused himself and got up to look after customers.

Mad Crow watched the couple dancing. 'I can't get used to that outfit of hers,' he said, shaking his head. 'You squint your eyes, and it could almost be two men dancing over there.'

'If she looks anything like a man, you've had way too much to drink,' Horn said.

'I know.' Mad Crow grinned broadly. 'Just kidding. Actually she's downright pretty, isn't she? Takes after her mother.'

'She is.' Horn didn't want the conversation to turn to Cassie's father. 'Aren't you supposed to be at the casino?'

'I guess. But Cassie's shift doesn't start until midnight tonight, and I thought I'd just take a little time off to spend with her.' He looked vaguely embarrassed.

'You two are getting along a lot better now, aren't you?'

'We are. And she's doing pretty well driving the cab. Never

thought I'd say this, but I'm starting to be proud of her.' He waved at the bartender. '*Garcon!* Two more over here.'

The jukebox shifted to an instrumental by Bob Wills and his Texas Playboys, and Cassie and the young man kept dancing. 'He's holding her awful close,' Mad Crow said.

'Relax.'

When the bottles arrived, Horn sat without touching his.

'Something on your mind,' Mad Crow said.

Horn told him about the events of the last few days. He approached the subject of Cassie and the police delicately but was relieved to find that she had already told her uncle about being called in for questioning. 'If you have a dark skin in this town,' Mad Crow said, 'you don't go looking for fair treatment from them. She knows that. We all know it.'

'I'm not too worried about her,' Horn said. 'She didn't do anything. Coby's a typical cop in a lot of ways, but he's not dumb, and I think he'll be fair. And even though he seems lazy every now and then, I think he really wants to find out who killed Rose.'

When Horn spoke of meeting Dolores Winter and her ex-husband, Mad Crow's expression took on a faraway look.

'I met her once,' he said. 'Did I ever tell you?'

'Nope.'

'It was during the war. You were probably off in Italy, and I was taking a break from my arduous duties in Special Services, lining up entertainment for the boys. One night I stopped in at the Hollywood Canteen, and next thing I knew, I was dancing with her.'

'You're kidding.'

'Huh-uh. As usual, the place was loaded with GIs buzzing around a handful of movie stars. I'd been working my way across the room to get a better look at Lana Turner, but she was surrounded. This great-looking redhead asked me if I wanted to dance, and a second later I recognized her.'

'Doll Winter.'

'None other than. She was wearing a tight skirt and white blouse with a ruffle in the front. It was hot in there, and she smelled very warm and talcumy, you know? We danced, we talked a little about her movies, and she admired my sergeant's stripes. Then she caught me looking at Lana, and she laughed. "Lana Turner always reminded me of a vanilla ice-cream cone just about to melt," she said. I thought that was wonderful. "How about you?" I said, feeling downright bold. "Takes a lot to make me melt," she said, looking me right in the eye. Lord. I forgot all about Lana Turner and was about to say something really witty when this gunner's mate from the Big Mo cut in. And that was the end of my romance with Doll Winter.'

The look he gave Horn was both sly and envious. 'You had lunch with her. And she's not married any more. You got any chance with her? Or does she prefer the Leslie Howard type?'

'Actually, she told me she likes cowboys.'

'You sonofabitch. You're going to get some of that, aren't you?'

'Leave me alone, Indian.'

'If you get a chance at that and you pass it up, don't ever talk to me again.'

Seeking to change the subject, Horn began describing Rose's letters to Willis Shockley. 'I'm starting to get an idea about what happened that night twenty years ago,' he said. 'And I'm beginning to have doubts about some people. Emory Quinn is one of them. He had a thing for Rose, and he's kept quiet about it. But what bothers me most is . . . I'm afraid Dex was somehow involved. It looks like he may have lied to me. About more than one thing.'

'Have you talked to him?'

'No. Not yet.'

'Talk to him. Maybe he can explain. Hell, men lie about women all the time, and it doesn't make 'em murderers.'

Cassie returned from dancing, her face flushed and happy. The Indian looked at his watch and got up. 'Think I'll stop by the shop on my way home,' he said. 'I'll get there just in time to clean out the cash register, kick out the riffraff, and lock the doors.'

'Guess I should leave too,' Cassie said.

Outside, Horn started for his car, but a wordless look from Cassie stopped him. Mad Crow, a little drunk, patted the gleaming white finish of his boat-like convertible. 'Have you heard the Lakota warrior's song to his horse?'

'Many times,' Horn said, winking at Cassie.

'My horse be swift in flight,' Mad Crow intoned, his hand still on the car. 'Bear me now in safety far from the enemy's arrows. And you shall be rewarded with streamers and ribbons red.' He got in and cranked the engine, then waved as the car roared out of the lot, throwing gravel behind it.

'Where's your cab?' Horn asked.

'Behind the building. Wouldn't want Yellow Cab to know one of their drivers is in here drinking, even if she is off duty.'

'Especially when she's not quite twenty-one. Was I imagining it, or did you not want me to leave just yet?'

She nodded. 'I met someone who knew Rose years ago,' she said. 'I think he knows some things. I'm going to see him now. You interested?'

It took him only a second to get over his surprise. 'Very.'

'Then follow me.'

Chapter Nineteen

Cassie led him over the Cahuenga Pass and down into Holly-wood. On the broad parkway that cut through the hill, she drove the big cab with her usual urgency, as if she were on a life-and-death mission. Even with the advantage of the Ford's oversized engine, he had to fight to keep up with her. When she abruptly changed lanes, cutting off a Hudson full of people and drawing an outraged blast of the horn, he heard himself mutter at her.

At Wilshire, the regular stop signals on the big street slowed her pace somewhat, and Horn began to enjoy the drive. It was almost midnight, and much of the city was asleep. Most of Wilshire's businesses were dark, but here and there a corner bar or drugstore glowed with light. A light rain, little more than a mist, began falling, and he switched on his wipers. He almost missed the sight of the cab pulling over to the curb, but he recovered and found a spot behind her. Cassie got out, waved ambiguously, and went inside a brightly lit liquor store. In a minute she emerged carrying a small paper bag. They drove on.

As he began to wonder how far she was going, Cassie took a quick left, and soon he found himself in a quiet, darkened neighborhood of big yards and sprawling homes. A block and a half north of Wilshire, she cut left again, darting into a driveway. He followed and saw the cab quickly enveloped in heavy, over-hanging shrubbery and tree branches as it negotiated a narrow loop of a circular driveway. Peering through the rain-slick wind-shield, he made out the ornate entryway of what looked like a large house. But Cassie kept going until she reached a side door, where her brake lights stopped him.

He got out and found her huddling in the doorway to keep

dry, her cabby's hat still on and her jacket collar turned up. 'He doesn't use the front door much any more,' she said as she pressed her thumb against the bell. He heard a faint ringing inside.

'What's going on?' he demanded. 'It's the middle of the night. Whose place is this?'

'He stays up late,' she said. 'Madge told me you've been looking for him. She calls him the gray man.'

What the hell? Before he had time to digest this, a light went on inside and the door opened. Horn could see a tall, stooped man with almost cadaverous features. He was wrapped in what appeared to be a bulky robe.

'Cassie,' the man said in a deep baritone.

'Hello, Alden,' she said in a voice that Horn would have called flirtatious in any other woman. 'All right if we come in?'

The man noticed Horn, and his look of pleasure at seeing Cassie left his face abruptly, replaced by apprehension. 'Who is this?'

'This is John Ray Horn,' she said. 'A friend. I told you about him, remember?'

The man's eyes swept Horn up and down, and he clutched his robe at the neck. His other hand moved to close the door. 'I'm not sure this is a good time,' he muttered.

'Come on,' she said in a wheedling tone Horn had never heard her use before. 'It's raining. Besides, I brought you something.' She raised the paper bag so that he could see it.

The man looked from Cassie to the bag, then questioningly at Horn. 'I've known him for years,' she said. 'You can trust him.'

Before Horn could appreciate the incongruity of Cassie vouching for his character, the man opened the door wider. 'I'm sorry to keep you out in the rain,' he said, gesturing in a courtly manner. 'Please come in.'

They stepped inside and, dripping slightly, found themselves in a large kitchen. 'Alden Richwine,' the man said in a melliflu-ous voice, rolling the R just enough to add weight to the name. He extended a hand to Horn. 'Excuse my, ah . . .' He indicated the bold plaid robe he was wearing. 'I wasn't expecting visitors.'

211

'I hope we didn't wake you up.'

'Oh, no, no. I was reading.' He indicated a book on a nearby kitchen counter. 'I'm very much the night owl.' Although Horn guessed his age at seventy or more, Alden Richwine had striking looks. He was tall and extremely lean, with craggy features crowned by a wide brow and a full head of wavy white hair, worn unfashionably long in the back and over the ears. As Madge had described, his face had an unhealthy pallor, as if he seldom went out in the sun.

Cassie opened the bag and pulled out a bottle of Paul Jones whisky, which she handed to him. 'For being a gentleman and inviting us in,' she said.

'Dear girl.' He laid the bottle on the counter and began pulling glasses from an overhead cupboard. 'Both of you must join me.' He showed them to a well-worn and oversize kitchen table. 'Would you like it neat, as I do?' Hearing no dissent, he poured their drinks as they sat down.

Horn looked uneasily at Cassie, who appeared to be enjoying a small, secret joke. She obviously knew more about this man and his connection to Rose than Horn did, and she was being of little help to him. He would have to find out as best he could.

Richwine politely turned his attention to his new acquaintance. 'Mr Horn, the charming Cassie tells me you and I have something in common.' He spoke carefully, in a theatrical version of an old-school British accent.

Horn gave him a questioning look.

'I believe you're an actor?'

'Oh. Yes, sir. I was for a while. I'm not any more.'

'And your current occupation?'

'I do whatever I need to get by.'

'Admirable.' Richwine nodded soberly. 'Myself, I've never left this gypsy profession of mine. From the moment when I was eight years old, standing in front of my classmates and reciting lines from Matthew Arnold, I knew I was condemned to the life of a performer, both the joys and the sorrows. First I appeared on the London stage, later in New York. Then I made the mistake of traveling to this desert, this artistic sinkhole, to help usher in something called the moving pictures. And I've been trapped here ever since, unable to—'

'You were here in the twenties? You worked in the silents?'

'Yes. As to the nature of that work . . . well, there were those who said I was a memorable actor, with a face made for the camera. But compared to the stage, it was all insubstantial. In London I had done Shakespeare – Gloucester, Claudius, Malvolio. Even, for one glittering engagement, Richard the Third. The drama critic for the *Guardian* said, and I quote, "He manages the difficult task of investing one of the Bard's darkest villains with an unaccustomed and somewhat startling nobility." ' Richwine closed his eyes briefly, savoring the critic's long-ago words. 'Then, to come to this place and make empty gestures in front of a man grinding a camera . . . it seemed beneath me. And yet I did it happily, for the money. I played heroes and villains, all of them voiceless, and I prospered. And then, when the movies found their voice and I was ready to unlimber my own once again, my best years were gone. I was too far past my prime.'

Noticing Horn's questioning look, he went on. 'You're wondering if you've ever seen me. Of course you have, my boy. In the background. As the doting grandfather, the roguish uncle, the devious lawyer. I'm still up there on the screen, only now I'm just part of the scenery.'

'I'm sure I've seen you, sir,' Horn said. Richwine was something of a windbag, he thought. Even his name had a showoff, actorish ring to it. But he seemed to be well intentioned. And he might have valuable information. Horn wanted to focus the conversation where it belonged. 'Do I understand you knew Rose Galen?'

Richwine didn't answer. He seemed to be giving Horn a fresh assessment. He turned to Cassie, an unspoken question in his eyes.

'John Ray knew her, Alden,' Cassie said reassuringly. 'They were friends too.'

'You didn't mention that, my dear,' he said reproachfully.

'I'm sorry.'

213

He looked at Horn again, and this time suspicion was written plainly on his features. 'How well did you know her?' he asked.

'Well enough,' Horn said. 'But that was years ago, when the two of us did a movie together. And then I lost track of her for a long time, up until just a few days ago.'

Richwine continued to stare, but some of the suspicion seemed to dissolve. 'Rose.' He sighed deeply and drained his glass. He offered to freshen their drinks, but they declined, so he refilled his own glass. 'Yes, I knew her. She was Rosemary Gale then. Did you know that?'

'Yes.'

'An exceptional woman. An enormous talent.'

'And you know that she's dead.'

'Of course I know,' Richwine said patiently. 'She died in my house. Can you wonder why I feel responsible in some way? But then I ask myself: what could I have done?'

'Your house? I don't understand.'

'Alden owns the rooming house,' Cassie said.

Horn took a moment to absorb this. 'So you would come by every now and then,' he said almost to himself. 'Both before and after she died.'

'Of course. Once a month or so.'

'Why didn't the residents know who you were?'

Richwine looked irritated. 'I'm sorry, Mr Horn. I didn't realize I was going to be subjected to some kind of interrogation.'

Out of the corner of his eye, Horn saw Cassie give him a cautionary look. He realized he was moving too fast. 'No, sir, I apologize for offending you,' he said. 'It's just that I've been looking for you, hoping you could tell me something I could use. Rose was important to me—'

'She never mentioned you.'

Horn sighed. 'Like I said, I had lost touch with her for a long time. I found her again just before she died.' He felt a wordless accusation taking shape in Richwine's attitude, and he glanced at Cassie, remembering her admission of guilt at having left Rose alone in an unlocked room. *All right*, he told the other man silently. *Maybe I feel guilty too, for not being around when she could have used some help.*

'She was important to me,' Horn repeated stubbornly. 'I want to know who killed her, even more than the police want to. If that makes me careless and rude sometimes, I apologize.'

Richwine waved the matter away. 'The good people at Rook House didn't know I was the owner because I preferred it that way,' he said. He yawned elaborately, covering his mouth with an elegant, blue-veined hand. For the first time, Horn noticed the other whisky bottle by the kitchen sink. It bore the same label, and it appeared to be empty. 'Only Rose and the manager knew.'

'How did Rose know?'

'We had known each other almost from the first day she began working in films,' Richwine said, his gaze lowered to the tabletop, his voice grown reflective. 'I knew her, worked with her occasionally, admired her greatly. When, for reasons best known to her, she decided to leave, she was gone for years. Then she reappeared, and it was obvious she was in need. As the owner of a residence for those of limited incomes, I was in a position to help her. I told the manager to give her the first vacancy.'

'Mr Richwine, do you have any idea who killed Rose?'

The other man stared at Horn for long moments, eyes almost hooded by the gray, overgrown hedge of his brows. Then he drained his glass a second time. A tiny tremor developed in his right hand, which sat curled around the glass. Horn noted his red-edged eyes and wondered how long he'd been drinking.

'Suddenly I'm very tired,' the older man said softly. 'The last few days have been . . . I pray you'll excuse me if I prepare for bed. And if it's not too much trouble, please lock up when you leave.'

Horn mumbled a polite response, berating himself for pushing too hard. Cassie got up quickly. 'Will you let me help you?' she asked Richwine.

'Of course,' he said, rising heavily as she put an arm lightly around his waist. 'The day a comely young lady offers to help me to bed and I decline, I'll know I'm ready for the last curtain.' He turned to Horn. 'Good night.'

'Good night, sir.'

They left the kitchen by a door that opened onto a hallway. He remained at the table, listening to their banter.

'Alden, you're not King Richard anymore,' she said. 'First, Second, or any other number. You should look after yourself better.'

'I am now Lear,' he responded in a voice with a trace of old thunder. 'And you . . . you are my kindly Indian medicine woman. My priestess.'

When their voices had receded, Horn left the kitchen. After about twenty feet, the dimly lit hallway opened into something larger. He switched on a light and saw a high-ceilinged room with an imposing tiled fireplace, a wrought-iron chandelier, and a sweeping stone staircase that led upstairs. The furniture was bulky, overstuffed, and well-worn. The oriental carpet was almost threadbare in places.

Turning on lights as he went, Horn visited the library, dining room and what appeared to be a parlor, whose French doors looked out on overgrown greenery. The library's shelves held mostly poetry, plays, and books on the theater. Overhead, a brown water stain marred one corner of the ceiling. Back in the main room, he mounted the wide steps, passing by ten-foot windows that marched upward alongside the stairs, each window set back from the stairway and framed by heavy velvet curtains. One pane in each tall window was of stained glass, depicting scenes from a fanciful menagerie that included birds, bears, and unicorns.

The upstairs held six doors, apparently to bedrooms. One was open, and he could hear Cassie and their host talking inside. 'I'll leave your water here, next to your medicine,' she said. Horn retreated quietly back down to the kitchen. A few minutes later, Cassie joined him.

'All right, talk to me,' he said as she sat down at the table. 'How long have you known this character?'

'Not long,' she said, still seeming to enjoy her secret joke. 'I waited a few days, to make sure he trusted me, before I invited you over. He's a nice old guy, isn't he?'

'How did you meet him?'

'Well, I knew you and Madge were looking for him. You should have a talk with her, by the way.'

'I've talked to her.'

'No, I mean about something new. I'll tell you later. Anyway . . . one night, as I was leaving for my shift, I saw him get out of his car and come up the front steps. He went in to see the manager. From Madge's description, I knew it was him. So I went out to where he was parked and looked over his car and thought up a quick plan. He has an old LaSalle, a 'thirty-nine with the Sunshine Roof. It's nice, but he doesn't take very good care of it. Anyway, I got an old rag from my cab and used it to plug up the tailpipe. Then, when he came out, I followed him.' Noting Horn's expression, she stopped warily.

'Nothing,' he said with a grin. 'Just sounds like something your uncle would pull.'

'After about a mile, his engine quit,' she went on. 'I came up and offered to take a look. Told him he should have it checked by a mechanic and asked if he wanted to take my cab home. He said sure. On the way, we got to talking. He loves to talk.'

'I can tell.'

'Once I got him home, I could tell he didn't have anybody to look after him. Cleaning woman comes in once a week; that's about it. He used to be rich. Look at this house, huh? But he doesn't make much money from acting any more, so most of what he has comes from the rents at Rook House—'

'From your conversation, sounds like the two of you are pretty cozy.'

'What's your point?' He saw a flash of the old Cassie in her look.

'Just that I never saw you act motherly toward anybody, that's all.'

'What do you know about me? And what do you care, anyway? He likes me. I enjoy listening to him talk, and the polite way he treats me. What's wrong with that?'

'Nothing.'

'I don't mind doing him favors, stopping for a bottle of Paul Jones or getting him a loaf of bread when he forgets to go out for groceries.'

He regretted what he'd said. 'All right, Cassie. That's good. I bet he appreciates you.'

'So now you've found him, like you wanted.' She looked at her watch. 'I need to go try to scare up some fares.' She got up, then looked at him expectantly. 'You coming?'

'No.'

'What do you mean?'

'I'm not sure. All I know is, I need to talk to him more. Ever since Rose died, I feel like I've done nothing. I've wasted time. This Alden, he's somebody I thought I needed to find, and now that I have, I've got questions that can't wait. While you were upstairs, I walked around down here, and . . . Something tells me I shouldn't leave this house until I either have some answers or else I decide that he doesn't have any.'

'So what are you going to do?'

'I'm staying here. I'll sleep on his couch. I'm used to couches. And when he wakes up, I'll be here, and we'll finish talking.'

She looked dubious. 'Don't scare him,' she said.

'I won't. Hell, I'll fix him some breakfast if it helps any.'

She stared at him, visibly distrustful. 'Be sure to lock up before you turn in,' she said finally.

'I will. Go make some money.'

'He likes his coffee with just cream.' She was almost out the door when his voice stopped her. 'What?' She turned, hand on the knob.

'I was just saying . . . you did real good. Finding him like that.'

Her eyebrows rose in exaggerated response. 'Gee, a compliment from a cowboy. I'm all twittery.'

'Make fun if you want to. But I mean it. You did good.'

She grinned delightedly. 'You're right, I did. Must be my Indian side.' Then she was gone.

Horn walked around the house again, checking doors and windows. Although neglected, the house was solidly made.

Noticing that the latch on one of the kitchen windows was loose, he rummaged through the adjoining pantry and found a drawer with an assortment of tools, including a screwdriver. He tightened the screws securing the latch.

He took one last turn around the house. What had just been a feeling an hour earlier now swelled into something more. It was almost as if the house were talking to him. No words at first, just a drone, like the animated muttering of party guests in an adjoining room. He started up the great, curved staircase, and his eyes came to rest on one of the panes of stained glass in the first window. Glowing faintly from the light of a nearby street lamp, it showed foxes at play in an emerald forest.

The words from Rose's last letter came to him. At the party where Tess died, amorous couples had hidden themselves behind curtained alcoves by the windows on the staircase, *where only animals could see*. The ending of the sentence had puzzled him, but he had dismissed it as the alcohol taking hold of an already feverish mind. Now he knew. The animals lived in the glowing glass of the windows.

As he stood on the stairs, listening, the house spoke to him in full voice. He could hear frantic laughter, the strains of a fast-paced Charleston, the heavy breathing behind the velvet curtains.

Somewhere upstairs, Rose was making her plans. A young girl's life was about to end.

He poured another glass of Alden Richwine's whisky, took off his shoes, and settled onto a sofa in front of the fireplace, covering himself with a dusty afghan that had been draped over one arm. It was almost two in the morning before he slept.

Chapter Twenty

Horn awoke to the clinking sound of the milkman depositing bottles on the steps outside the kitchen door. He got up and splashed his face in the kitchen sink, then went out to pick up the milk, which he deposited in the noisy old Servel. He noted a small puddle of water collecting underneath the fridge. Like its owner, Alden Richwine's house was showing its age.

He took a minute to look around the kitchen, locating the things he needed. He found the coffee pot and a jar of coffee and started a pot brewing. Muffled clanking sounds from somewhere deep in the plumbing told him his unwitting host was up and about. He broke some eggs into a bowl, added a little milk and some salt and pepper, and sliced up part of an onion. After about twenty minutes, he heard a door close upstairs. He was beginning to melt butter in the skillet when he heard Richwine's voice.

'What are you doing here?' A simple question, but delivered with enough theatricality to require an immediate and satisfactory answer.

'Good morning,' Horn said, half turning. 'I stayed here last night. Hoped you wouldn't mind.'

Richwine wore the same plaid robe. Unshaven and in the light of day, he looked even older and more worn-down. But his voice held the same command.

'This is outrageous,' he said, remaining in the doorway and looking warily at Horn. 'You were not invited, sir.'

'I know. And don't blame Cassie. She tried to get me to leave. But . . . look, I'm not a burglar. I'm just somebody who badly needs to talk to you, and who doesn't have any time to waste being polite. So I took the chance of offending you—'

'Bad manners, common behavior, always constitute an offense,' Richwine broke in. He sniffed the air, noting the breakfast smells. 'What are you doing?' Emboldened, he took a step forward. 'Are you feeding yourself? In my kitchen?'

'No, sir. This is for you.' Horn poured the eggs into the hot butter and left them to set for a while. He poured coffee into a cup, then opened one of the fresh bottles of milk and carefully spooned into the coffee some of the cream from the top. Stirring it, he handed the cup to Richwine. 'I don't know how you like your eggs, but I took a guess.' He returned to the skillet, quickly scrambled the bubbling eggs and raked them into a dish, which he laid on the table. 'I added some onions to these. Hope they're all right.'

Richwine rubbed a hand across his stubble as he looked wonderingly down at the plate. Finally he shrugged and sat down. 'Mr . . . Horn, is it? You're an unusual man.'

'Thank you, sir. I suppose.'

'And where exactly did you sleep?' Richwine tasted the eggs, nodded his head almost imperceptibly, and helped himself to another forkful.

'On your sofa out by the fireplace.'

'Not exactly comfortable, I would surmise.'

'It was fine. I usually sleep on a sofa at home. My place is small, and I don't have a bed.'

Richwine frankly appraised his guest. 'Cassie told me your work sometimes takes you into a kind of gray area, Mr Horn,' he said quietly. 'An area where you may come in contact with those outside the law, where it may not be clear if your own actions—'

'I've spent some time in prison,' Horn cut in. 'Right now, if anyone asks, I tell them I'm as law-abiding as anybody.' His voice turned abrupt. 'But I know what's on your mind. You live in a big house, and you find a man in your kitchen who's used to sleeping on a sofa. So you wonder about me. Well, I could have taken anything I wanted from this house while you were asleep,

221

and I didn't. If you'll talk honestly with me for a while, I should have no reason to ever bother you again.'

They sat silently for a moment. Then Richwine said, 'You may join me in some coffee, if you like. We can have it in another room.'

'Thanks.' Horn poured himself a cup. Carrying the whisky bottle along with his coffee cup, Richwine led him down the hall and through the main room to the library, where they sat in tufted-leather easy chairs the color of mahogany. The room smelled of old paper and bindings, with a hint of mildew.

Richwine set his cup and the bottle on a small, brass-topped table between them. 'And now you may ask me questions, and I reserve the right to answer them or not.'

'Fine. Let's pick up where we left off last night. Do you have any idea who killed Rose?'

Richwine cleared his throat, and his instrument of a voice softened. 'I've been asking myself that question since the day she died,' he said. 'Since the moment I received the telephone call from the police. There was talk that her murder may have been part of a robbery, since her purse was emptied. At any rate, I do not know who killed her.'

'I don't think it was part of a robbery, Mr Richwine. I think she was killed very deliberately by someone she knew. And I'd be very surprised if you didn't have an idea or two about it.'

'Why do you say that?'

'Because you're at the center of it. It all revolves around you. I've just figured out something important. Rose was not the only person to die in one of your houses.'

It may not have been possible for Alden Richwine's complexion to turn even more pale, but that seemed to happen. The man's jaw went slack as he stared at Horn. He uncapped the Paul Jones bottle and, with a not quite steady hand, poured a generous amount into his coffee cup.

'Well,' he said. 'Well. Do you mind if I ask—'

'What I've found out? Not at all. About twenty years ago you threw a New Year's Eve party in this house. Rose was your hostess. In one of the bedrooms upstairs, a young woman

222

named Tess Shockley was raped and killed. Oh, she didn't die right away. But she was dying when someone drove her to a hospital and dumped her on the doorstep. The police called it murder, and they never solved it. They never even found out where she'd been earlier. But we know, don't we?'

Richwine was silent, studying the contents of his cup as if seeking to discern the separate swirls of coffee, cream, and whisky.

'Tess's death changed Rose,' Horn went on. 'You could almost say it destroyed her. She said she was responsible, and maybe she was. All I know is, Rose's murder leads straight back to that party. She was killed because of what happened that night. Either out of revenge over Tess Shockley or because someone decided Rose had to be kept quiet.

'And now you know exactly why I'm here.' Horn let that statement hang in the air for a moment. 'If you say you don't know who killed Rose, I just might believe you for now. But you know some things about that night in this house twenty years ago, and you're going to tell me.'

'And if I don't?' Richwine's feeble smile said he already knew the answer.

'I'll go to the police with what I know about Tess Shockley. It was a long time ago, but it got a lot of attention back then, and policemen love to close the file on splashy murders. They may or may not believe everything I tell them, but if they only believe part of it, you'll become very interesting to them—'

'I didn't kill that girl,' Richwine broke in.

'I don't know if you did or not,' Horn replied. 'Maybe all you did was help keep her death a secret. But here's a joke for you: the police detective in charge of Rose's death is a man named Luther Coby, and his dream is to pin something on a big name. For a while, he thought he had me, but I convinced him I was clean – and besides, I was never more than a B-movie actor. You, Mr Richwine, would be a bigger fish. Maybe your best days are behind you, but you've had a distinguished career. My friend Coby would love to get his hands on you.'

His words were a combination of bluff, conjecture, and flattery, and Horn wasn't sure of their effect. Alden Richwine looked at him evenly before responding. 'You're quite the cardboard hero, aren't you?' he said, his voice carefully controlled but the sarcasm clear. 'I've seen a few of those cheap little morality plays you call westerns. I found them rather ludicrous, with their simplistic notions of good and evil and their neat resolutions, as if life's problems could be solved by killing a few villains with your – what do you call it? – your six-shooter, and riding over the hill. Well, I doubt that those solutions will translate into real life, Mr Horn, try as you might.'

'It was just a living. I never took it all that seriously.'

'Nor should you have. Five minutes of William Shakespeare, or even your Eugene O'Neill, are worth every line of wooden dialogue you ever spoke. But something tells me you're acting a part now – the lone avenger, that tired cliché of so many second-rate films. As such, you're not all that convincing. To begin with, you might consider outfitting yourself in some decent clothes.'

He paused, waiting for a response.

'Are you through insulting me?' Horn asked.

Richwine sighed. 'Let me see if I understand. Either I talk to you, or I talk to the police.'

'Something like that.'

'What do you want to know?'

'I want to know about the party. Everything.'

The other man nodded slowly, over and over, obviously thinking hard. 'You were wrong about one thing.' he began. 'Rose was not my hostess. I offered the use of my house, but the actual host was someone else. A man named Jay Lombard.'

A dangerous man, Horn thought, recalling Rose's description. Of course.

'Why did you offer your house?'

Richwine laughed wryly. 'Because I loved the spotlight. I was successful, I lived in a grand house, and I enjoyed showing it off. Also because Rose asked me. Lombard, you see, had just moved to town and was in the process of buying his own place. And, I should mention, because the idea of having a gangster and his friends in my house appealed to my sense of the dramatic. As it happened, everyone was invited, not just the bootlegging crowd. We had quite the turnout that night. Studio people mingled with gamblers, politicians with jockeys. It was written up in all the papers . . .'

'I don't get it,' Horn said. 'With all that going on—'

'How could the events in the bedroom be kept a secret? A combination of luck – gambler's luck, possibly – and great care. But I fear I'm getting ahead of myself. May I just tell the story?'

Horn nodded.

'Rose and I had worked together on what was to be her last film, a costume drama set in Italy. There was something about a hawk in the title. My blasted memory—'

'*Hawk of Tramonti.*'

'Yes. How did you know?'

'I'll tell you in a minute. You said you were in the film?'

'I played her father.'

Horn summoned up the memory of the last reel of the old film. He had been watching Rose, not the other person. The duke. The one who overacted, as Dex described him. Alden Richwine.

'I see. Well, I learned about it from Dexter Diggs, your director. He even ran part of it for me. And it wasn't her last film, as it turned out. She made one with me years later. But I doubt that she was any more proud of it than I was.'

'Dexter.' Richwine's tone was noncommittal. Horn tried to read his expression, but he saw nothing.

'Are you in touch with him?'

'No. Not since we finished working on the film.'

'Dex told me you two were good friends back then.'

'I suppose. But over the years . . .' He gestured vaguely. 'Friends lose touch.'

'You were telling me about working with Rose.'

'Yes.' Richwine grew suddenly animated, smiling broadly. He got up from his chair and went to one of the library shelves, where he picked through a series of thick file folders, finally selecting one. 'I keep souvenirs of everything in which I've appeared,' he said. 'Playbills and theater programs from stage productions. Later, in Hollywood, I collected photos. These are from that film.' He spread them out on a nearby desktop. Most were publicity photos and lobby cards, the latter meant for display in the theater. A few appeared to be candid shots showing Rose and other cast members at rest between shots or posing for group pictures.

'Here we are, the happy company,' Richwine said, pointing to one such shot, in which a dozen or so people, some in costume, stood in a row with arms around each other, smiling and mugging for the camera. 'Here's Rose, and here's the distinguished duke, her father. And, of course, our esteemed director.' Rose, standing near the center, wore ornate jewelry and a gown that trailed to the floor. Richwine was also elegantly dressed. Dexter Diggs, seated at the center, wore the jodhpurs and shooting jacket popular with directors at the time. Except for Richwine and Diggs, most of those in the picture looked impossibly young.

'Who's that?' Horn pointed to a tall, striking young woman next to Rose, her head inclined toward her and one arm around her neck. She wore tailored slacks and a silk blouse. But even as he asked, he recognized her.

'That's Dolores Winter,' Richwine said appreciatively. 'A friend of Rose, which is quite obvious here. She stopped by the set that day, as I recall. Some of us didn't even know her at the time. A beauty, wasn't she? And now she's become quite the movie star. I hadn't seen her for all these years until just a while ago, when she called me, quite out of the blue. She and that strapping husband of hers popped over here one day and took me out for a very enjoyable lunch.'

Horn was about to ask if Richwine could recall anything about her from that earlier period when his eyes strayed to another face in the photo. At the end of the line on the right stood a petite young woman, also in costume. She seemed little more than a girl, younger even than Rose, with a face and smile that Horn recognized immediately. It was Tess Shockley.

'Do you remember her?' Horn asked, pointing.

'Of course,' Richwine said somberly. 'Poor thing. She had a small part in the film. At the time, I'm sorry to say, she was not someone to whom I paid much attention. I'd give anything if she had not been in this house that awful night.'

As if looking for a reason to change the subject, his hands moved over some of the other items on the desktop, and his face brightened somewhat. 'This was taken on the set. It is, I believe, the best picture of Rose.'

Horn picked up the black-and-white photo. Dramatically lit, with deep shadows and bright highlights, it was a close-up of her profile by candlelight.

'I lie there in bed, oblivious,' Richwine said in a deep story-teller's voice. 'My sweet daughter stands over me, intent on murder. But then she spies the image of her dead, sainted mother, and her heart melts. My worthless carcass is spared.' He chuckled.

'Beautiful here, isn't she? It was part of Dexter's artistry with the camera, but also something that came from within the woman. They talk about inner beauty. I think we're being allowed a glimpse of it here. She seems to glow . . . I marvel at the way the light illuminates her cheek and her brow, almost as if all of it were outlined in silver.'

'I know.' Horn studied the picture for a few more seconds, then replaced it.

They sat down. Richwine took a deep breath, preparing to resume his story, when Horn broke in.

'Were you in love with her?'

'Good Lord, no. I was far too old for her. We even joked about that. I suppose I had a kind of older man's affection for her – who would not? But she was involved with someone at the time, and I chose to be noble about it. So I cast myself as the uncle who would joke with her and be available for gossip and conversation and confidences, and who would always protect her secrets. I think she treasured our friendship. I certainly did.'

'The secrets. What did she tell you?'

'I know what you want to hear. The scandalous details. She had been having an affair with Dexter Diggs—'

'I know about that. And also that Dex was becoming involved with Tess.'

227

'Oh? I'm beginning to doubt that I know anything useful to you, Mr Horn.' Richwine sounded almost regretful.

'Let me decide that. Please go on.'

'She also confided in me that she was trying to end another kind of relationship. Someone had attached himself to her, she said. It was becoming uncomfortable for her, and she was looking for the kindest way to end it.'

'She was a busy girl. Did she name that other person?'

'No. In fact, she seemed to go to great pains to protect his identity. I was given the impression that revealing the relationship would have caused the man great pain.'

'Because he was married?'

'Possibly, but she was quite willing to tell me about Dexter Diggs, who was most definitely married. No, this may have been something else. All I know is, she was very secretive about the whole thing. I never found out who the man was.'

'Anyway, you were talking about Dex.'

'Oh, yes. Rose was distraught over her breakup with him. He, it appeared, had taken a fancy to Miss Shockley, who was playing Rose's maid. Sometime near the end of filming, Dexter had told Rose of his new infatuation and that he and Rose were finished.'

'The way I heard it, he told her he really loved his wife,' Horn muttered. 'However you look at it, he was lying to somebody.'

'I suppose,' Richwine said.

'Tell me about the party. Rose was here, and Lombard, and Tess. Also Dex, I believe. Who else?'

'Scores of people,' Richwine said, shaking his head. 'They came and went. Some left before midnight. Many I recognized, many I greeted. Some were acquaintances, friends, others were faces familiar to me. But many others were totally unknown.'

'Give me some names you remember.'

'Oh, let me see. Clara Bow was here, with some football player. Even among this crowd, she caused a stir. Adolph Zukor and his wife—'

'Who was he?'

'You obviously don't know your Hollywood history. Mr Zukor

was head of the company that eventually became Paramount Pictures. They left fairly early in the evening, as I recall. Many mid-level people from various studios were here – producers, directors, screenwriters. A politician or two. I'm afraid I've forgotten most of the names.'

'Was there a guest list?'

'I never saw it. Jay Lombard and Rose handled the invitations. But even if I had it here, it wouldn't take into account those who came as part of an entourage, and others who were simply uninvited. We turned away no one that night, as long as they were well dressed.'

'Tell me about what happened in the bedroom.'

Richwine paused, thinking. He laid his head on the back of the chair and closed his eyes. 'It was about two o'clock in the morning,' he began. 'Rose found me in the dining room with some guests. She looked . . . odd. Almost feverish. She was wrapped in something – a heavy coat. I thought it strange. She looked as if she were going out, which made no sense. She caught my eye, said nothing, but I went to her. She said she had been looking for Jay Lombard. She whispered to me that I should follow her. Upstairs, she took me to the bedroom to the left of the landing. The door was closed. Inside, it was dark. We closed the door, and I turned on the light.'

Eyes still closed, Richwine swallowed heavily, causing his Adam's apple to bob dramatically. 'There on the bed was a young woman, naked. She had . . . there was a substantial amount of blood around her thighs. She was very pale. I remember the contrast, the darkness of the blood and the crimson coverlet on which she lay, and the paleness of her skin. She appeared dead. Then I saw she was breathing very shallowly. I approached the bed, and then I recognized her. It was Tess.'

'How well did you know her?'

'Not extremely well, but as fellow workers, you might say. We had had a few scenes together in the film and had spoken a few times. I thought her a lovely girl, very sweet, very interested in improving herself. Studious, almost. And, of course, I knew of her involvement with our director.'

'Was anyone else in the room? A man?'

'No.'

'Did you see anyone leave the room just before you went in?'

'No.'

'What happened next?'

'Well . . . there was some incoherent talk between Rose and myself. I naturally asked her what had happened, and she was evasive. She was insistent that we get help for Tess, but equally insistent that we not cause a stir. Without either of us being specific, I think I understood that Rose was at some risk over this, and that if I were not discreet . . . In other words, her fate depended to some extent on my behavior.'

'Did you think she was responsible?'

'I knew she had done something. When her wrap fell open in the front, I saw that her dress was dark with blood, almost as much as . . . But I didn't know exactly what. I think I instructed my mind not to go down that particular path, if you know what I mean. I thought the world of Rose and would not have wanted to cause her harm in any way. I asked her what I should do, and she said, "Go find Jay." That is what I did. Jay Lombard came to the bedroom, and he and Rose closeted themselves for a few minutes while I waited outside. Then they emerged, and it appeared they had a plan.

'Earlier in the evening, someone had removed the house fuses, cutting all the lights for about half an hour. Now I did the same. There was much screaming laughter, as before. While the house was dark, the three of us wrapped Tess in a sheet and carried her down the back stairs and out to Jay Lombard's car. He seemed to be in charge by then. Rose was almost in shock, and I was . . . I'm sorry to say, I was being amenable to whatever they wanted to do. As I said, my main thought was to protect Rose. We drove to the nearest hospital. The emergency entrance was quiet. We laid her by the door, and Lombard blew his horn several times. Then we left.'

He exhaled loudly and opened his eyes but didn't otherwise move. For a minute, the only sounds were of Richwine's heavy breathing and the distant noise of street traffic.

'That was it,' he said finally. 'The last time I saw Rose for many years. I was so horrified by the events of that night . . . It was as if, by mutual consent, we had decided that we wanted to close that chapter in both our lives. I never sought to contact her; she never sought me either.

'Years went by, and then one day she called. As I told you last night, she seemed in obvious need, and I found her a room at Rook House. We resumed our friendship, without speaking of what had separated us. Then, one night, we had dinner, and she brought up the subject. She told me she was tired of carrying around the guilt over Tess's death. She intended to go to the police and tell them what she had done. She wanted to warn me. But at the same time, she said she knew her responsibility was far greater than mine, and she didn't plan to incriminate me in any way. I was very grateful to her for that.'

'Did she ever tell you exactly what happened in the bedroom?'

'No, and I never asked. How could I?'

'Over the years, were you ever in touch with Jay Lombard?'

'Oh, yes. Even when I had lost track of Rose, he seemed eager to stay in contact with me, although we had never really been friends. He would call periodically and invite me to dinner. That sinister companion of his would always drive us.'

'When was the last time you saw him?'

'Oh, it was a couple of months ago, I think. We dined at the Hotel Bel-Air. He seemed somewhat agitated, which was unusual for him. He quickly brought up the subject of Tess and the party. He seemed to need my reassurances that I had no intention of ever talking about it to anyone.' He looked rueful. 'A pledge that I kept until today.'

Horn briefly described the letters Rose sent to Tess's parents. 'She told them that someone else was responsible for the murder too. Did she ever—'

'No. She named no one else.'

'Not even Dex?'

When the other man didn't respond, Horn pressed on. 'You

231

were good friends with him, but you haven't spoken to him in years,' he said. 'I think I can guess why.'

'No need to guess,' Richwine said, the melancholy now plain in his voice and his sagging features. 'I suspected him.'

'Why?'

'Perhaps because he seemed to be the cause of so much intrigue and unhappiness. Deceiving his wife, then throwing over Rose to take up with still another young woman. As much as I respected him professionally, I had only contempt for his personal behavior. Whatever Rose said about those events, both then and in the future, I always guessed that someone else had been involved along with her, someone capable of more violence. I have no reason to think Dexter would have deliberately sought to harm Tess, but considering all the outrageous behavior that took place in my house that night, one can easily imagine a scenario in which three people, inflamed by drugs and recklessness, may have lost control, with tragic results.'

Horn thought that over. He imagined a scene of three-way sex, orchestrated by Rose, that got out of hand. It was surprisingly plausible.

'In one of her letters, Rose mentioned an unidentified man being in the room, but she said nothing about Dex,' he said.

'My dear boy, wasn't that typical of her? She was protecting everyone but herself.' His eyes looked beyond Horn, beyond even the room where they sat. 'The guilt was too much for her,' he said. 'In some way I don't understand, it brought about her death. I should have tried to help her. If I had, she might be alive today.'

'You shouldn't think that.' Horn rose from his chair and stretched his arms overhead to work out the stiffness. 'I appreciate what you've told me,' he said. 'I'll see myself out.' Then he remembered something. 'Cassie said she saw you standing outside the rooming house one night, looking up at her window.'

'Yes. Well, it wasn't always her window,' Richwine said. 'I don't believe I need anyone's permission to look at it.'

'No, I suppose you don't. Is it all right if I go upstairs and have a look at the bedroom? I won't be long.'

'Go ahead,' Richwine said. 'Forgive me if I don't accompany you.'

He took the stairs up to the second floor, then turned and walked the short distance to the only bedroom at the left of the landing. He opened the door and flipped the light switch.

It was an ordinary bedroom, although it looked long disused, and the window curtains were drawn against the sunlight. The double bed, an old-fashioned four-poster with a canopy, was covered by what appeared to be a handmade crocheted spread that had once been white but was now a mottled ivory. The carpet and furnishings were worn, and everything sat under a layer of dust. Horn wondered if anyone had slept there in years.

He stared at the bed for a moment, imagining things he could only half see. Then he turned out the light and left.

Downstairs, his host had not moved. 'Thank you. I'll leave now,' Horn said. 'I think you should be real careful, Mr Richwine. Don't tell Jay Lombard or anybody else about our talk. Whoever killed Rose may be looking at anyone who had a connection to that night.'

Richwine's eyes were closed once again. 'I'm so tired,' he said with a faint smile. 'I'm not sure I really care.'

It was a little after ten in the morning when he left the house. He drove down to Wilshire and pulled in at the first cafe he spotted. Inside, he sat at a lunch counter and tore through an order of eggs, sausage, and toast, along with several cups of coffee. Then he asked for the biggest cinnamon bun in the glass display case.

The cafe had a phone booth just inside the door. Horn took his coffee cup and cigarette inside. He started to call Rook House, then remembered that Cassie had worked most of the night and would no doubt be asleep. She would be interested in the gray man's revelations, but he could report to her later.

He dialed the Diggses' number. Sometimes, he knew, location shoots ran over schedule, and he wanted to make sure that Dex

233

was still expected home that evening. Evelyn assured him that such was the case. 'We'll look for you around nine,' she said.

He was about to say goodbye when she spoke up. 'Oh, I have a message for you. Dolores Winter called earlier this morning.'

'Uh-huh?'

'She sounded agitated. Said she couldn't reach you at home and needed to see you.'

He thought about how tired he was. More than anything, he wanted to drive home and sleep for a while. 'I don't know if I can—'

'She said right away. And if you'd heard her voice, you'd know she meant it.'

'All right. Did she say where?'

'She said to tell you she'll be at the studio all day. And that she'd leave word at the gate.'

Leaving the cafe, Horn took Highland north into Hollywood and turned east on Melrose. Many who had known Rose, he reflected, had reason to feel guilt over her death. He certainly did, and Cassie as well. Quinn was going through some kind of torment. And now Alden Richwine. He wondered what was going through the mind of Dexter Diggs. And Jay Lombard. And Dolores Winter. And he wondered if any of those had been the one who knotted the cord around Rose's neck and strangled her to death on her bed, watching as she died.

On the radio, the Ink Spots were weaving their way through 'The Gypsy'. He had always enjoyed the song's mellow, soothing harmonies. Now he also responded to its message. Somewhere, the lyrics said, was a mysterious lady with the power to read your palm and tell you the direction your life would take. He needed the truth, and he wasn't totally confident of the fortune-telling powers of Ruby Renfrew, the Detroit Firecracker.

In his exhaustion, his mind churned over the dark visions thrown up by Alden Richwine's recollections. By the time the truth was fully known about that New Year's Eve, Rose was sure to be tainted by it in some way. Possibly Dex, too. The knowledge saddened him.

But he had acquired one good thing that morning, and he

took it out of a compartment in his memory and turned it over like a shiny new penny. It was the photo of Rose taken on the set of her last silent film. For too long now, he had carried with him the mental picture of her features twisted and made ugly by death. Now he had something to replace it with – a radiant image of a face at peace and transformed by love, its cheek and brow etched in silver.

Chapter Twenty-One

Medallion Pictures, Horn's old studio, was part of what movie people called Poverty Row, where studios churned out B-movies on limited budgets. He had never been on the Magnum Arts Studios lot, one of the landmarks of Hollywood. Although many of the big studios such as MGM and Warners were located in relatively unglamorous places such as Culver City and Burbank, Hollywood still boasted two of the giants, Paramount and Magnum Arts, anchoring opposite ends of Melrose Avenue.

He turned in at the main gate and stopped at the guard shack. As promised, his name was on the guard's list. The man handed him a visitor's pass and waved him through. 'Sound Stage Nine,' he said. 'I'll let them know you're coming. You can park just beyond the building.'

Horn drove along the road that took him past the elephantine sound stages. Along the way, he passed workers wheeling pieces of scenery and extras garbed for various productions. In one building, a warehouse-size door was open, and beyond it he glimpsed the bustle of a set under construction. He marveled at the enormity of the place. Back in the days when he was welcome at any studio, he had once visited the sprawling Metro-Goldwyn-Mayer to see a friend. MagArts, as this place was familiarly known, was easily as big as MGM and just as impressive.

He found the lot and parked the Ford. At the entrance to Sound Stage Nine was mounted a sign: *Yukon Queen Wardrobe Tests. Do Not Enter When Red Light Is On*. The light was on. He rapped lightly and heard a voice say, 'Come on in.'

As he stood inside in the relative darkness, he became aware

236

of a man sitting nearby on a folding chair. It was Lewis De Loach, Dolores Winter's husband. Ex-husband, he corrected himself.

'Hello,' De Loach called out. 'Come have a seat.' Horn went over and sat in a chair next to him. 'We were hoping you'd come by,' De Loach said, sticking out his hand without getting up. He wore rumpled khakis and a loud Hawaiian shirt, tail out, and he sat forward in the chair as if he were not quite comfortable. 'Doll's about to take a break. I'll walk you over in a minute.'

About fifty feet away, beyond a clutter of set construction, Horn could see the edge of a brightly lit area. 'She hates wardrobe tests,' De Loach said lightly. 'And make-up. And rehearsing. And everything that precedes the real thing. Once the camera starts rolling, she says, she takes a deep breath and says to herself: *Finally*.'

'I remember it that way too,' Horn said. 'Even though make-up, wardrobe, and all the rest took about five minutes where I worked.'

As he spoke, his eyes adjusted to the low light, and he noticed that De Loach's left arm, which was tucked protectively into his side, was covered by a plaster cast from wrist to elbow. He could also make out a brilliant shiner that was starting to spread its dark colors around the other man's left eye.

'What happened to you?'

De Loach shrugged, wincing slightly. 'Something strange. What happened to your face?'

'Nothing important.'

'It must be going around,' De Loach said wryly. 'Well, I'll let Doll tell you about it. If she wants to.'

'All right.'

'I was a little disdainful of your studio the other day,' De Loach said. 'Didn't mean to sound so prissy.'

'Don't mention it,' Horn said. 'I know what kind of work we turned out, and I don't go around bragging about it. To me, it was just a job.' *Bullshit*, he thought. *Every time you gave some kid your autograph and he gave you that hero-worshiping look, you thought you were hot stuff, didn't you?*

'I've had a little career trouble lately,' De Loach said. 'Nothing

237

too serious. But that was the reason I may have sounded a bit condescending. It wasn't your studio or your work I was commenting on – I've never seen any of your movies, although I'd like to. I was really thinking of Ben Greene and the other holier-than-thou bastards here at Magnum Arts who wouldn't know talent if it punched them in the nose. Which I came close to doing a couple of times.'

'Any problem in particular?'

'Creative differences,' De Loach said. 'I'm creative, and they're different.' He looked eager to change the subject.

'Actually, when you think about it, the western is important to us,' he said. 'It's our national epic, and the cowboy is our epic hero, the way Odysseus was to the Greeks and Roland to the French and Arthur to the English.' He laughed. 'Now I'm sounding like a screenwriter. I made my reputation with romances and drawing room comedies, and they never asked me to do anything else. But someday I'd like to try a western, something with a truly big theme. An uncomplicatedly heroic character.'

'I'm afraid you're too late,' Horn said. 'The kind of western I made is dead or dying. The ones coming along are all about characters with problems.'

De Loach sighed and made a face. 'Damn,' he said with a rueful grin. 'I'm always too late.' He looked over to the set area, where the bright lights had gone out. 'We can go now.' He got up slowly, bracing himself on the arm of the chair. As they walked into the cavernous interior, he limped slightly.

They passed an array of sets done in different styles and motifs, in various stages of being dismantled. Off to one side was a green and lovely garden with an ivy-clad stone fountain at its center. The fountain – which Horn could now see was not stone but papier-mâché – was draped in electrical cords, and resting on its rim was an empty Nesbitt's orange soda bottle and a partially eaten sandwich on wax paper, the remnants of a crew member's lunch.

'Here we are,' De Loach said. 'I know she wanted to see you, but I'll ask you to try not to stay too long. When you see her, you'll know why.' He walked away, still limping.

The wardrobe tests were being conducted on a small, gaudily decorated set that could have been a room in a fancy hotel, gambling hall, or bordello around the turn of the century. Nearby huddled a group of technicians, talking quietly and occasionally glancing toward the set and its only occupant, Dolores Winter. She wore an ostentatious but elegant off-the-shoulder gown in forest green, its waist nipped in severely, with matching high-heeled, lace-up ankle boots. Her hair was swept up in an elaborate, pillowy style, and she sat on what appeared to be a burgundy velvet love seat, knees spread ungracefully, head in her hands.

She looked up when Horn rapped his knuckles on the frame of the big thirty-five millimeter camera. At first she seemed to hardly recognize him. Her pale green eyes were rimmed with exhaustion or the residue of tears, or both.

'I told them all to get lost,' she said in a voice that almost cracked. 'No more tests for this little birdie today.' She sighed, straightening up. ' "You shoot the way I look, it'll break the camera." That's what I told them.'

'What's wrong?' He went over to stand by her. 'What happened to Lewis?'

'Oh, God.' She compressed her lips into a thin line, as if to squeeze some kind of resolve into herself. 'Someone tried to kill him.'

'When? Where?' He quickly sat down beside her.

'Last night. He'd been out with friends and came in late, sometime after midnight. Someone was waiting for him in the garage. Came up behind him when he got out of his car, started choking him, with a rope or something—'

'Choking him,' Horn muttered, almost to himself. *The way Rose died*.

'But Lewis fought. He's very strong, and he wouldn't give up.' Her voice caught for an instant, but she went on. 'They slammed into things. Two of Lewis's ribs were broken, and his left arm, and he kept fighting. I heard the noise, and came out. It was almost totally dark, but I could make out which man was which. I began screaming, hoping someone would come. I grabbed at the other man, tried to scratch him, hit him. I think it was the screams that finally made him stop. He turned around, swung his fist at me, and then he was gone.'

'Did he hurt you?'

For the first time, she laughed, but there was no mirth in the sound. 'Nothing they can't hide or cover with make-up.' She laid an index finger lightly on her left cheekbone. 'A very dainty bruise here, which you can't see. And this.' Half turning her back to him, she carefully parted her auburn hair at the crown of her head. He saw a small shaved spot covered by a circular bandage. 'Two stitches,' she said. 'When he hit me, my head hit the wall. I told the doc that if his work showed up on camera, I'd be back to pay him a visit with the same kitchen knife I used to kill my sad-sack boyfriend in *Storm Fury*. He laughed, because he thought I didn't mean it.'

'Did you get enough of a look—'

'No. I've gone over it in my head so many times. Just a figure in the dark. Not tall or short. Lewis told the police that since the man cut off his air at the beginning, he was never able to think very clearly during the fight. All he could really tell them was that the man was stronger than average. That's not much help, is it?'

'He's lucky,' Horn said. 'You both are.'

'I showed up at work this morning like a good trouper,' she said. 'I held myself together through make-up and fittings and all that shit. Then, when we got out here and they turned on all those lights, I just . . . I couldn't do it. All I could think about was that Lewis could be dead now. That, and . . .' She looked squarely at him, and he saw fear written plainly on her features. In the short time he had known her, he had seen nothing like it on her face.

'And what?'

'And I knew who he had really come for last night.' She shuddered, even though the heat of the tall lights still lingered on the set, and leaned forward, hugging herself. Fifty feet away, Horn could see the crew members waiting, talking in low voices. She seemed oblivious to them.

240

'He came for me. He thought he'd kill Lewis, take his keys, and unlock the door that leads from the garage to the house. And then he would come for me.' She shook her head, as if reluctant to recognize the truth. 'This is about Rose. I know it. Ever since you and I talked, I've had this feeling that I was on someone's list.'

'Why?'

She looked around, as if coming out of a trance. 'You got a cigarette?' she asked abruptly.

'Sure. If you've got the patience.' He pulled out the pouch of Bull Durham and reached for his papers, but she made a face.

'No offense, but I can't stand those. Come on.' She got up and led him past the camera and lights and off the set. As they passed the small group of workers, a man holding a clipboard stepped forward.

'Miss Winter—'

'Ronnie, I told you I'm not working today.' Her voice sounded close to breaking, like a tightly strung wire. 'I'm going home in a few minutes. Call Ben Greene if you want. I don't give a good goddam.'

She led him out of the huge building and down a narrow lane behind it. Lined up there was a series of small portable dressing rooms, each about ten feet square. Her name, Horn noted, was on the door to the first, and that of her co-star on the adjacent one.

'Bob Taylor's not here until next week,' she said, opening the door to her room. 'Mr Gorgeous Puss. I'm glad he didn't see me like this.' Inside was an elaborate, lighted dressing table, a rack that held clothing on hangers, a comfortable sofa and two chairs. She pulled a chair close to the sofa and indicated that he should sit. 'Excuse me while I swoon, like one of those Victorian ladies,' she said as she lay down. 'They had good reason. You ever try taking a deep breath in one of these fucking waist pinchers?'

'Not lately.'

'Poor Lewis,' she said. 'This is my fault, and he's been so sweet about it. Most people think he's frivolous – I admit I did too – but he has a kind of strength I never even knew about. I think I

241

actually look at him differently now. Oh, I'm not sorry we divorced. We were never cut out to be a married couple. But I've learned that he's a good man to have around in a crisis. He probably saved my life, just by being there.'

'Anybody would be proud to hear that kind of compliment.'

'My cigarettes are on the dressing table,' she said. 'Get one for me, and help yourself.'

Laying his fedora on the table, he found her pack of Pall Malls, lit one for each of them, and positioned the ashtray on the edge of the table where she could reach it. She took her first drag and exhaled mightily, sending a gust of smoke to the ceiling. 'That's better.' She looked at him more closely. 'You never told me what happened to your face. Did somebody try to kill you too?'

'I was in a fight.'

'Really?' She seemed almost amused. 'I suppose some actors are like that, wanting to be as tough in real life as they are in—'

'Believe me, I don't think I'm particularly tough,' he said. 'But let's talk about you. Why would you be on somebody's list?'

Her eyes followed the path of the smoke. She plucked a shred of tobacco from her lower lip. She shook her head, like a little girl refusing to recite a poem.

'Come on, Doll. Did you talk to the police?'

'Yes. That detective, Coby. He chews on his matchstick and looks at me out of the corner of his eye. Loves to talk about movie stars.'

'What does he think?'

'About last night? That we were very lucky. He suggested we hire some of the studio cops to moonlight at our place, watch things for a while. It was a good idea, and we've already done it.'

'Good. Did you tell him all this might be tied in with Rose?'

She nodded. 'But I didn't tell him why. I'll probably have to, though, sooner or later.'

'Tell me.'

'First you tell me something. Tell me I've got a good reason to confide in you,' she said, her voice rising. 'Nothing happened to Lewis or me until you started poking around, asking questions about Rose. If the police are such idiots, tell me why I should expect any more from you.' She was agitated, waving the hand with the cigarette as she lay there, making swirls of smoke in the air.

'Correct me if I'm wrong, but you called me over here.'

'Well, maybe I've changed my mind.'

'Do you want me to leave?'

'I want you to listen to me, goddamn it. You seem honest enough, but God knows you're not much to look at. You dress like somebody on a park bench. You used to ride a horse like some kind of a hero, but now you're not much more than . . .'

She trailed off, slightly out of breath from the emotion and the tightly laced corset under her gaudy dress. A look of discomfort briefly crossed her face. 'I'm sorry,' she said grimly, taking another fierce drag on her cigarette. 'I know I'm not making much sense, and it's embarrassing. I'm usually more in control. This has been a bad time.'

'That's the second or third time you've apologized to me,' he said. 'You better not make a habit of it.'

'Don't worry about that. I'm just trying to understand why—'

'Why you should have any confidence in me.'

She nodded.

'Well, I suppose I could start by saying that I want to find out who killed Rose more than I want anything else. I may not do this for a living. Hell, I may not be much to look at, either. But wanting it this bad gives me an edge over anybody who's not going to try as hard as I am. Maybe even the police.'

She nodded again, giving him a half-smile through the smoke. Her expression seemed to suggest he had said what she wanted to hear.

To put her more at ease, he told her about the events of the past two days. He described how Cassie had helped him locate Alden Richwine, and he related the old man's revelations. He summarized the contents of Rose's letters, but he held back specifics, largely out of consideration for Rose herself.

Dolores Winter lay facing him, head propped on one arm, fascinated. When he had finished, she asked, 'Which room was it?'

'Hmm?'

'Which bedroom in that house? Where was it, exactly?'

'Top of the stairs and to the left. It's the only one on that side. Why do you want to know?'

Her expression grew focused, almost hard. She looked like a woman preparing to defend herself against attack.

'I was there.'

'What?'

'In the house. During the party.'

He could think of nothing to say.

'Lewis and I could have died last night. You asked why I think it's connected to Rose. Now I'm telling you: because I was there, in that man's house, the night it all happened.'

'So you've been lying to me. Now who's the one who needs to worry about confidence?'

'All right. But I had a reason to lie. Listen, John Ray, I was never in that bedroom. I was just one of a crowd of indulgent, half-crazy people who saw in the new year that night and then went home. I'm not even sure I knew who Tess Shockley was, so even if she was later mentioned in the paper, I wouldn't have thought anything of it. There were hundreds of parties all over Los Angeles that night, and some of them were every bit as grand as the one we're talking about. But when you came to my house and asked about Rose, I vaguely remembered being at one particular New Year's Eve party where she was the hostess. I decided on the spot not to admit it, because . . . Look, in this business we're all trained to avoid scandal. So I lied. I did it without thinking.'

She looked his way, as if for reassurance, but found none. 'Now I know there's no point. I'm in this whether I want to be or not. And, God help me, so is Lewis, who didn't deserve what happened to him. I'm not keeping any more secrets – from you or the police.'

'Good for you.'

'You don't sound convinced. In fact, you sound sarcastic. Maybe I should just say to hell with you, Mister Hotshot Hopalong Cowboy Whoever-You-Used-to-Be.'

'You've got me confused with somebody else. He made more money than I did. Dressed better, too.'

'I mean it. I'm not answerable to you. If I lied, it was because I thought it was necessary. I'm telling you the truth now. Take it or leave it.'

'All right, Doll. Don't shoot. I'm on your side.'

She lay breathing hard, defiance in her eyes. After a few seconds, her expression softened a bit. 'I don't know why I called you,' she said quietly.

'Maybe it's because you think you can trust me. And you need somebody to trust.'

'Maybe.' She shook her head. 'I'd better not be wrong about you.'

He shook a fresh cigarette out of her pack, lit it, and handed it to her. 'What can you tell me about the party?' he asked. 'Who invited you?'

'I'm not sure I remember,' she said. 'It may have been Rose. Probably was, since I was just a nobody, and she would have been one of the few people I knew there. She looked gorgeous that night.'

'Who else do you remember?'

'Well . . .' She lay back, resting her head on one arm. 'The usual sprinkling of famous faces. The really big names usually didn't stay for long, since they would move on to their own private parties. I remember Alden vividly. I even spoke to him for a few seconds. He cut quite a figure back then, with his accent and his manners. The ladies loved him. And Rose's boyfriend, the gangster. I don't know if he was really a gangster or not, but part of the fun back then was the company you kept. Booze was illegal, so if you drank, you rubbed elbows with some very shady people. He was that type, you know? A little dangerous.'

He nodded. 'Rose called him the same thing.'

'And Dexter Diggs was there. He didn't really know me back then. I was just another girl in a fringed dress – red, if I remember right. But he was well known at the time, and I certainly recognized him.'

245

'Did you see him with Rose?'

She closed her eyes just as Alden Richwine had done, straining for the memory. 'This is where it gets a little fuzzy,' she said. 'I blame the champagne. I always loved champagne, and I recall they were serving something French and very good that night. I do remember one thing, a kind of isolated memory. Rose came up to Dexter in the main room. I was standing near the bandstand, and the band was taking a break. He looked very elegant in his tux, I remember. She spoke to him urgently, as if trying to get him to do something. Not long after that, he followed her upstairs.'

'Upstairs? You're sure?'

'I'm sure of that much, in spite of the champagne. I lost sight of them when they reached the top of the stairs, so I don't know where they went.' She opened her eyes and smiled briefly. 'Considering how long ago it was and the shape I was in, I'm surprised I remember anything.' Her face took on a pained look. She swallowed hard and rubbed at her eyes, smearing her make-up. 'Dammit,' she said fiercely. 'I'm thinking of Lewis again, and what happened to him. If he'd been killed last night, how could I ever . . .'

She rolled away from him, presenting her back. 'Would you help me loosen this, and the damn thing under it?' she asked, indicating the back of the dress. 'I can't breathe.'

He leaned toward her. She smelled of talcum. Her bare shoulders looked strong, but their coloring appeared unnaturally dark. He rubbed his fingertips lightly across her back, leaving a white streak as the make-up came off on his fingers. She laughed, causing her back to ripple.

'You've exposed the real me,' she said. 'Undo me, please.'

He fumbled at the top of the dress, and moved over to sit sideways on the sofa next to her. As he worked at the dress, her left hand clutched at his knee. 'I need something from you,' she said.

'What is that?'

'I think you know.' She sounded out of breath. 'I knew the day you came to my house.'

'Doll, somebody could walk in on us. I'm not sure this is a good—'

'No one will bother us. Lewis will make sure of that.'

The image of Lewis De Loach standing watch outside troubled him, but it was quickly replaced by the woman lying before him. The temperature inside the small dressing room had risen, and the white streak across her back looked like nakedness itself.

He worked at the dress, cursing the costumer who had made it. Underneath, he could feel the rigid corset, another barrier. 'These are all hooks and eyes,' he said. 'I don't know if I can—'

'Tear them,' she said. 'I promise I won't send you a bill for the repairs.' Her hand gripped his knee so hard it hurt. 'Go on. Tear them.'

Chapter Twenty-Two

On the way home, he dialed up the local news on the car radio and heard a man talking about more rain, a lot of it, expected tomorrow. But as he swung down onto Pacific Coast Highway, the afternoon sky was a white-flecked, placid blue crowned with a pale, wintry sun. Something might be coming, he thought, but it was still far out to sea.

At the cabin, he acknowledged his exhaustion and lay down for a while, but could not sleep. Doll Winter was still much with him – the look and feel and scent of her, the rustle of her ornate gown on the sofa as they both fought to get her out of it, her soft cries moments later. She was not like Rose, he thought. Not at all like Rose. But, as Mad Crow would say, a lot of woman. Even though she did not strike him as the clinging type, he now felt responsible for her in a new way, and the thought both pleased and troubled him. He was not unaccustomed to making space for a woman in his life. But it didn't feel right now.

Despite his tiredness, he got up, changed into his heavy, high-topped shoes, and went out to work on the drainage ditch. Laboring with the hand saw, he managed to cut several more branches off the formidable limb blocking the canal, but it remained mired in mud as if frozen in concrete. If he didn't manage to muscle it out by tomorrow, he knew, the rain could overflow the ditch and wash out much of the road. Harry Flye, his landlord, would not be pleased.

Back at the cabin, he left his muddy shoes on the porch, went inside, and drew a hot bath. He soaked for a while, sipping occasionally from a glass of Evan Williams on the floor by the tub. As he was toweling off, the phone rang.

'I used to have this fantasy,' the voice said. 'He'd come riding over the hill and sweep me up onto the saddle behind him, and we'd ride away. And he'd cross one leg around that thing – what do you call it?'

'The saddle horn.'

'That's right. And he'd strum on his guitar and sing something about love amid the cactuses, and I'd hang onto him very tight, lean my head against him, and hum along.' She paused. 'Does any of this sound workable?'

'Doll, I don't sing. Don't play the guitar either.'

'You weren't one of those cowboys?'

'Nope.'

'Damn. I want my money back, then.' He heard the sound of ice in a glass.

'I'm sorry.'

'Well, I just called to say I'm still tingling. And I know this isn't going to work out, because before long you'll find out just how shallow I am.' She sounded slightly drunk, but pleasantly so. 'And it'll be over, and no hard feelings. But I want you to know I intend to enjoy it as long as it lasts. And I don't know exactly how to put this without sounding maudlin, but I'm grateful to Rose for bringing us together.'

'Me too.'

'That's all I wanted to say.' She hung up.

Wrapping the towel around him, he opened a can of beef stew, heated it, and ate it out of the pot while he stood at the kitchen counter. He actually liked eating while standing up. Mad Crow had seen him do it once and could not resist ribbing him about it. 'Hey, cowboy,' he had said. 'Afraid your horse is going to run off if you sit down and eat with the gentry?'

After eating, he checked the door and windows, then positioned the Colt within reach, lay on the sofa and closed his eyes.

When he awoke, it was fully dark and almost time to leave for Dex's place. As he was getting dressed, the phone rang again.

'Hi.' It was Cassie.

'Hello, there.'

'I've just got a minute and thought I'd call, see how it went with Alden this morning.'

Background noise threatened to wash out her words. He could hear people's voices and vehicles. Then the loud, electric drone of a male voice intoning the name *Bakersfield*.

'I'm at the Greyhound depot,' she said, speaking up. 'Waiting for a fare. He asked for me.' A hint of pride in her voice.

'I didn't know you were so popular. You being new at this, and all.'

'You'd be surprised. I hand out a lot of cards, and sometimes people call later and say they want me. One of the other cabbies told me that's where the good money is – the regulars. This guy tonight wants to go up to Santa Barbara, and he's even offered to pay for gas. Maybe I'll overnight up there. They say Santa Barbara's a pretty town.'

'You'll like it.' He told her about his conversation with Alden Richwine. When he had finished, she was silent for a moment, allowing the noise of the terminal to take over. The amplified voice came on again, speaking in well-shaped tones of San Luis Obispo, San Francisco, and other locales with mellifluous Spanish names.

'Have you talked to Madge, like I asked you?'

'No,' he said, slightly irritated. 'What's this about, anyway?'

'I'm not sure. The other night, we went down to Broadway, to that bar where we all saw Rose. Madge and I got to talking. We've talked a lot, but she was always sober. That night, though, I was buying, and she put it away. Seagram's Five Crown on the rocks, one after the other. She can really hold it.'

'Cassie . . .'

'All right. Just listen. After her third or fourth, she started going on about Rose. And after a while, I could tell that the words weren't Madge's words, they were Rose's.'

'What do you mean?'

'Do you know about Madge's memory?'

'You mean the tricks she can do? Yeah. She brags about them.'

'They're not really tricks. She can stash lots of things in her head, and then pull them out whenever she wants to. In the bar, what she pulled out was something Rose told her. The two of them had been drinking in that same place one time, and being there with me reminded her of it. I got the feeling that she had wanted to hide what Rose told her because it scared her. Only the Five Crown brought it out.'

'What did she say?' He checked his watch.

Cassie gave a sigh of frustration. 'You know how drunks talk. It didn't make sense to me. I wasn't exactly sober myself, and I wasn't in any shape to take notes. All I know is, she – Rose, I mean – was talking about a party.'

'A party.' He leaned forward on the couch, straining to pick up her words against the noise of the bus station.

'And Tess. And something about the lights. And a man in a tux. The next morning, I cussed myself out for not being able to pay better attention, maybe write it down. I asked Madge about it, and she looked at me like I was crazy. Said she didn't know what I was talking about.'

'I'm going to have to leave pretty soon, Cassie. But I'll have a talk with Madge.'

'I've got a feeling we're getting close,' she said. 'To whoever killed Rose. Do you feel it too?'

'Maybe,' he said, suddenly uncomfortable with her heightened interest. 'But this is the time we need to be careful.' He felt the need to tell her about the attack on Doll and her ex-husband. 'You've been a big help. I don't want to see you take chances. Just last night—'

'I think that's him,' she said suddenly.

'Who?'

'My fare. Got to go.' He heard the low roar of the terminal for a second longer, then nothing.

On the way over to Dex's place, he worried about Cassie, but he could think of no way to rein her in. Horn had met her father only briefly and recalled him as a moody white man who liked to drink. Now he knew the man was a wife-beater as well. He had no idea how many of the father's dark impulses had been

251

passed on to the daughter. But she certainly seemed to share a few of her uncle's traits. At times, especially in his younger days, Joseph Mad Crow had shown a rash and intemperate side, gaining a reputation as a fist fighter and bar brawler. Pushed the wrong way, Cassie sometimes behaved as if she were his image.

Those worries, however, soon gave way to more immediate ones. He was going to ask Dex some hard and inescapable questions tonight, and he did not look forward to the answers.

It was only a little past eight-thirty when he pulled up in front of the Diggses' house and parked. Dex's Plymouth was in the driveway. Deciding to give them time to finish dinner, he rolled a smoke and made himself as comfortable as he could. With the ignition on auxiliary, he tried to find a listenable station, but most of the dial was infected with a low level of static. *Must be that storm they're talking about*, he thought, *the one that's taking so long to show up*. He managed to hear a few minutes' worth of Jack Benny, but Rochester had most of the punch lines, and his throaty delivery was no match for the static. Dialing up a clear-channel station in New Orleans, he landed in the middle of what promised to be an endless commercial for Hadacol. He turned off the radio.

Why'd they call Hadacol Hadacol? he asked himself as he got out of the car, resurrecting a stale joke that always seemed good for a groan.

I don't know. Why?

Hadacol it something.

He knocked, and Evelyn opened the front door. Although she smiled, she didn't offer her cheek. Instead, she said, 'He's running some film. You can join him.' She went back to the kitchen, which emitted the lingering, pleasant scent of a home-cooked meal.

Horn opened the inside door to the garage and was met with the loud hum of the projector. Dex sat in one of the two soft chairs, wreathed in cigarette smoke, face sharply illuminated by the reflected light off the screen that covered most of the garage door.

'Hey there,' Dex said. 'Come on in.'

As Horn stepped carefully inside and took the vacant seat, he looked up and was startled to see his own face, giant-size, staring back at him from the screen. The man on the screen wore a Stetson and his lips moved, but no words were heard.

'I've got the soundtrack turned off,' Dex said. 'I like it better this way sometimes. Just me and the pictures.' His right hand rested on the arm of the chair, wrapped around a tumbler half full of dark liquid and a couple of ice cubes.

'What the hell are you watching?'

'*Smoke on the Mountain*. Don't you recognize it?'

'Not hardly. I haven't seen it since it came out. Haven't you got a better way to spend your time than to watch—' He gestured at his own face.

'That big galoot? With all respect to his dramatic skills, he's not the reason I'm watching.'

The scene cut to a closeup of Rose Galen. She was listening, wordlessly and intently, to Sierra Lane. Then her lips moved, and her face grew animated with the conviction of what she was saying.

'Most of the hacks at that Grade B movie factory don't even bother to set up for closeups,' Diggs said, as if to himself. His words sounded lazy, almost slurred. 'But it makes a difference.'

The scene cut to a two-shot of Horn and his leading lady. Then, a moment later, a long shot showed them quickly mounting their horses and riding off. In the next shot, the camera tracked them as they rode at a gallop, both leaning forward urgently in the saddle, their weight on the stirrups, hands loose on the reins, wind in their faces.

Fearful of what his father would no doubt call the sin of pride, Horn had always tried to avoid admiring anything about his own movies. But he felt his breath catch at the image on the screen. First his eyes were drawn to Raincloud, the gray horse carrying the cowboy, running at top speed as effortlessly as dust swirling across the prairie. Although it had been years, he could almost feel the horse under him. Then, before he could reject it, a memory pushed its way into his mind – the feel of the pistol bucking under his hand as he snuffed out the horse's life in an act of mercy that hurt to this day. He focused on the two figures on horseback. One was a man he barely recognized. The other was Rose Galen, in the last film she would ever make.

'For somebody who started out barely knowing one end of a horse from another, she caught on pretty fast, didn't she?' Horn said.

'She did indeed.' Diggs got up, switched off the projector, and turned on the overhead garage light, then reclaimed his seat. 'Offer you anything?' he asked, tilting his glass suggestively.

'No, thanks.' Horn cleared his throat noisily. 'I need to talk to you.'

'That's what the good wife said.' Diggs looked at him expectantly.

'When we saw Doll Winter at the cemetery, she said Rose had told her a lot of things about you. For a while, I didn't know what she meant, but I've learned a lot since then.'

'What have you learned, John Ray?' Diggs spoke casually, as if nothing could surprise him tonight.

'That you and Rose were involved, during the time you worked on that silent picture together. Then you told her it was over, and you said Evelyn was the reason. But that was apparently a lie, because you were taking up right then with Tess Shockley. You were pretty busy, weren't you?'

After giving Diggs a second to respond to his sarcasm, Horn went on. 'Before long, Tess was dead. She died in a house owned by Alden Richwine, a man you know.' Horn saw Diggs' expression change briefly and almost imperceptibly at those words. 'We've known for a while that Rose had something to do with that. But now I know she wasn't the only one. It seems just the other day you were asking me if Rose and I had anything going on back when the three of us worked together. I have to laugh at that now—'

'I was curious, John Ray,' Diggs cut in. 'I wanted to know about the two of you, but I wasn't ready to talk about myself. I'm sorry I wasn't more truthful with you.'

'More truthful? Dex, you either held back the truth or you flat-out lied to me about almost everything.'

'I told you how Tess died. I helped you find out about that.'

'Yeah. Maybe you knew it was only a matter of time before I got to that on my own, and you wanted to look helpful. But you left out a few details about Tess. For one, you were screwing her. Hell, you never even bothered to mention that she had a part in the last movie you made with Rose. You lied to me, Dex.'

Diggs knocked back another inch of his drink. His movements were becoming slower and more exaggerated. 'Sorry to hurt your feelings,' he said harshly. 'I had the best reason in the world to keep secrets, even from you. It was Evelyn. I was married to her when all this happened. She's the best thing in my life, always has been. I had never been tempted to run around behind her back before then, and not since then. But during this time we're talking about, I was so goddam full of myself . . . I was the all-powerful director, the creator. Beautiful women looked to me for guidance, Rose and Tess admired me, and I . . . Hell, I loved it. In terms of the work I was doing and the way I felt about myself, you could say that was the high point of my life back then. Before this stuff started getting to me.' He waggled his glass gently, sloshing the liquid inside.

'Evelyn was smart enough to know that something was going on back then, but we've never talked about it. We don't need to. I've been a good husband to her ever since. If people learned about any of this, she'd be hurt. I wouldn't want that to happen.'

'Dex, listen to me.' Horn leaned forward, hands on his knees, trying to make eye contact. 'We're not just talking about you protecting your wife's reputation. This goes way beyond that. When Tess died, you were there in that house. You were seen with Rose, not long before . . . it happened. You went upstairs with her.'

'I didn't.'

'Another lie?'

'No. I never went upstairs. She asked me to go with her.

Wanted to talk about us, she said. I told her it was too late. I may have been a little drunk—'

'Everybody in that house was drunk, Dex, on one thing or another. They all use the same excuse.'

'All I mean is I may have been too abrupt with her. Unkind, even. At any rate, I didn't go with her.'

'I don't believe you.'

Diggs's shrug turned into an elaborate gesture that almost upset his whisky glass. 'Go to hell, then. You know, I've always given you credit for being pretty smart. Not book-educated, mind you, and not always good at making choices for yourself. But basically smart. If you can't hear the truth when it's spoken, then I've been wrong about you.'

'Not as wrong as I've been about you. Did you kill Rose?'

Diggs showed no surprise. Maybe it was the whisky. He sat in silence for a while. Then: 'I've never known anyone like Rose. Evelyn is the love of my life, but Rose . . . was unforgettable. I always regretted losing touch with her. And now that I know how she was living these last few years, I feel I should have done something. No, sir, I did not kill her,' he said, glaring now at Horn, emphasizing each word. 'I said the same thing to a certain ill-mannered police detective who came calling just the other day. Seems I'm on a list of suspects. I told him the truth, and he went on his way.'

Horn wondered at how quickly his old affection for Dexter Diggs could have vanished. 'I owe you a lot, Dex. For a while there, you were almost like a father. But if you killed Rose, I'll make sure you pay for it.'

Diggs made no answer.

'This is where you tell me I'm too old to go running around like the avenging cowboy of the plains, trying to do the sheriff's job,' Horn said. 'Alden Richwine told me that, except he used better words.'

He sat back in his chair, coolly studying the other man. 'You've always been strong,' he mused. 'And you're still pretty fit. You could have easily killed Rose. I just wonder if you could

256

have taken on Lewis De Loach. Were you really out of town that night, like Evelyn said?'

'The policeman mentioned that incident too. I think you're unbalanced.'

'Never mind. I wouldn't expect you to tell me the truth anyway. One more question, and then I'll leave you alone. Let's say you did go into that bedroom. Why would you want to kill Tess? Were you already dumping her, the way you did Rose? Did she threaten to tell Evelyn? And did Rose offer to help you—'

'Get out.'

As Horn closed the door behind him, he heard the whirr of the projector start up again.

Outside, he was about to start the engine when he saw Evelyn open the front door and come down the walkway. Leaning over toward the passenger side, he cranked down the window.

She wore a faded housecoat and slippers, and a scarf over what appeared to be a head full of curlers.

'Dex is sitting in there alone, drinking,' she said. 'You've made him very unhappy. Why would you want to do that?'

'I don't want to make anyone unhappy, Evelyn. I just want to find out who killed Rose Galen.'

'What does that have to do with him?'

Be careful, he told himself. 'I just don't think he's telling me everything he knows.'

She hugged herself and shivered. 'You'd better go inside,' he said.

'Not until you talk to me.'

'Then please get in the car.' He reached over and opened the door for her, and she slid inside, still hugging herself. He started the engine and opened the heater vent.

She sat staring straight ahead. After a moment's silence, she said, 'I knew about Rose, of course.'

'He said you had probably guessed.'

'It didn't take much guessing,' she said, laughing lightly, her face taut. 'They were obvious about it. Later, I heard there was someone else. No name, just someone else. All of it hurt me,

257

naturally. But somehow I knew Dex would never stray far and would always come back. And I was right.'

A faint snatch of music from the radio. It was Doris Day singing 'Sentimental Journey' in front of Les Brown's band. 'I always loved that,' Evelyn said, turning up the volume a little. 'It was one of those songs that told us the war was over and things would be getting better. Remember?'

'I remember the promise,' he said. 'Not that it happened that way, at least not for everybody.'

'Maybe part of that's your own fault,' she said. 'Have you forgotten how close the two of you used to be? How much Dex helped you when you were starting out? How many meals you ate at our house? Do you remember how many people were ready to turn their backs on you when you went to prison? Dex wasn't one of those. He couldn't hire you, naturally, because he would have lost his own job. But it bothered him, and he never stopped being your friend.'

'Evelyn—'

'So here you come, stirring things up. How can he help you find out who killed Rose?'

'I asked him about a New Year's Eve party twenty years ago,' he said, picking his words carefully. 'Rose was there, and so was he. A young woman named Tess Shockley, who worked on the film with Rose that Dex directed, died that night.'

'I vaguely remember that,' Evelyn said. 'It was in the papers, and Dex mentioned it to me.'

'Well, Rose may have had something to do with it.'

'No. That's hard to believe, John Ray.'

'I know, but I'm afraid it's true.'

'I'm sure Dex would help if he could. This party you asked him about – was it the one at Alden Richwine's house?'

'As a matter of fact, it was.'

'Why don't you ask me about it? I was there.'

He stared at her.

'Why do you look so surprised? Even though we were having problems then, he did take me out like a proper husband from time to time, you know. If he'd left me at home to go traipsing off to some glittering New Year's Eve party at a lovely house, I'd have killed him, and he knew it. And this particular one . . . well, it just may have been the most glamorous thing I ever attended. Naturally I'm going to remember it.'

Horn exhaled loudly. 'Evelyn, you're amazing. All right, tell me. What do you remember about that night?'

'Lots of gorgeous, well-dressed people,' she said almost in a sing-song voice. 'With too much money, too much bootleg hooch, too much everything. It was probably the wildest party I've ever attended. You know, Dex and I are not typical Holly-wood people. Although we drink, we've never touched drugs of any kind. Well, actually I smoked a reefer once, but it only made me sleepy.'

'What happened that night?'

'The lights went out a couple of times,' she said. 'We knew people were sneaking off and making love in some of the bed-rooms and behind the curtains on the stairway. It was all very naughty. I stood around taking dainty sips from a glass of forbidden champagne, feeling like Dorothy from Kansas. Only Oz turned out to be this depraved place, a place where I enjoyed visiting but couldn't imagine living.'

'Do you remember Rose being there?'

'Of course. It was her party. I hated her, but I had the satisfaction of knowing that Dex had brought me and that she was going to see us together. At the same time I admired her for her talent, and I thought she was the most beautiful creature there that night. With the possible exception of Dolores Winter.'

'Did you know Doll then?'

'Not really. Just from a distance. Years later, of course, she became well known. But even then she had a touch of the outrageous. You couldn't have missed her in that crowd—'

'This is important,' he broke in. 'Were you and Dex together all night?'

'Let me think.' She paused. 'No. There were times when I was in the ladies' room, or he in the men's room. There were the times when the lights were out—'

'How long would you guess?'

'The lights? Maybe ten minutes, fifteen. I don't know. We could have gotten separated during those times.'

'Did you ever see him with Rose?'

'Just once, I think. She came over to him while I was standing nearby talking to someone else. Naturally I watched them. She spoke to him with a lot of urgency. Then she left.'

'He didn't go with her?'

'No.'

'Are you sure?'

She looked at him curiously, then suspiciously. Her expression hardened. 'Someone told you otherwise?' When he didn't answer, she said, 'Whoever did is lying. Ask yourself why they would lie about that.'

'All right.' He leaned over and kissed her. 'Thanks, Evelyn.' She got out and walked toward her front door without looking back, her slippers making soft slapping sounds on the walkway.

Dolores Winter had told a different story, and this new version may have been nothing more than a wife's effort to shield her husband. It was likely that someone was lying, and not just about this. In trying to reconstruct the life and death of Rose Galen, he felt like a weaver trying to repair a damaged tapestry. Of the threads offered to him, some belonged there and some did not. If he wove with the proper threads, he would know everything. If not, the finished picture would be a lie.

It was eleven-thirty when he pulled up in front of the cabin. Once he was inside, the accumulated exhaustion of the past two days caught up with him, and he was asleep almost as soon as he lay down.

He dreamed lazily, and once he saw Cassie's cab drift by the cabin in slow motion. She drove with one arm hanging out the window, cap pushed back, a cigarette dangling from her lips. He called out to her, a gentle gibe about girl cabbies who try too hard to look the part, knowing she'd grin in response and come back with something even better. But she didn't hear him, and moments later the cab had drifted by. He couldn't see who rode in the back.

He slept until long past daybreak, had a bath and a lazy break-fast. He was in the bathroom shaving when the phone rang. It was Luther Coby.

'Something you need to know,' the detective said in a curiously pinched voice. Horn stood by the sofa holding the phone as Coby talked. Suddenly his legs felt strangely unsupportive, so he sat down, still listening, asking a few short questions. When they had hung up, he finished shaving and got dressed, taking care to put on a clean shirt and, for a change, a tie.

He drove downtown. On the way there, he thought of driving straight to Mad Crow's house, or at least stopping to call him. But he decided against either move. He feared what the Indian would do.

It was best, Horn reasoned, if he went to look at Cassie first.

Chapter Twenty-Three

When Horn asked the guard on duty at the Hall of Justice for Luther Coby, the detective appeared within a minute. He had a tentative air about him, and he greeted Horn in a low voice and guarded manner that did not fit him well.

Neither man spoke as they took an elevator down to the basement, where a sign painted on the wall said: *Office of the Los Angeles County Coroner*, and below that the line *County Morgue*. Coby led him down a brightly lit corridor to a pair of swinging, glass-paneled doors. From beyond them came a heavy medical smell that Horn guessed was embalming fluid. Just this side of the doors stood three gurneys lined up alongside the wall on the right, each bearing a form covered by a sheet.

Without hesitating, Coby went to the nearest gurney and, standing to the side, lifted the corner of the sheet.

For an instant, Horn felt almost sick with relief. It was not Cassie. Dear God. A mistake.

Then the full weight of it hit him. Of course it was Cassie, only a Cassie he had never seen. In death, she had become Rose. The same nightmarish bulge of the eyes, dark congestion of blood swelling the face, grotesque twist of the mouth with just the tip of the tongue visible between the teeth. Finally, in a needless confirmation, he noted the dark ponytail and the shiny black bow tie, torn slightly askew by the violence of the act that had left her this way.

Horn stepped back, fixing his eyes on a chipped patch of plaster on the wall. 'It's her,' he said. 'But you already know that.'

'We'll need . . .' Coby began, but Horn was walking away. He headed almost blindly down the corridor, finally finding a men's room. It was empty. He shut himself in a stall.

Tears did not come easily to him. They had not come after Rose's death – that was a time of shock and numbness, followed by overwhelming sadness. But Cassie's death was an even greater waste, and it touched him in a deeper way, leaving him overwhelmed. The tears arrived uninvited, like unwelcome visitors, and afterward he leaned over a wash basin and washed his face. Finally he rejoined Coby in the corridor.

They went upstairs to the lobby, where they stood amid a swirl of people – lawyers and defendants and uniformed police and court employees, all seeming in a hurry, their steps echoing off the marble floor. 'We'll need a next of kin,' Coby said in a voice that in another man would have sounded polite. 'Mad Crow, I imagine. Calling you was a courtesy. I thought you'd want to know.'

'I appreciate it,' Horn said. 'Let me call Joseph. I'd rather be the one to tell him.' *What a lie*, he thought. *The last thing on this earth I want to do. But I've got no choice.* 'I told you a lot of things the last time I saw you,' Horn said, trying to keep the tension out of his voice. 'Now you can tell me. What do you know about this?'

'Not as much as I'd like,' Coby said, pulling a match out of a vest pocket and sticking the wooden end between his teeth. 'I just happened to see an item on the ticker when I came in and recognized the name. A truck driver on his way up the coast pulled onto the shoulder to take a nap about three o'clock this morning, almost ran over a parked cab. Got out to take a look and found her dead in the front seat. Coroner will probably get to the autopsy this afternoon, but it's pretty obvious she was strangled.'

'The way Rose died.'

Coby nodded. His expression grew glum and resigned, as if he knew what was coming next.

'You thought Cassie did it,' Horn said. 'You told me so.'

'I thought she might have.'

'You're so fucking smart. What do you think now?'

'Don't talk to me like that,' Coby said, but there was little threat in his tone. 'All right. Looks like I was wrong. About that, anyway.'

'You sure as hell were. Wrong about me, too, but you haven't gotten around to finding that out yet. What else do you know?'

'Her dispatcher said a man called yesterday afternoon and asked for her by name, said he wanted her to pick him up at the bus station at eight o'clock for a trip up to Santa Barbara. Gave the name Carson. That's all they said. She told them she would probably overnight up there and come back today.'

She would have liked Santa Barbara.

'Whoever did it must have had a car waiting, or expected somebody to come along and pick him up,' Coby went on. The detective was staring at him almost warily, as if he could see the fury slowly building up inside him. 'One other thing,' he said.

'What?'

'He didn't get away clean. She stuck him with that knife she wore. It was still in her hand when they found her. There was blood on the blade, and a little on the seat. And it wasn't hers.'

'Good,' Horn said. 'I hope the son of a bitch bleeds to death. No, wait. I hope he doesn't bleed to death. And I find him.'

'All right,' Coby said. 'That's my job. Maybe you can call her uncle now. Before you do, have you found out anything else you want to tell me?'

Horn thought for a moment. He saw no reason to go over the slow accumulation of details over the past few days, especially since they had yet to yield a definitive answer. But there was one thing he should mention, in fairness to Dex.

'You've talked to Dexter Diggs,' he said.

'The movie director? Yeah, Dolores Winter told me about him when I asked her about Rose Galen and the old days. She told me he and Rose had a thing back then. I asked him a few questions, and I'll have more. Why?'

'He's an old friend of mine,' Horn said. 'I didn't like the idea, but for a while he was at the top of my own list. Now it looks like I was wrong, because I was with him last night at the time Cassie would have been driving up the coast.'

Coby pondered that, his face motionless, the matchstick wiggling between his lips in a little tongue-propelled dance of its own. 'He still could have killed Rose Galen. Could have gone after the actress and her husband too, for that matter.'

'That doesn't make any sense. All three of those things are connected. They have to be.'

'All right. I'll just throw out one thing I know about Mister Diggs. My partner Stiles has been checking in every now and then with Jay Lombard, just to see what he's up to. He has an expensive apartment at the Biltmore. The desk clerk there is good with faces, especially movie faces. According to him, your old friend Diggs went to see Lombard there two days ago. They had dinner in the dining room along with Lombard's big friend, and then the three of them went up to Lombard's rooms. Diggs left about an hour later.'

'What?'

'You look surprised.'

'I am surprised. I didn't know—'

'They even knew each other? You wouldn't expect them to, I guess. They don't seem to have a lot in common, except for Rose Galen.'

And a certain party, Horn thought. *On a certain New Year's Eve.*

'I hope you have a look at Willie Apples, for one,' Horn said. 'Just to see if—'

'He's got any wounds? You mean besides the ones we already know about. Sounds like you're trying to tell me my job again.'

After the detective had boarded the elevator, Horn stood there in the lobby amid the swirl of people. Dex and Lombard. What could they have to talk about? Murder? Or just covering up a murder?

He was full of an unfocused anger that was primed to fly in all directions, at all targets. Anger at Dex first of all, for not telling him he knew Jay Lombard. Dex had been at home while Cassie was driving her killer north along the coast highway. But could he still be connected to the two murders? If he knew Lombard and secretly met with him, the answer was yes.

Anger at Luther Coby for not caring enough. At Dolores

Winter and Evelyn Diggs, for telling contradictory stories about an important event. At Emory Quinn, for retreating into an alcoholic haze when he might be useful.

And, of course, anger at himself. For having to find out key information from a lazy, uncommitted policeman rather than on his own. For being as far away as ever from finding Rose's killer.

And for his own cowardice over what he now had to do.

Horn went to a phone booth in the lobby, pulled a nickel from his pocket, and dialed the Indian's number.

When they stepped off the elevator that had brought them up from the basement, Mad Crow walked blindly across the crowded lobby and pushed through the glass doors. Horn followed him. The Indian covered the sidewalk in big strides. Every now and then, someone coming his way would catch sight of his expression and quickly step aside.

As they reached the white Cadillac in the parking lot, Mad Crow stopped. He looked around, as if suddenly without purpose. A chill wind swept over Bunker Hill and down through the marble buildings of the civic center, while layers of clouds overhead stacked up in shades ranging from pearl to slate gray. One of the clouds spat a single drop of rain onto the Caddy's windshield, then another on the front seat.

'You need to get the top up,' Horn said.

'Hmm?'

'The top. It's raining.'

Mad Crow raised the top, and together they secured it with the twin handles over the sun visors. Then they sat inside, while the spitting grew to a dribble, then a drizzle, then a steady rain that thudded on the canvas with a sound that was almost comforting. The promised Pacific storm had arrived.

Mad Crow punched in the cigarette lighter. He flipped a Lucky out of his pack, offered one to Horn, then lit both with the glowing end of the lighter.

'She never got her tooth fixed,' he said slowly.

'I didn't know that.' Horn started to say he was sorry to hear it, but the tooth seemed such a small thing now.

'You know who killed her?'

'No. I wish I did.'

'But you've got ideas.'

'Lots of ideas. Too many, really.'

For the next twenty minutes Horn talked. Occasionally he paused, looking for a thread, or backtracked when he remembered something important. When he got to the subject of his visit with Doll Winter at the studio, he held back the extent of their sudden involvement with each other. He wasn't sure why. He didn't know if Mad Crow would envy him or deride him for being so easily detoured. At any rate, he had no time for self-examination. He finished up with the conversation he had had with Coby a little over an hour earlier.

Then he stopped, listening to the rain. He watched Mad Crow's hands tighten and loosen on the steering wheel, the knuckles whitening and then regaining color with each motion. Mad Crow's moods, he knew, ranged from near-placidity to explosiveness. He had no doubt of the direction his friend was moving in now.

'What about Dex?' Mad Crow asked.

'Maybe,' Horn said. 'We don't know for sure yet.'

'There's also this guy Quinn. Something not quite right about him. But I think I'm partial to Lombard and his cuddly friend. The wrestler. He likes strangleholds, doesn't he?'

'He sure does. Used one on you and me both.'

'If Rose had something on Lombard about the party, he could have decided to keep her quiet. And, being well connected, maybe he also could have—'

'Found out how busy Cassie had been lately, how much she was beginning to find out,' Horn finished for him.

'Then it wouldn't have been much of a stretch for him to call Yellow Cab, ask for Cassie, and send Willie Apples to keep the appointment.'

'What are you going to do?'

'Got arrangements to make,' Mad Crow mumbled, stubbing out his cigarette in the ashtray. 'I need to call her mother. As soon as I get up the courage.'

'That's not what I meant. Are you going to do anything crazy?'

'Do you mean am I going to saddle up and go wring somebody's neck? No. Like you said, it's too early for that. What I think I'll do right this minute is find myself a cozy little hideaway, preferably with good music on the jukebox, and get quietly drunk. Any objection?'

' 'Course not.'

'Thought I might head down to that place where we had our nice chat with Vitalis. Remember? The place where we saw Rose. Just a few blocks away, down on Broadway, right?'

'The Green Light.'

'That's it.'

'I'm not sure they'd be open yet.'

'I'll wait.'

'Listen . . .' Horn felt an urgent need to keep Mad Crow out of public places. Reacting to Cassie's death, he might indeed simply get quietly drunk. On the other hand, Los Angeles was littered with bars where Mad Crow, in his rowdier days, had begun getting quietly drunk and concluded things in quite another manner.

'I've got a better idea,' Horn said. 'Follow me on out to my place. We'll stock up on food and refreshments along the way, build a fire when we get there, settle in. I'll even put Rose Maddox on the phonograph. What do you say?'

'I don't like leaving her in that fucking basement,' Mad Crow said, his voice barely a whisper.

'There's nothing we can do for her now. Come on.'

The fire was going well. After playing its stack of records, the phonograph was quiet. They had put away the steak sandwiches and the beers and had started in on the fifth of Cobbs Creek. Horn drank sparingly, but Mad Crow worked his glass like a man trying to slake a thirst.

'Not going to bury her here,' he said moodily, looking into the fire. 'This shitty town wasn't for her. It messed her up, and then it killed her.'

'She was getting a handle on this place,' Horn said. 'She surprised me, the way she picked things up. You could be proud of her, Indian. Not just the cab driving, making money. But she had given herself something to do – finding out who killed Rose. Nobody asked her to do that. And she was making progress. I just feel bad that . . .' He couldn't bring himself to say the rest.

But Mad Crow knew. 'You feel responsible, huh? Like you steered her in that direction, even if you didn't mean to. Well, don't. I've got just as much reason to feel that way. Who do you think got her that cabby's job?'

They sat in silence for a while, listening to the crackling of the fire and the whish of rain and wind in the trees outside. Mad Crow, sitting on the couch, finished another glass of whisky, then closed his eyes. He seemed to sway a little where he sat.

Horn pushed lightly on his shoulder and tilted Mad Crow over onto his side, then lifted his feet onto the couch. He heard a mutter.

'What?'

'Carson. The one who asked for Cassie.'

'That's right. We know he wouldn't use his real—'

'Kit Carson,' Mad Crow said heavily, eyes closed. 'The scout. And Indian killer. Our man has a sense of humor.'

Soon he slept.

Horn could not. His head buzzed with unanswered questions, all against the backdrop of Cassie's face in death. He needed to purge his brain of the questions and, especially, the face.

Putting on his work shoes and an old pair of dungarees, he donned his GI poncho, grabbed the pick and shovel, and headed out to the drainage ditch. The runoff from uphill was backing up around the impacted branch and beginning to course out onto the road in three separate, mud-colored streams. The road would be washed out by tonight.

He dug away at the mud around the big branch with the pick, then scooped it out with the shovel as the rain patted loudly on the hood of his poncho. He worked that way for half an hour, grunting loudly, muscles burning, his vision narrowed by the hood, his hearing obscured by the pattering of the rain.

Then, a different sound, a loud *thwack*. Looking up, he saw Mad Crow attacking the limb with the ax from the tool shed, swinging it in great arcs, hardly waiting for the blade to bite in before wrenching it loose and raising it again. Unprotected by any rain gear, Mad Crow was already soaked. Something approaching madness lit up his eyes.

'*Not* going to *bury* her *here*,' he grunted in time to the strokes as wood chips flew. '*Some*place in the *hills* back *home*.' Pause. Swing. '*Not* in this *shit*-eating *town*.'

He swung the ax several more times, grunting loudly with each blow, then stood there, gasping. Horn took the ax from him and began working on the same spot. The chips flew in a new rhythm. When he tired, they swapped again, and soon the giant limb was mortally wounded. A final dozen strokes from Mad Crow, and the ax rang on concrete. The limb was severed. 'Come on,' Mad Crow wheezed.

He bent and grabbed the upper half of the limb at the severed place. Horn took hold of the stump of a smaller branch nearby. Together, sloshing in mud, they wrenched the limb free of the mud and muck and flung it sideways out of the ditch. Then, with twin shouts, they repeated the labor on the other one. A few minutes' work with the shovel, and now the ditch was open. The muddy water coursed freely down it, through the culvert under the road, and into the creek bed beyond. Miles away, it would darken the ocean.

'We done good, huh?' Mad Crow gasped, chest heaving. He raised his face to the sky. His eyes glistened, and Horn could not tell if it was solely from the rain.

'Let's get inside,' he said. They crossed the road and made it to the cabin. It was late afternoon, and the storm was hastening the darkness. On the porch, Horn wrenched off his boots, then his pants and shirt, and went inside, where he found two blankets. He wrapped himself in one and held out the other. Mad Crow, still out in the rain at the foot of the steps, had already shucked off all his clothes, which lay there in a muddy puddle. His ponytail, black and shiny, was plastered to his right shoulder. Coming up the steps, he took the blanket and folded it around himself.

'You making some kind of bad joke?' he said. 'Handing me a blanket? I feel *deep*ly in*sul*ted.' His words were slow and slurred, and Horn noted that Mad Crow was now finally, seriously drunk.

'Shut up,' he said. 'It's not a Navajo or anything like that. It's a plain old Montgomery Ward.'

Inside, Mad Crow fell onto the couch. 'Got to call her mother,' he said faintly. For a while he breathed deeply, then he muttered something.

'What?'

'I thought maybe she killed Rose.'

'No, you didn't.'

'Just for a little while,' he mumbled. 'Crossed my mind, is all. Thought, hey, that wild-ass niece of mine, she could have gotten crazy enough, drunk enough . . . You know what I mean?'

'No.'

'I thought bad of her. And I got to live with that.'

'Go to sleep, Indian.'

Finally, Mad Crow slept. Horn fed the fire until it blazed busily again. He locked the door, found the Colt, checked the cylinder, and positioned the gun close by. Then, blanket around him, he lay down in front of the fire and closed his eyes.

When he awoke, it was just before first light. Mad Crow was gone. So were one of Horn's shirts and a pair of trousers.

A scrap of paper by the telephone bore a three-word note in the Indian's scrawl.

I'M IN NOW.

Chapter Twenty-Four

Over the next two days the storm exhausted itself, leaving the ground sodden and the sky sullen, the color of a dirty slate roof. Spare raindrops fell like stragglers behind an army that had moved on to other battles.

On the morning of the second day, Horn and Mad Crow stood on a train platform at Union Station as workers unloaded a large wooden crate from a baggage cart and muscled it aboard a freight car. The crate was seven feet long and four feet high and deep, its contents handwritten on a bill of lading stapled to the lid, along with its destination – South Dakota. They waited around, smoking and saying little, until the train pulled out in a hiss of steam. Then they walked to their cars in the lot.

'What's on your mind?' Mad Crow asked.

Horn realized he'd been staring up at the terminal's tower, a modern-day reproduction of a mission bell tower from the days of Spanish California.

'Oh, just remembered Cassie picked me up here once. It was that time we came out to your place and rode for a while.'

'I remember. That was a good day,' Mad Crow said. 'Listen, what are you up to right now?'

'Well, I thought I'd ask a certain lady out for a drink,' Horn said. Cassie had left him with a piece of unfinished business. It might be nothing, but he needed to see if there was anything in Madge's memory that could help him.

'I'm going to the club early,' Mad Crow said. 'Got a few things to do, paperwork and such. You, uh, want to come along?'

Mad Crow wasn't the sort who asked for favors. Horn could

see his friend wanted company. 'Sure,' he said. 'The lady can wait. I'll follow you.'

It was still well shy of noon, hours before opening time, when they pulled into the asphalt lot in front of the casino, but some of the boys were already busy out front.

'What's going on?' Horn asked.

'They're taking down the sign,' Mad Crow said. 'It's the Mick's idea. Neon is too flashy, he says. Draws too much attention. We want to fit in quietly, he says. So we're putting up something artistic and hand-painted—' He pointed to an eight-foot-square sign leaning against the front of the building. Done in reds and greens, it bore the words *Mad Crow Casino* in a lettering that appeared to be formed out of sticks. 'Look Indian enough to you?'

'Don't ask me.'

Mickey Cohen, Mad Crow's silent but intrusive partner, was an expert in such matters as publicity and dealing with the law. Mad Crow quietly loathed the man. But after his last partner met a violent end and authorities in this unincorporated corner of Los Angeles County began demanding more of a slice under the table, Mad Crow reluctantly allowed the gangster to buy a minority interest in the casino. So far, it had been an arrangement that benefited both sides. But Horn knew Cohen, and he wondered how long the honeymoon would last.

They climbed the stairs to Mad Crow's office, where they looked down on the bar and poker tables. Lula, Mad Crow's secretary, brought in some ledgers and a handful of phone messages and placed them in front of him. Her eyes looked red and swollen, her appearance in somber contrast to the perky cowgirl outfit she wore. 'I'm just so sorry about Cassie,' she said. 'Everybody is.'

'Thanks, Sugar,' he said as she left. Thumbing quickly through the message slips, he separated one and handed it to Horn. 'This one's for you.'

The note read *Miss Turner called*, followed by a number in the FItzroy telephone exchange. The Wilshire district. Alden Richwine might have an FI number, but he certainly wasn't a Miss Turner.

'Mind if I use this?' Horn asked, picking up the receiver and dialing the number.

'Hello.' A well-bred voice. He couldn't quite place it. Then he did.

'I'm trying to reach Miss Turner,' he said. 'Miss Peggy Jean Turner, I believe it is.'

'This is she,' said Eden Lamont. 'You have a good memory.'

'Just for certain things. Now you take Peggy Jean Turner – how am I going to forget a name like that?'

'Please,' she said. 'If it were that memorable, believe me, everyone would still be calling me P.J.'

'That's even better. And think how that would look in lights.'

'I'm on a sort of errand,' she said, the banter gone from her tone. 'For Jay. I'm supposed to call and invite you to come see him.'

'Uh-huh,' he said. 'And you're doing the honors because Jay and me, we're not as close as we used to be. He's afraid I might still be peeved at him.'

'That's right. I'm supposed to invite you to come up to his apartment at the Biltmore this afternoon at three, if you're not busy . . .' Her voice trailed off, as if leaving something unsaid.

'All right. Tell him—'

'But when I spoke to you,' she said carefully, 'you told me you would rather not come up to his room. In fact, you were rather emphatic. Do you understand?'

'I think so,' he said. 'What else did I say?'

'You said it would be much better if you met in a public place. And then you thought of the pool. Do you know the pool?'

'At the Biltmore? Uh . . . Isn't it downstairs?'

'Yes. Down from the lobby. It's a very popular place. There are always people there, swimming and relaxing. So, when I realized that you couldn't be persuaded otherwise, I agreed. And we decided that you would see Jay at the pool at three.'

'Good. Do you mind if I ask why—'

'Maybe some other time.'

'All right, then. Will you be there?'

274

'It's very likely.'

'Thanks, P.J.'

He hung up. 'Who's P.J.?' Mad Crow asked.

Horn explained.

'Damn,' Mad Crow said, adding an exaggerated whistle. 'First Doll Winter, now one of the Goldwyn Girls. Ain't you the Errol Flynn?'

'I'm really something,' Horn agreed. He described the invitation from Lombard, and the unspoken warning from Eden. 'You interested?'

Mad Crow sat forward in his swivel chair, making it squeak in protest. 'I am more than interested,' he said. After days of lugubriousness, his face was now animated. Horn saw the old grin, the one that could mean anything from jollity to serious trouble. 'Remember what I said? I'm in the game. But we should go prepared.'

'No guns, Indian.'

'Of course not. You still have those brass knucks you told me about?'

'I don't walk around with them. They're at home.'

'A teddible pity,' Mad Crow said in a phony British accent. 'Here.' He opened a drawer and drew out two rolls of poker chips, tightly wrapped in paper, tossing one to Horn. 'For insurance. You like to go collecting with these sometimes, right?'

'If it's a bad neighborhood. At least poker chips won't get me arrested.'

'In these circumstances, I'd say the Biltmore is a bad neighborhood.'

They walked through the Biltmore's ornate, Spanish-revival lobby, with its high-beamed ceiling. In anticipation of their genteel surroundings, Mad Crow had changed into a dressier outfit at the club. He now wore a western-style suit of gray gabardine, the jacket adorned in muted, dark-gray embroidery around the pockets and shoulders. He had even traded in his usual fedora for a flashier Stetson in matching gray. Horn wore his usual nondescript outfit of slacks, tweed sport jacket, and hat. As they crossed the lobby, it was Mad Crow who drew the gaze of several guests. He obviously enjoyed the attention.

They took a flight of stairs down to the pool area.

The swimming pool was in a grotto of pale blue tile that covered floor, walls, and ceiling. Walls and floor and the occasional square columns were accented with more colorful hand-painted tiles that depicted Greco-Roman deities in oceanic settings. Doors led to a steam bath and exercise room. The air was still and humid, and the splashing of a few swimmers reverberated off the tiles.

There was no sign of Eden Lamont, but they quickly spotted Jay Lombard. He lay on a wooden deck chair against the wall on the opposite side of the pool. On the adjacent deck chair lay Willie Apples.

They walked around the pool and approached the two. Lombard lay with his eyes closed, his hair wet as if he had just emerged from a swim. He was wrapped in a voluminous white bathrobe. Willie Apples' jacket was draped over the back of his chair, but he was otherwise fully dressed. He raised his eyes from a comic book he held in his lap and watched them approach, expressionless except for his usual knitted brow.

Lombard heard their footsteps and opened his eyes. 'Mr Horn,' he said. His tone was wary, for he had quickly seen and recognized Horn's companion.

'Mr Lombard. You remember my friend, Joseph Mad Crow.'

'How are you doing?' Mad Crow said.

'The invitation was for you,' Lombard said to Horn.

'I know,' Horn said. 'But me and Joseph, we're doing things together these days. Hard to separate us, I guess you'd say.'

Lombard weighed this, as if confronted with a sudden change of his opponent's courtroom tactics. Then he quickly reached a decision.

'You're both welcome,' he said with a thin smile. 'Won't you have a seat?' He sat up and reached over for a small glass-topped table that stood nearby, pulling it closer. Horn and Mad Crow fetched a couple of small upright chairs and placed them by the table.

'Drink?' Lombard asked. He waved to a pool attendant. 'The bar doesn't usually deliver drinks down here, but if you're nice to the help, they'll make an exception.'

'Ginger ale would be fine for me,' Horn said.

'And me,' Mad Crow said.

'Two ginger ales for my guests,' Lombard told the attendant. 'A gin and tonic for me, and a pineapple juice for Willie.' He pulled a cigar and lighter from a pocket of his bathrobe and went through the slow ritual of lighting up. He seemed in no hurry to begin the conversation.

'Where's Eden?' Horn asked.

'She's around,' Lombard said, reclining again. His slight frame took up little space on the slatted surface of the chair. 'She may honor us with her presence later.' There was a slight edge to his voice.

'So why are we here?'

'I heard about Cassie Montag,' Lombard said. 'I know you were friends, and also that she was a relative of Mr Mad Crow. I've had my differences with both of you, but I want you to know I'm very sorry.'

'Thank you,' Horn said, glancing at Mad Crow. 'We appreciate that.'

'When we first met, you asked me about Rose Galen,' Lombard said to Horn.

'And you lied to me and turned your boy loose on me.'

'You abused my hospitality,' Lombard said mildly. 'I didn't feel I owed you the truth, and I asked Willie to make the point forcefully.'

'How's he doing, by the way?' Horn looked over toward Willie, who continued to study his comic book.

'Oh, he's fine. You're the one who looks a bit the worse for wear. Willie follows no particular rule book when he fights. He's a great improviser.'

'I'll remember that next time,' Horn said.

'Good. Willie is eager for a return match. I tell him to be patient.'

Horn surreptitiously studied Willie, looking for fresh wounds. He saw nothing obvious, but that didn't prove anything.

Mad Crow stirred in his chair. 'One of the reasons we're here,' he said, 'is to check up on old Willie. Has he had any exercise lately? Besides driving the fancy car, I mean.'

'No,' Lombard said, with some emphasis. 'He has not.'

'So, you're sorry about Cassie,' Mad Crow said. 'And you want us to know Willie has been behaving himself. Is that the reason for this get-together?'

'That, and a few other things,' Lombard said as the drinks arrived. To his left, against the wall, sat a fancy brass canister filled almost to the top with fine white sand. Pulling it slightly closer, he tapped the cigar ash off into the container. He turned to Horn. 'As I mentioned, I didn't choose to tell you everything about Rose Galen when you first approached me. I'm feeling more obliging now. What do you want to know?'

'Why don't we get right to it?' Horn said. 'Did you have her killed?'

'The direct approach. That usually goes over very well in court,' Lombard said with amusement. Then his expression turned serious. 'No, I did not. Nor Miss Montag either.'

'Somebody tried to kill Dolores Winter and her ex-husband the other night,' Horn said. 'Do you know—'

An unguarded look resembling total surprise passed over Lombard's face for a few seconds. Then he recovered. 'I don't know anything about that,' he said in a flat tone.

'Thanks for all the information,' Mad Crow said sarcastically. 'Could be God's truth, could all be bullshit.' He swigged most of his ginger ale. 'Anything else before we leave?'

'The police have been around, and you're the reason,' Lombard said to Horn, some of the politeness dissolving from his voice. 'I've nothing to be afraid of, but I won't pretend it's not an inconvenience. Whether we like each other or not shouldn't matter. My main reason for asking you here was to tell you what I can and assure you that my hands are clean. You'll either believe me or you won't.'

'All right, fair enough,' Horn said. 'Then you shouldn't mind a few questions.'

Lombard stirred his drink briskly, then gestured with the straw for Horn to go ahead.

'About twenty years ago you gave a party,' Horn began. 'It was New Year's Eve, and Alden Richwine let you use his house. Rose was your hostess. A young girl named Tess Shockley was killed there, in one of the upstairs bedrooms—' Lombard's eyes widened for an instant. Then he resumed his lawyer's face. Horn plowed ahead. 'When Tess was dying, you and Rose and Alden put her in a car and dropped her off at a hospital. For years, Rose kept it all a secret. But then she decided to tell it all, how she and another person had killed Tess. You were one of the people she talked to, not long before she was killed.'

Out of the corner of his eye, Horn saw Willie Apples lift his eyes from the comic book for a few seconds, then resume reading.

'I think Rose was murdered – or ordered killed – by the man who was in the bedroom with her at the party that night. It might have been you. It might have been Dexter Diggs, who was also a guest – and who came to see you here in the hotel just the other day. It might have been someone else. But I want you to tell me everything you can. If your hands are really clean, the police will eventually stop bothering you, and so will I.'

He paused to catch his breath. 'Talk to me, Mr Lombard. Make me glad I came to see you today.'

Lombard looked relaxed, his hands cradling his glass on his chest. He cleared his throat like a lawyer about to deliver his closing argument.

'First of all, Mr Horn, if you'd ever like a job as an investigator, I hope you'll give me a call,' he said.

'He works for me,' Mad Crow said harshly.

'Of course. Well, let me deal with your questions as best I can. First of all, I'm afraid I can be of little help to you as to the events of that New Year's Eve. I hosted a party. When something untoward occurred, I tried to render a service. Whatever I may have done that night, even if illegal, was of so little consequence that it's no longer prosecutable. If you think otherwise, you would find it impossible to prove.'

He adjusted the lapels of his bathrobe and ran his hands through his still-wet hair. 'With all that said, I can be forthcoming about some things. After several years, Rose re-established contact with me just a few months ago. She asked to see me, and we met in this very hotel. She told me she had decided to tell the truth about the events of that night—'

'Tell who?' Horn asked.

'The police. She said she had decided to speak first to me and some others as a kindness, so we wouldn't be surprised when she went to the police.'

'Exactly what was it she said she did?'

'I'm afraid she wasn't specific,' Lombard replied. 'Except to say she felt responsible for Miss Shockley's death.'

'Alone?'

'No,' Lombard said with some reluctance. He paused, weighing his words. 'She said another person was also responsible. She didn't say who.'

'You didn't ask? Weren't you curious?'

'Of course I asked. She said the confession was to be her own and not a denunciation of anyone else. I pressured her, saying the police would not give up until she told them everything.'

'And?'

'She told me she wasn't sure who the other person was,' Lombard said.

'Bullshit,' Mad Crow muttered.

'No, wait,' Horn said. 'The lights were out.' He turned back to Lombard. 'Isn't that right? The lights were out part of the time.'

'Well . . . yes. I hadn't really thought of that. But you're right. The lights went out that night, more than once. That could be what she meant.'

'Some lawyer,' Mad Crow said in disgust. 'You weren't trying very hard to get anything out of her.'

'Look, I was trying to show her some consideration,' Lombard said heatedly. 'It was an emotional moment for her. It's obvious that just speaking to me represented an enormous effort for her.

I didn't want to make it any harder than necessary. Also, I soon gathered that she was asking me if I would consider representing her, even though she had no money. Naturally, I couldn't have taken her case, because of my own involvement in the matter, however peripheral. As a lawyer, though, I could quietly give her advice, as unethical as that might have been—'

Mad Crow made a vaguely rude sound.

'It sounded to me as if she could implicate herself and another person in a capital crime, and I wanted to take my time, to be very methodical about gaining information. I was certain I would speak to her again, in my office, where I could take everything down. I was wrong. Not long after I saw her, she was dead.'

'She said she was speaking to you and some others before she went to the police,' Horn said. 'Did she name any of them?'

'Let me see . . . She said there were four – myself, Alden Richwine, Dexter Diggs, and Dolores Winter.'

'Did she mention whether she had talked to any of the others?'

'Besides myself? I got the impression that she had. Some of them, at least.'

'Did you stay in touch with Dolores Winter?'

'No,' he said. 'I didn't actually know her at the party. She was just one of the crowd. Later, of course, I became aware of her as an actress and even met her. But I didn't realize she had been at the party until Rose told me.'

'You've met her ex-husband, too,' Horn said. 'In fact, you know him pretty well, don't you?'

Lombard looked vaguely surprised. 'How did you know that?'

'A certain policeman told me.'

'Oh,' Lombard said with a slight grimace. 'Detective Coby. That's right, I helped her husband in a dispute with his studio, while they were married. That's when I met the estimable Doll Winter.'

'You stayed in touch with Alden and Dex all these years,' Horn said. 'Why? And while we're on the subject, what did you and Dex talk about when he came to see you?'

281

Lombard merely stared at him, lips pursed, as if weighing the benefits and hazards of answering.

'I know why he stayed in touch,' Mad Crow broke in impatiently. 'To make sure everybody kept his story straight. To make sure nobody got nervous and caved in. Lombard tells us whatever he did that night, he can't be prosecuted for it. I'm no lawyer, but I know the clock never runs out on a murder investigation. Maybe all three of these characters did something gruesome that night, along with Rose. And Jay Lombard, Esquire, appointed himself the drill sergeant to keep everybody in line. What do you think?'

There was some logic to that, Horn admitted. He waited for Lombard to answer.

The lawyer deposited his empty glass on the table and stretched his arms overhead. 'I think I've had enough time by the pool,' he said to Horn. 'Your friend has overstayed his welcome. I hope I was some help to you. We won't be talking again.' He jabbed the stub of his cigar into the sand.

'Bullshit,' Mad Crow said, his voice rising. 'Horse piss.' He seemed almost drunk. Mad Crow sometimes put on an act, feigned drunkenness or loss of control, the threat of violence, as a way of intimidation. Occasionally it worked.

Mad Crow placed his own glass on the table heavily, and the loud crack it made on the glass top could be heard around the pool. Several people turned to look. The white-jacketed pool attendant picked up a house telephone.

Mad Crow got up and walked over to where Willie Apples reclined. 'What's that you're reading, Willie?'

'*Plastic Man*,' Willie said, displaying the cover.

'He's great,' Mad Crow said with a chuckle. 'Turns himself into a table top, a beach ball, a fucking rubber band whenever he wants to. Can I see it?' He plucked the comic book out of Willie's hands, studied it for a second, and then tossed it over his shoulder into the pool.

'Hey,' Willie said, the crease between his eyes deepening. 'You shouldn't have done that.'

'Willie, my boy,' Mad Crow said, leaning over him, 'here's my problem. Somebody killed my niece two nights ago. Got in her cab and strangled her to death. Probably did it by putting an arm around her neck from behind, the way you tried with me once. You taken any cab rides lately, Willie?'

'Not me,' Willie said, his expression almost guileless.

'Naturally we're suspicious of the little lawyer you work for,' Mad Crow went on. 'If he told you to do something, you'd do it. For example, what would have happened if John Ray had taken him up on the invitation to come up to the hotel room today? Would he be coming down the freight elevator right now in a laundry cart? But my brain has been so busy lately, I suspect just about everybody. Dexter Diggs, for example. Now that we know he and your boss get together sometimes, that makes me suspicious too. If Mr Lombard asked you to do a favor for Dexter Diggs, would you do it?'

No answer. Mad Crow leaned in closer. 'Willie, I know you're a very tough guy. You proved it with me once, and with my friend another time. But I'm ready to take you on. Round Two. Did you know I can swim like a fish? Once I get you in that pool, I'll hold you under until you drown, I don't care how fucking strong you are, you—'

'Willie.' Lombard spoke carefully. 'Don't.' Willie Apples was breathing deeply, his forehead knotted like a wood carving, knuckles white on the arms of the lounge chair. But he didn't move.

'As long as we're making threats,' Horn said, 'let me say one more thing. If I hear anything has happened to the Anchor mission – fire, flood, or anything else – I'm going to send the police right to you. Cross my heart.'

Affecting a bored look, Lombard turned his attention to the lapels of his bathrobe.

'Come on, Indian,' Horn said. 'Let's go.' Glancing over his shoulder, he saw that the pool had emptied, the swimmers frozen in various eavesdropping positions around the sides. A man in a suit, apparently a hotel official, was talking rapidly to the pool attendant. 'We don't want to make a scene. The hotel might toss Mr Lombard out on his ear, just for attracting riff-raff like us.'

Mad Crow straightened up. 'When I'm ready,' he said. He strode over to the brass canister, faced in Lombard's direction, unzipped his trousers, fumbled with his fly, and positioned himself. 'Man, that ginger ale goes right through me,' he said with a giant sigh, never taking his eyes off Lombard's. So quiet had the pool area become, the muted splashing in the sand carried clearly through the tiled interior.

'That's better,' he said, zipping up. 'The pause that refreshes. Ten, two, and four.' He dug into his pocket, found a dime, and flipped it onto the glass-topped table. 'For the funny book,' he said.

Of the two dozen or so others around the pool, no one moved or spoke as the two men walked toward the doorway. As they passed a deck chair, Horn touched Mad Crow's elbow, and they stopped. Eden Lamont was just getting up, retrieving a large towel and draping it over her arm.

'Hello,' she said. She wore a bright yellow one-piece Jantzen and a smooth suntan. 'I saw your finale. It was very entertaining. I didn't want to interrupt, though. Jay doesn't like that. I'll go join the boys now.'

'Eden Lamont, Joseph Mad Crow,' Horn said.

'I'm sure you'll understand if I don't offer to shake hands,' she said.

For once, Mad Crow seemed at a loss for words. He just grinned.

'Thanks for what you did,' Horn said. He began to notice details about her appearance. One was a small, irregular ring around her left bicep. It looked like a tattoo in the palest blue, but it was a chain of faded bruises. And the left corner of her upper lip was slightly asymmetrical, puffy.

'Willie?' he asked, pointing to the arm.

'Jay,' she said. 'He's stronger than he looks. But I have to go join them now. Would you like to talk later?'

'If you have anything to tell me.'

'I believe I do.' She inclined her head slightly, indicating that he should step over to one of the columns, where they stood shielded from Lombard and his companion. 'No pockets in these things,' she said, reaching into the top of her swimsuit and plucking out a small, folded piece of paper. 'This is an address on Wilshire,' she said, handing it to him. 'An apartment building. I'll be in the lobby tomorrow morning between eight and eight-thirty. I won't be able to wait.'

She stepped out from behind the column, touched up her hair with one hand, and smiled in Lombard's direction. 'You'd better go now,' she said over her shoulder.

Chapter Twenty-Five

To Horn and Mad Crow, whose work and interests focused on quieter parts of the city, downtown LA was something of a novelty, a mix of sights, sounds, and smells, a place of tall buildings, jostling, well-dressed people, too many cars, honking horns, palatial movie theaters, jangling traffic signals, and trolleys that clanged and sparked. After leaving the Biltmore, they walked around until dusk, looking in the windows of stores and restaurants and at the passing parade on the sidewalk.

'Skirts getting longer,' Horn observed. 'You notice?'

'Uh-huh. And hats getting crazier.'

For dinner, they settled in at one of Horn's favorites, Cole's Buffet, in the basement of the Pacific Electric Building, for French dip sandwiches and draft beer.

Later in the evening, Horn dropped off Mad Crow at his place, then made the long drive down through the Valley and across the Santa Monica Mountains to the Pacific, where he picked up the coast highway north to Culebra Canyon. As usual after a storm, the night air was pure and cool. His headlights barely pierced the dark of the canyon road. Halfway to the cabin, he spotted a coyote frozen momentarily in the lights, staring him down, before it darted away with a flick of its scraggly tail.

Once home, he undressed quickly, pulled the Colt from under the sofa cushion, then lay down and covered himself with the blanket. His tiredness, he knew, was a combination of the sorrow of seeing off Cassie's body and the tension of the meeting with Jay Lombard. He wanted to pick through the latest bits of information, line them up for inspection. But an image of Cassie intervened. He saw her leaning out the window of her cab, cigarette dangling, looking him up and down and saying, 'What do you want?'

Then, in half-sleep, he saw a shadowy figure reach for her from the back seat, the flash of her knife blade . . .

She stuck you, didn't she, Mr Indian Killer? Was it bad? You killed her, but she managed to cut you. She was proud of her Indian side. Looks like you weren't ready for it.

There are two of us after you now. And we'll find you.

He was up early the next morning and, after shaving and cleaning up, on the road by seven-thirty.

The address Eden Lamont had given him was an eight-story building on the north side of Wilshire, its higher floors within sight of MacArthur Park, a few blocks to the east. The building was called the Buckingham. By Horn's rule of thumb, giving an apartment building a name usually signaled the intention of asking for an extra twenty bucks a month in rent.

Inside, the lobby was quiet after the hum of morning traffic on Wilshire, with a high ceiling, mirrored walls and overstuffed furniture. A uniformed doorman was behind a desk. In one of the front chairs near the window sat Eden Lamont. She wore a tailored suit, high heels, and a pillbox hat with veil wrapped around it. Beside her chair were two large suitcases, a vanity case, and a hatbox.

'Hello,' he said, walking over. 'You're all dressed up. So this is what a Goldwyn Girl looks like in the morning.'

'I'm not a Goldwyn Girl any more,' she said. A cigarette with a long ash sat unattended in an ashtray on the large table in front of her.

'Oh,' he said, uncertain as to whether he should offer sympathy. 'You don't seem glad to see me.'

'Sorry. I've got a lot on my mind. Would you like to sit down? We don't have very long.'

'You're going somewhere.'

'Out of town. I have a cab on the way, and a flight out of Glendale. I'll be gone for a while, actually. I'm going . . . well,

I'm going home. To stay with my parents, and decide what I'm going to do next.'

'Why?'

'Why am I leaving?' She reached for the cigarette and found it had gone out. He shook one out of her pack on the table and lit it for her. 'Do you remember the night we met? Of course you do. I had spent a lot of time with Jay, and I considered myself a fairly experienced girl. But until that night I had never seen anything like what happened out there in front of the car. At first I thought it was like the boxing match we'd just seen. But this was different – Willie was trying to hurt you badly. And the fact that Jay calmly ordered him to do it, that it seemed to be a natural part of their behavior . . . well, it horrified me. And it caused me to look at him in a new way.'

He studied her as she spoke, unsure as to how much he could trust her. In the short time he had known her, she had never given him reason to doubt her. But he reminded himself of the man she had chosen to be with, and he decided to retain a small, healthy dose of scepticism.

'From what I've heard, that kind of thing happens around him a lot,' he said. 'Just yesterday, you told me not to go up to his room, remember?'

'Yes. I'd heard Willie saying he wanted another chance at you. And Jay laughed and said it would be worth paying for damages to the apartment just to see it.' She shook her head. 'I suppose I was naive about Jay at first. But I'm also capable of changing my mind before it's too late. I decided to leave him.'

'Good for you. But what happened to the job?'

Something in her smile suggested self-mockery. 'There was a morals clause in my contract. Goldwyn Girls are supposed to be above reproach. Did you know that? They decided there was something wrong with the company I was keeping.'

'Let me guess.'

She nodded. 'Jay's been useful to Mr Goldwyn, but apparently that wasn't enough to cancel out the awfulness of my associating with him. So they terminated my contract. Mr Goldwyn told me himself, which was thoughtful of him.'

'I'm sorry.'

'It's all right. It may actually be a good thing, because it was the other reason I decided to leave. I enjoyed the work, but all the girls are just window dressing in these big, gaudy movies, you know? I'm better than that. I'll take some time off, and after a while I'll be back.'

'I'm sure you will. What does Jay think about all this?'

She glanced at her watch. 'He doesn't know yet. About the job or my leaving.'

'Is it smart to sneak away like this? He could come after you.'

'I know. He could find me easily. But he won't go to the trouble. Like a lot of powerful men, he enjoys having others attach themselves to him, bask in his importance. For a while, I enjoyed doing that. Now that I've lost interest, he will too.'

She seemed about to go on, so he waited.

'Some day I think I'll be ashamed of the time I spent with him. But not yet. Did you ever ride a bicycle?'

'Sure.'

'Well, my sister and I were real hellions on bikes, always daring each other to do things. There was this steep street a couple of blocks away from our house. We would race down it. I was the first to lift my hands over my head. Then she did it too, and before long she would put her feet up on the handlebars and hands in the air. I was humiliated until I learned to do that. One day I came up with the ultimate risk: feet up, hands high, and eyes closed. I won. I also broke my collarbone.'

'You a tomboy,' he said. 'That's hard to picture.'

'Here's why I'm telling you this silly story,' she said. 'I never thought I'd experience that ever again, that same feeling of risk and adventure and flirting with disaster. Until I met Jay.'

'I think I understand,' he said, remembering once again Emory Quinn's story of the woman at the fights with the fleck of blood on her glove. 'Is this the reason you wanted to see me?'

'No. Could I have one more cigarette, please?' As he lit it, she cupped her gloved hand around his, and he caught a pleasant, flowery scent. 'I wanted to see you one more time. You strike me as a decent man who's had a hard time. I also wanted to apologize for being part of that terrible night. And one last thing—'

'What?'

'When you spoke to Jay in the car that night, I could tell how important this woman Rose was to you and how desperately you wanted to know who killed her.'

'That's true.'

'I don't think Jay killed her. He can be brutal. But I don't think he's capable of killing anyone, or ordering anyone killed. That's just my intuition, and you can believe it or not. But I think Jay knows something.' She paused, thinking, then resumed, speaking slowly and carefully. 'A young woman was murdered in a car out on the highway the other night.'

He leaned forward. 'Yes.'

'The morning before you came to the hotel, I was with Jay in his apartment. We had been out late, and he was supposed to wake me up when breakfast arrived from room service. But I was already awake. I heard Jay's voice through the door. He was talking to Willie, and I don't think I've ever heard him so upset. I heard the words *killed another one* and something about a Yellow Cab and a lot of cursing, and then your name.

'By then, I'm embarrassed to say, I was standing by the door, where I could hear a little better. He said the words *He did too good a job*. Or maybe it was *I did too good a job*. And then, just as they left the room, he said one more thing. It sounded like *I hear the fucker's back in circulation*.' She laughed lightly. 'Not exactly Goldwyn Girl language, is it?'

'No. But it fits your pal.'

'Those were his words. Or almost. They were opening the door at the same time, and I couldn't be sure of the first part of the sentence. Then the door slammed. I went out, and there was breakfast, untouched, and the morning paper. That's where I found the story about the young woman, the cab driver, who was killed. Did you know her?'

'Yes,' he said. 'Jay mentioned her by the pool. But only to say how sorry he was to hear about it.'

'If she was a friend of yours, like Rose, I'm sorry. I want to stress again that I don't think Jay is responsible for killing anyone. He's capable of a lot, but not murder.'

She heard the doorman's voice and looked up. 'Your cab is here, Miss Lamont.' The man came over and picked up the two large suitcases. Horn got the rest.

'Glendale airport, please,' she told the driver when the bags were loaded. Turning to Horn, she said with a faint smile, 'That's all you're going to get from me. Unless I see you again.'

By now, his last remaining doubts about Eden Lamont and her motives had dissolved. 'I have a feeling I'll be seeing you in the movies. Goodbye, P.J.'

She removed her right glove and touched his unmarked cheek. 'Do you mind? This is all the goodbye I get from this goddam town.'

He drove west past the Brown Derby to where the tempo of Wilshire picked up a few beats, and he found a cafe. He sat there over eggs and toast and several cups of coffee, thinking.

Jay Lombard knew who killed Cassie. If that was so, he knew who killed Rose. For reasons of his own – reasons that could range from the charitable to the criminal – he had decided to say nothing about it. But the tough little lawyer knew, and Horn hoped that with the right tools, the information could be extracted from him. Maybe the police had the tools.

Paying up, Horn asked the cashier about a phone and was directed to the pharmacy next door. Once in the booth, he dialed Luther Coby's number at the Hall of Justice. The detective and his partner were working down in San Pedro that morning, Horn was told, and wouldn't be back until afternoon. He decided to try later.

Another nickel got him Mad Crow at home. The Indian enjoyed sleeping in, and he sounded only half awake.

'Remember Eden?' Horn began without much preamble. 'I just talked to her. She overheard Lombard and Willie talking about Cassie the morning the story showed up in the papers. Lombard was in a lather, yelling about somebody doing too good a job and being back in circulation.'

'Uh-huh. I'm not sure I—'

'Just listen.' Horn repeated everything he could recall from Eden's account. 'It's a little complicated, but I'm sure he was talking about the man who killed her. He knows who did it.'

'Sounds like he might, all right.' Mad Crow was beginning to wake up. 'Thanks, Nee Nee,' he said away from the mouthpiece. A moment later, Horn heard slurping sounds as Mad Crow started on his coffee.

'I've tried to raise Luther Coby,' Horn said, 'but he's not around now. We need to find some way to put pressure on Lombard to come up with the name.'

'Maybe not.'

'What?'

'Maybe we can narrow it down a little.' Fully awake now, Mad Crow repeated Eden's words. 'Suppose the man said *I did too good a job*, instead of *He did*,' Mad Crow said.

'That could have been it. She said she wasn't sure.'

'All right. Then the next thing was something like *I hear the fucker's back in circulation*. But she couldn't be certain because of the noise from the door.'

'That's right.'

'Suppose what he said was *I put the fucker back in circulation*.'

'*I did too good a job*,' Horn repeated slowly. '*I put him back in circulation*.'

'Right. If that's what he said, then it's pretty clear he was talking about—'

'A client.' Horn gripped the phone. In an instant, a disjointed image began playing across his mind like a home movie: a sandy-haired man, stooped over in the bright sun, hefting large rocks as the tendons in his broad forearms jumped under the skin like snakes. Horn muttered the beginning of a curse word.

'What is it?' Mad Crow asked. 'Do you know something?'

'Lewis De Loach,' Horn said.

'Doll's husband?'

'Right. Ex-husband. He got in some kind of trouble with his studio and was fired. Lombard represented him.'

'What was the trouble?'

'I don't know. I asked him once, and he danced around the answer.'

'Well, think about it for a minute,' Mad Crow said, his voice dropping into a ruminative rumble. 'It wasn't just a contract dispute. You wouldn't hire a hotshot defense lawyer for that. Maybe it was something more serious. Maybe even something criminal.'

'Well, if it was criminal, you'd expect the police—'

'Oh, my innocent friend,' Mad Crow said. 'Now I remember why you needed me to ride alongside you all those years, across the prairies and deserts and mountains, protecting you from all those evildoers—'

'What's your point?'

'Just this: if Lewis De Loach, who may have been still married to a movie star at the time, got caught at something dirty, it wouldn't have been the first time a studio chose to wash its own dirty laundry. In return for them not calling in the *federales*, maybe he agreed to go quietly.'

Horn was silent. 'You told me Lombard had some influence with Sam Goldwyn,' Mad Crow said. 'Maybe he had some with Magnum Arts too. So, even though he didn't exactly get De Loach off clean, it's possible he kept him out of jail. And if that's so, it would make sense for Lombard to say he put him back in circulation.'

'This is a lot of guessing, Indian. De Loach is probably too young to have known Rose back then. Doll said somebody almost killed him the other night, and he sure looked beat up when I saw him the next day at the sound stage where she was working. The only reason I can make room for any of this is because Doll was there the night Tess was killed, and she's connected to both Rose and De Loach. But I have a lot of trouble imagining—'

'I know,' Mad Crow said, his voice softening. 'She's a lot of woman, and you don't want to go down that trail. Like you said, it's a lot of guessing. So let's stop guessing and start digging. We need to find out what De Loach did that was so nasty even Jay

Lombard couldn't save his job. Who would have that information? More important, who could get it for us?'

Horn was silent for a moment. 'Dex,' he said finally. 'I hate to say this, but if anybody could find out, he could. He's worked in this town for a long time, and he knows some folks at just about every studio.'

'Good luck,' Mad Crow said wryly. 'How does he look to you now?'

'Oh, hell. He told me a lot of lies. And I still need some explanations from him. But he doesn't look nearly as likely as he did. I never wanted to believe he could have done it.'

'But you did, didn't you? Me too. I guess it's a good thing I didn't drive right over to his place the other day and wring his neck. So call him. What can he do except cuss you out and maybe run you down with that beat-up Plymouth of his?'

'He could do worse,' Horn said. 'He could stop calling me his friend. Maybe he already has.'

A telephone call won't do it, Horn thought, pumping a third nickel into the phone. He needed to see Dex face to face. Evelyn answered his ring and told him her husband was at the studio doing paperwork.

'I'm not sure he wants to talk to you,' she said.

'Can't say I blame him,' he responded.

He drove north through Hollywood and over the Cahuenga Pass and soon was pulling up in front of the main gate of Medallion. 'John Ray Horn to see Dexter Diggs,' he said to the guard in the shack.

'Uh . . .' The guard was in his thirties and solidly built. Horn didn't recognize him, but the expression on the man's face said the name had clearly registered.

'Just call him, will you?' Horn said in what he hoped was an ingratiating tone. 'He's in his office.'

After some hesitation, the guard dialed a number and spoke into the phone. Then, holding the receiver away from his ear, said to Horn, 'No, sir. He doesn't want to see you. And I've got orders to . . . *Hey.*'

In a second, Horn was out of the car and pushing his way into the shack. He snatched the phone out of the guard's hand as the man placed his other hand on the butt of the revolver he wore in a holster at his waist.

'I know who you are,' the guard said. 'You don't get in.'

Because of the confined space, they stood inches apart. Horn could smell the other man's hair oil and see a patch his razor had missed.

'I don't want in,' Horn said, keeping his voice low. 'I don't want to get anybody in trouble either. You know, I used to work here just like you do. One thing I remember is how Mr Rome didn't want you guys walking around with loaded guns. So either load it or club me with it. Or go outside, have a smoke, and give me a few seconds on the phone.'

They stared at each other so long, Horn began to see the comedy in the situation. *Showdown at the main gate*. Then, with a what-the-hell look, the guard allowed his expression to relax and stepped just outside the shack.

'Dex?'

'What do you want?'

'A few minutes of your time.'

'I'm busy.'

'I know. I wouldn't be here if it wasn't important. I'm getting close, Dex. To the answer.'

'You already found it, remember, cowboy? I'm your villain. It's time to call the sheriff and have me hauled away.'

'I thought so for a while. I'm not so sure any more.'

'Goodness gracious. I'm overwhelmed.'

'Come on, Dex. Five minutes. I won't try to get onto the lot. You can meet me here at the gate.'

'Why should I?' Horn thought he heard an opening, a crack in Diggs's obstinacy.

'We go back a long way, and you want to know the answer as much as I do. Rose was important to a lot of people. I've got an idea I want to tell you about. Five minutes.'

He could hear Diggs breathing into the phone.

'Please, Dex.'

A minute after he had thanked the guard and parked his car on the street nearby, he saw Diggs coming out, striding briskly, a grim set to his square jaw.

'Thanks,' Horn said. 'You want to go over to the Roundup? We'd be more comfortable there.' The Roundup, a cafe located a half-block away, was a favorite hangout for Medallion people, especially the wranglers who worked on the westerns.

'I'm fine right here,' Diggs said, looking at his watch, the meaning clear.

'All right.' They sat in the Ford, and Horn began talking quickly about his meeting with Lombard and his conversation with Eden. Halfway through his account, he suddenly realized that Diggs knew nothing about Cassie's death – had not, in fact, known Cassie at all. Awkwardly, he told of her efforts to find Rose's killer, then her own death.

'God,' Diggs said under his breath. 'I'm sorry. Especially for Joseph. I knew he had a niece, but . . .'

'She was special,' Horn said. 'She could be hard to like sometimes, because she was so mad at the world, and she lumped me in there too. But I watched her change. It was a little bit like watching somebody grow up, except with her it happened fast. She was on her way to finding out who she was and what was important to her.'

'What a waste. How is Joseph taking it?'

'Pretty hard at first. But now he's just plain mad, and determined, and we're working on this together.'

'I guess that's a good thing,' Diggs said. 'But the two of you sometimes were a bad influence on each other, as I recall . . .'

'We're older now,' Horn said. 'We won't be busting up any saloons.'

'Are you working with the police? The one who came to see me?'

'Sure.'

Horn quickly finished summarizing his talk with Eden. Diggs listened intently. Five minutes had long since passed, but he showed no sign of leaving.

'Lewis De Loach,' Diggs said reflectively when Horn finally stopped.

'What do you think?'

'Does it matter? I hardly know the man, except by reputation.'

'All right. Tell me about his reputation.'

Diggs thought. 'Brilliant. Good screenwriter, but doesn't like criticism. Great with a particular kind of acid dialogue. A little too quick with his fists. You probably know he's a kind of athlete, and he seems to enjoy picking fights over the slightest things. Usually wins. Ladies' man, too,' Diggs went on. 'Word was, he fooled around a lot while he was married to Doll Winter, dipped his wick in quite a bit of the talent pool at the studio. And there were rumors . . .' Diggs stopped.

'What kind?'

'I don't like to slander anyone without facts,' Diggs said.

'Go ahead.'

'No. I won't make the same mistake about him that you did about me.'

'Then don't,' Horn said. 'But would you find out what you can about him? Especially the reason he was fired.'

'I suppose I could try,' Diggs said without enthusiasm. 'Is this leading toward Doll Winter?'

'Maybe.'

'When I saw the two of you together at her house, I was watching you. You looked smitten, like a big tree ready to fall,' Diggs said. 'Now you're almost ready to believe she's capable of something awful. You're very changeable, aren't you?'

'Dex, if I was wrong about you, I'm sorry.'

'*If* you were wrong?'

Horn swallowed. 'You went to see Jay Lombard the other day. When his name first came up, you said you'd never heard of him. Why did you lie, and why did you see him?'

For the first time since sitting down, Diggs smiled, but there was no humor in it. 'I lied about knowing him for the same reason I held back the truth about me and Rose,' he said. 'I saw no reason to involve myself and dig up past indiscretions that could only hurt Evelyn. But it all comes out, doesn't it? I could

297

have saved myself the trouble. I'm going to have to get back soon,' he said, looking at his watch. 'Jay Lombard is a loathsome little man. I have no respect for him. But for years, he made an effort to stay in touch with me, and I went along. I sensed that he wanted to reassure himself that I wasn't going to incriminate him in any way in Tess's murder, and I suppose I was looking for the same assurances. We were like two criminals, each wanting to make sure the other kept his mouth shut about their crime. Except that I didn't kill her, and I have no reason to believe he did.'

'His girlfriend told me the same thing about him,' Horn said. 'For a shyster, he sure has a lot of people vouching for his character.'

'Maybe you should listen, instead of making up your mind so quickly,' Diggs said. 'Anyway, Lombard called me the other day, asking for another meeting. This one was different, because now Rose was dead too. We circled each other like suspicious dogs, each wondering if the other had anything to do with it. I assured him I knew nothing about Rose's murder, and I left.'

Horn remembered something from his poolside talk. 'Rose got in touch with Lombard to say she was going to the police, to tell the truth about what she had done,' he said. 'There were four people on her contact list, including him. The others were Doll Winter, Alden Richwine, and you.'

'She never talked to me about that,' Diggs said. 'I told you I hadn't heard from her in years, and that was the truth.'

'She planned to, though. She was checking off four names from her list, one at a time, but she was killed before she could get to the last one. It looks like one of the three decided that he – or she – didn't want Rose to go to the police.'

'For a while there, you had your eye on me, didn't you?' Diggs said. 'Now I gather it's Doll.'

'Beginning to look that way.'

They sat in silence for a moment. Then Diggs spoke. 'If it's her – if it's the two of them, for whatever reason – this won't be easy, John Ray. She's got a lot more clout in this town than you do. Hell, than either of us.'

'I know.'

'So be smart and tell the police. Where do I reach you?'

'My place or the casino. And if I'm not there, you could talk to Joseph. He's got as much of a stake in this now as I do.'

Diggs nodded, opened the door, and swung his legs out. 'You're a bastard, you know it?' he said with little emotion. 'You weren't very fair to me or to my wife. You're a typical preacher's son, quick to judge people and full of self-righteousness. But, as you said, we go back a long way. I accept your apology.' He got out and leaned back in the window. 'What are you going to do?'

'Right now? It's time I did something about keeping my last promise to Cassie.'

Chapter Twenty-Six

'That was good,' Madge said. 'I like meat loaf. Earl never would eat it. After hard times and then the war with all the rationing, meat loaf reminded him of how we had to stretch things to make 'em last. But I like a good meat loaf. With chili sauce. He died during the war. His heart. Did I tell you that?'

'No.'

'I was hoping he'd get a chance to tuck into a steak some day. Nothing too expensive, you know, just a cut of real meat.' She trailed off, looking vague.

'I'm sorry, Madge.' They had gone down the street to the diner for an early dinner, and now they sat in Madge's cramped room, she on the bed, he on the only chair.

Might as well get to it. He pulled the pint of Seagram's Five Crown out of his jacket pocket and twisted off the top. 'Why don't we put on some music and have a drink? Where are your glasses?'

'Well, ain't you nice?' she said, unpinning her little hat and laying it on the bed next to her. 'They're right over the sink.' She gave him a sharp look. 'How did you know—'

'You're partial to this brand?' He hesitated. Then, deciding there was no need to hold back the truth, he told her. 'Cassie mentioned it to me.'

'Cassie? You knew her?'

'We were good friends,' he said, fetching two glasses from the shelf then using the dish towel to give each a couple of extra wipes. He poured a generous amount into her glass and less into his.

'Well, I'll be,' Madge said, taking the glass. 'She never told me.'

'Probably had no reason to,' he said.

'So sad about her,' she said, taking a sip. 'So young. And so soon after Rosie. They had the same room. It's this place. There's death all over this hill. Everybody is sitting around waiting to die. The houses too. There's this place down the street—the bulldozers have come. They're coming for all of us.' She sat upright on her bed, legs straight out in front of her, clutching her glass. 'Just a matter of time.' A small tic attacked her left eye.

He went over to the record player, a timeworn portable phonograph much like his own, and picked through Madge's small collection of records. Most were sentimental songs from the war and earlier. He put on a Sammy Kaye recording of 'My Buddy', Guy Lombardo's 'We'll Meet Again' and 'By the Light of the Silv'ry Moon' by Ray Noble.

'See that one with the green label?' Madge said, pointing. 'Put that one on too. Rose gave it to me. Even taught me the words.'

The almost-new record was an instrumental version of a song called 'Angel Eyes'. He added it to the stack and started the player.

'Drink up,' he said, topping up her glass. The music seemed to put her into a relaxed mood, something unusual for Madge, and she closed her eyes and hummed along.

They sat that way for a while. Periodically he would get up to freshen her glass. The sky began to darken outside.

The last record dropped onto the turntable. It was a slow ballad, the melody woven by a throaty tenor sax suggesting a late-night memory of something irretrievably lost. As the sax sighed out its final notes, Madge stirred on the bed and sang, slightly off-key: ' 'Scuse me while I *dis-ap-pear*.'

He had heard those words before. From Rose. On the last night of her life.

Two-thirds of the bottle was gone. He took the glass out of her hand, nudged her gently to make sure she was awake, and said, 'Madge.'

'Huh?'

301

'Let's talk about Rosie.'

'Okay.'

'How she told you about the party.'

'Party.'

'You remember. The party from a long time ago. It was in a big house.'

'Big house.'

'That's right. With music, and people all dressed up. I know you remember what she said, because you told Cassie the same story not long ago. The two of you were at the Green Light, remember?'

'Rosie never hurt anybody.'

'I know. Her friends know that. But I need to find out exactly what she said to you. My guess is, you and Rosie were drinking one night, and she just started talking to you, because she trusted you. You put it away in your head, like you did with everything you thought was important. Now she's gone, and only you can tell me what she said. She'd want you to. I was a good friend of hers too, just like you were.'

'Long time ago. Where's my glass?'

'Right here.' He handed it to her, let her sip from it, and then placed it carefully on the bedside table. The room was fast going dark, but he didn't turn on the lights.

'It's in your memory, Madge. That special memory of yours. Nobody else could remember it the way you could. It's time to bring it out again. There was music, and a man in a tux, and—'

'*The lights went out.*' She sounded almost surprised, as if the memory had suddenly reared up in front of her.

'Yes. The lights went out. What else?'

Nothing from her for a long minute, only her heavy breathing, louder than the faint traffic noises from outside and the occasional sounds of others moving about the rooming house. Then she began talking.

'And she screams. It's the dark. The dark scares her most of all. But no one can hear her because of the music and all the people, crazy now and stirred up in the dark.'

The voice was Madge's, but the words didn't seem to fit her. Rose's words.

'And the man – he just suddenly . . . He's holding her arms, and when she screams, he turns loose of her and runs out of the room, so fast he hits the door, and then he's gone. Frightened of her screaming. But so lucky, that man, to go when he does. So very lucky.'

Madge spoke in a monotone, like an actor rehearsing, rushing through a particularly boring part. She had retained Rose's words but not their emotion.

'Tess still struggling, both of us wrestling on the bed. What do I do now? My plan falling apart. Dexter won't come, and no one will help me show what a tramp she is. I feel like a fool. I'll have to . . .

'Wait. Who's that? Someone in the doorway. Doesn't look like the same man. But hard to make out – just outlined by faint light somewhere in the hall. Candlelight? Carrying something. Champagne bottle. Comes in, and seems to understand what's going on. Maybe even waiting outside, until the other one left. Tess growing wild now, thrashing about. But I'm stronger, and I hold her from behind, under her. My eyes are closed now, but I feel the extra weight on both of us, and I know what's going to happen. My plan. I smell strong aftershave. Familiar. Almond. I always liked it . . .

'Tess gasping. I feel crushed under both of them. My hand brushes against satin lapel. Violent movements. Take that! Do you like that? Dexter will see her like this. I'll find him, and this time I'll make him come to this room.

'I struggle to get out from under both of them. Suddenly Tess screams again, but different this time. More of a groan, an awful, animal sound. I feel wetness on my legs, stickiness. What is it? Oh, no. My dress is . . . Oh, no. Can't be. I reach around her, feel the bottle, huge and hard. Sticky, just like . . . Oh, no. I push with both hands, hard as I can. Something feels wrong. Can't be. The mattress shakes, once, twice. I hear the door open and close. Tess and I are alone.

'She groans again, twitches once. Then quiet and still.

'Wet. I smell it now.

'What have I done?

'Tess.

'I'm lost . . .'

These last words were delivered in a thin, reedy voice, as if Madge had used up the last of her strength. She half lay, half sat on the bed, head on her chest.

'Who was it?' Horn asked, unsure if he was talking to Madge or Rose. 'The man in the tux – who was he?' The only response was a tiny snoring sound.

He got up, turned on the light, and tugged on her legs until she lay fully prone. He arranged a pillow under her head, found a blanket, and spread it over her. 'You sleep good,' he whispered. He opened her purse and put a few dollars in it. Then, taking her door key, he turned out the light, closed the door, locked it from the outside, and slid the key under the door.

He walked for a while, too excited to get in his car. Without aim or direction, he walked all over Bunker Hill, the narrow streets lit feebly by lampposts, the houses looming tall on either side, lights in some of the windows. The decay on the hill almost vanished at night, and the houses reassumed some of their old gentility, like an old dowager in an almost-forgotten movie who dimmed the gas lamps in her parlor until they flattered her.

He was haunted by Madge's voice, Rose's words. He had no doubt they were genuine. Through them, one more piece had fallen into place. Driven by jealousy and revenge, Rose had arranged and taken part in a rape, but one that turned horribly wrong. The result was death, and Rose's responsibility was clear. She had not planned or foreseen the death, but to her that did not matter. All those years, she carried the guilt, and it impelled her to throw away her career, to descend into poverty. Once again, Horn saw Emory Quinn's bloodied knuckles, and thought, *No wonder they found each other. Both of them had learned how to punish themselves.*

After such a life, finally telling the truth may have seemed to Rose a way to lighten the guilt, if only slightly. Could any punishment imposed by others equal what she had already done to herself?

He found himself nearly back at Rook House and his car. In front of him was a vacant space that only a few days earlier had been a rooming house. A bulldozer sat parked amid the rubble, waiting for its driver to return tomorrow and finish the job. To his surprise, he silently expressed the hope that Madge would die before the bulldozers came for her.

As he drove away, he could still hear the thin voice, breaking with tiredness.

I'm lost . . .

The next morning he was at the Anchor mission before nine. As he parked nearby, he spotted Emory Quinn sitting on a folding chair on the sidewalk, his back against the building, eyes on a book in his lap. A dozen or more men sat or sprawled nearby, some wrapped in blankets.

'Strange place to be reading,' Horn said as he approached.

Quinn looked up. 'We turn everybody out in the morning and mop the floors. We needed to do that even more today, because somebody threw up in the sleeping area in the middle of the night. Anyway, the whole place will smell like disinfectant for a while. I like to come out here.'

'What are you reading?'

'Oh, something about a book with seven seals.'

Horn looked more closely at the black, pebble-grained Bible in Quinn's lap. 'I know that one,' he said. 'The book no man can open. My daddy used to make me and my little brother memorize verses. Revelation was one of his favorites, because he knew it scared us, and scaring people was one of the things he did well.'

'Religion can be misused,' Quinn said. 'Just like money. Or a gun.'

'We don't need to argue. I came by to see how you're doing.'

'You mean since the last couple of times we had words? I'm doing all right.' Each of his knuckles, Horn noticed, bore a small scab.

'There's a book I'm opening,' Horn said. 'When it's open, things will come out.'

Quinn tilted his head, waiting.

'I know now what Rose did. I thought you might want to know too.'

'Did she do like she said? Kill somebody?' Quinn returned his eyes to the page, as if to turn away from the answer.

Horn spoke carefully. 'Not everybody would call what she did murder. But the police might. And I can see why she did.'

'I don't need to know any more,' Quinn said, eyes still down. 'I knew her, and that was enough. Some of the people who come in off the street to be fed here still ask about her. I don't have the heart to tell them she won't be back. Whatever else she did, on balance she added to this life, instead of subtracting from it.' He looked up. 'Do you know who killed her? Was it Lombard?'

'I think I'll know pretty soon.'

'What are you going to do about it?'

'It's not just my decision. A friend is involved in this too. Both of us are going to have to decide what we want to do.'

Quinn lifted the book from his lap. 'There's something in here about that too.'

'I know all about that,' Horn said, laughing. '*Vengeance is mine; I will repay, saith the Lord*. That's a big joke. Men take vengeance on each other all the time.'

'That doesn't mean it's right. Do you think Rose would—'

'I'm not Rose. Whoever killed her is going to pay for it. If the police get to them first, I won't mind. But if they don't . . .'

'Not long before she died, Rose asked me to pray for you.'

The thought did not comfort him. Hearing a voice call out across the street, Horn turned around. Two workmen were atop the marquee at the Follies Theater, attaching ropes to the giant likeness of Ruby Renfrew. Down below, leaning against the box office, stood her brightly colored, oversized replacement, a dark-haired stripper in a dancer's pose and a costume that seemed mostly bananas. Horn could just make out the lettering: *Rosie Torres*, it said, *the Cuban Spitfire*. Slowly they began to lower her predecessor to the pavement.

'So long, Ruby,' Horn said under his breath. 'You didn't do me much good, did you?'

He turned back to Quinn. 'Did she ever ask you to pray for anybody else?'

Quinn thought for a moment. 'Just that friend of hers, the woman who's been so generous. The one she called Doll.'

Braving the smell of Lysol, Horn went inside to use the phone in Quinn's office. He dialed three digits for the Hall of Justice, then lowered the phone, hesitating. If Dolores Winter was behind Rose's death, he desperately needed the help of the police. Dex was right: she carried more weight, more credibility, than any has-been movie actor and ex-convict. But Horn lacked all the answers, and he now saw a danger in talking to Luther Coby before he could make a convincing case against her. The detective, it appeared, had a most unprofessional crush on the actress. If Coby was not impressed by Horn's collection of hunches, he might alert her and spoil everything. No, it was too early.

Instead, he dialed the number for Mad Crow's office at the casino.

'Where are you?' Mad Crow asked abruptly.

'I'm at the Anchor mission on Main, downtown.'

'Where you been? Dex called me almost an hour ago, said you weren't at home.'

'What did he want?'

'I'll tell you. Listen, you're on the way to where we need to go. Be waiting out front, and I'll pick you up.'

A little over a half-hour later, Mad Crow pulled up in the white Caddy, its top down and white finish gleaming. 'I was afraid you'd come to this sad end,' he said, looking around at the silent forms huddled on the litter-strewn sidewalk. 'Once an idol of the silver screen, now just a castaway, a piece of driftwood on the beach of life.' Pointing across the street, he asked, 'Who's the dollie in the bananas?'

'Will you just drive the goddam car and tell me where we're going?'

The convertible left a patch of rubber on the pavement. Mad

307

Crow headed north to First Street and swung left. 'Dex turned up something on Lewis De Loach, and it didn't take him long,' he said, raising his voice to be heard as the air rushed over the windshield. 'He won't name the tattletale, only that it's somebody who used to work in management at MagArts and left in a huff. A junior producer would be my guess. Apparently this individual is happy to spread a little dirt over his former employer. Anyway, it turns out De Loach got himself in a mess over a lady. A very particular kind of lady. And *we* . . .' His voice rose dramatically, a radio announcer's voice. 'We got her *name* and – yes, indeedy – her *address*.'

For the next ten minutes, Horn listened intently to what Diggs had uncovered. Then it was his turn to describe his evening with Madge. When Mad Crow parked the Caddy, they were on a quiet residential street in Hollywood. 'That's the place,' Mad Crow said, pointing to a well-kept bungalow fronted by an orderly lawn. 'Let's go say hello to Miss Myra Poole.'

They mounted a short flight of steps to the front porch, where Mad Crow rang the bell. A woman in her forties opened the door, dressed in an elegant-looking silk house coat with lace at the edges. She had until recently been beautiful, Horn thought, and she was still worth a second look. She smiled without speaking, her face betraying no curiosity.

'Afternoon, ma'am,' said Mad Crow. 'Edna, isn't it? I'm Roy. I called earlier. This is my friend Gene. We'd like to spend some time with Myra.'

She smiled noncommittally. 'I'm afraid Myra doesn't do twosomes,' she said.

'Oh, no, that's all right,' Mad Crow said. 'My friend was wounded in the war. He just likes to watch.'

She smiled again. 'Of course,' she said. 'Then that will be twenty for one of you. Myra's busy at the moment. Please come in.'

They sat in a parlor decorated with plush furniture and ersatz Victorian lighting fixtures, heavy on nudes. A pretty young girl sat in a corner reading a magazine, legs crossed and garters showing, and a bull-necked, well-fed young man in shirtsleeves and suspenders sat nearby, lips moving as he worked a cross-word puzzle.

After about ten minutes, a door closed somewhere at the side of the house, and they saw a man adjusting his hat as he moved down the sidewalk toward the street.

'Separate exit for customers,' Mad Crow said. 'Damn, I like a well-run operation.'

A few more minutes passed, and then Myra came out. She was in her late twenties, average height and dark-haired, and she wore the house uniform of peignoir over nylons, high heels, and frilly lingerie. Like the madam, she may have been beautiful once, but in her case it had faded much more quickly, to be replaced by something furtive and flinty.

'Hi, boys,' she said. 'Come on back.' She led them to a small bedroom at the rear of the one-story house. Inside, she began to shrug off the dressing gown. 'Which one of you—?'

'You can keep that on, Myra,' Horn said. 'All we want is to talk.'

'Are you cops?' she asked. 'You're not the regular ones.'

'No,' he said.

'You from some church? You want to save my soul? I've got no time—'

'That's not it, either.'

'Edna said you didn't look quite right, and she told Howie to sit outside the door. He used to play football. All I have to do is yell for him.'

'You won't have to do that, Myra,' Horn said. 'We've got money, and we'll pay for your time. Then we'll leave.'

She thought about that, twirling the sash of her gown around one finger. 'All right,' she said finally, sitting on the bed. 'What about?'

'Lewis De Loach,' Horn said as he and Mad Crow sat in the two chairs facing her.

'Oh, no,' she said, her posture growing rigid. 'No.'

'We already know all about it,' Horn said. 'Let me explain something. We're private detectives, hired by De Loach's ex-wife, Dolores Winter. You may have heard of her. We know

309

what De Loach did to you and how it was hushed up by the studio. Now Miss Winter has found out, and she's afraid the whole story may come out and damage her reputation. You know how these actresses are, always worried about publicity. So she hired us to make sure nothing comes out. And, when we started investigating, we found out that you got cheated out of money that was coming to you.'

'What do you mean?' She still fiddled with her sash, but he detected a flicker of interest in her expression.

'You got – let's see, what was the exact amount? I've got it written down here somewhere,' he said, patting his pockets.

'Two thousand,' she said. 'One for me, one for the house.'

'That's right. Well, we found out that the studio okayed a payment of four thousand. Apparently half of that never reached you, and we have reason to believe that it wound up in the pocket of Mister De Loach.'

Her eyes widened. 'The prick,' she said.

'Exactly,' Horn said, adopting a look of concern. 'Naturally, Miss Winter wants to make sure you never have any reason to embarrass her. We intend to put pressure on the studio to pay you the additional two thousand. All we need is just to, you know, confirm the events that occurred.' Horn glanced at Mad Crow and saw the beginning of a furtive grin.

'I suppose,' she said. 'But . . . double my fee?'

Horn looked at Mad Crow, who frowned and checked the contents of his wallet. 'All right,' the Indian said.

'Okay, then.' She reached for a stick of Teaberry chewing gum on the bedside table, unwrapped it, and began working on it.

'This was, I don't know, a couple of years ago,' she said, crossing her legs and swinging one foot slowly up and down. 'He came here one night and asked for a girl. Nobody knew him, and he gave some dumb name. John, or something like that.' She laughed. 'Dick. Anyway, he looked nice and was well dressed, and he saw me up front and picked me out. We came back here, and I could tell he was real drunk, but I can usually handle drunks. So we did it. And he paid, and even tipped me.

'And then he said he wanted to do it again, but I would have to help him. I said sure, if he paid again. He said he would. And he reached in his pocket and got out this little rope, except it was very soft. And he said he wanted to put it around my neck. He said it would make the fucking go better for me. But I could tell he really meant better for him.'

The two men looked at each other.

'I know,' she said, chewing vigorously. 'Sounds crazy, right? I'd never tried it, but I'd heard of it. Some people like to do it that way. I just didn't want to get any marks, you know? Like I said, he was very drunk, but he was well behaved, and he kept saying he liked me and wouldn't hurt me. So I said okay.

'Stupid,' she said, shaking her head. 'Very, very stupid. As soon as he started, I could tell it was too tight around my neck. I tried to tell him, but he was already on top of me and pulling it tighter, and I just couldn't breathe. His face was getting very red too, and his eyes big. I tried hitting him and scratching him, but I could feel myself passing out. Last thing I remember hearing him say was, *I could kill you now.*

'When I woke up, everybody was yelling and pulling at him. He was still on top of me, passed out drunk. They found his driver's license and some other things in his wallet. Edna didn't want the newspapers to get hold of it, so she called the studio herself, and they sent somebody to get him.'

'And they quietly paid up,' Horn said.

She nodded. 'I heard later that the sick son of a bitch lost his job. I said hurray. You know I had bruises for weeks?'

Horn and Mad Crow exchanged nods and stood up. Mad Crow produced the money, and they both thanked her.

Outside the door, the stocky young man lounged in a straight-backed chair against the wall, the crossword puzzle replaced by a policeman's nightstick in his lap. 'Howie,' Mad Crow said pleasantly as they passed him.

They had almost reached the exit when they heard the madam in the rear of the house, her voice raised in fury, followed by a ringing slap and a loud sob from Myra.

'Better get out of here,' Horn said. They made their way up

the walk toward the Cadillac as they heard the madam scream, *'Howie!'*

The young man came barreling out the front door and down the steps. Ignoring the door, Mad Crow vaulted into the driver's seat and began stabbing his key at the ignition. Realizing that their pursuer was too close, Horn turned to face him.

Howie was a few inches shorter and much broader, all chest, shoulders, and belly. 'Edna says you need to come back in,' he said with a pugnacious air, lightly tossing the billy club from hand to hand in a practiced motion.

'Not today, Howie.' Behind him, Horn heard the big engine roar to life.

'Get in!' Mad Crow yelled.

'If he goes, I take you inside,' Howie said, catching the stick without looking at it. His upper lip was adorned with the wispy beginnings of a mustache.

Horn realized he had little choice. 'You play football, Howie?' he asked. 'If you did, I bet you weren't first string. You were probably too dumb to memorize the play book, am I right?'

In the second it took for that to sink in, the young man's face began to clench, and Horn threw a kick, catching the stick in mid-flight, the heavy heel of his shoe following through into Howie's stomach. He felt the layer of fat and the heavy muscle underneath. Howie staggered back but did not fall. Stunned, he looked around for the nightstick. Horn flipped over the door into the passenger seat as Mad Crow gunned the engine and Howie lurched forward, club again in hand.

'Don't hurt the car!' Mad Crow wailed. As the Caddy peeled out, Howie took a mighty swing at his only target, the right rear taillight. Even over the engine noise and the screech of rubber, the sound of shattered glass was unmistakable.

Eight blocks later, Mad Crow was still cursing.

Chapter Twenty-Seven

'You know where we can find this guy De Loach?' Mad Crow drove automatically, his mind clearly somewhere else.

'Hmm? Well, I know where he lives. It's up in the hills. With Doll.'

'Point me there.'

'Why?'

'You know.'

'Now wait. Be patient for just a little—'

'Oh, that's great. *Be patient*, ladies and gentlemen. This coming to you from the man who threw away his job just so's he could pound little Bernie Rome Junior into oatmeal mush. Let me tell you something: Sierra Lane was patient. You ain't.'

'I want him as bad as you do,' Horn said. 'His number'll come up. In the meantime—' He looked down the street. 'That place has a phone. Can you pull over?'

Mad Crow parked in front of a cafe on Las Palmas, a block south of Hollywood Boulevard, then got out to check the damage to his car. 'The punk took off some of the paint job too,' he said mournfully. 'I ought to go back there—'

'I'll try to make this fast,' Horn said as he entered the cafe. Inside the phone booth, he dialed Luther Coby's number. The detective's partner, Stiles, answered. 'Hold on while I try to radio him,' the detective said. 'I think he wants to talk to you.'

A minute went by. 'Give me your number, and he'll call you back,' Stiles said. Horn rolled a smoke while he waited. Before long, the phone rang, and he heard Coby's familiar, disinterested voice.

'I need to tell you a bunch of things,' Horn said.

'I'm listening.'

Haltingly, he went over what he had found out since his last encounter with Coby. He mentioned the long talk with Alden Richwine in the house where Tess Shockley died, the revelation that Dolores Winter had been at the long-ago party, the tense and frustrating poolside meeting with Jay Lombard. Finally he went over what he had learned from Eden Lamont and, most recently, Myra Poole.

When Horn finished, Coby was silent for what seemed like a long time. All that came over the phone was the faint sound of a matchstick being nudged from one side of the man's mouth to the other and back again.

'Where are you right now?' Coby asked.

'At a cafe on Las Palmas. Why?'

'Never mind. I was thinking of getting you to meet me half-way, but then I remembered I'm due in court in half an hour. But I want to see you tomorrow. All right?'

'I guess. What is this about?'

'It's about all this detective work you've been doing,' Coby said. He sounded almost in good spirits. 'I've got to say you've done all right for an amateur. Almost as good as some movie cowboy detective. But you're on the wrong track.'

'What do you mean?'

'Let's start with this Eden Lamont. She left town, right?'

'Uh, yeah. Yesterday morning.'

'What if I was to tell you she's got herself a room at the Beverly Hills Hotel? Actually, one of those fancy bungalows. And that she checked in under a phony name and gets room service to bring all her meals?'

'I'd say it's some kind of a mistake.'

'Huh-uh. It's her, all right. I'm going over there tomorrow to surprise her, have a little chat. I'd like you to come along. With you there, maybe she'll open up.'

'Why not go there now?'

'I told you, I got to be in court. Getting a little pushy, aren't you? I'll tell you how we handle this, all right?'

314

'At least tell me what she's doing there. And how did you find her, anyway?'

'Some of your questions are going to have to wait. But as to what she's doing there, it's pretty simple. You've been led skipping down the garden path.' Coby now sounded absolutely jovial. 'She had a job to do for Jay Lombard. The lady's an actress, remember? Her job was to get you thinking in a certain direction, and it worked.'

Horn cursed under his breath.

'Her story about Lewis De Loach was pure bullshit,' Coby went on, 'just a shyster lawyer song and dance, and you fell for it. I've got to hand it to Lombard. He's even slicker than I figured.'

'This is crazy,' Horn said, the anger tightening his voice. He felt like a fool, but he wasn't ready to admit it.

'Don't feel bad,' Coby said. 'He's outflanked better men than you. Made me look pretty stupid once, that time I told you about.'

Horn exhaled loudly, causing static over the phone. 'So the reason for all this was—'

'Was just to give Lombard time to maneuver. He's cleaning up the mess he made, and part of that involves getting rid of anybody who could eventually figure things out.'

'You're saying he killed Rose? And Cassie?'

'I'm saying his thug Willie killed them. And I'm saying you could be next. In fact, you probably are. You need to be careful until I'm able to pick up those two. You got any weapons?'

'You know I'm not supposed to—'

'Sure, you're not supposed to. But do you?'

'I've got something at home,' Horn said carefully.

'All right. We'll worry about the niceties later. For now, I think you should lay low tonight, then meet me in the lobby of the hotel tomorrow morning at nine. If we can get this Eden Lamont to roll over on her boyfriend, I can have him in the tank by tomorrow night. All right?'

'I don't know,' Horn said, still feeling resentment and anger at himself for not being more perceptive. 'What about the hooker's story? That wasn't made up, was it?'

'No,' Coby said. 'That happened. De Loach is a twisted character, no doubt about it. But he's never killed anybody, far as I know. The fact that he likes to get rough with the girls made him a convenient patsy for Lombard—'

'What about Dolores Winter?'

'She's something, isn't she?' Coby said.

'You know what I mean.'

'You a little sweet on her? If so, I wouldn't blame you. Anyway, I think she's clean. Don't forget, she and De Loach got banged up pretty bad the other night.'

'So that was Willie too?'

'In my opinion. We'll know for sure before long.'

Horn had a thought, and not a pleasant one. 'You said Lombard's cleaning up his mess. That means Doll could be on his list—'

'She's already got protection, remember?'

'And Alden.'

'Uh-huh.' Coby sounded thoughtful. 'Him I'm worried about. I'm going to send a uniform over to watch his house. But these things take time, and we probably won't have anybody in place until sometime tomorrow.'

'Can you move him out in the meantime?'

'I tried,' Coby said. 'He's a stubborn old guy. Won't go anywhere.'

Horn held the phone without speaking.

'Don't feel bad,' Coby said, and this time Horn thought he could hear genuine solicitude. 'Look on the bright side. At least *you're* not on my list any more.'

'I'll see you tomorrow,' Horn muttered and hung up.

Out on the street, Mad Crow noticed his expression. 'What's up?'

Horn got in and began talking as Mad Crow drove. When he had finished, Mad Crow took his eyes off the road to stare at him for a moment. Absentmindedly, he tugged at the brim of his hat, then reached back to fiddle with his ponytail. 'I don't get it,' he said at last.

'Me neither,' Horn said. 'All I know is, half of what I've heard lately is lies, and I've got no idea which half.'

When Mad Crow didn't respond, Horn looked over at him. 'You still want De Loach?' he asked.

'Don't know,' Mad Crow said slowly, appearing to study the road ahead. 'This puts a different light on things, doesn't it? I suppose I can give the man a little more time to walk around upright and enjoy the bounty of this world. So . . . all right. Just lie low tonight, like the man says, and go see the lovely Eden tomorrow. If she's at the hotel, the two of you'll get something useful out of her. If she's not, then this Coby isn't half the cop he pretends to be, and I'll keep my rendezvous with Mr De Loach.' When Horn started to object, he quickly added, 'With you along to referee, naturally. All right?'

'All right,' Horn said. 'But the thing that worries me most is Alden. He could be next—'

'*You* could be next.'

Fifteen minutes later, the Cadillac stopped behind Horn's car next to the Anchor mission.

'You got a parking ticket,' Mad Crow observed.

'That makes everything just about perfect.' Horn got out. 'Can you wait a minute?'

'Sure.' Mad Crow looked across the street, where Rosie Torres and her bananas were now installed high above Main Street. 'I'll just sit here and enjoy the view.'

Inside the mission, he saw no sign of Emory Quinn. He went straight to Quinn's office behind the stage, sat at the desk, and dialed 'O' for the operator. A minute later he was calling the switchboard at the Beverly Hills Hotel. When he reached the front desk, he said, 'Miss Peggy Jean Turner, please. I don't have her room number, but I think she's in one of the bungalows.'

After looking, the clerk said in practiced Beverly Hills tones, 'I'm sorry. We have no one by that name registered here.'

'How about Miss Eden Lamont?'

Another pause. 'I'm sorry, no.'

He replaced the receiver. Finding Eden there would have confirmed Coby's story. But not finding her proved nothing. She could be using any name. Or she might not be at the hotel.

Something was wrong. There was no time to sift through all the various stories, the clashing accounts he had heard in recent days. But a few isolated memories swam up to the surface like bubbles from something that lived far below.

Of all the conflicting stories he was being told, he was still unable to sift through the faulty recollections, half-truths, and outright lies to find any nuggets of truth, and his failure made him angry. Just one example was the question of whether Dexter Diggs went upstairs with Rose on that New Year's Eve. According to Dolores Winter, he did. According to Evelyn Diggs, he did not. One was clearly lying, or mistaken.

Another example: Eden Lamont either had left town for good or was holed up at an exclusive hotel and would receive a surprise visit tomorrow morning along with her room-service breakfast. Either she or Coby had lied to him.

Time was running out. Before long, Horn was going to have to gamble on who was trustworthy and who was not. A few lives, he thought, could depend on it.

One more call, and when Alden Richwine answered, his voice sounded far away and somewhat sleepy, as if he'd been awakened from a nap.

'Alden? It's John Ray Horn. Did I wake you up?'

'Why, no,' Richwine said tonelessly. 'I'm just . . . Who is this, please?'

'It's John Ray Horn.' *He's drunk*, Horn thought. 'I'm sorry to bother you, but I'd like to come over. Right now.'

'Well, I . . .'

'It's important. I'll see you in a few minutes.' He hung up without waiting for an answer. *If he's drunk*, Horn thought, *he'll be easier to handle*.

He went out to the car. 'I'm going over to Alden's house,' he said to Mad Crow. 'Whoever's next on the list, it's clear that Alden can't look after himself, and Coby said there might not be anybody watching his house until tomorrow. I'm going to stay with him until the cops show up.'

Mad Crow looked doubtful. 'All right, buddy,' he said. 'But you're talking about a long time. I'll help. How about I come over and relieve you sometime tonight?'

'What are you going to do until then?' Horn's suspicion showed on his face.

'You still think I mean to call out De Loach? I had a quieter evening in mind. Dinner, maybe a couple of drinks.'

'Drinks'll just make you sleepy, and it could be a long night,' Horn said. 'Why don't you take in a movie? I think there's a new Burt Lancaster playing over on Broadway.'

'Really?' Mad Crow showed interest. 'I ever tell you about the time I arm-wrestled him on the bar at Musso's?'

'Many times.'

'Okay. Well, then I'll show up around ten or so. You can go home, get some sleep, and be all fresh and clean-shaven for your meeting with the lovely Eden.'

'Thanks, Indian. I appreciate it.'

'You got an equalizer?'

'Hmm? Oh . . . No, not with me.'

'What kind of cowboy goes around without his trusty hog leg?' Mad Crow got out and unlocked the trunk. He rummaged around inside and came up with a large knife in a scabbard. 'Remember this? Cassie's.' He pulled it smoothly from its sheath. 'I gave it a good cleaning, but I left this.' He pointed to a tiny fleck of blood on the blade near the base. 'Just to remind me that somebody needs to finish the job.'

He rummaged deeper. 'Here we go.' He held up a dusty .22-caliber revolver. 'Not exactly heavy armament. Remember that time at the dump? I slaughtered every bottle and tin can for miles.' He handed it to Horn. 'It's loaded. I don't have any more shells in the car, but you know what they say. If you need more than six or eight, chances are you're already dead.'

'Thanks.' Horn stuck the pistol in his belt. 'I mean it.'

'Don't mention it.' Mad Crow got behind the wheel. 'Cassie was buried today,' he said, looking straight ahead. 'I've been to

319

that cemetery once, years ago. It's not very fancy. A lot of the markers are plain wood. But it's kind of a pretty place. You can see the Big White River from there, and a stand of evergreens. And the Black Hills are off to the west . . .'

He started the engine. 'You got any idea how much I want this guy, whoever he is? I dream about him sometimes.'

'I know,' Horn said. 'Me too.'

He drove west out of downtown. On his way through Mac-Arthur Park, he saw ducks on the water of the little lake, spotlighted in a brilliant circle of sunshine that had just poked through a dark-underbellied cloud that sailed overhead in the shape of a huge galleon. At the same instant, a few raindrops spattered his windshield.

'Devil's beating his wife,' he muttered, echoing one of his mother's folk sayings from her mountain upbringing. He had never quite understood that description of light rain amid bright sunshine, but it had always struck him as strangely appropriate.

By the time he turned into Alden Richwine's driveway, the sun was hidden again, the raindrops were growing fatter, and a stiff breeze caused a palm frond to rock nervously back and forth on the gravel driveway. He parked by the kitchen door under drooping greenery, heavy with moisture, that almost blotted out the sky.

'Alden?' He knocked on the kitchen door but got no answer. He walked around to the front door and swung the heavy knocker, with the same result. Retracing his steps, he followed a damp pathway around to the back of the house, where he found himself in the small garden, with access to the library and living room through two sets of French doors.

The library was unoccupied, but he saw a light in the living room. Stepping carefully up to the glass doors, he could make out two people sitting in large wing-backed chairs before a table. In the nearest chair, partially glimpsed in profile, was Alden Richwine. In the other, facing him, was Dolores Winter, who sat with head bent, apparently studying something on the table.

He could see no one else in the room. With one hand on the

grip of the .22 in his belt, he tried the door handle. It turned, and he stepped into the room.

Dolores Winter looked up, recognized him, and smiled a welcome.

'Hello, Doll,' Horn said. Richwine did not move. Horn wondered why he had not seen her car outside. Then, as he came around the nearest chair, he saw that Richwine's expression was vacant, his jaw slack. And a vertical line of blood neatly bisected his forehead and the ridge of his nose.

Horn jerked at the pistol grip just as a faint noise caused him to turn to his right. Too late. Something slammed against the side of his head, sending him reeling, reaching out for support. His left hand found the armrest of Richwine's chair. Trying to steady himself, he pulled the pistol free of his belt just in time to feel another blow, this one at the back of his head. It cracked like a thunderclap. Then nothing.

Chapter Twenty-Eight

He stood just outside the bedroom door, full of pain and sick with knowledge. Inside the room, he knew, terrible things were about to happen. He had only to open the door, step inside, and stop it. He could save Tess. And Rose. All he had to do . . .

But the door was locked. And the pain in his head was a raucous Charleston, with every squeal of the trumpet threatening to split his skull wide open.

From inside the bedroom, he heard a scream. And he could do nothing . . .

He opened his eyes, then shut them. Even the light from the floor lamp seemed too bright. Voices spoke. A shoe nudged his shoulder. 'I would imagine that floor's not very comfortable. Get up and join the party.' He almost recognized the voice.

Strong hands lifted him, then deposited him. He opened his eyes again. He was slumped in one of the large wing-back chairs. To his right sat Doll; farther away, Alden.

A figure moved into view, and the voice spoke again. 'It was thoughtful of you to call,' Lewis De Loach said, sounding almost friendly. 'It allowed us a little time to prepare our welcome.'

Horn felt surreptitiously at his midsection. The pistol was gone. He heard a sound and looked to his right. Alden Richwine was truly the gray man now, with skin the color of mottled parchment. His eyes appeared unfocused, and a faint rasping noise came from his throat. His bathrobe looked even more tattered than before. The thin line of blood that ran from hairline to the tip of his nose was dried and dark.

'What did you do to him?' Horn asked. Even those few words

made his head throb anew. He reached up, feeling for the source of the pain, and found two patches of matted and sticky hair.

'We just tapped him on the noggin,' De Loach said. He wore dark trousers, a hand-painted tie in an abstract design, and a dress shirt with the sleeves rolled up. Horn's pistol was in his belt. 'When he understood you were coming over and we would be lying in wait, so to speak, he threatened to get unruly.'

'I'm sorry, Alden,' Horn said, but he wasn't sure if the other man understood.

'And he had been so cooperative up to that point,' De Loach went on. 'He helped us find what we were looking for.' The suggestion of boyishness had left his face. The veneer of gaiety in his manner barely covered his tight-wound nervousness.

'You're looking a lot better than last time,' Horn said to him.

'Oh, you mean the arm and all the rest?' De Loach held up his left arm and worked the wrist back and forth, grinning delightedly. 'I recover quickly.'

'It was never broken, was it?'

'No, no, just play-acting. Except for Doll's little head wound. We decided that would be our touch of authenticity.'

'And the black eye?' As soon as Horn asked, he remembered a comment from Dexter Diggs and realized that he knew the answer. '*Doll likes to do her own make-up*,' he muttered.

'Exactly,' De Loach said. 'You're finally getting it all sorted out. Just a little too late, that's all.'

His expression suggested a mixture of amusement and pity. 'You don't look particularly heroic today. In fact, you're quite a mess. I made a point of seeing one of your movies just recently. Curiosity, mostly. It caused me to change my mind about writing a western. The problem is, the western doesn't reflect real life in any significant way. The cowboy may be heroic, but he's also made of cardboard. The plots are simplistic, the acting is . . . well, the less said about you and your friend, that Indian character, the better. No offense, but I think I'll stick to writing for adult audiences.'

'No offense,' Horn said, wanting to keep him talking. 'You

mentioned that Alden helped you find something. What was that?'

De Loach was about to answer when Horn heard Doll's voice. 'These,' she said. He turned to see her gesturing to a dozen or so large photos strewn over the top of the oaken coffee table.

He looked at her. She was dressed for an evening out, in a midnight blue satin number with long sleeves and a square neckline embellished by a simple string of pearls. Her hair was brushed out, ungathered, and lustrous in the light from the floor lamp. Her expression was hard to read, but he knew he was looking at a new Doll. The acting was over. This woman was all business, and she regarded Horn almost as she would a stranger.

Moving slowly to keep down the throbbing in his head, he picked up one of the photos. It was a group of people, unposed. He glimpsed a circular staircase in the background, the same staircase that began its winding journey to the second floor only about thirty feet from where he sat. Details of clothing, along with the presence of a few costumes, told him the rest. It was the New Year's Eve party.

'Alden took them,' Doll said in a conversational tone. 'They were candid shots; he was just playing with his camera. When you visited him, he showed you things related to Rose's movie, but it never occurred to you—'

'To ask if anyone had taken pictures at the party,' Horn finished.

'That's right. For years I never knew about them until just the other day, when he mentioned having them. And I knew I couldn't leave them with him. So, since it was almost time to deal with Alden anyway, and since we had a date today to take him out for a drive and then have dinner, we thought this would be a good time to take care of everything. *And . . .'* She smiled for the first time, as if in appreciation of the convenience of it. 'And then when you called to say you were coming over . . .' She let the rest hang in the air.

'You must have thought I was really dumb,' he said.

'Don't be too hard on yourself,' she said. 'You're just not as smart as I am.'

He continued looking at the picture but saw nothing unusual. His eyes refused to focus properly. She took it from him and handed him another. 'This is the only one that really matters,' she said.

He studied the black-and-white image. More elegantly dressed people, more costumes. A servant carrying a tray of champagne glasses. A glimpse of the band off to the right, the trombone player bent over his instrument.

Then he saw it, in the background. A slender figure in a tuxedo mounting the stairs, one graceful hand on the railing, the other carrying a bottle. The man in the . . . No. Not a man in a tux.

Dolores Winter.

The face, in profile, was twenty years younger but unmistakable. *She stood out in the crowd*, Horn recalled. *Evelyn said so*.

'You recognize me, don't you?' she said. 'My hair was cut very short then. This is the only shot of me taken that night. I thought it best not to leave it lying around. Some people might put two and two together.'

His head still hurt, but the throbbing was starting to lessen a little. 'Why did you do it?' he asked.

'Be careful what you tell him,' De Loach said to her. He stood on the other side of the table, listening to them, his eyes occasionally darting around the room.

'Shut up, Lewis,' she said without too much concern. 'John Ray is curious, and I owe him a few answers. It's not as if he's going to run off and tell the police, is it?' She turned to Horn. 'You mean Tess? It's a little complicated. I didn't mean for it to turn out that way, actually. I'm sorry, in fact. But you see, I was in love with Rose.' She stopped and looked almost embarrassed. 'Can you imagine the scandal sheets getting hold of that today? *"Star Confesses to Depraved Love."*

'I'm afraid I was too aggressive with her. I frightened her off, and she told me I should get over this . . . this *crush*, she called it. I hated her so much for putting it that way, minimizing what I felt. By the time of the party, I was in a . . . I guess you could call it a kind of quiet rage. She barely noticed me that night. She was

325

too busy with Dexter and others. I just wanted to hurt her, any way I could.

'I'd seen her go upstairs a couple of times, to that same bedroom each time, and I knew something was going on. This time I followed her. I suppose I was drunk, like everyone else that night. I had only a hazy notion of what I wanted to do. But I had the bottle . . .'

Her voice grew reflective. 'Do you know this is the first time I've ever told this to anyone? The whole story, I mean. I suppose that's a compliment to you.'

Sorry, he said to her silently. *Flattery won't work with me any more.*

'You could have told me, sweetness,' De Loach said to her.

She ignored him. 'When the lights went out, I was at the top of the stairs,' she said to Horn, 'and a moment later I heard a scream from inside and felt a man brush past me. I had no idea Tess was in the room. I thought Rose was alone. I went inside and felt my way to the bed. She was there, naked. And with another woman, but I didn't care about that.'

'How could you mistake Tess for Rose?' Horn asked.

'It sounds crazy, doesn't it? But it was a natural mistake. They were very similar physically. And I later found out that Tess was wearing Rose's perfume that night.'

That's right, he recalled. *Rose said so.*

'And you,' he said slowly, remembering Rose's feverish words filtered through Madge's drunken monologue, 'were wearing a man's aftershave.'

'Now, how in the world did you—' She stopped. 'Well, you're right. My way of completing the portrait, you might say. It was actually a sweetish scent, and it went very well on me. But to finish answering you . . . I admit I wasn't thinking clearly. I suppose I wanted Rose to be the naked one, the one I could . . . I hated her so much, all I wanted was revenge. I used the champagne bottle on her, and I didn't hold back. The other woman was holding her, keeping her from . . . I couldn't believe my luck. But then suddenly I heard Rose's voice – it was all muffled, coming from underneath – and I felt her hands pushing me away, and I knew the terrible mistake I'd made. It was too late. I left the room as quickly as I could, and then left the house. Days later, I saw the story in the paper, and I finally realized what had happened.'

'That you had killed her.'

'Don't be self-righteous with me,' she said, her voice grown ugly. 'What I did was terrible, but what Rose did was no better. Years later, when she decided it was time to talk to me about it, she made it clear what had been in her mind that night. She hated Tess as much as I hated Rose. Neither one of us meant to kill anyone, but the fact remains that we both took part in a rape.'

'Difference is, Rose was ready to admit what she'd done,' he said to her. 'You were just ready to keep killing people.'

She didn't answer. 'In a minute I'm going to have to shut your mouth,' De Loach said to Horn, fingering the gun at his belt.

'And I imagine you're the one who did the killing for her,' Horn said, turning to him.

'With great pleasure.' De Loach bowed slightly from the waist, as if to acknowledge a compliment.

'I'd guess you're also the one who's been sneaking around my place.'

'Let's just say I identified you early on as a potential problem and wanted to know more about you.'

'How long have you been strangling women?'

De Loach's smooth manner deserted him for a second, replaced by a look of hatred. *Don't forget how dangerous he is*, Horn told himself. Then De Loach assumed the mask again. 'Has Myra been talking about me?' he asked with mock concern. 'I thought we paid that poor thing enough to ensure her silence. But apparently not. Let me make a mental note to visit her again.'

'You haven't answered the question.'

'Well, then, my has-been actor friend, the answer is, none of your business,' De Loach said lightly. 'Doll may want to tell all tonight. I prefer to be known as a man of mystery.'

'But I can guess some of it,' Horn went on. 'We're talking about strangling, not killing. Just a sex thing, wasn't it? Just for fun. At some point, Doll must have found out what you like to do. Maybe it was around the time Myra made such trouble for you. Or maybe Doll always knew what you liked to do. Hell, maybe she likes it too.' He glanced at her but could see no reaction.

'Then one day Rose told her that some of the old secrets were going to come out—' He stopped and turned to her again. 'Did Rose know it was you who killed Tess? Or were you just afraid that she might put too much attention on you?'

'I think she knew, or at least guessed,' Doll said in a small voice. 'But she never said so. Maybe she wanted to leave herself room for doubt. Rose, you see, believed she was responsible for everything that happened that night.'

'But you decided she had to die,' Horn said. 'And old Lewis must have seemed like a gift from heaven. A man who gets a kick out of strangling women. *Do me a little favor, Lewis.* Is that how you put it?'

She was silent. 'Don't tell him any more,' De Loach said to her.

'You had already divorced him,' Horn said. 'Maybe that was the reason you took him back. You suddenly realized what a talented man he was.'

De Loach started to come around the table, his hand at the gun. 'Don't hit him,' Doll said, sounding more irritated than concerned. He stopped.

Horn eyed De Loach cautiously, trying to judge how far he could go in trying to get them to talk to him.

He studied the distance between himself and De Loach. Too far to get at that gun, he conceded, and the table was in the way. He did not want to get hit again, but he recognized the need to get De Loach within reach. Maybe he would have to bait him some more.

The tension made his head throb anew. His stomach growled, and he was aware that he hadn't eaten since breakfast. Was he going to die hungry, and with a headache? The thought made him profoundly depressed.

There was also fear, of course. His old enemy from the war. He had fought it and been defeated by it, and it had left him feeling less than a man. Thinking about his make-believe heroics up on the screen simply made the memory of the war more painful. Since then, he had been visited by his old enemy only rarely. He had found an uneasy accommodation with fear that night up at the old Aguilar estate, and once again the night he stood in the glare of the big car's headlights as Willie Apples came at him. He had learned that he could momentarily push his fear aside by focusing on something more important than himself – a life that needed to be saved, for instance. He glanced over at Alden. Would that be enough?

Now, as he felt the old feeling begin to gnaw at him, the growing weakness in his limbs, he wondered if any of the old tricks would work. Two of the people in this room planned to kill him, and there seemed to be little he could do about it.

He thought he saw a movement in the corner of his eye, around the French doors. Carefully, he looked without turning his head, but saw only the wet garden greenery hanging limply just beyond the glass.

De Loach had seen the look. He followed Horn's gaze to the doors. 'You've probably noticed it's almost dark,' he said. 'And earlier than usual, because of the rain. We've been waiting for the dark.'

Horn understood. 'I suppose that's when you kill us,' he said. He tried to sound resigned, beaten down, when all he wanted was the feel of De Loach's windpipe under his thumbs.

'Well, actually, we don't want to mess up Alden's lovely house,' De Loach said. 'We'll take you out to the car, and then we'll do our business somewhere up in the hills where it's nice and quiet.' No longer guarding his speech, De Loach was warming up to his subject. Horn could hear the self-satisfaction in his tone, the need to brag.

'Of course,' De Loach went on, enjoying the moment, 'if you make a fuss about leaving, we'll just have to shoot you here. But that would involve dragging you out to the car, which is something I'd prefer not to do.'

Time was running out. Horn needed to get the other man within reach.

'I know you think you're a real desperado, Lewis,' he said, 'but anybody who goes around strangling women can't be much of a real threat.'

De Loach regarded him, his eyes pale against his freckled skin.

'Poor Rose didn't put up much of a fight, did she?' Horn continued. 'In fact, she was probably asleep when you snuck in there. Not much to brag about, was it?'

'Watch your mouth.'

'But I bet Cassie was more of a challenge . . .' Horn stopped. He had to know. 'Why did you kill her?'

De Loach allowed himself a smile. His answer came easily, conversationally. 'It was her idea,' he said, indicating Doll, as if the answer were obvious.

'Why?' Horn demanded. 'What did she do?'

'Enough,' Doll said evenly, reaching down to her purse, which sat on the floor near her chair, and coming up with a cigarette and her lighter. 'You mentioned to me how helpful she was in sniffing around for you, how she had managed to locate Alden. I thought she had done enough damage, and I didn't want to wait for more.'

Horn felt sick. His words had painted a target on Cassie, allowing her killers to take aim.

Alden Richwine stirred in his chair. 'Cassie.' The name came out as a croak. 'You killed Cassie?'

Horn regarded him. 'Alden, are you all right?'

Richwine's eyes were fixed on De Loach. 'Answer me.'

'He killed her,' Horn said. 'He was getting ready to tell me about it.' Inside him, the sickness began turning to rage, and he focused all of it on Lewis De Loach.

'Villain,' Richwine said. The word came out as a curse. 'Monstrous villain. Damnable—'

When De Loach's hand went again to the pistol in his belt, Horn quickly interrupted. 'She pulled a knife on you, didn't she, Lewis? Bet that surprised the hell out of you. Where did she cut you?'

'She tried, but she couldn't do much,' De Loach responded

330

with a shrug. 'Just a little nick across the base of the neck. My shirt collar covers it nicely.'

'Still, not much for you to brag about,' Horn said, shaking his head. 'You ever kill a man, Lewis?'

De Loach stared at him.

'I don't mean a woman. You ever try to strangle a man?'

'Don't listen to him,' Doll said, her voice controlled. 'He's just trying to get at you.'

'You'd better mind your mama or she might spank you,' Horn said. 'Answer me, Lewis. You feel like coming over here and trying your little trick with me? Or are you afraid?'

De Loach's mouth twisted, and he started around the table. Horn's hands and arms tensed. Just before De Loach got within reach, Horn heard a sound from behind, in the entryway of the house. It was the front door closing, followed by quick footsteps and a shout.

'Hey!'

De Loach stopped, the fury on his face dissolving. Horn turned around, blinking his eyes against the pain in his head.

Luther Coby walked into the living room.

'Don't go all to pieces on me, Lewis,' Coby said. 'There's plenty of time to take care of him.' His hat and suit coat were lightly speckled with raindrops. He walked over, lightly pushing De Loach aside, and said to Doll, 'I moved his car a few blocks away. We're just about ready.'

'When the time comes,' De Loach muttered, looking at Horn, 'I want him.'

'Sure, if it makes you happy.' Coby stood looking down at Horn, a matchstick busy in one corner of his mouth. 'Awake, huh? You figured everything out?'

Horn stared back, his brain working furiously. 'Not quite,' he said, straining to sound unconcerned. 'But I'm working on it. I guess Eden Lamont's nowhere around the Beverly Hills Hotel, is she?'

'Not as far as I know,' Coby said with a chuckle. 'But I thought that was pretty fancy footwork on my part, coming up with that story as quick as I did. Just wanted to throw you off a little, that's all.'

'What was supposed to happen when I—'

'When you met me there tomorrow? I guess you haven't worked out the details. You see, you never would have made it there. Sometime tonight, I'd have paid you a visit, gotten you to open the door, and put out your lights. You coming over here—'

'I know. Doll told me. It just made things a lot easier for you.'

'Exactly.' He leaned to the side, studying Horn's wounds. 'Doesn't usually take me two licks to put a man out with a gun butt. I must be slowing down.' Noting Horn's look, he laughed quietly. 'So you thought you owed Lewis for your headache? Nope, that was me.'

He looked out the window, then at his watch, and turned to the others. 'It's about time. I don't want to use my car for this.' He turned to De Loach. 'Go get the Lincoln and park it by the kitchen door.'

'Yes, sir,' De Loach said with exaggerated subservience. 'Right away.' He looked around the room. 'Where's my raincoat?'

Even though slumped in his chair, Horn felt his whole body tense. For the first time, he felt something approaching panic. Soon De Loach would leave, but there was no way to separate Luther Coby from his gun. And yet he would have to try. For Alden's sake, and his own. He couldn't just go quietly.

'So what brought you into this?' he asked Coby.

'You need to ask?' the detective said.

'That little retirement cottage in Del Mar.'

Coby nodded. 'We got a saying in homicide. All over the department, in fact. Retirement doesn't come cheap.'

'Some cops do, though, I bet,' Horn said, wondering what it would take to set the man off. 'What was your price, exactly?' When Coby didn't answer, Horn looked over at Doll. 'Was it just money? Or something else?'

For the first time, Coby looked slightly uneasy. As he watched the man's responses, Horn again thought he saw a slight movement, this time in the corridor that led from the living room past the pantry to the kitchen. He glanced over at Doll to see if she had noticed as well, but her eyes were on him, waiting to hear what else he had to say.

Horn pressed on. 'Doll can be pretty persuasive when she wants to be,' he said. 'I've had a little experience in that department. If she did you any favors to get you on her side, my guess is she had her eyes closed all the time. Did you even notice?'

Coby stopped chewing on the matchstick and shook his head in a weary manner, as if to signal that he'd heard enough.

'Don't listen to him, Luther,' Doll said. Standing several feet away, De Loach adjusted the collar of his raincoat and waited, clearly enjoying the drama.

'You ever hear some of the things she says about you when you're not around?' Horn said to Coby. *I need to get him closer.* 'She likes the word *fat*. Another one is *lazy*. And then there was something about the way you smell—'

Watching Coby, he missed the swift movement of Doll's arm. Her open palm rocked his head sideways. It threw him off, left him unprepared for Coby's move, barely a second later, as he drew his short-barreled police revolver, shifted it quickly to his left hand, and slammed it against Horn's right temple and ear, driving his head against the back of the chair.

'Behave,' Coby muttered. 'Any more conversation, and I shoot you right here.'

The front sight of the pistol had torn skin and cartilage, and blood began to trickle down the side of his face. The pain was intense, but it had a curious side effect. The fear was now pushed deep inside, in a place where he thought he could manage it. He could feel adrenalin starting to course through his system. All he needed was a target for it.

Doll leaned over, holding out a handkerchief. She dabbed at his cheek and jaw. 'That was your fault,' she whispered. 'Does it do any good to say I'm sorry? Or to say I wish I'd met you some other way, some other time?'

He pushed her hand away without looking at her.

Her face went blank. She withdrew the handkerchief, spotted with his blood. 'Lewis, will you get the goddam car?' she said, raising her voice. Then, to Coby: 'Collect all those pictures.'

The detective replaced his pistol in its holster, knelt in front of the table, and began gathering up the prints. His face was barely a yard from Horn's knees. *I can almost reach him. It has to be now.*

De Loach turned and started for the pantry corridor. Horn's every muscle tensed. As soon as he was out of sight . . .

Then, an unexpected sound. Footsteps from the corridor. All of them turned as Mad Crow emerged. He walked slowly and deliberately into the living room, both hands showing innocently, but his eyes were wide, and his face held a wild energy. De Loach had halted in surprise, and now Mad Crow stopped about two paces away. Horn heard Doll's wordless intake of breath. At the margin of his vision, he saw Coby, still kneeling, pull out his pistol and half turn toward the intruder.

'Lewis De Loach, I presume,' Mad Crow said. 'Or is it Carson?'

'I know you.' De Loach's tone suggested curiosity as much as concern.

' 'Course you do,' Mad Crow said. 'From the movies, maybe. Or my dreams.'

'What?'

'Lewis, look out!' Doll shouted.

Coby's gun wavered. De Loach was in the way, and he waited for a clear shot. Quickening his step, Mad Crow closed the gap, reaching for something at his hip. De Loach took a tentative step backward, his left hand sweeping away his raincoat as his right reached for his gun.

Mad Crow's face broke into that fearsome grin, showing his teeth. 'Present from Cassie Montag,' he growled as he whipped the hunting knife from its scabbard and drove the blade into the other man's stomach. De Loach, his back to the others, hunched his shoulders and made a small, clenched sound.

Coby's arm steadied as he took aim at what he could see of Mad Crow. He squeezed off a shot, but it missed, sending a chunk of chipped plaster off the wall. The blast from the gun was shockingly loud.

Mad Crow slightly turned De Loach, getting a grip on the front of the man's raincoat with his left hand. In three quick moves, he withdrew the blade, raised it, and then sliced it backhanded across De Loach's throat. It sounded like the parting of a ripe melon.

Coby was taking aim again, trying to rise, but now Horn was out of the chair and launching himself across the table head first. Coby swung his gun hand to meet the attack. Horn went for Coby's throat with his right hand and the gun with his left. In the same instant, he knew he would not make it.

The gun spat fire. The blast this time was deafening. Horn felt the bullet tear through the web of skin between his thumb and forefinger, heard Doll scream behind him. His hand closed on barrel and cylinder, and he forced the barrel upward as his other hand closed on Coby's throat and his weight drove the detective backward onto the floor.

Coby was strong, but Horn was driven by a demon. The gun, slippery with his blood, went off one more time. Horn loosened his grip on the man's throat and began using his fist. Coby tried to cover up with his free hand, but Horn drove in – face, neck, stomach, wherever he found a target. Somewhere in the background he could hear Alden Richwine's voice, vigorous once again, urging him on. He punched with all his strength, hearing Coby grunting and also hearing great, sobbing groans that he realized were his own.

He punched until he felt the detective's grip loosen from the gun.

Then he reached over, took the pistol shakily in his right hand, and placed it against the other man's temple. The gesture said, *I've got you*. Horn's finger was tight on the trigger, his hand shaking with rage. Coby, eyes bulging, sucked in his breath. Horn's finger froze, unable for an instant to follow through.

Then Coby's knee drove upward into his groin, and Horn shouted in pain. He felt the other man's hand scrabbling at his waist, reaching for . . .

He pulled the trigger.

Chapter Twenty-Nine

Horn heard Mad Crow's voice. He let the gun slip from his hand and pushed himself up from Coby's body, then unsteadily got to his feet. His head ached; he staggered and almost fell. The smell of gunpowder stung his nostrils.

'You okay?' Mad Crow asked again. De Loach lay on the floor, curled up into a rigid ball, occasionally shuddering as he made faint liquid sounds. A small pool darkened the carpet under him. But Mad Crow's attention was already elsewhere. 'Look,' he said.

Dolores Winter sat in the chair, both hands grasping her stomach, where the dark blue of her dress glistened redly from her rib cage to her lap. Horn went over to her.

'He shot me,' she said through clenched teeth. 'Luther. Can you believe that? He didn't mean to, but . . .'

As he watched, a patch of brighter red invaded the darkening stain. He had seen wounds like this during the war. The aorta was nicked or severed. The blood would not stop.

'This *really* hurts,' she sighed. 'Can you get a doctor here?' She raised her knees slightly, as if to relieve the pain somewhat, then dropped them. 'Please.'

'I'm afraid I won't be able to do that,' Horn said.

She looked at him searchingly, seeking something in his face and not finding it. 'Are you going to be that way?' she asked almost teasingly, attempting a smile. Her face was growing pale under the rouge, and her eyes seemed to be losing some of their color and clarity.

He didn't answer.

She removed her left hand from her stomach and extended it toward him. He took it.

'Cowboy,' she said, sounding as if she were tired and ready for bed. 'Big cowboy hero.' She squeezed his hand hard.

'Tell the doctor to hurry.' Her voice was down to a whisper. 'Be sure and tell him I'm getting ready to make a movie. With Robert Taylor.' Her eyes closed. 'Mister . . . Gorgeous . . .'

Her hand went limp.

'Come on,' Mad Crow said. He stood nearby, supporting Alden Richwine. 'We've got work to do.'

They helped Alden over to the sofa where Horn had once slept, and they made him reasonably comfortable with a pillow under his head.

'Alden, I'd like you to meet my friend Joseph Mad Crow.'

'Are they dead?' Richwine asked.

Horn turned around. All three were still. 'I'm afraid so,' he said. 'Don't look at them, all right? Just lie here for a while.'

'We should call the police.' His eyes darted to Coby's large form. 'Or . . . someone.'

'Later. Just rest.'

Out in the kitchen, the two men washed carefully in the sink. 'You were a little early,' Horn said.

'Yeah. Turns out that Lancaster movie doesn't open 'til this weekend. They had something with Esther Williams, but I wasn't that hard up. So I thought I'd just come over here, and we'd make a pot of coffee and sing campfire songs.'

'Thanks, Indian.'

'You're making a mess.'

'Oh. Right.' Horn noticed that his injured left hand, showing a small, jagged tear at the base of the thumb, was dripping blood on the rim of the sink. He held it under the faucet again.

'You thinking what I'm thinking?' Mad Crow said. 'We call the cops and we're asking for it.'

Horn nodded. 'Me especially, since I just killed one. And he happens to be the same one who went around telling people he suspected me of murder.' He paused. 'I thought he was reaching for another gun. Turned out he wasn't.'

'Does it matter one way or the other?' Mad Crow asked. 'To me, it's simple: if he'd lived, you would've died. Eventually.'

'I suppose.' Horn studied his hands. Except for the wound, they appeared clean, but he rubbed them together under the running water for several more seconds.

'So what do we do?'

Horn winced as he touched a wet dish towel to his ear. 'I think we're going to have to make up a story that doesn't have us in it,' he said. 'And just hope Alden can tell it right.'

Grabbing a clean towel, he dried his hands and, with Mad Crow's help, wrapped a handkerchief around the wound on his left hand.

For the next five minutes they talked. Then, carrying towels, they returned to the living room, where Alden seemed to be napping. Stepping carefully to avoid tracking blood around, they retrieved Mad Crow's gun from De Loach's belt and cleaned it, then wiped off Coby's gun and placed it in De Loach's hand. Mad Crow wiped off the hunting knife. He went out to the kitchen, found a large knife with roughly the same size blade, then returned, stained it with De Loach's blood, and wrapped the fingers of Coby's right hand around it.

They surveyed the living room with its three bodies. 'It's a godawful mess,' Horn said. 'But it could make sense. Two weapons, two killers, three dead.'

'All right,' Mad Crow said. They roused Alden and helped him out to the kitchen, where Horn found a bottle of Paul Jones and three glasses. The three sat at the kitchen table. Horn and Mad Crow told their story. Then they told it again.

'What do you think, Alden?' Horn asked. 'Can you tell it that way?'

Richwine downed a healthy slug and nodded his head. 'Yes, I can,' he said. His cheeks were gaining some color. 'You gentlemen saved my life.' He shook his head. 'I'm deeply ashamed not to have been more perceptive about those three individuals. I thought two of them were my friends. And the policeman . . .'

'They fooled a lot of people,' Horn said. 'Can you go over the story, the way you'll tell it?'

'All right.' He sipped from his glass and began, haltingly at first. He had planned to go out for a drive and then dinner with Dolores Winter and Lewis De Loach. But Coby joined them, and things turned ominous. They beat him until he produced the photos. And they made it clear that they planned to kill him.

At this point, Richwine's story became more creative, and his delivery more confident.

'Naturally, I questioned them,' he said. 'Miss Winter admitted having caused the death years ago of Tess Shockley in this very house. To keep her role secret, she admitted having dispatched Mister De Loach, her former husband, to murder Rose Galen and—' He paused to clear his throat. '—and Cassie Montag, who was a wonderful young woman. And admitted bribing Detective Coby to help her cover up both deeds.'

By now his voice had regained much of its old strength, and he began embroidering his story with gestures.

'A dispute, however, developed. It seems Miss Winter had promised the detective a sum of money for his services, and he demanded much more. He mentioned the high price of a home he was buying in Del Mar. They argued. A fight ensued. I was, I confess, somewhat dazed from my beating and unable to follow every detail. But it appeared to me that Mister De Loach had somehow got his hands on the policeman's gun and threatened him with it. The latter obtained a knife from the kitchen. They grappled. De Loach was stabbed, and the policeman was shot. Other shots went astray, one of them striking Miss Winter.'

Richwine stopped, slightly out of breath. 'Somewhat baroque, I admit. But on the whole, a rather convincing performance, don't you think? You know, when I portrayed Horatio in the Old Vic's *Hamlet*, a total of four bodies littered the stage at the final curtain, one of them a woman, and no one suggested that it was unbelievable. Three dead in my living room . . .' He looked pensive. 'I think I can make our story sound credible.'

'Oh, Lordy,' Mad Crow said. 'I wonder if anybody's going to buy it.'

'I think they will,' Horn said. 'Three bodies, two weapons, and a story that explains it. A story told by a distinguished actor.'

Horn got up and washed the three glasses. Then he rolled up the two stained towels. 'We'll take these with us. I think you can call the police now, Alden.'

'This was quite an adventure,' Richwine said at the kitchen door. 'Quite possibly the last of a full life. And a secret for the three of us to keep down through the days. Do you mind if I call you John and Joseph? Good Anglo-Saxon biblical names, both of them.'

'My friends call me John Ray.'

'Oh, yes. That curious southern American custom of giving one's children a whole string of given names. As if one were not good enough.'

'You're being snooty, Alden.'

'One of the privileges of age.'

They leaned against the fender of the Cadillac, looking out over the gentle green hills and spreading oaks. It had been another blustery morning, but a stray sunbeam had found one of the farthest hills and, depending on the movement of the high clouds, looked as if it might pay them a visit if they stayed long enough. Because it was Sunday, families were dotted around the grass, some of them carrying bouquets of flowers.

'Funny old gal,' Mad Crow said, indicating Madge, who stood next to Rose's marker down the slope about fifty feet away from them.

'Yep,' Horn agreed. 'She can do a trick with a dollar bill. Maybe we'll show you later.' Bandages covered part of his left hand and his right ear. His fedora hid the other two wounds, which were now mostly healed.

'What are you looking at?'

'This?' Horn held a piece of note paper covered with writing, some of the words crossed out. 'It's just a letter I've been working on. To Tess's father. I'm looking for a way to tell him it's over—'

'Without telling him everything.'

'Right.' Horn put the letter in his pocket.

Mad Crow flicked his cigarette butt out over the close-cut

grass in a long arc. 'I, uh . . .' he began, then tried again. 'I never killed a man before. Did you know that?'

'I never thought about it one way or the other.'

'I figured you must have done something during the war, because of where you were, even though you never wanted to talk about it. That night up behind your house, when they came after Clea . . . I guess you could say I was ready to do it then. As it turned out, I didn't have to, and I was glad. This time I had to. And I wanted to.'

'If anybody deserved it, he did.'

'One thing, though,' Mad Crow said, looking at someplace far off. 'I think I enjoyed it a little. Because of Cassie. That sound funny?'

Horn didn't answer.

'Oh, hell,' Mad Crow said. 'Never mind.' He looked over at the spot where Madge stood. 'Nice place for Rose to be.'

'Doll paid for it.'

'Really?'

'Before she died, she said something about how she was no worse than Rose.'

'You believe that?'

'No. But I have learned some things about Rose I wish I didn't know.'

'Well . . .'

'She did something a long time ago, something that put a mark on her. It was like she took on a huge debt, to herself and other people, and she spent the rest of her life trying to pay it off.'

'Do you think she—?'

'If you *can* pay off something like that, I think she did. By the end.'

Madge came up the slope and joined them. She wore the same tattered coat, but it was topped this time by a brown velvet hat with a jaunty feather. Even though Horn had never seen the hat before, he knew it. 'This is just awfully pretty here,' she said. 'I'm happy for Rosie.'

341

'I thought you'd like it,' Horn said. 'Now, are you hungry? There's this place in Glendale that serves up great steaks.'

Madge beamed at both of them. 'Well, ain't you nice?'